Remember Me

Remember Me

Melissa Bowersock

Draumr Publishing, LLC
Maryland

Remember Me

Cover art by Patricia Storms.

ISBN: 1-933157-02-X
PUBLISHED BY DRAUMR PUBLISHING, LLC
www.draumrpublishing.com
Columbia, Maryland

Printed in the United States of America

Remember Me

Chapter One

She woke up, terrified.

One eye opened on a small room with white walls, white sheets over her in a white bed, drawn white Venetian blinds. The other eye didn't open at all.

In a quick, instinctive action, she attempted to put her hand to her eye—right hand, right eye. The hand was bound, the arm splinted and secured to her side. With her good left eye, she stared at the bandaged, cast arm and white bandages.

She put her left hand to her face. Her right eye was patched, taped, and the tape extended like a cap over most of her head. She had smaller bandages on her chin. At the movement of her arm, her ribs ached. They were wrapped, too.

She was in a hospital; she'd been hurt. But she didn't know how. She didn't know what hospital in what city. She didn't know anything that had happened to her, and she didn't know who she was.

In a sudden surge of panic, she tried to sit up—pain in her ribs grabbed her at her sudden intake of breath—and she looked around. She was in a private room so there was no second bed, no place for anyone else to be. The door was closed. If she were in a mental hospital, which she felt was a distinct possibility, it would be locked. A quick glance at her unbound left wrist allayed her worst fear, but didn't reduce the panic building inside of her. She had to do something! A nurse's button squatted on her bedside table and she jabbed at it. There was no sound. She hit it again, pushed it down and held it. There was a whisper of movement from behind the closed door.

A nurse strode in, tall and slender, concerned, curious. She wore a tight smile.

"Good morning. How are you fee—"

"What's happened to me? Why am I here? Who am I?" The voice burst from her, unfamiliar and high with panic.

"What?" The nurse looked taken back. Quickly, professionally, she readjusted. "Now, calm down, Mi—"

"Tell me who I am!" she pleaded piteously. "Please tell me who I am!"

She didn't recognize the doctor, but at this point she would have been suspiciously surprised if she recognized anyone. The nurse had skittered out of the room so fast that she knew she was seriously ill. She forced herself into a semblance of composure although she was still quaking inside.

The doctor was average height, mid-forties, with short, curly, salt and pepper hair. He had a quick smile, reassuring yet without the impersonal blandness of the nurse. His eyes were gray and quick, haloed by crow's-foot wrinkles. He brushed past the nurse at the door and breezed in.

"Good morning," he said. "I'm Dr. D'Angelo. I'm glad to see you're awake. I expected you to come out of the anesthetic yesterday evening, but with all your injuries, I'm just as glad you slept."

She stared at him, her mind straining to remember him, to remember anything. It was all a blank.

"I don't—should I..."

Dr. D'Angelo smiled compassionately. "You don't know me. The only time you may have seen me before was when you were already under the effects of the anesthesia." His smile faded. "The nurse tells me you don't know who you are. Is that right?"

She was afraid she might cry. She nodded, feeling her chin quiver, wanting this man to comfort her, console her, give her back her life. "I, I..." Her voice broke.

"That's all right," Dr. D'Angelo said as he took her hand and patted it while she struggled to swallow her tears. "It must be terribly frightening for you. You are safe, though, and you'll be fine in a few days, physically at least. Do you mind if I check something?"

She shook her head. He pulled out a penlight and leaned toward her to shine it into her good eye. Whatever he saw when he held her eye open with practiced fingers seemed to satisfy him. He sat back in his chair.

"We were afraid you had some internal hemorrhaging, but I don't think so. You do have a severe concussion, though. Your right arm is broken, and your shoulder was dislocated. Your right eye is all right, just some close cuts that required stitches, and I was afraid you'd rub at them in your sleep. We can take the patch off now. Oh, and you bruised a couple of ribs."

"What happened to me?"

"You were in a car accident. You don't remember anything about it?"

She shook her head. "Can you—tell me who I am?"

That smile again. "Your name is Eleanor Cole. You're twenty-four years old, and you were in a very serious accident. The driver of the car was killed. From what I can gather, you took the brunt of the impact on the right side of your upper body, which is why you feel so lopsided. We had thought you were extremely lucky to come out with a concussion when, by rights, you might have had your skull crushed. Is anything I'm telling you bringing any memories to mind?"

"No, none of it. Does amnesia always do that, blank out everything? I feel so lost."

"I'm not surprised. Amnesia's a funny thing. We still don't understand it. Sometimes it can affect people partially, blocking out only parts of their memory, although mostly that's a psychological mechanism. Yours, I would guess, is strictly physical, and that kind very often produces a complete blank."

"It is permanent?"

"Again, we're not sure. Sometimes it'll clear up in a few days, sometimes never. I've seen cases where it comes back little by little and cases where the patient wakes up one morning and boom, it's all back. I'm afraid that's not very professional, but we just don't know. It's not a very promising picture, but I don't want to give you any false hopes."

"I see." Intellectually, she did. Emotionally, she felt like Alice in Wonderland, fallen down a rabbit hole and unable to get back or even to see where she fell from. Dr. D'Angelo was nice, but he wasn't a fixture in her life. She had a name and an age, but other than that, she had nothing. She was entirely alone.

"I hate to ask this, but do you feel up to some simple tests? Nothing difficult, just blood and pulse, simple reflexes, that sort of thing. Maybe later we'll do a brain scan just to be safe."

"Will you be able to tell why I can't remember?"

"I don't know. It's doubtful."

"All right. Whatever you have to do is all right."

He studied her for a moment, then rose to go. "I'm sure you don't feel lucky right now, but perhaps later, you'll be able to look back and see it. You really are a very lucky young woman."

The nurse administered the first tests. Eleanor submitted to her instructions without protest. She allowed her temperature to be taken, her pulse, even a small blood sample and endured it all without a word.

She didn't feel like an Eleanor. Eleanor sounded like a comic name for an elephant, or at the very least an aged, maiden aunt. What kind of parents had she had that would name a baby Eleanor? And where were Mr. and Mrs. Cole anyway? Did they know that their daughter was dead and that a newborn, frightened girl cowered in Eleanor's body?

"What city is this?" she dared when the nurse removed the thermometer.

"Denver."

"Colorado?"

"Yes. Do you know the city?" The nurse went about her duties but watched Eleanor curiously.

"No. I just know it's in Colorado." She hesitated to ask her next question. "Is there...has there been anyone waiting to see me?"

"Yes, Mr. Cole's been quite anxious to see you. Do you think you'd like to have a visitor?"

"I don't know." She was half relieved, half panic-stricken. At least someone was here who knew her, someone from her past life. That was comforting. But what would her father think when she didn't recognize him? And where was her mother? Dead? She wasn't sure she wanted to have her father come in and be a total stranger.

"He's been waiting all night. I think he slept in the waiting room," the nurse went on. "I don't know if the doctor had a chance to talk to him or not, but I know he's very anxious to see you if you feel up to it."

"What about the tests?"

"I'm almost done with what I have to do here, and the doctor's ordered a brain scan. That will be in a little while. You have time."

"Well," she swallowed, "I guess so. Can I—can you take this bandage off my eye? Dr. D'Angelo said it was okay."

"Sure," the nurse answered with a smile and peeled the tape off Eleanor's tender skin. "Is that better?"

"Yes. At least I don't feel like a fish anymore, staring out only one side of my face. Thanks."

"You're welcome. I'll just run these things to the lab and then let the desk know you can see Mr. Cole. If you want anything, just buzz."

"Thank you."

Eleanor felt around her right eye. There were three or four small cuts woven with stitches. She realized Dr. D'Angelo was right. She was lucky. It was difficult enough coming to terms with her amnesia but how much more so would it be if she were blind? Just the thought made her shiver.

She wished she'd thought to have the nurse open the blinds. She knew it was mid-morning, but she had no idea what day it was or what season. She'd like to look outside. Maybe once her father got over the initial shock, he would open them for her. She wondered what he would look like.

There was the whispering behind the door that signaled someone's entrance. A different nurse, younger, more girlish, pushed open the door.

"Mrs. Cole?" she called cheerfully. "Your husband is here to see you."

Husband?

The word was a cold steel sword piercing her body, impaling her on the bed in frozen fear. God, she was married! The idea of meeting her husband bound up her brain in a functionless vise. She pressed back into the pillows and stared at the opening door like a rabbit at an approaching snake.

As soon as she saw him, she realized she had good cause to be afraid.

He was huge. His thick, black hair only missed the top door jamb by a fraction of an inch, and his shoulders filled the entire width of the frame. He came in casually yet there was a tautness to his walk, a tension in his carriage that frightened her. But his eyes—his eyes were enough to elicit a whimper of fear from her.

They were black and as deep as a bottomless pool. They looked like the kind of eyes Satan might have—commanding, examining, discerning. They swept her in a contemptible gaze. His entire face was arranged in a forbidding frown. She felt a chilling feeling wash over her, a feeling that he would much rather have seen her dead.

"Good morning, Elly," he said. His voice was deep-timbered yet she heard the bite of sarcasm. "How are you feeling?"

She couldn't answer. Her throat worked soundlessly, her mouth opened, but no words came out.

"Speechless, Elly?" He stood close by the bed, his hands held behind his back as if to keep from slapping her. His black brows frowned down at her. "What's the matter, did you use up all your powers of communication on that marvelous little note you left me? Or didn't you expect to see me here? You don't have anyone else now, you know. Just me."

It sounded like a threat. Elly squirmed. She didn't like this man. She wished a nurse would come.

"I'm waiting, Elly," he said crossly. "If you're expecting pity for your wounds, you can forget it. Well? No tears? No explanations? Your note was so well worded. I'm waiting for a live performance."

"Have you..." her voice was barely a whisper. "Have you talked with Dr. D'Angelo?"

"Last night. He told me what all you've got splinted and bandaged. You don't really expect me to feel sorry for you, do you?"

"I don't expect anything," she managed. "I don't remember anything."

His scowl deepened. "What do you mean, you don't remember anything? Don't try to pass this off, Elly. It won't work."

A needle of irritation worked beneath the fear she felt. The man knew he was threatening-looking, and he played it for all he was worth. She found a trace of stubbornness to use against his bullying.

"I'm not trying to 'pass off' anything," she said coldly. "I have amnesia. I don't know you or anything about any of the things you're saying. I can't remember anything at all."

His black eyes sparked to life and he studied her face, his look leaving her cold. The planes of his face were like cool stone. She tried not to shrink away from the hatred she felt emanating from him, but it was almost a physical force.

"Don't be stupid," he growled low in his throat. "Are you trying to tell me you don't remember writing that note? I have it with me, you know. Or you don't remember packing and leaving? It's gone too far to play games, Elly."

"I'm not playing games, and I'm not trying to tell you anything except that I don't remember." She was surprised at the anger she felt, too surprised to notice how her voice had risen or how her husband's jaw tightened.

"If you don't remember anything, then why did you look like a scared rabbit when I came in? You wouldn't be afraid of me if you didn't remember."

"I didn't know you were my husband. They said Mr. Cole; I thought they meant my father. And when you came in, you looked like you wanted to finish what the accident didn't. Why shouldn't I be afraid? Apparently, I have good reason to be."

"You're damn right you do," he agreed.

"Look," she said. "I don't know what it was that I supposedly did to you to make you so mad, but—"

"You don't know what you *supposedly* did?" he sneered. "Well, let me tell you, Mrs. Cole." He pulled the doctor's chair up and leaned over the back of it. "You wrote me a wonderful note telling me what an emotional cripple I was, packed your bags and ran off with your lover. That's what you did."

Elly was stunned. "No. You're lying."

"I wish I were."

She couldn't face those black, bottomless eyes. Shaking her head, she looked down. "It's impossible. I don't feel like I could have done that. I ought to be able to feel something." Try as she might, she could summon up no names, no faces, no emotions except the confusing ones struggling inside of her right now. Expecting her to claim those emotion-charged actions was unthinkable.

Then she remembered something Dr. D'Angelo had said.

"The doctor said the driver of the car was killed." She stared up at her husband guilelessly. "Was that...?"

"Yes."

She nodded and looked away. "I don't see how it can be true, what you're telling me. I don't even know his name. I don't feel sad. I don't feel—anything."

"His name was Adam," Cole supplied through clenched teeth. "You know, like the first man?"

His tone alerted Elly and she tried to read his eyes. There was something else there, an inference.

"It doesn't mean anything," she said. "I'm sorry I can't spar with you about it; I don't know my lines."

Their eyes locked in an unforgiving tug-ofwar. Elly could see that her husband had no plans to let her off the hook for what she'd done, but she refused to be bullied. She didn't feel guilty and she wouldn't act like it, regardless of the way he glared at her. If their marriage had been so filled with hate, maybe they were better off divorced. Maybe, once she got her bearings, that was the course of action she'd have to take. It was ridiculous to fight with a man she didn't know.

"Mrs. Cole? Oh." The tall nurse pushed in, then stopped at the sight of the hulking Mr. Cole standing so oddly over his wife. In the split second before he turned away, she could feel the tension. It was obvious they'd had words.

"I'm sorry, Mr. Cole, I'll have to ask you to leave now. Mrs.

know who I can turn to, who I need. It's frightening to even think of meeting people I'm supposed to know and finding them total strangers."

"I'm sure it must be very strange." He stood, clipboard under his arm. "Well, let me know if there's anything I can do. I'll check back with you after dinner."

"Thank you." She braved a smile for the one person in the world who seemed to care for her. She didn't even want to think about leaving the safety of his jurisdiction.

"Oh, Doctor," she called when he was almost out the door. He turned back. "The man who was killed? In the car?" He nodded. "Was his name Adam?"

"Yes. Adam Wolfford."

Her bedside phone jangled her out of a troubled sleep. She instinctively reached with her right hand, remembered the cast and lay it against her side. It was a little difficult to learn to do things with her left hand, but she would manage.

"Hello?"

"Mrs. Cole? Dr. D'Angelo. Did I wake you?"

"Not really," she lied. "What time is it?"

"Almost seven. I'm afraid I'm running late; I had an emergency up here on three, and I'm not going to get back to you tonight. What I called for though was to find out if you want to see your husband. He's been harassing the girls at the desk for over an hour, I guess, until I could get free. He's very determined to see you."

Elly could well believe that. No doubt he wanted to do a little more headhunting.

"It's up to you," Dr. D'Angelo continued. "If you feel up to it, it's all right with me."

"Um, I think maybe no more today," she said. "I am tired and I still need time to think. Maybe tomorrow he and I can decide what I should do."

"Good. I don't want you immersed in emotional problems just yet. I'll call down to the desk and have them tell Mr. Cole you're sleeping. He can come back in the morning if he's so determined."

"Yes."

"All right, then. Did you have dinner? Everything okay?"

"Fine."

"Any questions you want to ask, anything I can help you with?"

"No, really, everything is fine. The only thing I want is my memory, and since I can't have that, I'll have to make do with what I've got."

She dreamed she was in a house, a huge white house with towers and gables and tall, leaded windows. She had to go inside, although she didn't know why, and instead of rooms she found nothing but hallways. Long, dimly-lit corridors led in all directions, turned left, turned right, went on to infinity it seemed. At first she thought the walls were black, but as she chose a corridor and started down it, she realized it was paneled with mirrors—long, slender framed mirrors. Each mirror leaned at a slightly different angle than the ones on either side of it, so the collage of images they formed was a shattered, piecemeal picture of bits of frame and countless reflected mirrors. In none of the mirrors did she see herself.

She walked on, rationalizing to herself that the mirrors were all at odd angles to her and that was why they were so curiously blank, but as she neared a corner she approached a larger mirror set heavily against the wall. Its face shown silver as she neared, and flattened to a dull gray as she came around its edge. When she stood in front of it, she stopped and turned her head slowly to its face.

It reflected everything but her.

When she assured herself she was awake, she had to lie still for a moment just to calm her pounding heart. Her left hand shook even as she pressed it to her chest, and her mouth was cottony. She caught her breath, then slid from the bed and made her way to the bathroom. The harsh, white light was almost blinding.

She peered at herself in the bathroom mirror. Her face was not familiar.

She had blue eyes, dark with large, fearful pupils that seemed to try to hide in her face. Her features were ordinary, her nose average. She had neither high cheekbones nor a wide mouth. The only way to describe herself was, perhaps, nondescript.

Except for the right eye. Uncovered, it still bore four small cross-hatched cuts that radiated outward toward her hair line. She touched a finger to the brownish stitches. One of them puckered, drew her skin upward in a parody of a childlike imitation of an Asian. Yes, her right eye had a definite slant to it.

She wondered if Dr. D'Angelo had noticed. Perhaps the pucker would smooth out once the stitches were out. She's have to ask him.

Her cap of bandages was gone, but a three-inch square patch covered her right temple. She touched it gingerly; it was tender. Behind it, her hair was dark brown and hung lifelessly. It was blunt-cut just above her shoulders, and she apparently wore it without bangs. It looked very dull.

Well, she thought, at least I have a face.

For the first time she allowed herself to think about what Dr. D'Angelo had told her earlier. What would the baby look like? Her, or her dark, storm-cloud faced husband? She put a wondering hand on her stomach. Eight weeks wasn't much. It wouldn't move or even show for months. She had seven months to picture a face for it. Blue eyes, black eyes, or—God, she'd almost forgotten—what about Adam?

She returned to her bed and fell heavily into it, the weight of the world pressing her down. It was all a huge, horrible practical joke, with her as the butt. Her former self had somehow gotten her into a hundred messes and then had conveniently vanished, leaving the new-born, memoryless Elly to clear them up. For some reason her marriage was a disaster, she was pregnant with a choice of fathers, and her lover, or at least the one man she trusted enough to go off with, was dead. It wasn't fair that she be the one, she with no hindsight, to make sense out of the problems she'd had no hand in creating. And how could she possibly hope to handle having a baby when she was a baby herself, not even a day old? It was all ridiculous, crazy, insane. And depressing. Turning restlessly into her pillow, Elly felt tears welling in her dark blue eyes. Not even one day old, and she cried herself to sleep.

"Good morning, Mrs. Cole. Sleep well?" Dr. D'Angelo settled himself cheerfully on the straight-backed chair.

"Well enough, I guess. I think I could have used one of those frequently joked about sleeping pills, though."

He smiled at her humor. "Sorry. No sedatives for pregnant ladies. Maybe today you'll feel more like walking. If we can tire you out, you'll sleep better."

"I hope so. I've got so much to think about that my brain isn't able to gear down. By the way, I did think of some questions I'd like answered."

"Oh? Good. I hope I can answer them." He waited patiently.

"Well," she began slowly, "I'm not sure how to word it exactly. I was wondering why I know some things and not others. I knew Denver was in Colorado, I knew how to turn on the TV, how to open the blinds. Why can I remember unimportant things like that and not remember my name or even what I look like? I had to look at myself in the mirror last night before I knew what color my eyes were."

Dr. D'Angelo was nodding. "Yes, it's usually that way. Very rarely we'll hear of someone who needs to be completely re-taught, and I mean in everything—eating, walking, talking. Usually that sort of thing is bordering on catatonia, though, and that's a whole different ball game. No, most amnesiacs are like you—the transparent knowledge of things we seldom think about is retained while anything dealing with the personality itself is suppressed. Again, as frustrating as it is, it's not unusual."

"Frustrating is putting it lightly. Well, second question: I noticed my right eye looks a little slanted by the stitches. Will that be permanent?"

"Oh?" He cocked his head at her, his quick, gray eyes dodging across her face. "Well, I'll be. It sure is. I hadn't noticed. That shouldn't be a problem. Some of the swelling still needs to go down, and after a day or two you'll probably notice the difference is less. Still, if it's enough to bother you, we can do a little corrective plastic surgery. That part is easy."

"I'm glad something is." She managed to return his smile. "I guess the only other thing is, do I get released today?"

"How do you feel about it?"

"I don't know. Scared. I have no idea what I'll be going to."

Dr. D'Angelo nodded. "Actually, I'd just as soon keep you one more day, just to be safe. By tomorrow morning we ought to be able to remove those stitches, fit you with a surgical girdle for your ribs and get that bandage off your head. At least you can go home not looking like a war casualty."

"All right. I can't say that I mind."

"I didn't think you would. I'm not awfully worried about your physical condition. You're a tough, young woman. A lot of women would have lost that baby in an accident like that, but you must have deliberately shielded your abdomen with your head and shoulder. I've seen your records from your gynocologist in Colorado Springs and I can't see that you'll have any problems with your pregnancy. All in all, you're in pretty good shape."

"Physically," she amended.

"Physically. Which reminds me. If you want any kind of counseling—psychological, psychiatric, whatever—we can set it up for you. It might make it easier to come to terms with your predicament, although I would say from what I've seen that you're a pretty level-headed person."

"Thanks, but I don't think it would help. I'd probably fail the Rorschach. No, I think what I need to do is go home, wherever that is, and try to start where the me before left off. Somehow I've got to start at the beginning."

"Sounds commendable to me." He rose to leave. "Which brings us to the fact that your husband is waiting to see you. Do you feel up to it?"

She sighed and suppressed a shudder. "I guess so. He wants answers as much as I do, and at this point it looks like the only way to find them is by talking it out."

Dr. D'Angelo stared down at her a moment, pity foremost in his eyes. "If you need me, I'll be on the floor. Just buzz the nurse."

"I will. Thanks."

A nurse ushered Cole in, a slightly more reserved Cole, although his eyes sparked dangerously as soon as they settled on his wife. He kept his posture and carriage unprepossessing until the door clicked shut behind the nurse. Then, Elly realized uncomfortably, he reared up to his full height like a bear going to battle. It wasn't a consoling sight.

"Dr. D'Angelo said he's going to release you tomorrow."

Elly ignored his lack of greeting. "Yes," she said simply.

"Well?"

"Well what?"

"What are you going to do?" He stood at parade rest over her, his look at once commanding and daring.

For the first time she considered the fact that he didn't want her. Not that she could blame him, knowing how brazenly she had left once, but she had thought by his fiercely determined attitude that he still had some feeling for her. Hate binds as well as love, she reflected, and it was certainly hate she saw emanating from his eyes. But maybe it wasn't the binding kind.

"Well?"

"I'm not sure what I'm going to do," she said thoughtfully. "I don't think I have a lot of options. I might ask you, since you so obviously feel nothing but contempt for me, what do you care what I do?"

He looked patently shocked. "You are my wife, you know."

"That doesn't really answer the question."

"It does for me. You have a home, a career, a circle of friends. Where else would you go?"

She shrugged with practiced unconcern. "I don't know. I just have to wonder why you want me if I humiliated you so badly by leaving. You don't love me—or who I was. I know that much. Why should you want me back?"

He began to pace and looked for all the world like a huge black lion in a cage. Elly wondered if he were as brutally strong as he looked.

"I need answers," he said grudgingly. "I can't deny that I'm angry and resentful of you. I'm not offering you a place of honor in my home, but I need answers. You can give them to me."

"Me?" She almost laughed. "I had to be told my own name and you expect me to have answers for you?"

"Not right away, no." He turned a stubborn look to her. "I'm not unreasonable. I know it'll take time for you to remember. But when you do, I want to know why."

"Why what?"

"Why you left me."

It was the last thing she expected him to say.

"Dr. D'Angelo said I may never regain my memory."

"I don't believe that. I think you will."

"And if I don't?"

His look darkened in rejection. "I guess we'll never know until the time comes."

"I thought you said I left a note," Elly remembered.

"You did."

Suddenly she felt she was on shaky ground. Just the mention of the note brought a scowl to his face.

"Did I explain anything in it?"

"It was too emotional. It's not valid."

"May I see it?"

His head snapped up as if she had suggested something unforgivable. "No."

She roused in irritation. "Why not?"

"Because it's not valid. It was an emotional attack on me and it just was not a practical explanation. It had no bearing on the actual situation."

"I would think if it were the last thing I wrote to you that it would have a lot of bearing. I may have been finally able to write what I had been feeling and not saying or, or—"

"No!" he roared. "We won't talk about the note! Forget about it. It doesn't matter."

Like hell, Elly thought. His sudden thundering outburst quelled her own response, though. She wished she knew if he'd ever hit her.

"All right," she agreed, thin-lipped. "At any rate, I have more or less thought that I should go back home, wherever that is. I figured if I was ever going to remember, I would have to start where I left off before. I guess we're both agreed on that."

He settled somewhat under her response. He looked relieved in a restless sort of way.

"Good. I'll pick you up tomorrow, then. About noon."

"There's one more thing," she said. Her coolness evaporated and she plucked nervously at her blanket. "It may make a difference, but you have a right to know. Dr. D'Angelo told me I'm pregnant."

There was a moment of silence but she couldn't bring herself to lift her eyes to his face. She had a feeling she wouldn't have been comforted by what she saw there.

"I know," he said finally.

"Did — did the doctor tell you?"

"No. You did."

Chapter Two

The next morning Elly was understandably nervous. She fidgeted while her stitches were removed, winced when her temple bandage was peeled off and stood staring restlessly out the window while a nurse helped her with her surgical corset.

It was autumn outside, October thirteenth, she'd found out. Through her second story window she could see trees below shredding in the wind, losing bits of red and yellow leaves. Far to the west the Rocky Mountains reared up behind Denver, a few elongated gray clouds being propelled above their peaks. It was an odd day to begin a new life. She would have felt more comforted if it were spring. Spring was the time of new beginnings; autumn was the time of dying.

Dr. D'Angelo appeared while she was eating her lunch and settled himself in his usual chair.

"Ready to go home, Mrs. Cole?"

"As ready as I'll ever be," she sighed.

"It must be frightening."

"Yes, it is. But I don't suppose it'll be the first time, or the last. I'm guessing I'm going to feel like this a lot in the next few months."

Dr. D'Angelo nodded sagely. "It's amazing to me with all the advances in modern medicine, all the high technology, that we can't do more for amnesiacs. I probably shouldn't tell you this, but I feel very frustrated, very ineffective letting you go off like this. Trial-and-error has never been one of my favorite methods of healing."

"I'm sorry I'm such a problem," Elly said. She smiled and the doctor laughed.

"Lord, don't apologize to me!" he said. "But you're right; I shouldn't be crying my problems to you. You're the patient, not me. I, of course, being human, am seeing things from only my viewpoint. Very selfish of me."

Elly's smile was warm and affectionate. "You've been extremely kind to me. I don't know what other sorts of medical experiences I may have had, but I can honestly say that you're the nicest doctor I know."

"A very safe assumption, since I am the *only* doctor you know."

They laughed together. It felt good to Elly to laugh. She wondered how long it had been since she had done that.

"Well," Dr. D'Angelo said, slapping his knee and standing up, "I guess I'd better leave you to your lunch. Your husband will be here soon." The humor faded from Elly's eyes at the mention of her husband. "Now, now," he said. "Let's be positive. I think Mr. Cole is going through a rather traumatic experience himself, and you both will need to help each other."

"Does he know that?"

Dr. D'Angelo looked disturbed, then determined. "It'll be up to you to make him know." She started to protest but he waved her off. "No, listen. You both have a lot of reordering to do, a lot of rethinking. You, I think, are the stronger of the two in this situation because you don't have a lot of preconceived emotional roadblocks in your way. You are intellectually aware of the situation and you're starting out completely fresh, a clear unmarked slate. Your husband on the other hand is caught up in the emotional vestiges of your lives before; he's going to have to unlearn everything he knows about you and see you as a new, different person. It's going to be extremely difficult and you're the one who's going to have to stand against his preconceptions and show him who you are. It won't be easy."

"Thanks."

"But I think you can do it. You're a very strong, resilient young woman. I'm expecting good things from you, Mrs. Cole."

Elly met his animated gray eyes and couldn't keep from smiling. "Are you sure, Dr. D'Angelo," she asked, "that you don't teach self-help courses in positive thinking in your spare time?"

When Cole came, she was standing at the window, her overnight bag packed on the bed. The clothes he had brought for her earlier were uncomfortable and increased her nervousness. She didn't feel like wearing a gray pleated skirt, white blouse and matching gray jacket. Even the low-heeled shoes seemed out of sorts. And she hadn't been able to wash her hair; she felt dowdy.

The opening of the door alerted her to his presence and she turned to face him. Whatever his eyes found unfamiliar in her expression, they seemed reassured by the outfit. He drew himself up and faced her across the room. "Ready to go?"

She couldn't bring herself to answer as flippantly as she had Dr. D'Angelo. "Yes."

"The nurse is bringing a wheel chair."

They didn't speak again. When she had settled into the wheel chair and been taken down to the elevator, Cole stood stony-faced beside her, his hands clasped in front of him, untouchable. Elly tried to conjure up the strength Dr. D'Angelo insisted she had, but found that it wasn't as prominent without him. So much for positive thinking.

Cole had apparently taken care of signing the release forms earlier; Elly was wheeled to the wide, automatic glass doors and out. While the nurse held her chair, her husband brought the car forward—a dark blue Ford. It didn't look familiar.

They pulled away from the curb into the stream of hospital traffic. Elly looked back at the huge building, tried to pinpoint her room. There seemed to be millions of windows.

"Sorry to be leaving?" Cole asked dryly.

She didn't turn around, not until she was ready. "No. Just—it's the only place I know. It's hard to explain."

"I imagine."

She ignored the sarcasm in his voice.

"How long does it take to get to Colorado Springs?"

"About an hour."

"That long?"

"What did you think?"

"I didn't know. I thought it was closer. You came every day."

"I stayed at a motel until yesterday."

She nodded. As Cole pulled onto the freeway and slipped into southbound traffic, Elly let her eyes wander over the scenery, tripping from one building or landmark to another.

"Have I—we—lived in Colorado long?"

"Three years. Why?"

"It's awfully pretty. The colors of the leaves are so striking against the mountains. And the snow—is there always snow on the Rockies?"

"In some places. We had a storm about a week ago that dumped a lot of new snow."

"I see." She watched the landscape glide by, a child with her first view of a passing parade. "It's very pretty."

There was an answering snort from the driver's side of the car. "You didn't want to move here."

Elly turned around frontward and studied her husband's dark profile. "Why not?"

"You didn't want to leave your family."

"In New Mexico?"

"Yes."

"Did we live in Carri—Carrizozo?"

"No. Alamogordo."

"Is that close to Carrizozo?"

"About 65 miles away. A lot closer than Colorado Springs."

"Oh." She shifted her attention around the car, to the closed ashtray, the tree-shaped air freshener, and finally to the scratchy feel of her skirt on her knees.

"How long...have we been married?"

Cole glanced at her curiously. "Four years."

"Then we'd only been married a year when we moved here."

"That's right."

That struck Elly strangely. Even at a young twenty-one, after being married a year she would have thought she'd have been able to leave her family, particularly when they lived in another city anyway. She had no doubt that there was more to the situation than Cole explained, but she wondered if he could explain objectively. She decided now was not the time to ask.

The freeway extended on southward, a steady stream of mid-day traffic. Elly glanced to the east occasionally, catching glimpses of the Great Plains between the curtaining swells of low hills. The Rockies marched alongside to the west, seeming to extend on forever. It was an interesting place, she decided, with the wall of mountains on one side and the great open expanse of the plains on the other. It must have been strange to her after living in the desert.

"Oh —" The brooding gray of a thunderhead to the southwest caught her attention and she pointed. "You can see the rain." Somewhat flustered, she kept her eyes on the distant squall. A sheet of gray mist slanted down out of the belly of the cloud.

"You were going to say something else," her husband said. She felt his eyes on her and blushed nervously.

"I...I was just going to—to...Oh, this is so stupid, not knowing! I don't—I don't know your name."

Again that half-suspicious, examining stare. She ignored the fact that her face was crimson, her blood warm.

"Graydon," he said.

Graydon Cole. She said it to herself a couple of times, familiarizing herself with the sound of it. "It sounds English," she said finally.

"My father was English and Irish."

"What was your mother? You—you don't look English. You look..."

"What do I look?" If not for the set of his jaw, Elly almost thought he sounded amused. She pushed on.

"Oh, I know you think it's stupid to have me ask all these questions, things I should know, but I just don't have any idea. You look—Italian, or even Spanish. Your dark hair and all."

"I'm black Irish. It's not a common strain and a lot of people think I'm Italian or possibly Welsh. But basically black Irish."

"I see."

They drove on in silence. He seemed to be deep in thought, no doubt cursing the fact that he had to explain his lineage to his wife after four years of marriage. She felt like a reprimanded child, not understanding, but not allowed to ask why.

"I'm sorry to make you repeat yourself," she forced herself to say calmly.

"I'm not repeating myself."

"I mean, explaining your ancestry and all."

"You never asked before."

Elly's eyes swiveled to meet his. Yes, he was definitely amused now; she could tell by the sparkle in his eyes. Somehow that was worse than his contempt. She looked quickly away.

"You never asked me much of anything before," he said.

"I didn't? Why not?" She was annoyed. She didn't want him laughing at her.

"I don't know. Too shy, I guess. Or it wasn't important."

Maybe not exactly important, Elly thought, but she'd been curious and she'd wanted to know. Maybe she had been shy before. She certainly felt shy now, but her overriding need to know seemed to outweigh all other considerations. Her brain was like a dry sponge, sucking up the smallest bits of information to feed its rampaging thirst. Everything else was unimportant in comparison.

"Speaking of parents," Graydon said, "I called yours Saturday night to let them know you'd been in an accident, but were all right. That was before we knew you'd lost your memory, though. Then, Sunday when I found out, I called them again. I figured it'd be better to let them get used to the idea before you spoke to them. Your mom is upset, of course, and wants you to call her as soon as you can, but I told her it'd be a few days."

Elly took it all in, wondering what these mystery parents looked like. She couldn't even conjure up probable faces.

"Thank you," she said. "I—I hadn't thought about calling anyone. I guess I'll have a lot of explaining to do to friends and all." A thought struck her, one she hated to ask. She and her husband were communicating at last and she dreaded spoiling it. She had to know her ground, though. "Does—anyone know, I mean, like my parents or our friends about my—leaving?"

Graydon's jaw tightened perceptibly as Elly knew it would. "No. You were very discreet. You didn't tell anyone, at least not that I know of. That'll be one less complication you'll have to explain to anyone else."

But no chance of not explaining to you, she thought. God, there was so much she needed to *know*! It was so frustrating.

"Dr. D'Angelo said I worked for the Colorado Springs School District," she said to change the subject. "What job did I have?"

"Substitute teacher, part-time only. You arranged for that, too. You took a leave of absence, pending possible transfer. You still have two months and three weeks of leave to go."

She had been very thorough, hadn't she? It was appalling. She must have planned her escape for a while, covered all the bases. She wondered where she would have transferred to.

"And you're in the Air Force," she continued, "but I don't remember what rank."

"Colonel."

"Is that very high?"

"One step below General."

"Oh." She was impressed, particularly because he didn't seem to care if she were impressed or not. "What do you do?"

"Teach at the Academy."

They had borne steadily down on the darkening thunderheads and now Elly saw that they were about to drive directly under them. Great slashes of gray rain streaked down, flooding the windshield in a sudden slap of water. The onslaught of the downpour jolted Elly, and she jerked instinctively away from the windshield. Graydon pulled on the wipers but stared at her with a suspicious eye.

"What's the matter?" he demanded.

Elly was embarrassed to realize she was trembling. "I don't know," she breathed. "Just the water hitting the windshield, I...it just scared me. I guess I wasn't expecting it."

But she had expected it. She'd been watching the clouds advance, she had seen the curtain of rain. She had known when the downpour would strike them, and it still scared the hell out of her. Why, she wondered. What was so terrifying about rain?

"Are you all right now?" Graydon asked.

"Sure." She forced herself to sound calm, even crossed her legs leisurely to prove it. "Does it rain a lot here?"

"Yeah. Not like some states, like Washington, but we get a lot of these thunderstorms or squalls up from the Gulf coast. I think Colorado has the most unpredictable weather of any state. It can be clear and sunny one minute and hailing like crazy the next."

"It must be hard to stay ahead of it."

"It is. You just have to learn to wear light clothes and take a jacket with you wherever you go."

"I'll remember that," she said.

Try as she might to be casual, she realized Graydon was keeping a wary eye on her. Apparently she was not normally afraid of rain. The knowledge that she had developed a phobia out of her amnesia was disturbing. She wondered what Dr. D'Angelo would think of it.

It was less disquieting to stare out the side window, so Elly did that. "Is Aspen far from here?" she asked.

"Half way across the state. Do you remember it?"

"Just the name. Have I been there?"

"We were there last year, in November. We spent Thanksgiving and the week after there."

She could conjure up images of tiny skiers zigzagging down powdery slopes, but nothing else. And she could have just as easily seen a picture like that on a Christmas card. It was hopeless.

"What's the matter?"

"Nothing."

"You sighed like the weight of the world is on you."

"I guess I feel that way. It seems like there's so much to know and so much to figure out, and I'm only learning a fraction of it at a time. It's so frustrating."

Her voice was pensive, her eyes fastened unseeingly on the Rockies. She wouldn't face Graydon—she knew he wouldn't be sympathetic—so she didn't see the curious, wondering look in his eyes. For a brief moment the cold stone of his face softened until he thought about what this woman—memory or not—had done to him. He returned his eyes bitterly to the road.

"I guess that goes for both of us," he muttered. They drove in silence.

Once they had passed the crags of Castle Rock, Graydon snapped on the radio to a weather station. The clouds had multiplied until they crowded the sky ahead, and everywhere the slanting sheets of rain poured down. At first Graydon turned the wipers on, then off, then on as they passed through the intermittent storms, but finally he had to leave them on. The freeway was a silver-sheeted road ahead. Traffic slowed down. According to the radio it was only three o'clock, but to Elly it looked like six or seven.

"Looks like we're in for a big one," Graydon remarked. He checked over his left shoulder before changing lanes to pass a slowpoke. Elly didn't watch out the front window.

"How much further is it?" she asked.

"About a half hour. See those buildings ahead on the right? And the missiles sticking up in the air? That's the Academy."

The green sign said *Visitor Center* and Elly counted three rocket-like missiles canted into the air at a deadly angle. Beyond the square building where cars of all states were parked was a conglomeration of more buildings, all off white, all reaching up the slope of the Rockies' foothills. Among the array of buildings were open spaces, field, courts, parade grounds.

"What do you teach?"

"I'm a flight instructor. Ground school and in the air. It's just as well the storm hit while I'm off. I couldn't get anything off the ground today even if I wanted to."

The Academy slid by.

"You can't see Pike's Peak now, but it's there, beneath those clouds." He pointed to a slope lost in the low-ceiling cloud cover. "It's just above that clearing."

"What is the clearing?"

"The railroad up to the top."

Elly nodded. "Where is our house?"

"It's in Manitou Springs, a suburb of Colorado Springs, to the west. We're above the city, just below Pike's Peak." He pointed. "It looks like it's raining there, too."

When they came off the freeway and began a confusing course through curving, hillside residential streets, Elly found herself sitting up with nervous anticipation. As Graydon drove, she studied every house that came into view, hoping one would spark a memory. None did.

They pulled into a short, upgrade driveway next to an

impressive-looking gray house. The charcoal gray might have looked drab, Elly realized, if not for the stark white trim on the doors and windows. The sloping lawn and carefully bordered shrub gardens were neat without being austere. It was a nice looking house.

Graydon unlocked the door and let her go in first. Her eyes fairly attacked everything they met, trying vainly to wrestle the tiniest bit of familiarity from any object in sight.

The living room was inviting. Warm, rust-colored carpeting expanded from beneath her feet across the living room and into the dining room. A natural wheat colored couch reclined in front of the fireplace; a matching flame-stitched chair was off its corner. The end tables were a rich mahogany and there were pillows—rust and turquoise and orange—arranged casually about the furniture. A huge freeform wooden clock reigned above the fireplace.

"Does anything look familiar?" Graydon asked

She'd almost forgotten him but his voice startled her back to awareness. "No. Nothing."

He didn't seem surprised. "The kitchen is here, off the dining room." He led the way, gesturing off-handedly at the heavy oak dining room set, the wood-and-tile kitchen. "Down the hall is my den," he pushed open a door—bookshelves and a computer on a desk, a recliner and a small TV set. "Here's the one bathroom"— blue and white—"here's the spare bedroom"—a calico bed spread, probably handmade—"and here's the master bedroom." This last was dark woods and blues with patterned drapes and a full wall of mirrored closets. A decorative chain connected hurricane lanterns that hung on either side of the bed.

Elly froze at the sight of the room. It still meant nothing to her, jogged not one tiny piece of her mental block loose, but she suddenly remembered that she was married to this huge, brooding stranger beside her, had shared this bed with him. Maybe even created the growing life inside of her here.

"I—uh, where should I—can I use the spare bedroom?" It was an effort to ask and not demand, and yet she was fairly sure Graydon would be just as glad to have her across the hall and out of his way. She wished she had thought ahead to this so she could have discussed it coolly.

"Help yourself," he said. "Your clothes are still in the closet. Do you want me to move them for you?"

"If it's all the same to you, I can do it."

"Suit yourself." He started back down the hall, paused at the doorway of his den. "I've got some phone calls to make. If you need me, just knock."

She nodded understanding. Knock. Don't think you can come barging into my life without announcing yourself. You don't belong here. This is not your house, your home, any longer.

Even when the den door had clicked shut behind Graydon, Elly still felt the chill. He'd brought her home, showed her around; now it was up to her to amuse herself. Let me know if you remember anything, she thought bitterly, otherwise stay out of my sight.

A heavy sigh escaped her and she immediately broke it off. She couldn't waste time and energy feeling sorry for herself. There were too many more important things to do, to discover. Pity was a worthless emotion, not to be included in her vocabulary. She had work to do.

The closet was full. When she pulled open the mirrored, bi-fold doors, she was shocked by the amounts of dresses, suits, skirts, pants and tops. No matter what else she had lacked in her marriage to Graydon, she had not lacked clothing.

Curiously she pored through it all.

She was struck by the overriding sense of correctness, of matching color and fabric, of coordination. It was not the wardrobe of a woman used to bargain basements or close-out sales. Like the gray wool she had on, all the outfits were perfectly matched, perfectly accessorized. It was as if they had all been chosen to effect an image. It was not an image that Elly felt comfortable with.

She ignored the dresses and pulled out a few skirts, some pants, some basic tops. Designer jeans hung hidden in the recesses of the wardrobe and she took those, too. Shoes were carefully boxed on the closet floor. She found some low pumps, some espadrilles, a battered pair of tennies. They would be more comfortable than the heels and slings she left behind. Encumbered by having only one useable arm, she began the tedious process of transferring her booty to the spare bedroom.

It was obviously an unused room, or at least not used very often. There was a mirror on the back of the door but none over the bureau, and the heat was turned low. Elly turned it up to 68°. Beneath the calico bedspread, the bed was made up with fresh sheets, all ready for the infrequent guest. It was a small room, but it would suit her well enough. She hung up all her new clothes and emptied out her overnight case.

When she'd arranged things in her room, she checked to see if Graydon's door was still closed. It was. She stepped quietly from her room to prowl the rest of the house.

The bathroom was so uncluttered that it looked hardly used. The counter top had a tooled wooden towel stand with a small guest towel on it and a small, flower-shaped blue soap. Otherwise it was bare. A wicker basket on the back of the toilet held several issues of magazines—*Ladies' Home Journals* and some ski magazines. His and hers, she thought grimly. Everything, she found, was put away, either in the medicine chest or in the linen cupboards along one side. The Coles apparently were very neat, tidy people.

Elly poured over the things in the cupboards. Soap, towel, toothpaste, shaving cream. Some moisturizer. She needed that. In the shower she found shampoo and rinse and a big, fibrous loofa. She'd love to wash her hair but with her arm in a cast she wouldn't be taking any showers, just baths, and anyway, she couldn't very well wash her own hair with one hand. Or could she? The image of her scowling husband performing such ministrations was not comforting. She'd learn to do it with one hand.

Still, it seemed that the bathroom was spartanly supplied. She couldn't place what else might be there that wasn't. Her things, of course, were in her room—brush, toothbrush, deodorant, cologne. Maybe that's why it looked so bare. Her thoughts wandering, Elly glanced at the smiling woman on the cover of the magazine and then lifted her eyes to the image facing her in the mirror.

It was her face. She knew it now; dark blue eyes, (one slightly slanted though less than before) regular features, dark brown hair. She looked ghostly, though, as pale as the white wall behind her. She rechecked the face on the magazine. It looked vibrant, alive. Compared to it, her own face looked dull. She needed color in her face, at least a bit of blusher or some eye shadow.

That was what was missing—makeup! How silly, she thought. Hadn't she worn makeup before, or had Graydon thrown it away in a fit of temper at her leaving? She checked the medicine cabinet again. Nothing. She'd have to buy some.

Which brought up another question, she realized as she went into the kitchen. She had no money; she wasn't working. She was just going to have to talk with Graydon and decide a few things. She needed *some* money. And the shopping—surely she had done that. The kitchen pantry was full. She found shelves of canned goods, rows of preserves—did she can all those things? The refrigerator was stocked with all the essentials: milk, butter, eggs, fruit, vegetables, lunch meat, bread. The freezer was packed with white-wrapped meat. Whoever did the shopping was very thorough. She wondered if Graydon expected her to cook dinner.

She checked the clock—it was after four-thirty. What time was a good time to eat dinner. Six? Seven? No time sounded better than any other. She'd just have to guess.

A prickling at the back of her neck alerted her to the fact that Graydon was there. Her back to the dining room, she had been lost in thought and hadn't heard him on the deep carpet. She spun to find him staring at her.

"Are you finding everything okay?" he asked. His voice was a mixture of sarcasm and satire.

"Yes." God, why did he do that to her? Just a look from him and she turned red.

"You looked very absorbed. Was it about anything important?" While he talked, he brushed past her to the cupboard for a glass. He filled it with cold water and downed half of it before turning to wait for her answer.

"I, uh, was just wondering if I should start dinner. I didn't know what time you were used to eating."

"Do you know how to cook?" There was that satirical lilt again.

"I—yes, I think so." She was getting mad now. "Dr. D'Angelo said it's normal to remember small things, everyday things; it's just the important emotional things I've forgotten."

"*Just* the important things? Isn't that enough?"

"Well, I certainly didn't do it on purpose!" she snapped.

"You act like I did it deliberately just to annoy you. Dr. D'Angelo said—"

"I don't want to hear any more about what Dr. D'Angelo said." Graydon's voice was suddenly flat and final. His eyes turned hard.

"Why not? He's the doctor who knows more about my condition than anyone else. He understands—"

"Oh, does he? More than I do, of course? Well, he's not married to you and he wasn't humiliated by you, so leave him out. From now on, we don't discuss Dr. D'Angelo." He dared her to argue, his eyes challenging her over the rim of his glass as he sipped water.

Elly was furious. "You're very used to having your own way, aren't you?" she asked. "You're used to having me cater to your temper tantrums and fits of jealousy. Look, I don't know how I was before, but if I cowed down to you then, I won't now. You've no right to bully me around."

In a lightning move, Graydon had a hold of her good arm. He yanked her up with an angry jerk.

"And just where did you learn that? Did Adam teach you not to cow down? Is he the one who said you weren't a complete woman if you didn't stand up to me?"

"I don't know what you're talking about. Let go of my arm."

"If you don't know what I'm talking about then why are you continuing to act like you did when you left? You were never such a bothersome bitch before you met that jackass artist. Explain that to me if you can."

"Let go of my arm." Her voice was a low command. "You're hurting me."

"Oh? I wasn't sure if you'd forgotten how strong I was. You only forgot the important things, after all." He glared at her and his hand, if anything, tightened its grip.

"Am I supposed to give in to you just because you're stronger than I am? Was that the way it was before?" She winced as he increased the pressure; it felt like the small bones of her wrist were being crushed. "Damn you, let *go* of me!" she cried. "No wonder I left! If this is the way you handle things, I'm surprised I stayed as long as I did!"

He flexed his fingers, tightening his hold all the more. The pain made her yield so that her arm twisted with his hand, and her shoulder began to throb. All she could see was his face, close and angry and dangerous. She panicked.

Without thinking she kicked out and the toe of her shoe caught him full on the shin. Immediately his hand opened, she jerked free and before he could recover she was running down the hall. Once in her room, she slammed the door and reached for the lock.

There was no lock.

She leaned against it, casting about for anything she could block the door with. Before she could find anything, he was there, pushing on the door, shoving her back. With one impatient heave he smashed the door open and she went spinning across the room. She caught herself on the window sill and waited for him to close in. Her hand went instinctively to her stomach.

"What are you doing, protecting Adam's brat?" he asked. Breathing angrily, he blocked the doorway. His face was contorted with rage and his hands curled into fists. He didn't approach her, though. "You're good at that, aren't you? You let yourself almost get killed to protect that thing."

"How do you know whose it is?" she demanded. "Maybe its yours."

"That's not what you said in your note. You told me it was his. You said you knew."

"So what do you want me to do?" she asked angrily. "Get down on my knees and apologize? Beg forgiveness? I can't apologize for things I don't remember doing. I won't."

Graydon stood in the doorway like a huge, hulking bull, his nostrils wide.

For a moment Elly thought he might actually stride over and backhand her, but he was able to maintain his distance. For the moment.

"This isn't the end of this," he promised. "One way or another we're going to resolve this thing, and if you can't remember how things were, you know how they are now. I've never taken any crap off a woman yet, and I'm not about to start, so you'd better make up your mind to it. This is my home and things get done my way. Now do you understand that?"

"Yes, sir," she hissed. "Or should I say, yes, sir, Colonel Cole?"

The effort he made to keep his temper in check was a physical one, and luckily it succeeded. Elly was sure he could have killed her if he chose to.

"I'm going out, both to cool off and to get some dinner. I just can't see going to jail over you. But you'd better think about everything else I've said, and you'd better learn to live with it. Just because you can't remember doesn't mean it didn't happen. Remember *that*, at least."

Elly was a frustrated maelstrom of anger and fear. She stayed at the window, her shoulder wedged against the frame, until she heard the Ford start up, back out and drive away. The car lights splashed across the window briefly. She cringed from the light. She couldn't have felt more afraid if the car itself were bearing down on her.

When the sound of the car had droned away into silence, Elly went to her bed and sank gratefully down onto it. She was shaking with the residue of the conflict, with misery and with confusion. Whatever had she done to deserve this? How had she gotten herself into such a mess? It was impractical, even impossible to even think of finding a way out of this maze of disaster. It was more than she could ask of herself. For the second time in her three days of consciousness, she cried herself to sleep.

Chapter Three

When she woke up, it was dark. She was on her stomach, her cast beneath her and now both her arm and her ribs ached. She rolled over onto her back. The light from a street lamp lit the opening of the window like a backstage light behind a prop. It was raining outside.

There was no clock in her room. Over the heavy silence of the rest of the house, she could hear the frantic ticking of the living room clock as it tried to keep pace with the rain outside. But there were no other sounds.

She forced herself up off the bed and went to the window. Her head pounded with the effort. To her right outside she could see the jutting corner of the garage, the slick grade of the driveway, but no car. She breathed a little easier.

The bathroom light winked on over the medicine cabinet and even its diffused brightness hurt her eyes. She looked like hell in the mirror—hair limp and tangled, one cheek creased from sleeping on a wrinkle in the bedspread, her eyes red and puffy. The healing cuts near her right eye looked inflamed and angry, but when she touched them, they weren't tender. Obviously crying was not her greatest beauty aid. She'd have to do less of it.

She poked her head out the door and checked the living room clock—8:43. She wondered when Graydon would be back. Maybe there was an officer's club at the Academy and he would stay there for the night. It certainly wouldn't bother her if he did. She needed time to think.

Taking advantage of her possession of the house, she started bath water and went to the kitchen. She was starving.

She knew she ought to eat well, for the baby's sake at least, so she poured a glass of milk and made a ham and cheese sandwich. It was nice not to have to eat bland hospital food. Carrying her dinner with her, she retreated to her room for clean things to wear after her bath.

When she crossed to her bureau and opened a drawer, she was startled at its emptiness. How stupid, she thought. She hadn't brought any underthings from Graydon's room. Thank God he wasn't here to see. She could go in his room and get some without worrying about sparking his awful temper.

There was a triple dresser in his room, and she had to try all three top drawers before she found hers. It was filled with sensible cotton hip-huggers and brand name bras. She pulled out a pair of panties, found a loose cotton nightgown in the next drawer, and carried the rest of the contents back to her room. On her second trip, she investigated the bottom drawer and found more lingerie, some hand knitted slippers of variegated yarn, scarves and pantyhose. The slippers were too gaudy; there had to be something else she could wear to keep her feet warm.

In the closet she found regular slippers of honey-beige plush. They were better, but still not exactly to her liking. She'd just as soon have a pair of knee-high socks. Maybe later, she thought, and took her things to the bathroom.

It felt marvelous to soak in the warm water. She found that once she took off her sling, she could rest her cast on the edge of the tub so as to keep it out of the water and still be comfortable. She leaned back and relaxed. It was heaven.

Eleanor Cole, she thought, what in God's name are you going to do? She didn't see how she and Graydon were ever going to be able to communicate on an objective level. She was willing to keep trying, but how long until he took a swipe at her with one of those huge fists and smashed her head in? She made up her mind that if he ever laid a finger on her again, she'd leave. She'd done it before, and she'd do it again. She could even do it now, tonight.

There was no one to stop her.

And go where, she thought. She had no money, no job, and no practical knowledge of how to go about getting either. She didn't know who her friends were and her parents were hundreds of miles away. As a matter of fact, she thought with a humorless smile, she couldn't even remember her maiden name. It was almost laughable.

All right, she said to herself, so you can't leave. Then figure out away to settle this before he kills you.

The problem, she decided, was that they let their discussions get too emotional. Instead of reasoning like adults, Graydon read implications into everything she said or did, baited her, goaded her and she lashed out in defense. That would have to stop. Dr. D'Angelo, she decided, was right. It was up to her to re-educate her husband. She had to control herself enough to make him understand, to make him re-evaluate her personality. If she left it to him, they would keep fighting and nothing would get accomplished.

So, she thought, no more hysterics, no more tears, no more vindictive outbursts. From now on, she would be in control. She would face him eye to eye and make him see.

The thought of his eyes boring into her sent shivers up her spine. Ducking carefully under the water, she began the complicated task of washing her hair.

When she finally climbed out of the tub, she felt much better. Newly clean and newly resolved, she felt more able to draw on that strength Dr. D'Angelo said she had. She pulled a huge blue towel off the rack, knowing it could just as easily be Graydon's as hers, and dried herself off.

Naked, she surprised herself. Even allowing for the splinted arm, bruised rib cage and stitched head, she had a good figure. Dressed in shapeless hospital gowns and that sensible gray suit, she hadn't thought much about it, but she certainly hadn't felt very attractive. Now as she turned in front of the mirror she realized that she could be. Her breasts were high and full, her waist tapered and her hips rounded. Her legs were fairly long and well-turned. All in all, with her dark hair combed out, she wasn't bad looking. Why, then, did she feel surprised to find out?

Actually, she didn't like her hair. It was blunt, bland. She'd like to have a little more shape to it, have it do something beside just lie there. Later, she thought, when everything she did wasn't so suspect, she'd make a change. Right now, she was sure any changes she made would be immediately pounced on by Graydon.

While she dressed, she thought about her husband. It wasn't hard to figure that he was immensely jealous. Any allusion to Elly's leaving—or to Adam—was enough to infuriate him and even the mention of Dr. D'Angelo's name too often had sparked a green-eyed response. If she wanted to keep all her teeth, she'd have to remember to watch how she spoke.

And that was another thing—he was certainly adept at giving orders and he expected nothing less than absolute obedience. It had been humiliating to have him talk down to her as if she were a child overstepping her bounds. Perhaps before she had not minded. But that was foolish. More than likely, she was too afraid of the brute to butt heads with him, at least until Adam came along and offered her a way of escape. Elly could easily understand why she had opted to say her goodbyes and anything else in a note. She had no doubt planned to be miles from Colorado Springs by the time Graydon read it. She probably knew a confrontation would result in nothing but a show of force—his.

Robed and slippered, she padded to the kitchen. It wouldn't be long before she climbed back into bed, but the idea of a hot cup of tea sounded good. Surprisingly, a tea kettle sat on the stove. Maybe at least there was one part of her that had filtered through the block. She filled it and set it on a burner, then sat at the dining room table to wait.

She wondered what Adam had been like. He had to have been very different from Graydon or else why would she bother to leave one for the other? She wished she knew what he looked like.

An idea struck her. In her overnight case she had seen a clutch purse underneath her robe. When she'd unpacked, she had thoughtlessly laid it on her bureau and forgotten it. Now she went for it and brought it back where she could empty its contents on the dining room table.

Car keys and a cell phone spilled out, clanking on the table. At least he trusted her to drive. She found a wallet and pulled it open. Yes, here was a driver's license, complete with a picture of her unscathed face. A very plain, expressionless face. Flipping through the plastic photo mounts, she found a snapshot of herself and Graydon standing in front of a hedge. Graydon's arm was possessively around her waist, but her own hands were clasped chastely in front of her. There was no inscription on the back.

Another picture, a young man of about twenty-five. Could that be Adam? She read the back: "Managed to get this of Bryan last Christmas. He'll probably never let me take another one." And below that, in different handwriting was "Dec. 02."

Her brother. He had similar features, the same color hair, but his eyes looked gray. According to the date and to the age difference Dr. D'Angelo had mentioned, he was twenty-four, her age now. He looked infinitely more at ease at twenty-four than she felt.

The last picture was of an older couple and Elly guessed they must be her parents. There was nothing on the back to tell her so, but the woman was of average height, close to fifty and had blue eyes. The man was quite a bit taller and larger, his face boxy and florid-looking. He hung an arm lazily across his wife's shoulders and grinned cockily at the camera. Elly didn't like him. He reminded her too much of Graydon.

Other than that, her wallet told her nothing. She had credit cards, a social security card, School District ID, and a parking pass. There was a checkbook with scenic checks on a joint account: Graydon A. Cole and Eleanor K. Cole. She didn't even know what the 'K' stood for.

The tea kettle burst to life in a puff of steam and began to squeal. Elly fixed her cup of tea—it took her a few minutes to find the teabags; the canisters were put away in the pantry—and returned to her investigation of her purse. It was almost like digging through layers of artifacts in an archeological dig, she thought; such small bits of evidence from which to reconstruct so much. She dumped out the rest of the contents.

A brush clattered out, a compact mirror with no place for powder, a stick of lip balm and a pack of gum. There were miscellaneous papers: a gas receipt, a telephone number scribbled on a torn scrap, a dry cleaning ticket and a coupon for fifteen cents on pantyhose. Frustratingly there was nothing that could tell her any more about the woman she used to be.

She felt the lethargy of discouragement settle over her as she scooped everything back into the purse. She had known it wasn't going to be easy, but it was beginning to feel like she was butting her head against a brick wall. Not only was she making very little headway, but the emotional toll was practically debilitating. She had to wonder if it was worth it.

Sighing, she took her tea and her purse back into her room and propped herself comfortably on the bed. Much as she would like to lie down and forget the whole thing, she knew she couldn't. She had to keep at it, even if it meant antagonizing Graydon to near violence. If only they could come to some sort of an understanding, they could work at it together. There had to be some way they could work it out without destroying each other.

Warmed and soothed by the tea, Elly slid down beneath the blankets on her bed. She decided to wait up for Graydon so she could approach him about her idea, but her ribs still ached so she got as comfortable as she could. She left the light on so she wouldn't fall asleep.

When she woke up later, her room was dark.

She was first alerted to morning by the sun driving its needles of light directly into her eyes. Her window faced due east and the rain-cleared sky held back none of the sun's brilliance. She rolled over and promised herself she'd pull the shade at night from now on.

Then small noises came to her—the dull thud of a cupboard door closing, the free-floating surge of water through pipes, the sound of shoes on the kitchen tile. Graydon was up.

She dreaded meeting his eyes. This morning he would have one more criticism of her to add to the others. She had managed to drive him out of his own house by her failure to stay in line and caused him to ramble about the city for hours until he had cooled his temper. She could imagine how glad he would be to see her this morning.

Trying valiantly to steel her resolve, she rose to meet him. "Hello." He was measuring coffee into a coffee filter. After a cursory study of her, he returned to it.

"Is there anything I can do?" she asked. "Make breakfast?" Her voice, although responsive, was not pleading. She would not have him think she was groveling.

"I don't eat breakfast. If you want some, help yourself." He shoved the filter basket into the coffee maker and snapped it on. The coffee can was returned unthinkingly to a cupboard Elly no doubt would have had to hunt for. Then he headed her way. "I'm going to get the paper."

She exhaled silently in relief as he strode by.

With his dominating presence out of the kitchen, Elly felt safe in going in. She wasn't particularly hungry, either, but she poured the baby a glass of milk. She needed something to keep her hand from shaking.

There was one woven placemat on the table and Elly searched drawers until she found more. She lay one at the seat across from Graydon's so the width of the table would separate them. No sense courting disaster.

When Graydon returned with the paper, he seemed not to notice Elly at all. He checked the coffee, noting it hadn't begun to fill the pot, and settled himself at the table. In seconds he was engrossed in the front page.

Elly slid into her chair across from him.

"You're not going to the Academy today?" she asked. She had noticed he wore black slacks and a pullover sweater. She was sure even a colonel had to wear a uniform.

Graydon rustled the newspaper. "No. I had already planned on taking off at least through today."

Because of me, she finished silently. She rested her cast on the table and wrapped her left hand around her glass. It looked as though Graydon was going to leave all of the patching up to her.

"You need to know where things are," he continued. "I'll take you into the city and show you. Just pay attention so you don't get lost."

His admonishment pricked her temper. Immediately she squelched it. She would not rise to his baiting; she would keep control.

"Graydon," she said as evenly as she could, "we have to talk.

We have to declare a truce or something."

He lowered the paper from in front of his face and his black eyes studied her suspiciously.

"Why?" he scoffed.

"Because we're not getting anywhere like this. Look, we both want answers; we agreed on that at the hospital, but we aren't going to accomplish anything by fighting. I don't want to fight with you."

"What do you want?" he asked belligerently.

She breathed deeply to steady her voice. "I want to know who I am."

He didn't change his expression. "You know who you are."

"I know my name, yes, I know a few facts about where I live and where I work, but I don't know who I am. Not really. Graydon, please help me find out who I am."

The silence was heavy between them. Graydon stared uncertainly into her eyes as if he might find the key to the mystery there, and Elly suffered his investigation as stoically as she could. Staring back at him, she knew things had not been easy for him, either. There was uncertainty behind the black stone of his eyes. If only he would help her, she would do her best to help him, too.

"What do you suggest?" he asked finally. "Twenty questions? This is your life, Elly Cole? I can't teach you everything you ever knew."

"I know, I'm not asking that. I just want to have a solid foundation that I can start from. If we could talk objectively, without fighting, I think—"

"I hate you, you know."

Elly felt as if he'd kicked her in the stomach. All the breath rushed out of her and she gripped the table edge to steady herself. There was not a flicker of pity in her husband's face as he watched her struggle. There was nothing there but blackness.

Elly gulped air. Her heart hammered as if it would break free of her already bruised rib cage, and she sank back against the chair to ease the ache. Gradually she regained her breath. Graydon waited moodily for her to recover.

"I know that," she said when she felt able to talk. "I can't say that I blame you, not if I did what you say."

"There's no 'if' about it. You did."

"All right; I'm willing to concede that. But I can't do anything about it until I know why I did those things. And I can't do that alone."

The coffee began to dribble noisily. Graydon got up and pulled a cup out of the cupboard. Instead of returning to the table as Elly expected, he leaned against the kitchen counter and crossed his arms over his chest.

"You're asking help from the wrong person. The only reason you're here at all is because I want to resolve, in my own mind, why you left. If I could do that without you, you'd be out on your ass, memory or not. I have absolutely no desire to do you any favors at all."

Their eyes locked. Elly felt powerless against him. He was her only hope, and without his help, she was stymied. Without the knowledge he could give her, what chance did she have of regaining anything of her past life at all? "I guess, if you feel that way, there's no point in my staying here." She looked down at her splinted arm and tried to draw on her inner strength. There didn't seem to be much left. "If you'll tell me my parents' phone number, I'll call them and see if they'll send me a plane ticket."

"Sorry. You're not leaving. Not yet."

Elly looked up in surprise.

"I told you. I want something from you. You'll stay until I get it."

Now she was mad. "So you're going to keep me here like a prisoner, belittling me and bullying me around as long as it pleases you? Do you honestly think I'm going to stay under those circumstances?" She laughed humorlessly. "Sorry, that's not my idea of the way to find out. If that's how it's going to be, I'll leave first chance I get, and you'll never know the answers."

"Neither will you. Is that what you want?"

"No, but I don't want to be treated like a skeleton that's come rattling out of its closet, either. If you won't help me, what difference will it make if I stay or go? I want to know, I want to understand, but if I can't, at least I want to be treated like a human being."

Graydon frowned angrily. "So what do you suggest, since you

seem so ready with solutions."

"A truce," she sighed. "That's all. If we could try to get along, just until we know if and when I'll get my memory back. It won't be easy, but it's worth a try." Graydon's lack of an agreement drove her on. "Look, I promise you I won't interfere; I'll stay as far away from you as you want, and I'll try not to ask stupid questions. I'll be as little trouble to you as I can manage. It shouldn't take me more than a few days to learn your routine around the house, and then I won't be such a bother to you."

"And you won't defy me?" he pressed. "I don't take kindly to being kicked in the shin in my own kitchen."

Elly dropped her gaze at the memory of last night's battle. "I'll try," she said. "I can't promise I won't fight back if you start badgering me, but I'll try. You've got to try, too. You'll have to control your temper. I can't answer any of your accusations, not yet, so you'll just have to try to understand. But if you're willing, I am, too. I know we can do it if we'll just compromise a little. I know we can."

Graydon turned his attention to the coffee, still dribbling. His expression gave nothing away and Elly held her breath. As hard-headed as he was, she could imagine his squelching the whole idea just on pride. His ego was as big as he was.

"You won't give me any guff?" he asked.

"No, not if I can help it."

"You'll do what I say?"

"Within reason."

He looked up. "All right, we'll try it. But the first time you start pulling that independent crap on me, that's it. I won't tolerate that."

Elly gulped, crossed her fingers on her left hand, and nodded. "Okay."

Graydon reached for the carafe. "You want some coffee?"

She fairly devoured the paper. As Graydon sipped steaming black coffee and leafed through section after section, Elly pounced on whatever he set aside and scoured the headlines. Some things came home with the helpful newsprint; she knew who was President, she knew about the mid-east crisis and the consuming drive to find more oil or a good substitute. The tragedy of over a hundred people dying in an air disaster sounded sadly familiar. A picture of smoldering rubble brought back the knowledge of an earthquake in Turkey. She was delighted to know that she had retained so much. Her eyes must have shown it.

"See anything familiar?" Graydon asked.

"Yes, quite a bit. It seems like I know the general state of the nation. And some of this foreign policy stuff is familiar. Yes, I remember quite a bit." She couldn't help but be excited. She wanted Graydon to share in it with her.

"Well, at least we know you're not hopeless," he said. "Why don't you get dressed? I'll take you downtown."

Elly almost had to call for help. She slid on a pair of jeans and then had a heck of a time buttoning the button with only one hand. After wrestling with it for several minutes, she got it. She found out if she pulled her sweater sleeve over her cast first, she could slide the turtleneck over her head with one hand easily. Pirouetting before the mirror, she thought the camel-colored sweater went well with the dark blue jeans. Now the only problem was tying her shoes.

"Graydon?" she called, coming down the hall. He was waiting, finishing the last of his coffee. His jacket hung over his arm. "I hate to ask but would you mind tying my shoes? I can't do it."

"You've got better shoes than those old tennis shoes," he said. "Why don't you wear something else?"

"But these will be comfortable," she said. Graydon didn't look pleased. "Okay, okay, I'll wear something else. Do you have any preferences?" She circled back toward the bedrooms.

"Wear your boots. They zip up the side."

"Boots, boots," she chanted as she searched the big closet. Ah, there they were. Tan leather with three-inch wood heels. Not exactly her idea of comfortable, but she'd wear anything to keep on Graydon's good side. Plopping down on his bed, she pulled them on and zipped them. Easy, she thought.

"Do you want to drive?" he asked when she came out again.

"Oh, not really. I'd rather be able to concentrate on streets and places than have to worry about driving, too. Do you mind?"

"No. I'd just as well. Let's go."

The blue Ford was cold and Graydon let it warm up for almost a minute. Elly had pulled a suede coat out of the closet and snuggled into it until the heater began to put out warm air. A plume of vapor clouded behind the car.

"Cold?" Graydon asked. He slipped the car into reverse and turned around to back out.

"A little. It's nice that it's not raining, though."

"Yeah."

When he had the car headed down the street, Elly was able to look out her window and see Colorado Springs. It looked huge, sprawled out below like a dark maze. Everywhere were trees bending gracefully in the wind. "This is a nice area up here," she observed.

"It should be. The houses cost enough."

"We must be fairly well off, then?"

"Well enough. A colonel's pay is pretty good."

Elly nodded. "My job, then—my teaching job—that was just a supplement?"

"Right. You don't have to work. You never did."

Elly quieted. She had a feeling she was in dangerous territory again. From what she knew of Graydon so far, she figured he would be the type who would not want his wife to work. It would fit.

So why had she gone to work? Being a part-time substitute wasn't much of a career, but maybe it had been enough. Since they had apparently not planned a family in four years of marriage, maybe she had felt a need for some sort of outside interest.

"If you were to take this street all the way down, it would take you clear to Colorado Springs. The freeway's faster, though."

Elly noted the streets. Colorado Avenue was the main thoroughfare. They lived on Alder, at 2633. She'd memorized that before they left the driveway. "This street takes you over to the freeway." This was Beaten. She filed it away.

The freeway traffic was light, but it was after 9 a.m. and most rush hour traffic was gone. Today is Wednesday, Elly told herself, Wednesday October 14. The fourth day of her life. She was looking forward to it.

Graydon drove silently for awhile and then steered the car

down an off ramp. Elly had noted the multitude of houses giving way to businesses and now they drove past motels, fast food outlets and small commercial buildings. She read all the signs she could: Nelson's Saw Shop, Speedy-Mark, East Slope Motel, Hamburger Hut. None of it jarred memories loose but she kept looking eagerly ahead. They were coming to a shopping center.

The Big Value Market squatted at one end of the mall, a large department store at the other. In between, scores of small shops advertising in an array of signs. "Anything look familiar?"

"No; I feel like it should, but it doesn't."

He was unperturbed. "Well, this is probably where you'll do most of your shopping. Do you want to go inside?"

"Not unless you want to. I can do my poking around later. As long as I know how to get here, I can find my way around all right."

Graydon circled the lot and headed further east.

"I'll take you downtown. Once you see the way the town's laid out, you ought to be able to get around without getting lost."

The four-lane thoroughfare extended down toward higher buildings and more traffic. The two-way streets gave way to one-way streets, and eventually they crossed a maze of wide avenues divided by grassy median strips. Everywhere were high-rise office buildings, restaurants, theaters and scores of smaller businesses.

"I didn't think it was this big," Elly said.

"It's approaching the half million mark," Graydon explained. "It's the second biggest city in the state after Denver. This is the freeway, I-25, going north to Denver. If you keep on the freeway from Manitou Springs, you can go right to it."

"Is that the way you go to the Academy?" she asked.

"Yes. If you ever need to go there, it's easy to find from the freeway." He drove around the city center and started back westward. "I'll take you by a couple of schools you taught at; maybe you'll see something you recognize."

"What grade level did I teach?"

"Primary, first through third. Up ahead is Washington Elementary. You were there just a couple of weeks ago."

It didn't spark any memories. As Graydon drove by, Elly studied the layout of the school, noted the hundreds of children playing on the grounds. Try as she might, she couldn't force her brain to recognize any part of it.

"I'll take you over to Jefferson. You were there just a little more than a week ago."

"What's that?" Elly asked, pointing. At the bottom of the slope ahead and a little to the south was a huge building, seeming to sprawl across organized grounds.

"The Broadmoor. It's a hotel complex. Has its own golf course and everything."

"Is it a resort?"

"Sort of. It's pretty famous, I guess, and very, very expensive."

"Have we ever stayed there?"

Graydon laughed. "No, the closest we ever got was going to the zoo, just above it on the hillside. See those roads criss-crossing the slope? That's the zoo walk."

Somehow it surprised Elly that Colorado Springs would have a zoo, but she didn't know why. She decided she'd like to see it some time.

"Here's Jefferson Elementary."

Another meaningless school. Elly felt defeated. How could she not remember a place she'd been just the week before? It was discouraging.

Graydon appeared to notice her flagging interest. "You want to see any more?" he asked.

"I don't think so," Elly sighed. "Not unless there's something you think I should see."

"I can't think of anything." He turned back toward Manitou Springs. Elly noted street names and his general direction, but otherwise everything around her was lost in futility. They passed another school and it, like the others, held nothing for her. An interesting mural covered one whole outside wall, but other than appealing to Elly's sense of color and line, it was meaningless. She didn't even comment on it to Graydon.

Back at the house, she went to her room to hang up her jacket. She returned to the kitchen to find Graydon scowling through the refrigerator.

"Would you like some lunch?" she asked, "Or do you eat

lunch?" She was careful to keep her voice and expression patently innocent. Graydon evidently decided to let the reminder pass unnoticed.

"I was thinking of making a sandwich," he allowed.

"Would you like me to do it? What kind do you want?" Surprising even herself, Elly brushed past Graydon for the bread and got a knife.

"Some of that salami, I guess." He retreated to the dining room and let Elly have the kitchen. She was conscious of his eyes on her as she worked.

"Mustard and mayonnaise?"

"Just mustard."

"Oh." She put the mayonnaise back.

"You like mayonnaise," he said. "Aren't you eating?"

"I saw some soup in the pantry and thought I'd have that, instead. I'm still cold from being outside."

Graydon carried the morning's paper to the fireplace and added it to a pile of others on the edge of the hearth. "Do you want me to start a fire?"

"Not unless you were going to anyway. I'll warm up in a few minutes. Do you want cheese?"

"Yeah. There's some sharp cheddar in there."

"I see it."

Elly put the sandwich together and brought it to Graydon where he sat at the table. He couldn't disguise his curiosity as she brought him a napkin, then set about fixing her soup. He was distrustful of this domestic gentility.

"I was looking through my wallet last night," she said, "and found some pictures. I think they're of my parents and my brother. Do you know?"

"They are."

"Do you have any more? Like a photo album or something? I thought I could look through them and see if anything strikes me."

"We have one," he said around his sandwich. "And a lot of loose pictures that never got put in. I'll get it."

Elly was about to protest, being afraid she was becoming troublesome again, but Graydon was already on his feet and headed for his den. When he returned, he had the photo album and an envelope crammed with snapshots. He laid them at Elly's place on the table. She put her soup on a low burner and came to leaf through them.

The pictures in the album were the oldest. There were a few landscapes, desert scenes mostly, and some large, sand-colored buildings.

"Where's this?" she asked.

"The base at Alamogordo. I was a test pilot there for three years."

As if in illustration of his words, the next page held several pictures of various fighter jets, sleek delta winged, needle-nosed planes, some in flight, some on the ground. A younger Graydon stood beside a few of them.

"Wasn't it dangerous?" she asked. The jets looked satanic, every bit of their design for only one purpose—killing. It gave Elly chills.

"Sometimes. The closest call I ever had was having one of the damn things stall on me at 6,000 feet."

Elly looked up, eyes wide. "How awful. What did you do?"

"Fiddled with it until I got it going again."

"How close to the ground were you then?"

"Two thousand. I had plenty of time."

Elly shivered. It didn't sound like near enough time to her, but she had no idea what the capabilities of the weird-looking jets were. She turned another page.

She saw herself staring back. She was much younger, nineteen or twenty, she guessed, and stood shyly in front of a parked blue Ford. Her dark hair was pulled back on top but hung down past her shoulders. She smiled painfully.

"How old was I here?" she asked.

"Just twenty, I think. Your birthday's in July, and I think that was taken in August."

"July what?

"Fifteenth."

"You like blue Fords, don't you?"

"Not particularly. The Air Force does, though."

Of course, she thought. How silly of her not to know they

were government cars.

"I think your soup is boiling," Graydon said.

She jumped up. She'd been so engrossed in the pictures, she'd forgotten all about the soup. Mollified, she got a bowl and poured the steaming soup into it.

It smelled good and she realized she really was hungry. Setting her bowl on one side of the photo album, she resumed her reconstruction of her past.

"Who's this with you?" She'd found a picture of Graydon arm in arm with another uniformed young man. They grinned at the camera.

"Friend of mine, Bud Louellen. He died in a plane crash about six months after that was taken."

"Oh, how awful. Did I know him?"

"He was best man at our wedding."

Elly didn't know what else to say, so she said nothing. Looking at these pictures was more difficult than she'd thought.

"Where is this?" She saw herself again, this time standing in front of low buildings connected by covered walks.

"The Community College in Alamogordo. That's where you were going to school when I met you."

The pieces were beginning to fall into place. She'd left home to go to school, had met dashing Graydon Cole, a devil-may-care test pilot, and gotten married shortly after. They'd stayed at Alamogordo a year, then moved here so Graydon could teach.

"Was I majoring in education?"

"That and English Literature. You got your BA there."

"Where did I get my teaching certificate?"

"Here. At Colorado College."

"In three years?"

Graydon smiled grimly. "You're very intelligent. You challenged a lot of courses and passed. That saved you a lot of time."

Elly didn't feel intelligent. She must have been very determined to teach. Why? Was it a way to get out of a loveless marriage?

Surprisingly, the next pictures were of their wedding. They stood smiling happily in a small chapel, Graydon in his blue uniform and Elly in a knee-length summer dress. Bud Louellen stood beside Graydon and a strange girl stood next to Elly.

"Who's this?"

"Bud's girlfriend, Sue."

"Is this in Alamogordo?"

"Yes, in the small chapel."

"Were my parents there?"

"No."

Elly looked up. She heard distaste in Graydon's voice. "Why not?" she asked.

"Because we didn't take the time to invite them," he said shortly. "It was sort of a spur of the moment thing."

Elly backed off. She had learned enough to know when she was questioning too much, and she had no desire to incite Graydon's temper. There was something between him and her parents, though.

"What about your parents?" she asked. "You never mention them."

"That's because they're dead."

"Oh, I'm sorry. Did I know them?"

"No. They died years before we met. My dad died in a car accident, and my mom had a stroke about two years later. It's been a long time."

"Do you have any brothers or sisters?" Elly turned the pages of the album, scanning over pictures of deserts, mountains, sand dunes.

"Two sisters, one older and one younger. One's in Chicago and the other one's in Los Angeles."

"Have I met them?"

"No. We never see each other. We have nothing in common."

Elly thought that was sad, but knowing how bull-headed and stubborn Graydon was, somehow it didn't surprise her. She turned more pages.

"Where's this?" It was a snowy mountain scene, with Graydon bundled up and goggled on skis. "Aspen?"

He laughed. "Not hardly. That's Telluride, a little resort in western Colorado. We were there the winter after we got married."

Finally another picture of her parents, her brother, too. It was an earlier picture than the one in her purse. Her mother smiled sadly, dwarfed by her towering husband and tall, slender son. Elly decided not to comment on it.

"That's the Academy," Graydon said about the next page. "Here's Pike's Peak on a good day."

"Oh, where is this?" she asked. She found pictures of huge, towering rock formations, all of them thrust upward out of the earth like spines of a giant animal. The frozen sedimentary layers ran vertical to the ground and at the base of the spurs stood tiny people.

"Garden of the Gods, just north of here."

"How neat. I'd love to see it."

Graydon looked thoughtful. "Maybe we'll go there one weekend, then. You've been there before, but maybe you'll remember something when you see it again."

"I'd like that," she said. She went on to pictures of the zoo, herself in front of a monkey cage, Graydon in front of the elephant pit. The photo album ended with a shot of the Broadmoor.

Elly took the time to finish her soup. It had cooled while she had been so caught up in the pictures, and now she gulped down spoonful after tepid spoonful. Without her attention so distracted by the album, she became aware of a scratching noise.

"What's that? I hear something."

"Probably that damn cat," Graydon said.

Elly went to see. "Is it our cat?" She opened the back door and instantly a big orange Morris-cat bounded in and leaned lovingly into her ankles. His purr vibrated against her boots.

"No, he's just a neighborhood tom that decided he'd like to live here. Put him back outside."

"But he's cold," Elly said. When she leaned down to pet him, his fur was cold to the touch. "Poor baby, you're freezing outside, aren't you?"

"I don't want him in the house," Graydon said forcefully. "He's got fleas and God knows what else. Put him out."

"All right." Elly scooped the cat up with her good arm and held him close for a minute. His purring sounded like a distant airplane turning up. He kneaded her sweater with big, orange paws. "What's his name?"

"I don't know. I think you call him Chester. Put him out before he thinks he belongs in."

Elly opened the door and dropped Chester out on the mat. He did an immediate about face and would have run back in, but Elly closed the door on his face. She watched him out the window as he stretched up on his back legs and clawed at the door again.

"He sure wants in," she sighed. "Poor thing."

"Poor thing, hell. Didn't you see how fat he is? He probably gets fed at every house for a mile around."

He doesn't want food, she thought, he wants a warm lap to sit on. Already she decided Chester could come in whenever Graydon was gone. Not now, though.

She didn't want to press her luck. She returned to the table and began to sort through the loose pictures in the envelope.

She realized that neither she nor Graydon had been avid photographers; there were stray shots of Christmases, the new house, skiing in Aspen, and a class of Graydon's beside a fighter. Occasionally, Elly ran across some of other people, and they were almost always Air Force people—at parties, retirement dinners, or faculty get-togethers. On almost every picture she could see the stamp of Graydon's lifestyle, but on none of them could she see hers. It was almost as if she had meekly allowed Graydon to enfold her in his world, a world in which she could only be a spectator. It was an unsettling feeling.

"What's the matter?" he asked as she scooped the pictures back into the envelope.

"Nothing. Just ... there aren't very many for over four years, are there?"

"Sorry. If I'd known you were going to lose your memory, I'd have taken more." Elly held her tongue. How sensitive he was! One less-than-positive remark from her, and he was ready to fight. She smoothed the disappointed frown from her face and stood up.

"If you'll tell me where these go, I'll put them back."

For a moment she thought Graydon was going to continue his attack, regardless of whether she fought back or not, but then his expression changed. "I'll put them back," he said.

"That's okay, I can do it. You don't have to..."

But he was already there taking the album from her, his huge hands pulling it from her grip easily. With the exception of last night when he'd grabbed her wrist, she'd never been so close to him and just the bulk of him was frightening. She felt somewhat relieved when he moved away toward the hall.

Elly took her bowl to the sink and put on water for tea. What now? She wondered what else they could do to keep from staring at each other, to keep from thinking of the pain they had caused each other. She heard the sound of Graydon's returning footfalls and busied herself with the tea.

"Unless you have any more questions for right now, I've got a few things to do in my shop," he said.

"No, I don't have any more questions," she lied. "Thank you."

Graydon seemed to hesitate. "If you do, I'll be—"

The ringing of the phone interrupted him. In one stride he was at the end table and had the phone before it rang again.

"Hello?"

Elly measured sugar into her cup. The water was close to boiling and she turned it off before it could start squealing.

"Just a minute," Graydon held the phone toward her. "It's for you. Dr. Lynch's office."

"Who?" Elly panicked. She'd never heard of him. Who was it? What was she supposed to do?

"Dr. Lynch. Your gynecologist." Suddenly Graydon's voice was commanding. "Come on, take it. They won't bite."

Elly went to him. She took the phone in her left hand and sank heavily onto the arm of the couch. Somehow Graydon's presence beside her was both assuring and frightening. "Hello?"

"Mrs. Cole?"

"Yes."

"This is Dr. Lynch's office. We just got word back on your transcripts that we sent to Denver, but in view of your accident, the doctor said he'd like to see you again this week. I know you were just in last week, but he thought another check-up would be a good idea. Will it be possible for you to come in tomorrow or Friday?"

"Come in?" She looked up at Graydon. His expression was no

help. "Uh, I guess so."

"Which day?"

"Uh, I don't know." She pleaded with her eyes. He remained silent. "I guess either one. Wait." She held the phone against her shoulder. "Do I have a car?"

"In the garage," he said.

"All right," she told the receptionist. "Either day."

"How about tomorrow at 11?"

"Fine."

"Good. We'll see you then."

"Oh, wait! Where—what's the address?"

"The address?" the receptionist asked. "It's the same as it's always been. Ten forty Cascade."

"Oh, of course. I just forgot. All right, eleven o'clock tomorrow."

"Fine. See you then."

Elly hung up the phone, shaken. "Where is 1040 Cascade?"

"Downtown. I'll draw you a map."

His curt reply barely penetrated the haze Elly was in. She had forgotten the panic of interacting with total strangers, strangers she was supposed to know. It was devastating to think of venturing into a sea of unfamiliar faces alone. She wished Graydon could go with her.

"I guess it's just as well," she said more to herself than to Graydon. "I'll have to get back into the swing of things sooner or later."

"Into the swing of things, yes," Graydon said sarcastically. "A good choice of words, Elly."

Elly glanced up at her husband towering over her. Oh, God, she thought, not again, not now. "Graydon, what are you—"

"Isn't that what you were doing to begin with—swinging? Isn't that how you managed to get pregnant? You knew I didn't want any children so you found someone who did."

"You didn't want children?" she asked, stunned. "At all? Ever?"

"No, why should I? It's too uncertain a world to be bringing babies into it. No, you knew I didn't want children, so you found that traveling artist, conned him into taking you away from here and got pregnant with his bastard.''

"You don't know that; you can't be sure.''

"The hell I can't! You taunt me with it every chance you get, and every time I think about it, I get so furious, I could just—''

Elly cowered away from her husband. She knew how mad he could get, and now, with his nostrils flaring and his hands pulled into fists, she wondered if he had finally reached a breaking point.

"Graydon, please,'' she said, edging away. "I haven't taunted you; I haven't even mentioned it. You're the one—''

"You taunted me in your note!'' he roared. "You bragged about it to me! You bragged like the scheming little bitch that you are!''

That note again, Elly thought. Why in God's name had she written that thing?

"Graydon, please don't. I'm not taunting you now, I just can't help it. I tried not to let it interfere. Today when we talked and we made that truce—''

"The hell with your goddamn truce! I can't stand it. Every time I look at you and I think about that bastard's child in you, I just want to rip him apart with my bare hands. You're my wife, mine!''

Elly scurried around the other side of the couch, out of Graydon's reach. An idea struck her, an absurd idea.

"You're not—sterile, are you?''

That brought him up short. "Sterile? God, no. Where the hell did you ever get an idea like that?''

Elly realized that if her question hadn't cooled his anger, it had at least sidetracked it. She wasn't sure what to do with it now, though.

"I—I don't know. It just seemed like you were awfully defensive about the fact that someone else—''

"As if I *shouldn't* be?'' he demanded. "Did you think I was the type who couldn't care less if my wife let any scum that came along take her to bed? For god's sake, Elly, of course I'm defensive. You're my wife, married to me. If it didn't mean anything to you, it did to me.'' Graydon had begun to pace the living room, looking dangerously like an enraged bull. Elly stayed behind the couch.

"I think it must have meant something to me,'' she said

plaintively. "I don't feel like I could have married you for nothing. There had to be something there. I must have loved you."

"Do you think so?" Graydon asked with a raised brow. "I thought so—at first. But not now, not any more. You couldn't have, not and do what you did."

"But what about you? Did you love me? I know you hate me now, but was it different before? Did I change that much?"

Graydon stopped pacing and impaled Elly with his brooding eyes. His mouth twisted into a sneer.

"Yes, I loved you. Now I look back and I think the only reason you married me was to get away from that brow-beating father of yours, but I loved you just the same. You were different; you needed me."

In his voice Elly heard the strain of some far away memory. Graydon seemed to be thinking back, back to some time she had lost. She wanted to cry. "I need you now, Graydon," she whispered.

Bracing herself behind the couch, she reached out to him with her voice and her heart. The tears were welling up now, casting a sheen over her lake-colored eyes.

"It's too late now." Graydon took the piece of herself that she offered, twisted it into junk and threw it back at her. "Way too late. You killed it, Elly. You killed all the love I ever had for you. You've got what you wanted; you'll have your child. But you won't have me."

Elly heard the locked door of Graydon's voice, heard the hopelessness of their marriage and sank heavily onto the couch. She could no longer hold the tears back; they pooled over her lashes and made shiny, irregular paths down her cheeks. She was too miserable to even swipe at them with her hand.

Graydon stood silently across the room, watching her for a long moment. His anger was gone, but in place of it was an uncomfortable dissatisfaction. He hated it when she cried. It made him feel like a huge, blundering bull. Just like it had those last few times they'd made love. Only then he had cared, he told himself; now he didn't.

"I'm going to my shop," he announced coldly. Without waiting for a reply, he breezed out of the living room and disappeared through the basement door. Elly gathered a pillow into her arms and cried.

She prayed for the surcease of sleep. After crying herself weak, she had holed up in her room and paced or lain wide-eyed on the bed until darkness fell. She had heard Graydon moving around the kitchen, fixing his own dinner. Later, when the door across the hall had closed, she had ventured out for a glass of milk. Finally she had scurried back to her room, undressed and slid miserably into bed. When her tired brain could no longer wrestle with the complexities of the situation, she slept.

Chapter Four

Graydon was gone. Out her window she could see the place where the blue Ford should have been. She wasn't sure if she felt better or worse. She didn't want to be alone.

A hot bath eased some of the physical soreness she felt, and the massage of washing her hair seemed to help the headache. She looked awful, though—drawn and gaunt. How long could she go on like this?

By the time she had managed to dress herself—boots and all— it was almost ten. She decided to leave for the doctor's office early, just in case she had trouble finding it. While her tea water boiled, she looked up the phone number in the directory and scribbled it on the simple map Graydon had left on the table. She found some English muffins and toasted them for breakfast, promising herself she'd eat more for lunch.

Surprisingly, she found Cascade without too much trouble. Ten forty was a modest, single-story complex of doctors' offices, a pleasing design of stucco and wood. Elly parked the marine blue BMW—Colonel's pay, she reminded herself—across the street and waited until her watch said 10:55. She decided it would be less disturbing to wait in her car than in the office where an over-zealous receptionist might complicate things.

Dr. Lynch's office was halfway down the court. Elly pushed through the door and looked around. No one else waiting—good.

She stepped up to the receptionist's window.

"Good morning, Mrs. Cole," a cheerful voice said. A woman, mid-thirties with short, strawberry blonde hair smiled from the desk. "How are you today?"

"Fine," Elly hedged, returning the smile uncertainly.

"You can go on in. First room on the right. I'll be right there."

Elly went where directed and studied the room as she pulled off her coat. The examining table lay waiting, the silver stirrups pushed aside. Along one wall was a sink, the counter top crowded with glass canisters and plastic bottles. Tongue depressors and cotton balls filled the canisters like candy.

The receptionist-nurse came in. "Doctor said he just wants to make sure you're all right. You were very lucky. The first trimester is the most critical one, and in an accident like that, the chances of keeping the baby are small. We want to make sure the little guy is okay."

Elly murmured non-committally. She didn't feel very lucky today.

"If you'll get undressed, here's a gown and a sheet. Doctor will be with you in a minute."

When he came in, Elly was seated on the table, her sheet around her.

Dr. Lynch didn't look familiar.

"Hello, Mrs. Cole. How are you feeling?"

"Fine," she repeated. She studied him obliquely, trying to find a recognizable characteristic. Older, fiftyish, salt-and-pepper graying hair and a close trimmed, almost white, beard. Small framed and slender, he looked a little like how Elly imagined Freud had looked. He even had small, wire-rimmed glasses.

"I talked with Dr. D'Angelo for quite a while," he said conversationally. Ignoring Elly's state of undress in his best professional manner, he sat on a wheeled stool and flipped through her file. "You were very lucky. But I also understand you have amnesia?" At the question, he raised curious eyes to her.

"Yes," she said.

"You don't remember me?" He pulled his glasses part way down on his nose, as if this might afford her a better view.

"No. Not at all."

Dr. Lynch looked mildly disbelieving. "Do you remember being here last week?"

"I don't remember being here at all. None of it's familiar."

He tried to assimilate this, but Elly could see that it was a new experience for him, too, and out of his range medically.

"Very odd," he muttered to himself. With a gnarled index finger, he pushed his glasses back up his nose and turned back a few pages in her file. "Well, let me start at the beginning, then.

"You were in last March for your usual pap smear and everything was fine, except you had been experiencing some difficulty with circulation in your legs. You apparently had heard a lot about the pill fouling up the works, blood clots and so forth, and asked me to fit you with a diaphragm instead, which I did. I had you come back in May just to see how you were doing, and you were fine." He pulled his glasses down again. "You remember any of that?"

"No."

Stubbornly, he went on. "I told you to keep track of your ovulation so you'd know when your unsafe days were, and you did that pretty well. You have an early cycle; you ovulate only seven or eight days after your period. In May you didn't seem to have any difficulties, and you said your circulation was improved. No pins and needles, no aching knees. All well and good."

He flipped a page.

"Then on—let's see—September 26, you came in because you'd missed a period. You said you were very, very regular and never skipped. We did tests and you came back positive."

"Pregnant," Elly affirmed.

"Yes, pregnant." Dr. Lynch paused thoughtfully. "You came in last week on your own."

"What for?" Elly asked.

"To ask about having an abortion."

Elly wasn't surprised. Once the doctor voiced the word, she realized that the idea had been lurking beneath her consciousness all morning. It would make everything so much simpler. Not only would she not have to be concerned about someone else's life when she couldn't even come to terms with her own, but perhaps it would eliminate some of Graydon's hostility. The fact that she had been unfaithful would remain, but there would be no burgeoning seed of sin in her, no reminder to Graydon of her betrayal.

"And what did you tell me?" she asked.

Dr. Lynch took off his glasses and laid them on the counter. "I thought it highly unusual that a healthy young woman, married, fairly affluent, would want such a thing. I advised against it."

Elly turned her attention away from the doctor's piercing eyes and concentrated on her toes. "And what if I still want it?" She heard a deep sigh.

"You have problems in your marriage, yes?"

"Yes."

"I advised you before to go for counseling; I still do. You told me your husband does not want children, you said he would be violently opposed. After these weeks, is he still opposed? He hasn't come around at all?"

"No," she said miserably. "He hates it." She couldn't bring herself to explain.

"That is a shame," Dr. Lynch said. He shook his head slowly. "Life is so precious and yet we still abuse it." He closed her file. "Will you go for counseling?"

"I—no, I don't want to. I don't think it would help. I know it wouldn't help."

No amount of counseling could rebuild the bridges she'd burned behind her on her flight. Nothing could. "I want the abortion."

Dr. Lynch drummed his fingers on the countertop, toyed with his glasses. "All right," he said heavily. "First things first. Lie down and put your feet in the stirrups. I'll call the nurse."

When she left the office, Elly felt driven in a grim, determined way. She had set into motion actions that would clear her future of the mess that had been her past. The appointment date for her brief hospital visit was jammed protectively in her wallet. For better or worse, she would not bring an unwanted child into the web of her destruction.

She stopped at the shopping center on her way home to browse through the stores. There was nothing she needed, but the thought of the empty house was depressing. It seemed barren, lifeless—the way she would be soon. She tried not to think about it.

In a drug store, she strolled past jewelry and cosmetic counters. The image of herself in the mirrored wall startled her. God, she thought, do I look that bad? Her face was as drawn and pale as if all the blood had been leeched out of her, and her dark blue eyes were dull. She looked half dead. Probably, she thought, because part of me will be dead soon. But only a very small part.

It'll be better, she told herself. Once she and Graydon had resolved their differences—one way or another—she would go away, be independent, alone, self-sufficient. She would start a new life some place else. Later, she could have babies. Later, when she knew who she was.

The decision to take control of her life filled her with a fierce determination. As her second act of independence, she bought some makeup.

At home, Elly prowled the house. No longer concerned with the baby's health, she concocted a sandwich of salami and cheese and bell peppers, and sipped a beer. When that didn't seem to relieve her driving restlessness, she locked herself in the bathroom and toyed with the new makeup. Experimenting like a child, she applied eye liner and shadow, washed if off and tried mascara and rouge. She put on face after face, standing back from the mirror and considering the images she saw. Frustratingly, it all seemed garish and overdone. She settled on faint shadings of blusher and a trace of blue shadow smudged subtly toward the outer edges of her eye. Not professional, she thought, but at least she had color.

A quick rattling sound at the front door caught her attention. She stood suspiciously behind the front drapes and peeked out the window—only the mailman. When he had crossed the inclined lawn and disappeared into the next yard, Elly stepped out onto the porch to see what was there.

Typical, she thought: ads, junk mail and bills. There was nothing that looked like a personal letter and nothing at all addressed specifically to her. She'd give it all to Graydon. Shivering in the cool air, she started back inside.

And kicked Chester. The cat had come from nowhere, gotten directly in front of her feet and had tumbled sideways into the living room off her foot. Immediately she was contrite, heaving the front door shut and kneeling down to console the bewildered cat.

"Poor baby," she cooed. "I'm sorry. I didn't see you. You'll have to let me know where you are or learn not to get in the way. Are you okay?" She stroked Chester's cold fur and he roused himself from his roll to lean into her hand. His motor started up with satisfaction.

"Oh, you're all right," she scolded. "You little faker. And here I was feeling sorry for you."

Chester blinked his big yellow eyes at her and preened against her fingers. "Come on, then," she said standing up. "You can keep me company." While she laid the mail on Graydon's desk—noting the exclusively male quality of the den—Chester sauntered to the kitchen and rubbed his big head playfully against the cabinets. When Elly followed him, he kept at his pleasant habit almost obsessively and meowed up at her.

"Are you hungry?" she asked. "You shouldn't be. You really are fat." Chester cried again and switched his attention to Elly's ankles.

"All right. Let's see. I don't have any cat food. How about salami? You think you'd like that?"

He loved it.

Elly wedged herself into a corner of the couch and coaxed Chester onto her lap with a piece of salami. The big cat fanned his whiskers forward inquisitively, sniffed the salami, then took it daintily in his needle-edged teeth. While Elly held a hand beneath his chin to catch crumbs, Chester devoured his tidbit. In seconds he was teasing for more.

"You really are hungry, aren't you?" Elly said. She broke off piece after piece of meat until Chester was down to nothing but the end. That, too, disappeared down his throat. Then, precariously balancing on her stomach, he cleaned his paws and face, turned around several times and went to sleep.

"Oh, Chester," Elly groaned. "Why do you have to look so comfortable? I'm going to have to get up soon and start dinner. Graydon's mad enough at me as it is, and if I don't do some of the work around here, I'm sure it will just make him worse. Chester, are you listening to me?"

The cat flicked an ear at her, but otherwise lay still. Only the soft undulation of his belly fur gave any evidence that he was even breathing. Elly stroked the orange marbling of his side and let him sleep.

She made spaghetti. She found all the things she needed and it was improbable that Graydon would dislike something that she obviously had stocked up on when she knew what she was doing. Chester slept soundly in the warm indentation where Elly had been on the couch until the sauce began to simmer, then he planted himself in the middle of the kitchen floor so he could enjoy the wafting aroma. Elly had to walk around him every time she did something, but she never made him move.

She had no idea what time Graydon normally came home from work. She was sure the academy had classes all day and with the drive and all, she figured about 5:30 or so. Going on that assumption, she put vegetables on low heat, set the table and had garlic bread ready to go into the oven. Not bad for a one-handed mental defect, she thought.

He got home at 5:15.

She hadn't even heard the car. He pushed the front door open, stepped inside and saw Chester. The cat had gone to meet him.

"What's this cat doing in here?" he growled.

"Oh," Elly breathed. Damn! "I just let him in a second ago. He was scratching at the door. Here, I'll put him out." Hauling the cat up in one arm was a struggle, but Elly wouldn't let Graydon do it. If he did, he'd notice that Chester's fur was quite warm. Elly sidestepped Graydon to the door and tossed the cat out with a silent apology.

"Don't let him in any more," Graydon said. "That'll only teach him to scratch on the door; he's already clawed the paint off the molding."

Elly tried to look properly chastised as she returned to the kitchen. If Graydon noticed her lack of agreement, he didn't say anything. He followed her and stood frowning as she put dinner together.

"You do like spaghetti, don't you?" she asked after several moments of unsupportive silence.

"Yeah." He pulled off his jacket and left her, then returned a minute later with his tie pulled loose and the top button of his shirt undone. Elly stole glances at him. She'd never seen him in his uniform before. For some reason the dark blue made him look twice as big and not unpleasant.

"Did we get any mail?" he asked curtly.

"It's on your desk."

He went to the desk and leafed through it, giving Elly the chance to set food on the table without his incriminating supervision. She had no idea what Graydon drank, but found a bottle of red wine and set a glass of it at his place. She began to pour herself milk, thought better of it and got a wine glass instead.

"Dinner's ready," she called.

Once seated, Graydon looked over the fare critically. Elly expected some disparaging remark, steeled herself for it, then was surprised when it never came. Instead her husband served himself a good-sized portion and began to eat.

"At least that's one thing you haven't forgotten," he said finally. "You still make good spaghetti."

It was a grudging compliment, one Elly accepted in the spirit it was given. She said nothing.

"You're awfully quiet," he remarked.

"I thought you might like to enjoy your dinner, since anything I say seems to set you off." Her cool reply earned her a disapproving glance. She ignored it.

He ate thoughtfully for a minute, looking all the while to Elly as if he were regrouping an offensive.

"Any breakthroughs today?"

"No, not in my memory, if that's what you mean."

"Is there any other kind?"

This wasn't how Elly wanted to do it. She had planned very coolly to drop the bomb in his lap, setting him back on his heels and for once letting him feel what it was like to be on the defensive. She didn't want him prying it from her piece by piece.

"I was going to let it wait until later," she said, sliding back her chair, "but I suppose you have a hardy digestive system." She got her purse and pulled out the preparation guidelines for the hospital check-in time, things to bring, when to stop ingesting all food. She laid it ceremoniously in front of Graydon.

"Do you think you can arrange to drive me to the hospital that evening? It shouldn't take too much of your time."

Graydon scanned the paper, flipped it over and checked the back. He looked suspiciously at Elly.

"What's this for?"

"An abortion," she announced regally.

Graydon dropped the paper. "An abortion? Are you crazy?"

Elly sipped her wine as casually as she could manage, but actually her mouth had suddenly gone cottony.

"No, I'm not crazy. I would think you'd be delighted to know Adam's child will be flushed down a toilet." She lifted wide, innocent eyes to him. "Aren't you pleased?"

Graydon scowled. In a restless motion that made Elly flinch, he shot from his chair and paced around the end of the table.

"That wasn't what I wanted," he said.

Elly toyed with the stem of her glass. "What do you want, then? Would you rather kick me in the stomach yourself? That might be more gratifying for you than just driving me to the hospital."

Graydon's fist landed on the table and made everything, including Elly, jump. "What the hell do you think I am, some kind of a monster? Just because I don't want my wife bearing some other man's brat..."

"That's exactly why I'm doing it. You won't have to worry about it. You won't have to think of my carrying his baby, you won't have to see it later. I can't think of a better solution."

Graydon took his seat across from her again and held her eyes. "I didn't ask you to do this," he said.

"I know." She couldn't meet his stare. "But I think it will be better this way. It's one less complication to think about. Whenever we get to the point where we don't need our ... partnership any more, it'll be just be you and me going our separate ways. No third party to consider. Very cut and dried."

She kept her eyes down. She was afraid if she let Graydon stare into them, he'd see the lie of her words. She had to stay strong through this.

Her determined silence wore Graydon down. "Well," he said, "I guess it's your decision. Personally, I don't like it. I didn't want you to do it, but...if this is what you want."

"It is," she confirmed.

Graydon pushed the paper across to her. "What about your other injuries? Your ribs? Won't they affect this surgery?"

"They shouldn't. My ribs don't bother me any more and abortions are very simple these days. It's practically like a D & C. I should be able to come home that night."

"I don't like it," Graydon said.

Elly didn't reply. They finished their meal in silence.

While Elly did the dishes, Graydon disappeared into his den and closed the door. Chester scratched at the back door, and although Elly tapped at him on the kitchen window, she didn't dare let him in. With one hand she rinsed the dishes and loaded the dishwasher. Keeping busy kept her mind off the future.

When the kitchen was clean, Elly had nothing to do. She prowled the unrestricted areas of the house—the living room, hall, and her room—and finally pulled the morning paper off the stack on the hearth and curled up with it on the couch. If nothing else, she could keep up on world events.

Graydon came out after awhile, not much improved for his solitude.

"Graydon," Elly asked, "did I have any hobbies? I mean is there anything I can do around the house except cook and clean?"

Graydon moved around in the kitchen behind her and for a moment she thought he wouldn't answer.

"You like to read," he said finally.

"That doesn't seem very constructive," she said, mostly to herself.

"I suppose you worked out all your constructive impulses when you were teaching. Why don't you call the school district and see if you can cancel your leave?"

Elly was surprised by the rational sound of Graydon's suggestion. She twisted around to eye him over the back of the couch.

"I thought you didn't like me to work," she said.

Graydon, pouring himself another glass of wine, shrugged. "I don't. But obviously what I like is of no concern to you. You do exactly what you please so what does it matter what I think?"

Elly might have nodded. Now the sarcasm was coming out,

now the bitterness. There was no topic of conversation that was safe from it. She returned to her warm curl and watched her husband as he took a seat in the chair opposite her.

"Isn't that being a little one-sided? Just yesterday you told me you had no desire to do me any favors and now you get your back up because I show a little independence. That's not consistent."

"You owe me," he said flatly.

"Oh? What do I owe you?"

"You owe me for the humiliation you caused me, the anger, the trouble, not to mention time and money. I gave you all the things a woman could want—a nice house, a car, steady income—and you stepped on it and walked out. I gave and you took. Now you owe me."

"And I gave nothing to the relationship?" she demanded. "I gave no time, no effort, no money? If that's true, why did you keep me around? Why have a wife who was nothing but a freeloader?"

"You weren't a freeloader," he argued. His jaw had begun to tighten.

"Well then what was I? Did I care about what you wanted then? Did I go along with all your little eccentricities, your rules? If it upsets you so much now that I'm not, I must have once."

"Yes, you did," he admitted angrily. "You respected my opinion. You dressed decently instead of running around in jeans like an over-age school girl, you didn't wear that crap on your face, and you didn't pick fights. But that was all before you met Adam."

Elly side-stepped the reference to her lover. "So now I'm supposed to repay you for all your expended energy by dressing the way you want, walking around like a drab and saying 'yes, sir' when you sound off to me? Will that heal the rift between us? Will that make up for the humiliation?"

"It'll come a damn sight closer than the way you're acting now." He ground the words out between clenched teeth.

"You don't want a wife," Elly said, "You want a puppet."

"You don't know what the hell I want," he retorted.

"Then tell me," she said. "When I try to understand, you don't want me to ask questions. If I try to fit in, you criticize me. I'm pregnant, and you can't even stand the idea of my having a baby so

I arrange for an abortion and you don't like that, either. Obviously you can't stand the sight of me, everything I do annoys you, but you don't want me to leave, you don't want me to work. What do you want from me, Graydon? Tell me what you want me to do."

For the first time Elly felt as if she had more control than Graydon. He met her eyes briefly, stared down at his glass and then drained it in one gulp.

The alcohol didn't appear to help him in his uncertainty.

"I don't know," he said grudgingly. "I don't know what I want you to do. Sometimes I think about what you did and I'd just like to toss you out on your ear and then sometimes..."

Elly waited. "Sometimes what?"

"Sometimes I think it doesn't matter and we could go back, maybe try it again. But you," he said, suddenly accusing, "you're like a different person now. I look in your eyes and it's like looking at a stranger. You look like Elly, you sound like her, but you don't act like her. Elly didn't defy me, she didn't try to make me over. She accepted me, she adapted to me. I don't know." He groaned. "I wish we could all go back to a month ago, before you started acting crazy, go back and just wipe it all out like it never happened."

"But we can't," Elly said.

"No." Graydon's voice was hard. "We can't."

For a moment, neither of them spoke. An evening wind barreled off the mountains and rattled around the house.

"What are we going to do, Graydon?" Elly asked quietly.

Graydon stared into the eyes of his wife, dark blue eyes wide with uncertainty, wide with reaching out. For a brief moment he saw her as that stranger so newly dropped into the mess of his marriage, unknowingly blamed for it all, courageously seeking an answer from the one man who insisted on hating her. Something stirred in Graydon, something he had not allowed for a long, long time. He leaned forward in his chair and locked his hands together.

"Elly," he said. "I think one thing we have to do is have this baby."

Elly's jaw dropped.

"But you hate it," she said. "Every time we talk about it—"

"I know," he interrupted, "but I don't want you to go through an abortion. Elly, for God's sake, I was raised Catholic, so were you. I can't justify it. I don't want you to do that."

"I was taking the pill," she said. "I have a diaphragm. Dr. Lynch told me that. If we're Catholic..."

"Not very devout, I'm afraid—we haven't been to church in ages—but birth control is one thing; abortion is another." He gazed seriously at the woman curled up on the couch. "I don't care whose it is, I don't want you to have an abortion."

Elly sat forward on her heels. "But the reminder," she said. "I—I don't want those kinds of scenes, Graydon. I can't handle those accusations you heap on me, that awful hatred when you think about it. I'm trying to be strong, but I can't be strong for seven more months and longer. You can't ask that of me."

Graydon held his head in his hands, seeming to search inward for an answer. He came up empty.

"I don't want you to have the abortion. Listen, have the baby. We can give it up, maybe. After all, it doesn't have a father at all and you—well, do you really feel like it's your child? You don't even remember conceiving it. It shouldn't be difficult for you to have it adopted."

Elly crossed her arms over her stomach instinctively, but she considered Graydon's proposal. It was more reasonable than abortion, she thought. She'd been ready to sweep the baby from her half-formed, but having it and giving it into a good home would be a thousand times better. The only thing was—once she had it, could she give it up? Better not to ask.

"What about you?" she asked. "How would you feel?"

"Not as bad as if you aborted it. And not as bad as if—if I thought it meant something to you, because it was Adam's."

"I don't even know who Adam was," she sighed.

"I know," Graydon said. "That's just it. I think it was hard for me to realize but I understand that now."

"Understand what?"

"That Adam means nothing to you—to the new Elly. When you said you had arranged for the abortion, it finally hit me that you really don't know him and you don't have any of the feelings for him you had before. Knowing that, I think I could accept your having the baby better. Having it and giving it up."

"Does that mean no more interrogations?" she queried.

Graydon had the grace to look uncomfortable. "Yes."

"Because I can't live with that," she continued. "I won't. I'm so screwed up and unsure of things now that all I have to go on are my own gut feelings and when you pile criticisms and accusations on me like that—"

"I said I won't. Let's just leave it at that, all right?"

Elly knew enough to back off. "All right."

"And no abortion, right?"

"I guess so."

"You don't sound very sure."

Elly shook her head as if to clear it. "It's just hard for me to reconcile. You've been so violently adamant about it all along and now, when you have the chance to see it completely done away with, you choose not to. It's hard for me to understand."

"I'm not a monster, Elly. I'm not some kind of demon that demands child sacrifices." He got up and abruptly began to pace. It made Elly nervous. "This has been a bad few days. You've got to know that it hasn't been any easier on me than it has been on you, maybe even worse in a different way. You woke up to a new life that you knew absolutely nothing about. I had just seen my life completely destroyed and had no idea how to repair it. You at least could sort of start out fresh; I was still trying to find all the pieces of my life, trying to figure out why it shattered. It hasn't been easy."

Elly remembered what Dr. D'Angelo had said. She had the advantage because she did not have to re-learn a new order in her life; Graydon did. And, she realized, he *was* re-learning.

"So what now?" she asked.

That brought Graydon up. "What do you mean?"

"Where do we go from here? We can't go on like we have been, bickering and fighting. I need to know what's expected of me. If I'm no longer a prisoner here, what am I?"

Graydon frowned. "What's wrong with just staying here until you get your memory back? Or until the baby's born, for that matter. It's not uncomfortable here, at least not now that we've been able to reach an understanding. I should think that would be preferable to going out on your own."

A thought struck Elly. "What about our friends, our families? What about people who knew I had left?"

"No one knows."

Elly wasn't sure she was hearing right. "What?"

"I said no one knows. You left last Friday. On Saturday night I got the call from the hospital. I didn't tell anyone—I barely had the chance to, even if I wanted to, which I didn't. I took off work those first few days, and well, I've never really explained to anyone. Why should I? It's no one else's business."

"What about me? Did I tell anyone? My parents, maybe?"

Graydon shook his head and finally came to sit down again. "No. When I called them Saturday night they didn't know a thing about it. Adam was already dead. I just told them you'd been in an accident."

"Friends?" Elly said.

"Not that I know of. At least no one that's said anything to me."

Elly thought the matter over. In a way, it was easier like this. There was no one to explain to, no one to stare accusingly at her, pityingly at Graydon. She had an accident. She lost her memory— period. No excuses. "But the baby—" she remembered.

Graydon shrugged. "When it's born, we arrange the adoption and tell people it was stillborn. No one needs to know anything else."

Very patent, Elly thought. For some reason it seemed too much so, but she didn't know why. Just a funny feeling she had. She shook it off.

"Well?" Graydon asked. "Does it sound feasible to you?" His eyes bored into hers, willing her to agree.

"I think so, yes."

"Then we have a deal." He looked relieved.

"A deal," Elly said in a wry voice. "Like to shake on it?"

Graydon stared at her outstretched hand. At first he looked unsure, but Elly kept her eyes level with his, her expression sincere. Reaching across the space that divided them, Graydon took her hand. The span of his hand was huge, unfolding hers by double. They shook.

"Now," she said, rousing from her corner of the couch, "would you like another glass of wine?"

Elly felt better. She and Graydon at last were on common ground. It was uplifting the next day to call the doctor's office and cancel her hospital appointment.

Feeling only minor guilt, she let Chester in to pad around the house after her as she picked up and cleaned. The only thing he objected to was the vacuum, and when Elly pulled it out of the hall closet, he went to crouch on one of the dining room chairs and stare at her until she put it away. Then he came back for more petting.

When Elly soaked in the bathtub, Chester compressed his huge bulk on the thin edge of the tub and batted playfully at the water. Once he almost fell in, and Elly thought he was so funny. The sight of the pompous-looking orange cat scrambling for a foothold sent her into hysterics. After that, Chester sat on the bathroom floor and only occasionally awarded Elly with a look over the rim of the tub.

Elly dressed and combed out her hair. She still didn't like it. It hung limp and lifeless, even with the frequent washings she'd been giving it.

"I think, Chester, old boy," she said to the cat, "It's because it's so thick and all the same length." She rummaged through a drawer and found a pair of scissors. "Ah, this ought to do the trick."

While Chester watched curiously from the back of the toilet, Elly tried to cut her hair. She had good ideas on how to do it, but it seemed that every time she went for a particular section, her cast wouldn't reach or her fingers turned uncoordinated in the mirror. She had hacked off shorter lengths here and there, and the front didn't look bad; but when she angled the mirror so she could see the back, it looked like a hatchet job. She realized there was no way she could effectively cut the back, not with only one good hand. Sighing a little at her own stupidity, she put the scissors away and looked up beauty shops in the yellow pages.

She heard the phone ringing as she returned the BMW to the garage later that afternoon. The sound of the bell made her rush inside instinctively, but once in, she slowed. Who was it? What would she say? She was paralyzed with uncertainty until she thought it might be Graydon. She answered it.

"Hello?"

"Elly? Elly, how are you?" A female voice asked enthusiastically.

"Uh, I'm fine," Elly said. "Who is this?"

"Elly, it's me, Linda. Listen, I wouldn't even bother you at home, but the accident summary came across my desk for the insurance company and when I saw it I couldn't even believe it. Gods you were lucky! How are you doing? Do you need anything?"

Elly sat down. "Uh, no, really, I'm doing all right. Just this cast gets in the way sometimes." Who was Linda?

"Your right arm, too; that's tough. Well at least you don't have to worry about teaching for awhile as long as you're on leave. I was wondering; you said you were going to get away for awhile and sort things out—how's Graydon taking all this?"

"Pretty well," Elly hedged.

"Good. Maybe he'll come around. It's too bad he has to be on such a macho trip. He's such a hunk, you'd never know it to look at him. Well, maybe this will all turn out for the best."

"Yes, I hope so," Elly said.

"Well, I just wanted to see how you were and see if you needed anything. I'll let you go now. Maybe we can get together for lunch soon."

"Yes."

"Call me at work if you're coming downtown, and I'll meet you. I might have something new to tell you."

"New?"

"Yeah. His name's Harris—do you believe that?—but he's absolutely gorgeous. I'll tell you all about it, providing there's anything to tell. I'm hoping he'll call me this weekend."

"Oh, I see. How nice."

"Are you sure you're all right, Elly? You don't sound too chipper."

"I, uh, I'm a little tired. That's all."

"Oh, well, I'll let you go. But call me, okay? Just because you're not a working girl any more doesn't mean you can't associate, you know."

"No, of course not," Elly said. "I'll call you."

"Good. Take care."

Elly put the phone down. Who was Linda? Did she work at an insurance company? And how did they know each other? Chester jumped into Elly's lap and began to knead her stomach; she stroked him automatically. This Linda obviously knew part of the story, but not all. Damn, Elly thought, I should have gotten her phone number. Maybe she could tell her something about before—she said I told her I was going to get away for awhile, sort things out. Did Linda know about Adam? Or had Elly covered her tracks there, too? She wished she knew.

"Ouch!" Chester purred contentedly, even as he punctured Elly's skin. She pulled the cat off her lap and went to the kitchen to start the tea kettle boiling. Why couldn't she remember anything? She felt that if she could remember something, even the smallest detail, it might set up a chain reaction and eventually it would all come tumbling back to her like dominoes.

But no time to sit and wish now. It was time to start dinner.

By the time she heard the front door open, the house was filled with the warm scents of fried chicken, mashed potatoes, gravy and buttery peas. The table was set and Chester was out. Elly felt relieved that she had managed to coordinate everything so well.

"Something smells good," Graydon said. He came to peer into the kitchen, took one look at Elly and stopped.

"What the hell did you do?" he demanded.

"What? Oh." Elly saw his eyes on her hair. "I got my hair cut. I didn't like the way it just hung there."

Graydon did not look pleased. "It looked fine the way it was."

"Well, actually," Elly explained as she put food on the table, "I tried to trim it myself and I made such a mess of it, I had to have someone fix it. It's not much shorter really; just layered and a little fuller. Do you think it looks bad?"

Graydon pulled off his jacket before he answered, letting Elly know how he felt before a word was spoken.

"I liked it better before," he said.

"But it was so plain."

"It looked better."

Elly took the hint. "Well, I'm sorry, Graydon. I really didn't think you'd mind, but it's done now, so unless you want me to buy a wig, I guess I'll just wear it until it grows out." She dismissed the subject. "Dinner's ready."

Graydon ate, but not without casting quick, secretive glances at his wife across the table. Elly thought it best to ignore them. No sense inviting discord into their tenuous relationship.

"Do you know who Linda would be?" she asked. "Girlfriend of mine or something?"

"Why?"

"I got a phone call today from her. I figured she must work at an insurance company because she said she saw the accident summary on insurance papers. She seemed to know me pretty well."

"Linda Dahl, probably. She's a clerk or something at the school district. I think you two used to have lunch together fairly often, and she's been to some of the school functions we went to. I didn't care for her personally."

"Why not? She was very friendly."

"Too friendly. She's a run-around divorcee. She makes eyes at anything in pants."

Elly nodded. It had to be the same one. Apparently Elly had been privy to her affairs.

"What did she want?" Graydon asked.

"Just to know how I was and if I needed anything."

"What did you tell her?"

"Nothing, really. I didn't have much of a chance. She did almost all the talking."

"Good. I didn't particularly like your hanging around with her, anyway. You can find less brazen friends than she."

Again Elly was struck by Graydon's desire—or need—to so completely control Elly's life. It nettled her but she let it slide. She was sure the time would come soon enough when she and Graydon would clash again over one of their bids for power.

"Do you have weekends off usually?" she asked.

"Yes. Why?"

"I just wondered. I wasn't sure if you'd be going to work

tomorrow or not." He didn't seem in a hurry to expand on the subject so Elly continued. "Do we usually do anything in particular on weekends?"

"No. Why? Do you have something in mind?"

Elly shook her head. "Just wondering."

Graydon continued eating, but he turned thoughtful. "Actually I had considered taking you a few places you might recognize. Maybe something will jar loose."

Elly held in her immediate enthusiasm, trying to match her mood to Graydon's. "I'd like that, if it's not too much trouble. I'm sure you have a lot of things you might want to do."

"Not too much right now," he admitted. "It's too cold for yard work and not cold enough for skiing."

"Do we go skiing much?" she asked.

"Not as much as I'd like. We go to Aspen or Telluride once a year, maybe twice if we can manage it. I was thinking of going some time between Thanksgiving and Christmas."

Elly thought that might be fun. She didn't remember skiing, but if she learned once, she was sure she could learn again.

"Where would you like to go tomorrow?"

His question surprised her. While she'd been picking at her chicken, he had taken the opportunity to study her unwatched and now she looked up to find his black eyes on her.

"Oh, I don't know," she hedged. "Wherever you want to take me."

"No, you pick," he said. His voice was conversational, but underneath Elly heard the command.

"Well," she mused, thinking back to all he had said, the things she'd seen, "I know—Garden of the Gods."

He didn't seem surprised. "I thought you'd say that."

"It's my favorite place?"

He nodded.

"I wonder why." She tried to imagine the place but the only images she could conjure were the ones from the pictures.

"I don't know. Maybe it reminds you of New Mexico."

Throughout the rest of the meal, Elly was content to leave Graydon to his unwinding silence while she became more and more excited about the outing. When he finally pushed his plate away, she cleared the table cheerfully and hummed while she did the dishes. Graydon took up a position on the living room couch to sort through the mail and finish reading the paper. It was odd, but knowing he was comfortable enough to return to his small routines without watching her like a hawk or sulking like a child made her confidence soar. She felt more optimistic than she had since she woke up five days ago.

The phone rang. Its sound sent an immediate chill down Elly's spine and she quieted. Too much bad news comes by phone, she thought.

"Hello?" Graydon's voice. "Oh, hi... No, she's here... She's fine. She has to go back for check-ups, but otherwise just the cast on her arm is the only thing... Well, yeah, but, like I said— No, nothing... Well, I wouldn't say that; some things she does, but not people, places— Sure, just a minute."

"Elly? It's for you. It's your mom."

Elly froze. For a heartbeat, she heard the clock ticking, the sound of wind outside.

"Elly? Did you hear me?"

"Yes. I...I'm coming." Quickly she dried her hands and went to Graydon. He had the receiver held against his shoulder. "What should I...I don't know what to say," she whispered.

"Just talk," he said. "She knows you don't remember. Just tell her you're okay."

Elly took the phone. It was warm where Graydon had held it but her own hands felt like ice. She spoke haltingly into the receiver.

"H...hello?"

"Eleanor? My baby. How are you?" The woman's voice was high, warbling with emotion. Elly had to sit down and Graydon made room for her on the couch.

"I'm fine."

"Oh, honey, we were so worried about you. Graydon said you lost your memory."

"I did."

"But you know me, don't you?" The voice cajoled, yet Elly heard the quivering of uncertainty.

"Uh, no, I don't. I've been looking at pictures, though..."

"Oh, honey!" The voice began to sob.

"Oh, please," Elly said, "please don't."

There was a scuffling on the other end of the line, indistinct sounds mixed with muttered voices. Elly waited.

"Elly? This is Dad. What did you say to your mother? She's bawling like a baby."

"I—I—"

"What's this crap about amnesia? Is that true?" Elly fit the voice to the big over-bearing man in the pictures. It matched.

"Yes, I don't remember anything."

"Holy Christ," the man said. "Not even us? Or Graydon?"

"No," Elly said again, "nothing."

She heard the man's breath expel harshly into the phone. "What about the accident? Are you okay?"

"Yes, fine. I have a cast on my right arm, but that's all. I'm really okay." Elly was relieved to get onto a more understandable subject. Trying to explain her amnesia to people not emotionally prepared to accept it was too difficult.

"Wait, your mother wants to talk to you again." More scuffling. Elly held her breath.

"Eleanor?" The voice quivered but was a little stronger.

"Yes?"

"I'm sorry. I didn't mean to cry. It was such a shock. I just couldn't believe..."

"I know," Elly sympathized. "It's hard for me to believe, too."

"Do the doctors say when you'll get your memory back?"

"They don't know. It could be anytime." Elly couldn't bring herself to say it could be never.

"Oh. How are things with Graydon?"

"Fine."

"You two aren't quarrelling any more?"

"Uh, no, not very much." Elly stole an embarrassed glance at her husband. His black eyes were fastened to her face. "He's been trying to help me remember, telling me things. He's been very patient."

"Good. He was always so cold to us but, I don't know. You just can't tell about people sometimes." The woman drew in a sighing breath. "Bryan will be here for Thanksgiving, Elly and we'd love to have you and Graydon, too. Do you think he could get away long enough to bring you down? You haven't had Thanksgiving with us since you moved there, you know."

"Uh, Thanksgiving?" She alerted Graydon with her eyes. "Gee, I don't know. I'll have to check and see what his schedule is. Can I let you know?"

"Of course, dear. We'd so like to see you. When we heard about the accident, the first thing I thought of was my baby dying all alone away from home and it was just awful. I wish you'd move back to New Mexico. We miss you so much."

"I—I know. But you know, Graydon's job."

"Yes, yes, I know. And Graydon always did have to have his way. Well, talk to him, will you, honey? See if you can get him to come."

"I will."

"Maybe—maybe coming home will help you remember. Maybe once you see us, you'll remember."

"It's possible," Elly hedged. "We'll talk it over and let you know."

"All right, dear." Another sigh. "I'm just glad you're all right. Oh—your father wants me to hang up now. He hates it when we get the bill for these calls. You'll try to get Graydon to come?"

"I'll try, yes. I promise."

"Okay. Oh, honey, I hope you'll remember us."

"Me, too. We'll call you in a few days and let you know about Thanksgiving, okay?"

"Okay. Goodbye, dear."

"Goodbye."

Elly hung up the phone, exhausted. She leaned back into the soft cushions of the couch and closed her eyes. "God," she said.

"Your mother gets pretty emotional," Graydon said. "I probably should have warned you."

"You didn't really have time. I suppose I should have been thinking ahead to this, though. I'm finding that I avoid planning for these confrontations." She opened her eyes and stared at the ceiling. "I wish it didn't rock people back on their heels so when I don't remember them. They take it like a personal criticism, as if

I'm doing it on purpose. I feel like I'm twisting a knife in them."

Graydon was quiet. Elly hadn't meant to include him, but couldn't help but wonder if he were thinking back to that first day in the hospital.

"What about Thanksgiving?" he asked finally.

"Oh." Elly sat up. "They want us to come down there. She said my brother will be there. I told her we'd think it over."

"And?"

"And what?" Elly asked.

"Do you want to go?"

"Well," she said, leaning back again, "I don't know. Personally, I mean for myself, I'd kind of like to. I'd like to meet them, see if anything is familiar, but then I'd be scared to death, too. Talking to them on the phone was bad enough. I don't know if I could cope with a stranger hugging me and crying and carrying on. I guess what I'm saying is that it might do my subconscious some good, but I don't think my conscious mind would care for it."

Graydon settled back into the corner of the couch so he could face Elly. He considered what she had said.

"You can't run from it," he said. "You'll never know if you do."

"Yes, I thought of that. Sometimes I think that would be easier; just forget the past twenty-four years and start fresh now. But I know I would never be able to walk away from it and not wonder. No, I can't run. I'll have to face it sometime." She met his gaze. "What about you? Do you want to go?"

He looked uncomfortable. "I ought to tell you something. I don't want to prejudice you when you'll be meeting them essentially for the first time; you really need to make your own judgments. But I don't like your parents. I never have."

Elly nodded. "I had that impression already. And I also have the impression that it's mutual."

"It is. Matter of fact your father and I have come close to blows. That's one reason I jumped at this teaching position. The farther away from New Mexico the better, I thought. They hated me that much more for taking you away from them."

"Is my family close?" Elly asked. "Was I close to them?"

"Oh, it's hard to say. There was a closeness, but it always

felt strained to me, not the cheerful, loving closeness you see on those happy TV families. It was more like a defensiveness. When you objected to moving here, I felt you were doing it out of an obligation to your parents rather than because you really didn't want to move."

Elly tried to imagine feeling obligated to those two strangers on the phone. She failed.

"I'm having trouble even trying to think emotionally about people I don't know," she said. "I guess I'll just have to wait until I meet them to see how I'll feel." She turned to Graydon. "You still didn't say whether or not you wanted to go."

"We probably should, if nothing else because if we don't we'll never know if it might help you remember."

"All right," Elly said, feeling not at all confident. "We'll go."

Chapter Five

Saturday dawned overcast, and the low clouds crawled heavily across the sky like huge, rumbling boulders. Elly didn't care.

"You still want to go?" Graydon asked over breakfast. "There's no cover at the Garden of the Gods except a little concession building."

"Oh, yes, please," she begged. "I don't care if it rains."

Graydon lifted an eyebrow at her curiously. "Okay, if it means that much to you."

"It does."

She even tied her own tennis shoes. At first she grabbed the boots that zipped so easily, but they had three-inch heels. If the terrain were as rough as it looked in the pictures and the ground were the least bit wet or slippery, Elly was afraid she'd trip and fall and—with her luck—break her other arm. While Graydon was in the bathroom brushing his teeth, she hurried into his room and stole a pair of white knee-high athletic socks, then contorted her body enough so that she could tie lop-sided bows on her shoes. She made sure she was already half way out the door before Graydon might see.

The drive over was surreal. Elly rode attentively, studying the way for familiar landmarks. There were none. She had a peculiar feeling of deja vu, though, as if she felt she had been there before but she hadn't—and yet she knew she had. It caused her skin to prickle.

She knew it before they reached the entrance road. The skin of her entire body felt hot and tingly, and her head felt light. While Graydon steered the car around the turns of the road, Elly could see the rock spires looming up closer and closer, higher and higher. And she remembered.

The feeling was so overwhelming, so unique, that Elly sat soundlessly and let it break over her like a warm, welcoming wave. She peered excitedly out of the car at the winding concrete walkways she remembered walking on and at the huge towers of rock—towers she remembered climbing. When Graydon pulled over into a shoulder parking area, Elly was out of the car and walking before he could turn the key.

"Elly?" he called. "Wait. Elly! What are you doing?"

She was enthralled. She came to a halt at Graydon's call but could not stop staring and smiling and remembering. It was glorious.

"Elly?" he called. "What's the matter with you? What are you..."

Her maniacal grin broke into laughter. Like a convict recently free of prison, Elly hugged herself, breathed in the cool air, and laughed.

"I remember!" she cried. Dancing from one foot to the other, Elly spun around. "I remember being here! We walked the paths at first, but then we took the dirt trails instead." To illustrate, she broke for a narrow trail leading up the loose dirt toward the higher rock. "We took this one clear through the top and down the other side. And on the other side, there's more trails, and more rolling hills and there's white rock, too, just like these red ones, but a whole spine of white rocks jutting up all in a row. I remember! Graydon, I remember!" Still laughing, she spun around and ran back down the trail to Graydon. As stunned as he was, her smile was infectious and he laughed with her. Instinctively, he reached out to hold her still by her shoulders.

"That's great," he said. "What else?"

Elly flicked her eyes around like a child in a toy store,

discovering new joys in every direction.

"We always have a hot dog at the concession," she said. "And they're always terrible, but we eat them anyway because we never remember to pack a lunch. There was a field trip of little kids here, third-graders, I think, and we couldn't go anywhere without falling over kids; they just seemed to be everywhere. Later I ran away from you and hid and kept moving to different spots and you tried to find me and you almost got mad because I wouldn't come out."

"What else?" Graydon pressed.

"And when I finally did come out, we were standing there," she pointed down the walkway. "And I was trying to make you not be mad and you kept scowling at me and it started to rain, great big drops, and we had to run for the car, but before we got there the rain turned to hail. That was that weird storm with those great big huge hailstones, stones as big as shooter marbles and we were afraid they'd break the windshield. See? I remember it all!"

"Elly, do you know how long ago that storm was? That was over two years ago! Remember the picture in the paper of the hailstones?"

Elly's smile faltered. "Picture?"

"Yes. Don't you remember? It was the picture of a hand, a man's hand holding four or five of those hailstones, and they looked almost as big as golf balls. It was on the front page of the paper."

Now her smile vanished altogether.

"No. I don't remember that. Maybe I didn't see it. Maybe you saw it but I didn't."

Graydon shook his head. "I showed it to you. You cut it out and sent it to your parents."

"Oh." Elly's voice was small. Her eyes turned shiny and in the space of a second Graydon saw her go from jubilant to morose.

"Elly," he said, giving her a little shake, "don't. So what if you can't remember it all? We didn't expect that it would all come back in a rush of white light. You've remembered something; that's what's important. That's what counts. The rest will come."

"Yes," she agreed, but she didn't sound convinced. She focused on Graydon. "Why does it do that? Why does it let me remember part of something and not all?"

"I don't know," he said. "It doesn't matter. It will come. It's started now and the rest will come. You know that now."

She nodded and pulled slowly out of his hands. She turned her back to him and stared up at the high crags. Suddenly she looked very small and vulnerable to Graydon.

"Elly," he said softly. "Come on. Let's walk."

They went everywhere. Side by side or single file, they walked the paths and climbed the trails. Graydon let Elly set the pace and she picked a zig-zag path through the rocks. Small things delighted her—coming up a rise and knowing what lay beyond, standing at the top of a crag and feeling the moisture-laden wind. When, climbing first, Graydon might have extended a helping hand down to her, she kept her head down and scrambled resolutely with her one good hand. Watching her build her memory along with her strength was enough to keep Graydon from interfering. He studied the changes in her with quiet awareness.

They ate hot dogs at the concession and browsed through the usual tourist knickknack section. Elly exclaimed over a small sand-painting paperweight and Graydon bought it for her. It was going on two when they retraced their steps back to the car.

"Where now?" Graydon asked.

Elly looked blank. "Now? Aren't we going home?"

"I thought since you were doing so well, you might want to try your luck someplace else." He started the car and steered it around toward the exit road. "Any ideas?"

Elly thought back to the pictures she'd looked at and to Graydon's short tour the other day. A ground squirrel dashed nervously across the road in front of them. "The zoo," she said.

"All right," Graydon nodded. "The zoo."

Under darkening clouds, they drove past the Broadmoor. Elly didn't remember it. It seemed awfully garish, even ostentatious. She was glad they'd never stayed there.

At the zoo, Graydon parked the car and paid their admission. The first animals were up a sloped walk. Elly could already feel the muscles in her legs binding in protest, but she forced them on. She'd pay tomorrow, though.

The ungulates were first. Along with some other die-hard

tourists, Elly and Graydon strolled past the camels, okapis and giraffes. The giraffe pit had three slow-moving adults and one half-grown calf who undulated around in a comical, slip-shouldered canter. Elly joined the group in front of the pit and watched the slew-footed antics of the calf.

"Isn't he cute," she laughed. "He's so gangly. All legs."

"Looks more like a colt than a giraffe," Graydon said behind her.

"Except colts aren't nearly as sure-footed. He's been tearing around for ten minutes and he's never lost his footing. I wonder which one's his mom? The big ones all look completely disinterested."

"They're probably just as glad Junior's so good at keeping himself entertained."

A man nearby laughed. "Just like humans, huh?" he asked Graydon. His eyes swept over the big, dark-haired man and the woman in front of him. "Wait'll you have kids, then you'll know what it's like."

Elly blanched. She heard Graydon's placating, "Hmmm," felt his hand on her shoulder propelling her out of the crowd. They started on up the walk.

At an intersection, Elly picked the left fork and they entered the primate section. All sorts of monkeys screeched and squalled as they flung their agile bodies about on ropes and swings. Every so often Elly would pause at a cage to watch.

"Anything?" Graydon asked.

She shook her head and let a small sigh escape. "No. It's just a zoo. Did I like to come here?"

"I don't think it was high on your list. Sometimes you'd get depressed seeing the animals pacing their cages. We didn't come here a lot."

Elly turned on down the path. Below them the cat houses vibrated with periodic roars. "I'd like to see the tigers," she said.

"I know," Graydon said. "You like cats."

He was right, it was depressing. The big Siberian tigers paced restlessly, their beautiful fur matted in places by grime, their big, broad tongues out in a nervous pant. They walked the perimeter of their cage, turned, walked back. Occasionally one would roar.

"It stinks in here," Elly said in a low voice.

"Hmm," Graydon agreed. "It must not be cleaning time yet. Want to go?"

"Yes, I think so. I'm sorry to drag you up here and then not want to stay. I probably should have quit while I was ahead."

"Don't let it bother you. At least you remembered something; that's what counts. The rest will come."

They started back down the terraced ramp toward the parking lot.

"Oh, look," Elly said. She pointed to a retaining wall where a family of chipmunks teased for popcorn. Two boys stood well back, tossing kernels and howling as the little fellows scrambled to be first. "The poor little things act like they're starving."

"I doubt it," Graydon said sardonically.

"Oh, but look at that one, that littlest one—he never gets any. The big ones always beat him to it. Poor thing." Checking the ground, Elly found some stray kernels. She edged closer to the wall and tossed them near the littlest chipmunk. Frightened by her nearness, he scrambled back over the wall. One of the larger ones immediately raced in for the food.

"No, you big bully," she told the intruder. "That wasn't for you. Darn." She hunted the ground for more. The boys had been called away and there was very little popcorn left.

Graydon stood back and watched Elly's second attempt with raised brows and crossed arms. Ignoring the fact that she looked silly sneaking up on chipmunks with a few kernels of dirty popcorn in her hand, Elly tried again. This time the little one got one kernel before the others descended on the rest.

"I wish I had more," she muttered. She scoured the ground again.

"All right," Graydon sighed. "Wait here. I'll go get some."

Elly smiled shyly at her husband as he headed for the concession stand. There was one piece she missed, near the wall. She scooped it up and stationed herself close to the wall, holding the popcorn up and calling to the chipmunks with little clicks and kissing noises. Five of them edged nearer, each with a spindly little tail held nervously over its back.

"Excuse me."

Elly turned just her head. The chipmunks scattered. A tall, slender man a little older than Graydon stood ten feet away with a camera at his chest. He grinned.

"Sorry. I didn't mean to scare them. I wondered if you would mind if I took a picture of them. You had them all lined up like trained tigers."

"Oh, no, of course. Let me see if I can get them all back again." Returning her attention to the chipmunks, Elly pursed her lips and began her clucking noises again. The chipmunks darted in closer, each one coming a little farther than the one before, hoping for the tidbit.

Elly heard the camera click.

"Do you think you could get one to take it from you?" the man asked. He inched closer with slow, steady movements until he was only three feet from Elly.

"I'll try. Come on, babies. Come and get it." She held the popped kernel up high so all the chipmunks could see it. They dashed and darted like haywire circuits, starting and stopping with unbelievable speed. When one planted his tiny back feet and reared up ramrod straight, Elly lowered her hand. The masked bandit reached his little paw up, grabbed the popcorn and whirled. The camera clicked.

"Did you get him?" Elly asked.

"I think so. They're awfully quick, aren't they?"

"Yes." Elly returned the man's smile. He was very personable looking. "Are you from Colorado?"

"No, Florida. I'm just passing through, really, I—"

Elly's smile faded. Over the man's shoulder she caught sight of Graydon boring down on them like a dark, angry torpedo. In one hand he had a box of popcorn. His eyes snapped fire.

"Oh, no," Elly groaned.

"What—?" The man glanced over his shoulder, saw Graydon and turned full around. Graydon's long, angry strides brought him up next to Elly in seconds.

"Graydon," she said quickly, "this man took a picture of the chipmunks. I had one more piece that I found and I had five of them begging for it."

"How nice," Graydon said through clenched teeth. "There

are a lot of things to take pictures of here, aren't there? Better things besides chipmunks." His inference was not lost on the photographer.

"Yes, well," he flicked his eyes to Elly, then back to Graydon. "Thanks for your help. If you'd like a copy of the picture, I could—"

"Oh," Elly said quickly, "we're not much for pictures. We don't even put them in albums. Thanks anyway."

"Okay, sure. Well, have a nice day."

Escaping the chill, the man sauntered off.

Elly took the popcorn Graydon offered and dumped it on the retaining wall, a veritable chipmunk buffet. Before she had shaken the last of it out, the little rodents were already attacking the front of the pile.

"He was only being friendly," she said with her back to Graydon.

"He can be friendly to someone else."

"You were rude."

"I didn't like the way he looked at you."

Elly emptied the box and tossed it into a trash can. The chipmunks were scrambling around furiously, each one trying to gather up as much popcorn as possible without losing what they already had. Even the little one had his mouth full. It might have been comical five minutes earlier. Elly turned to face Graydon, her lips thin with anger.

"And how was he looking at me?" she demanded. "Was he leering? Was he slavering at the mouth? I thought he looked like a normal, friendly person who happened to want a picture of chipmunks."

"He didn't have to come to you for it." Graydon defended himself. "I don't like your talking to strangers."

"Obviously. I could tell that by the way you came rampaging up here like a rutting bull."

"For Christ's sake," Graydon swore. "You're over-reacting, aren't you? I happen to not want you being approached by strangers. Is that so awful? Lots of people are like that. It's common sense."

"I'm not the one who's over-reacting. If you'll recall, a week ago you were a total stranger to me, and that man was a lot more friendly-looking today than you were then. Anyway, I'll talk to anyone I please."

That hit Graydon wrong, and Elly knew it right away. He grabbed hold of her good arm in that innocent-looking steel grip and spoke down to her in a deadly quiet voice.

"You're my wife and I won't have you talking to strange men. If you're going to act like a flirt, you can damn well do it someplace not associated with me."

Elly couldn't believe her ears. "A flirt? I didn't even see the man until he spoke to me. I was minding my own business. Graydon, what's the matter with you?"

"We're going," he said, and he began to propel Elly down the incline.

"Graydon, stop it," Elly said. She tried to pull her arm from his grip but she couldn't without completely upsetting her own balance. He continued to drag her along. "Graydon, let go of my arm. You don't have to push me around like a bulldozer."

"You think you're free to do as you please, huh?" he said through clenched teeth. "First it's painting your face like a goddamn whore, then cutting your hair and now this. I won't stand for it. You're not going to play your little games behind my back this time, Elly. I won't let you."

"Graydon! What's the matter with you? I'm not playing any games. Will you let go of me? Damn it, you're going to pull me clear off my feet!"

They reached the exit and Graydon handed Elly through the turnstile. Luckily the car was close. Elly was afraid he'd jerk her over onto her face and drag her to it if it had been further away.

"Get in," he commanded.

"Graydon, listen to me..."

"Get in the car, Elly. We're going home."

She got in. Graydon slammed her door shut and climbed in the other side. Frowning like a troll, he started the car.

"Graydon, I don't know what your problem is, but you've got it all wrong. I wasn't doing anything."

"Let's not talk about it," he said.

"No, I *am* going to talk about it. I don't understand you. That man did absolutely nothing. He didn't make a pass at me, he didn't even act like he wanted to. And I don't paint my face. I looked awful when I got out of the hospital. My face was so pale, I disappeared into the walls. All I have on is a little blush and some eye makeup. What's wrong with that?"

"I don't want you wearing makeup," he ordered. "You don't need it."

"Maybe I don't need it, but I look a little bland without it. It's only blusher. It doesn't hurt anything."

"I don't want you wearing it!" His voice had risen to a near shout, but his hard-headedness was driving Elly crazy. She ignored the signals he sent.

"Well, I don't want to look like a ghost. Do you mind? And I like my hair this way. I think it looks better. What's wrong with wanting to look good? You sound as if you'd like me to walk around looking like a frump."

"I want you to look like a married woman, goddamn it! You wear those ass-tight jeans and tennis shoes and you look like a flirty little school girl. I want you to look your age, and I want you to look married!"

"That's what it really is, isn't it?" she flared. "You want me to look married. You want a stamp of ownership on me so no one else will look at me, isn't that it? You'd probably like it even better if you could lock me in a closet all day and just take me out at night when you're around. Damn it, Graydon, I'm a woman, not a doll, and I want to feel like I'm a woman. So what if I wear makeup? So what if other men look at me? That doesn't mean I'm looking back, it doesn't mean I'm flirting. A woman likes to look good, she likes to know men admire her. A woman needs that."

"You never needed it before."

"How do you know? Did you ask me if I liked being a faceless frump? Did you give me a choice? Or did you just say: You are not to wear makeup—period? A woman needs recognition as a woman. It has nothing to do with flirting or looking whorish. It has to do with feeling confident, with feeling good."

"Married women don't have to do that. They've got a husband. They don't need to look good to anyone else."

"Bullshit."

For a second Elly was afraid Graydon was going to backhand her. His color rose and he glared at her warningly, then returned his attention to the road.

"You're really pushing it, Elly. You know how I feel about these things. When we get home I want you to scrub that crap off your face, and I want an end to this nonsense. You're married to me, and I'm the only one you should be concerned about dressing for. Now that's final."

Elly fumed. She recognized the low, commanding tone of Graydon's voice but the threat of maltreatment couldn't allay her own anger. She swallowed once to moisten her tight throat and answered in an equally low, serious voice.

"No. You can't bully me. I'll dress the way I want."

Graydon had difficulty believing his ears. "What did you say?"

"I said no. You don't want me for your wife; we're only acting this out until I get my memory back. What do you care how I dress? As soon as I answer your questions, you'll kick me out anyway."

"You're not going to live in my house as my wife and look like a liberated single woman. You're not going to humiliate me any more than you already have. I don't want to have to worry about you any more, I don't want to have to wonder if you'll be there when I get home or if I'll find a clever little note instead. Now that's it."

"Graydon," Elly sighed, "do you really think I'm entertaining thoughts of leaving? My God, that's the farthest thing from my mind! I'm adjusting to my amnesia, I'm able to do some ordinary things, but I hardly feel capable enough to start a romantic relationship. Can you imagine my trying to explain myself to a new man? Hello, I'm Elly, but don't ask me anything else about myself because I don't know. What a joke!"

"It's not funny, Elly," Graydon said hoarsely.

"Damn it, I know it's not funny. But you're being ridiculous. I'm not going to leave. I don't have a lover, I don't even want one. All I want is my memory."

Graydon kept his eyes fastened stubbornly on the road ahead, but his jaw was tight. "That's what I thought before," he said.

"That you wouldn't leave. I never would have imagined it in a million years, but you did." He turned cold, steely eyes on her. "You're not going to do it again. I'll kill you first."

At that moment Elly actually thought he could. His face was frozen in a vicious, bitter expression that chilled her. Any reply she might have had was forgotten. She hunched down into her jacket and let Graydon attend to driving up their street in silence.

Once in the house, Elly thought it best to skitter to her room and let Graydon cool down. Unfortunately, he had other ideas.

"Go wash your face," he ordered.

Elly stopped midway down the hall, turned and drew herself up. She faced him across the living room. "No."

The whole house was quiet. Elly noted how Graydon's hands pulled into fists, how his nostrils flared. He looked for all the world like a boxer in his corner, psyching himself up for the bell. Elly came into the living room.

"Graydon, I don't want to fight with you, but I can't let you tell me what to do, either. I give you my word I won't leave as long as you still have questions—as long as you don't try to control me. I promise."

"And I'm supposed to believe that?" he asked. "After what you did? Listen, you lying little bitch, I'm not going to be humiliated by you again. You're not going to wear makeup and there had damn well better not be any men so much as glancing at you, or I'll rearrange your face so they'll never want to look again. You're my wife."

"God," Elly said in disbelief. "Were you this jealous before? Were you this psychotically possessive all the time? The more I listen to you, the more I think that I didn't leave because of Adam. I think I left because you drove me away."

The flat of Graydon's hand connected with Elly's cheek in a loud crack. Elly reeled away from him for an unsteady moment, then covered her tender, burning cheek with an incredulous hand. Tears of anger and frustration welled up in her eyes until her vision blurred and she struggled to keep from crying. Her voice quivered.

"I don't know," she whispered, "if you've ever hit me before or not. I think anyone can make a mistake once, and that was yours. Twice and it's not a mistake. If you ever raise a hand to me again, so help me God, I'll walk out that door and you'll never see me again."

Before Graydon could reply, the tears had clouded Elly's eyes and threatened to spill over. She caught her breath in a ragged gasp, spun on her heel and ran sobbing down the hall. The noise of her door slamming reverberated throughout the silent house.

It was an hour before Elly stirred from her bed. She knew by the feel of her skin that her face was puffy and red, that her eyes were bloodshot and that her makeup had pooled into dark smudges beneath her eyes. Her whole body ached from the effort of crying. She pushed herself up into a sitting position and took a shuddering breath.

The house was quiet. Had Graydon left? She hadn't heard him, but with her own sobs ringing in her ears, that was not surprising. No doubt he had gone out to cool down. If not, she was sure he would have followed her to her room and blasted her again. It was difficult for either of them to leave an argument alone.

Walking unsteadily, Elly went to the bathroom and splashed cool water on her face. It felt a little better, but in the mirror she saw that it did nothing for her looks. Graydon would be pleased. She looked ugly.

She was hungry. She left the bathroom light on until she could turn on the kitchen overhead and walked through the darkened living room.

Graydon sat on the couch.

Elly caught a panicked breath at the hulking silhouette where she had expected nothing. Graydon's head turned slightly.

"I—I didn't know you were still here," she stammered.

"I'm still here." His voice was barely audible, a low-timbered murmur.

"It's dark."

"I know."

"Do you want me to turn a light on?" Haltingly she moved toward the lamp. Graydon eased almost painfully back against the couch and shook his head.

"Elly," he said. She froze. "Elly, Elly, why do we do this?

Why do we fight like this?"

His voice did not sound like the voice of a man who was in control. The sharp edge of confidence was gone, the underlying steel of surety was missing. He sounded hollow. If Elly could have seen his face, she thought it would look drawn and tired.

She came around the end of the couch and stopped a few feet from him. With tortured hands he scrubbed his face, then ran his fingers through the black sheen of his hair. When his hands dropped down, he looked at Elly. He looked defeated.

"Graydon," Elly said softly. "I don't want to fight. It just seems that—we can't agree. We're just—different."

"We didn't used to be," he said in a tired voice. "It used to be good for awhile, Elly. It was good."

The yearning in his voice tore at Elly's heart and instinctively she dropped to her knees in front of him. She laid her hands uncertainly on his knees.

"Tell me," she said. "Tell me how it was."

Graydon's eyes bored into hers, their depths lit by the memories of better days. In the half light his face looked ghostly, surreal.

"You were afraid of me at first," he said slowly. "You blushed every time I looked at you. It was as if ... as if you couldn't believe that I could actually care for you. Then when we started going out, I remember how you used to defer to me ... in everything. You were so unsure. Every time you looked at me with those dark blue eyes, round as saucers, I'd feel all warm inside. I wanted to protect you. I wanted to just fold you into my arms and keep you there always. And you enjoyed it—or seemed to. You never questioned me, Elly, you never argued with me."

"Were we happy?" Elly asked. "All four years, were we happy?"

"I don't know. I guess, like all things, the excitement wears off. I thought we were happy enough—content. You never complained. If you weren't happy, you never said anything to me. You're so different now. You question everything that was normal before. I don't understand you."

Elly took a deep breath. Treading on shaky ground, she wanted to try to explain how she felt without opposing Graydon. If only she could keep this fine edge of balance.

"Maybe," she began slowly, "I was used to the way things were. They had always been that way with you, so I didn't think that it could be different. Maybe we just got into a routine and we both took it for granted. Now, not knowing how I was before, I see everything with new eyes. It's all strange to me. I'm not used to the idea of trying not to look attractive, I'm not used to your possessiveness. And I'm not used to giving in. All I have to go on now is how I feel, my inner feelings, and when you get that way, I feel as if I'm being smothered. I can't stand to feel that way, Graydon. It panics me."

"You used to need me," he said quietly.

"I still do. I need your help. I need your support."

"But you keep defying me. You push me away. I feel like I'm trying to hold on to you and you keep twisting away."

"Don't hold on quite so tightly, Graydon, and I won't. Give me some room to grow. That's what I'm doing, growing. Let me have a little bit of freedom, and I won't turn away."

He looked unsure. Elly leaned closer, tightening her hold on his knees. "I loved you before, Graydon; I must have loved you. Let me be myself and … and let me find out if I can love you again. Let me find out who I am. Let me find out if I can like myself first."

Carefully, Graydon moved forward and covered Elly's hands with his own. His bent head looked very sad to Elly, sad and lonely.

"All right," he barely whispered. "All right."

Somewhere, Elly knew, there was a sensitive soul inside the shell of the big man. She vowed to find it.

Chapter Six

Sunday morning was a little like the morning after, except there had been no night before. Elly returned Graydon's morning greeting shyly and busied herself with breakfast. When she glanced his way and caught him watching her, she blushed. Everything they had said and shared had seemed so right at night with nothing but the glow from the hallway; in the morning it felt strange, not as intimate. For the first time she allowed herself to wonder what kind of a lover Graydon was. The immediate heat that flushed her face warned her to think of other things.

"Do we have any plans for today?" she asked casually.

"No. What do you want to do?" Graydon held the paper in his lap at the table but he barely glanced at it. All his attention was on Elly.

"I picked yesterday," she said. "You pick today." Without asking, she began to fry bacon. Graydon had already started the coffee.

"Hmmm," Graydon tapped his chin with a thoughtful forefinger and glanced out the window. "It doesn't look too bad outside. Want to take a drive up to the mountains?"

"I'd like that," Elly nodded. "I think I like being outside." With the bacon sputtering on the griddle, Elly slid into her chair across from Graydon. She held his look with her eyes. "Do I look all right?" She had put just the barest hint of makeup on, just enough for some subtle color but not enough to notice. Graydon appraised her silently.

"I want to look good for you, Graydon," she said. A silent plea went out from her. She held her breath while he studied her. His eyes were alert but impassive and for a moment she thought he would object. Finally he half shrugged. A barely perceptible nod prefaced his words.

"You do look good."

Elly released her breath with a happy sigh of relief. Graydon tried not to smile, but one corner of his mouth tugged up. With Elly grinning like a schoolgirl across from him, he couldn't keep it. They both laughed.

"Would you like eggs with your bacon, sir?" she asked lightly.

"Sure," Graydon said. "Why not?"

They drove up to the snow. Graydon warned Elly ahead of time so she wore her boots, and they took the BMW. He'd had good wide tires put on it when he'd bought it so Elly would have less trouble driving in snow and ice, and so it handled much better than the Ford.

He headed first for Pike's Peak. They climbed a zig-zag road up out of Manitou Springs and as Elly watched, the city dropped farther and farther below. Up ahead was a layer of clouds, but Graydon said they would probably go clear through them.

"Did I like Pike's Peak?" Elly asked.

"I don't know. I don't think you ever said. Why?" He glanced at her curiously.

"Just wondered." But a feeling was building up inside of her, a funny, sick feeling. Instinctively she curled her good arm around her stomach. The ragged edge of anxiety flirted with her consciousness. She stared out the window and tried to ignore it.

The road curved again and again, climbing ever higher. They drove into the moisture-laden clouds and had to use the wipers to clear the mist from the windshield. Elly had nothing to look at but fog. She felt awful.

"We're almost there," Graydon said. "I hope we get through these clouds."

Elly's stomach began to ache, not a regular stomach ache, but a high, nervous ache. She began to sweat.

"Graydon?" she asked. "Am I afraid of heights?"

"No, why? What's wrong?"

"I—feel awful. Can you stop? Can you pull over at a turnout or something?"

"What is it? Are you sick?" Graydon divided his attention between looking for a turnout and watching Elly.

"No, I don't think so. I don't know what it is."

"Wait. Here's a place I can stop." He pulled off the road, threw the shift into park and turned to Elly. "What's wrong? Do you hurt?"

"I feel just terrible," she moaned. "Like—I don't know—like I'm afraid or I'm nervous. Are you sure I'm not afraid of heights?"

"I'm positive," he said.

"I—I don't want to go up here. I have an awful feeling about it. I feel like something terrible will happen."

"That's ridiculous," Graydon said, not unkindly. "Nothing's going to happen. Why are you holding your stomach?"

"I don't know. I just feel like—like I have to protect the baby. I don't understand."

"The baby?" Graydon's voice grew faint with a sudden thought. "Do you remember being here before?"

Elly shook her head. Some of her rationality returned since they were no longer heading toward the top, but she still felt anxious. She pressed the heel of her hand to the fluttering spot in her abdomen and stared at Graydon.

"The last time we were here was in spring," he was saying. "We came up to ride the train, just because we hadn't done it for awhile, but we got into an argument on the way."

"What were we arguing about?"

"You wanted to have a baby."

Elly felt the tumblers fall into place. "So that's why I feel so anxious. Was it a bad argument? I feel … terrified."

"It was as bad as we'd ever gotten into before. I'm afraid I wasn't very reasonable. In fact, I think I was pretty overbearing."

"Was I afraid?"

Graydon sagged against the wheel. "Probably. As I recall I was pretty adamant about the whole thing. You broke into tears and we drove home. After that nothing else was ever mentioned, and I just forgot about it."

Elly looked down at her stomach. It wasn't even rounding out yet. "I guess maybe parts of me remember more than others. It's going away now."

"Do you want to go on up?" he asked.

"No, I don't think so. Let's go some place new, okay? Some place where I don't even have to think about what happened before."

"I shouldn't have come this way," Graydon said. "If I had thought—"

Elly laid her hand on his arm. "No, it's okay. Don't even think about it. We're both learning. Let's just go someplace else."

Back down the road, they broke through the clouds and found a roadside meadow calf-deep in snow. Elly pulled on the gloves that Graydon had found for her and had the door open almost before he could get the car parked. She clambered up over the plowed roadside and immediately went hip-deep into the snow bank.

"For God's sake, Elly, wait," Graydon called. "You're going to kill yourself out there like that." He pulled on his own gloves and crunched out to her.

"I can't get loose," she laughed. "I'm stuck." Hip deep and one-armed, she had no leverage with which to carry herself out of the hole she was in. She waved her good arm at Graydon for help.

"Hold on," he said. Hands clasped, he pulled her forward and she managed to free one foot without falling over on her face. Ahead the snow leveled out to a decent depth and they walked without trouble.

"It's so pretty!" Elly cried. She scooped up a ball of snow and tossed it in the air. "Do I like snow?"

Graydon had to laugh. "As I recall, you love snow. You never saw it until we came to Colorado."

"Really? How odd. I must not have traveled much then." She bit the snow and the cold hurt her teeth.

"You didn't." Graydon made a snowball and pitched it at a tree. "You hadn't been anywhere."

"Had you? Or are you from Colorado?"

"No. I was born in Minnesota, but we moved a lot. I joined the Air Force right out of high school and from then on I did a lot of traveling. Any new duty that came up, I went for it."

"Do you like to travel?" Elly asked.

"I used to a lot more. Now I don't mind staying in one place as long as I can get out and go places if I want. Like when we go skiing."

"When are we going to go?"

"Well," Graydon paused playfully to get Elly's attention. "I thought we might take the week after Thanksgiving and stop at Telluride on the way back from New Mexico."

"Oh, good!" Elly said. "Telluride sounds so funny. I'd love to see it."

"Then we'll go."

"Good. Now you can help me build this snowman."

They built a snowman and had a snowball fight and walked beneath the trees that dumped soft piles of snow on them and Elly got soaked. Her boots, she realized, were not really actual snow boots and before an hour was up, her toes were hurting. The only thing that was really warm about her was her right arm, and that only because of the cast. When they trudged back to the car and sat puffing inside, their body heat immediately steamed up all the windows.

"I think I haven't done anything like this for a long time," Elly panted. "My legs feel like rubber. I'll probably be so sore tomorrow I won't be able to walk."

"Probably," Graydon agreed. "We don't get out as much as we used to."

"Ooooh." Elly collapsed back against the seat. "That was fun."

"Was it?"

When Elly looked over she found Graydon studying her, this time with a new look, a wondering look. She smiled shyly.

"Yes, it was," she said. "Thank you, Graydon. It was the most fun I've had."

"Well," he said, starting the car, "we'll have to do it more often, then."

Quickly he touched her gloved hand, squeezed it and pulled the car out onto the road. His attention was immediately given over to his driving.

Elly smiled. She was cold outside but she felt very, very warm inside.

They had gone farther north then Elly realized and came out of the mountains on a small secondary road near the Academy.

"I'm going to stop for a minute and pick up some papers that I should have brought home Friday. Do you mind?"

"No, I'd like to see it." Elly sat up and glanced around at the buildings as they drove the deserted streets. The long two-story buildings reminded her of college, even though she couldn't remember college. The parade grounds and fields, though, looked strictly military.

"Come on," Graydon said as he parked the car. "I'll show you around."

"Isn't there anyone here?" Elly asked. She stripped off her sodden gloves and left them in the car. Graydon led her to a building door and unlocked it.

"The dorms are over there," he waved behind them. "This section is usually pretty deserted on weekends."

They walked the empty halls, Elly's heels making hollow clacking noises on the floor.

"Is this where you teach ground school?"

"Yes. All the classroom instruction is done here. The rest—"

A door opened halfway down the hall and a briskly walking man, older than Graydon, stepped out. He saw them.

"You know him," Graydon said quietly to Elly.

"I do?" She was too surprised to feel panic.

"Yes. Colonel Mayfield. Just follow my lead."

Elly swallowed, or tried to. The man was already striding toward them, his long, narrow face split with a friendly grin, his brown eyes studying Elly. She managed to smile back.

"Well, Graydon, you putting in overtime, too? And brought your own helper? Hi, Elly, how are you? Didn't expect to see you up and around so soon."

Colonel Mayfield took Elly's left hand in an undemanding hold. He was probably forty-five, with medium brown hair and a basset hound face. As tall as Graydon, he was a good forty pounds lighter.

"I'm fine," she stammered. "Thank you."

"Hey, Graydon," Mayfield said, "you said she was in pretty bad shape. She looks darn good to me." He turned back to Elly. "I always told you if this ornery old bastard ever gave you a hard time, you could move into my place." He winked.

"And what about Clare?" Graydon asked archly.

"Oh, Clare," Mayfield laughed. He sighed dramatically. "Yes, I suppose an old goat like me ought to keep to my own age bracket. Oh, well. Can't blame me for trying. How long will you have that cast on, Elly?"

"A month or maybe six weeks. I'm hoping just a month."

"Well, don't baby it. Get that old circulation going in there and you'll be as good as new in no time."

"No; yes," Elly stammered. "I'm not. It—it feels pretty good already."

"Good. Say, Graydon," Mayfield said abruptly. "Why don't you two come over for dinner Saturday night? You haven't been over in a while and I know Clare would like to cook something up, keep Elly from having to do it. We could play cards or something. What do you say?"

"It's up to Elly, Don. If she feels up to it..."

"'Course she does, don't you Elly?" Don turned his eyes quickly back to Elly.

"Uh, well, I guess so."

"Good, good. Clare'll be pleased. She says we never entertain. She'll be glad I asked you. What time? About seven?"

"Seven's fine." Graydon arched an eyebrow at Elly.

"Good. Well, I'm on my way out. You working?"

"No, just picking up some test papers. We've been up to the snow."

"The snow, huh?" Don sighed again. "To be young again. Must be great."

He stepped close to Elly and put a fatherly hand on her shoulder. "But we really know who's keeping old Colonel Cole young, don't we, Elly?" He laughed at his own joke. "You're looking good, Elly, real good. To hear Graydon tell it, you were on death's door. I expected to see you hobbling around on crutches and white as a sheet." He shook his head. "If it'd been Clare, she'd have stayed in the hospital for two weeks just to get rid of the dark circles under her eyes. Well, see you two later. Take care, Elly. Keep that circulation going."

Elly held her breath. Don clacked down to the door behind them and left the building. Graydon touched Elly's arm and started forward. She waited for a blast of jealous possessiveness.

"See?" he said in a normal voice. "You did fine."

Elly released her breath. "He—he's awfully friendly isn't he?" she asked.

"Yeah, if there's anything Don is, it's friendly. Crazy old goat. He's a good man, though." Graydon led her to another classroom, unlocked the door and let Elly in first.

"It doesn't bother you when he ... when he talks to me like that?"

"Don? No. It used to. The first few times we went over there, I almost decked him, but after the second time we had a little heart-to-heart talk and I realized he was only kidding. He really does love Clare. She's his strength. But he's that way with all women—young, old, ugly, you name it. He's just friendly that way."

Thank God, Elly thought. She couldn't face another ordeal like the one last night. Especially when Don so pointedly said how good Elly looked. She was sure Graydon would want to drag her to a drinking fountain and scrub her face clean as soon as Don left. She breathed more easily in relief.

"Here's what I need," Graydon said. Elly hadn't even been paying attention. Graydon gathered up a sheaf of papers and bundled them into a folder. "Come on, I'll show you around."

"Do we go over there often?" Elly asked as they relocked the classroom.

"Where?"

"The Mayfield's."

"Not really. Maybe once every other month or so. Let's go this way." He led her out a different door.

"Is Clare nice?"

"She's okay. She's older than you, of course, and kind of overbearing, but you two get along okay. Over here is the ..."

Elly didn't hear much else. She tried to conjure up a mate for Don Mayfield, but the only thing she could come up with was a female basset. She was patently terrified of meeting them socially, especially when Graydon obviously wanted to pass her off as normal. She was positive she couldn't spend a whole evening with people and not act different. She said so to Graydon.

"You'll do fine. Don didn't notice anything. Anyway, if something comes up we'll just say that you have lapses of memory. That should be normal with a concussion."

Elly wasn't so sure. "What kind of cards do we play?"

"Tripoly."

"What's that?"

"Michigan rummy. It's easy. One hand and you'll know how to play."

"Do I like to play?"

"I think so. You ready to go home?"

"Yes."

"Good. I'm starving."

That evening Graydon brought in firewood and lit a fire. After dinner, Elly made a cup of tea and sat by the hearth with her back to the fireplace. The wind picked up outside. It began to rain.

"Are you still worried about meeting people?" Graydon asked. He had brought his own cup of coffee in and sat on the couch facing Elly.

"Yes," she sighed. "I was just thinking about next Saturday and then Thanksgiving. I didn't tell my parents for sure; I ought to call them and let them know."

Graydon agreed. "You want to do it now, get it over with?"

"I suppose I should. It would be better than sitting here thinking about it."

Graydon brought her the phone and the phone book. She sat dumbly.

"What's wrong?"

"I don't remember their last name."

"It's under the H's. Hatcher."

"Hatcher," Elly told herself. "Hatcher. I hope I can

remember."

"Just say Mom and Dad. It's easier." He smiled.

It was amazing how much difference his support made, Elly realized as she dialed. Having him sitting across from her, his eyes on her, watching her made it all so much easier. Better, too, than having him scowling at her. At least she didn't feel so alone.

The phone rang. Once. Twice.

"Hello?" The high, warbling voice.

"Hello—Mom?"

"Elly? Eleanor, dear, how are you? We've been waiting for you to call. I wanted to call Saturday, but your father wouldn't let me. We already called Bryan twice. How are you, dear?"

"Oh, fine, Mom, I'm really feeling pretty good. How are you?"

"Oh, about the same as always," she said heavily. "But what about Thanksgiving? You will come, won't you?"

"That's what I called to tell you. Yes, we're coming."

"Oh, good. I'm so glad. Graydon doesn't mind?"

"No, of course not. He thought it was a good idea."

Mrs. Hatcher sighed. "Well, how long can you stay?"

Time to punt, Elly thought. "Not long. Just a day or two. It's going to be kind of difficult..."

"Yes, I suppose your doctor doesn't want you to get too excited. Will you have your cast off by then?"

"I'm not sure. Probably. But I should still take it easy." Elly crossed her fingers. Graydon sipped his coffee to avoid smiling.

"Well, whatever your doctor says, that's what we'll do. Have you—are you getting better? I mean have you..."

"I've remembered some things, yes," Elly offered. "It's going to be a slow process, but I'm sure I'll get it all back eventually. It'll just take time."

"Yes, I suppose it will. Well, I'm glad you can come. We'll be looking forward to it. Did I tell you Bryan will be here?"

"Yes, you did."

"Good. He wants to see you."

"And I want to meet—uh, see him, too." Elly racked her brain for something else to say. "Well, uh, I probably shouldn't keep you any longer."

"Will you let us know exactly when you're coming? I need to plan my grocery shopping."

"Oh, sure. I'll, uh, write to you and tell you exactly as soon as I know. I'll make sure you get it in plenty of time."

"That'll be fine, dear."

"Well, uh, I guess I'll let you go now, Mom. Thanks for inviting us."

"Of course. Write soon. And take care of yourself."

Elly dropped the phone into its cradle. "Oh, God," she moaned. "How can I spend days with people I don't know? What will we say to each other? It doesn't get better; it gets worse."

"It's different on the phone," Graydon said. "Once we're there you can look around, ask questions, get them talking. Your mom will talk your ear off if you get her away from your dad. It'll be a lot easier."

"I hope so. We won't stay long, though, will we?" she looked at Graydon hopefully.

He had to laugh. "Any other time you'd be begging me to stay as long as we could. But no, we won't. We'll drive down and just stay two nights and tell them we don't want to tire you. Then we'll go straight to Telluride."

"Thank God. At least when we're alone, I can be myself." She pulled her knees up to her chin and sighed. Outside the rain was beating down harder than ever. The wind had picked up. "Listen to tha—"

Graydon's look stopped her in mid word. His face had taken on a sober, thoughtful look, his eyes on her yet far away. He looked as if he were brooding about something.

"Graydon? What is it? What's wrong?"

"Nothing." Quickly he pulled his features into their familiar order and took a sip of coffee.

"Are you mad? Did I say something?" Elly unfolded herself and sat up. "What did I do?"

"Nothing, really. Forget it."

"Graydon, I don't want to make you mad. We've had such a nice day; if I said anything, please..."

"It's not you," he said. "Or I should say, it's not you now, the way you are now."

"Than what?"

He appeared to wrestle with himself, crossed his legs restlessly, uncrossed them and turned toward Elly. "It's silly. I was just wondering when you said that if you could be just yourself before when we were alone. I thought I knew you backwards and forwards for four years and all of a sudden, out of the clear, you did something so completely... out of character. And when you said that, that you'd be glad when we could be alone so you could be yourself, I began to wonder if you were ever really yourself with me before."

"Oh." Elly pulled up her knees again. "I see what you mean. And I don't know. That's weird to me, too, how I can seem to be so different from what I was—or from what I'm told I was. It doesn't make sense."

"No," Graydon murmured, "it doesn't."

A noise caught Elly's ear. "Is that the rain?"

"Sounds like it."

"But it's only in the back." She rose to see. On tiptoe, she leaned over the kitchen sink and looked out the window. A horrible-looking dingy thing clawed at the door. "Oh," she cried. "Poor baby!"

As soon as she opened the door, Chester ran in. His feet left little muddy paw marks on the floor. His fur was so matted from rain that he looked more like a giant guinea pig than a cat. He cried to Elly.

"Poor baby," she repeated. "You must be freezing. Here. Let me dry you."

She got an old dish towel from the drawer and dropped it over Chester, then began to rub him vigorously. He didn't think much of the idea. While Elly rubbed, he tried to get a foothold on the slick floor and get away, but Elly held onto him. Finally, when he was no longer dripping, she bundled him up in her good arm and carried him into the living room.

"Not that damn cat," Graydon said.

"Graydon, look, he was all wet and it's cold out there. Poor thing. He could die out there like that."

"Cats don't die that easily," Graydon muttered. "Put him outside. He's all dirty."

"But he's cold. It's freezing outside. I'll keep him on my lap and he won't get anything else dirty."

"Except you. Elly, he's a mangy tom. He's got fleas and worms and God knows what. He belongs outside."

Elly hugged the toweled cat to her. "Please, Graydon. Just for a little while. Just until he gets warm. Please."

"Jesus," Graydon swore, but he had already lost. The way Elly looked, standing there like a waif with that damn cat bundled up in her arms was too much for him. He couldn't remember ever seeing her eyes so blue and pleading. It triggered something inside of him.

"All right," he said curtly. "But just until he gets warm. Then he goes out."

"Promise," Elly said. She plopped down on the hearth and let Chester knead a comfortable spot on her lap, then once he was settled, she draped the towel over him again. He purred.

"Don't get any ideas," Graydon said. "This isn't going to become a routine." He was a little disgusted with himself for giving in, but Elly looked so damn defenseless.

"I know," she murmured. "But it's really storming out there."

Graydon nodded, listening. "Maybe we'll get snow. It wouldn't surprise me. I've heard it's going to be a rough winter."

Elly just smiled.

The rain hadn't let up when Elly flicked off her bedroom light and pulled the blanket up to her chin. If anything, it had gotten worse.

She had little trouble going to sleep. Her whole body was exhausted, and within minutes she had turned in to her pillow and slept soundly. The rain rattled at her window.

She dreamed. She was in a car, riding on the passenger side, and it was raining. There was someone sitting on the driver's side, but she didn't know who it was. For some reason she couldn't see. Her head wouldn't even turn. But it was all right. She was uneasy, but not scared. It was all right.

The rain streaked the windshield in slowly melting, merging strands of reflected light and it was hard to see through the glass. She tried to see around the streaks, but everything beyond was blurred. Her discomfort grew. She knew that if she couldn't see very well, neither could the driver. The rain clattered sinisterly on the roof of the car.

There were red lights up ahead. Tail lights lit up like a racetrack Christmas tree, one pair on top of another on top of another. They had to slow down, quick.

It was slippery. The car began to slide.

Elly put her hands out toward the dash of the car, but it was so far away she couldn't reach it. She had nothing to hold on to. The taillights skidded closer.

Then a blinding white light stabbed her from the left side. It was a headlight, slanting angrily in from across the driver's seat. It blinded her and instinctively she put a hand up to shield her eyes. Then she saw the driver. It was a man—but he had no head. The white light blazed across his empty shoulders like a beacon from a human lighthouse. Elly screamed. Recoiling from the light, she fell in slow motion toward the cold steel of the car door on her right. She screamed and screamed and screamed.

"Elly? Elly! Wake up!"

She came up fighting. The weight of a body across hers was so heavy—like metal, pinning her. She twisted beneath it, swung her cast and narrowly missed connecting.

"Elly! For God's sake, wake up!"

"No!" she screamed. "No, let me go! Let me out!"

"Elly!"

Graydon's voice, a near shout itself, rang familiarly in Elly's mind. She opened her eyes, saw gratefully that he had a head, and threw herself into the harbor of his chest. In a second Graydon had rocked back into a sitting position and folded Elly in his arms. She clung to him in remembered terror.

"Oh, Graydon!" she sobbed. "It was awful! I dreamed I was in a car and it was raining and there were cars ahead but we couldn't stop and then one came at us from the side. I looked over and— and the man didn't have a head! It was awful. It was terrible."

"Okay, Elly, it's okay." Graydon tightened his arms securely around her and rocked her. "It's just a dream. It's okay. You're safe. Everything's okay."

Elly cried into his chest. The tears came from some place deep inside and flowed as if from an endless source. She tried to talk and her voice croaked.

"Shh," Graydon soothed. "Get it all out, Elly. Cry it all out. It's okay. Everything's okay."

When she was finally able to lift her head a little, she felt his soaked shirt cling to her cheek. Graydon relaxed his hold on her so she could sit up.

"I'm sorry," she breathed shakily. "I—I feel so stupid."

"Don't," Graydon said. One large hand rubbed her back. She leaned into it.

"It was awful. I don't think I've ever been so terrified." She shivered.

"I guess once things start breaking through, they come any way they can. It's just too bad it had to come like this."

Elly had the strength to look up curiously at Graydon. "What do you mean?"

"The accident. That must be what it was. Don't you remember?" Elly tried to think, but all she got was chills. Graydon pulled her close again and she sank gratefully against his shoulder.

"No, I don't remember. Is that what happened? Do you know how it was?"

"I talked to the police. They said there'd already been one accident because of the slippery roads. Apparently you came up on the stopped traffic and couldn't stop in time. You—or I should say Adam—cut the wheel to try to go left and went directly into the path of an oncoming car. That car fishtailed out of control and plowed into the driver's side, killing Adam instantly. You were thrown into the right door. You must have been knocked unconscious. At least you were that way when they pulled you out."

Elly swallowed. "Was Adam—did he—was he decapitated?" She shuddered at the word.

"No. I don't know why you dreamed that. Maybe because you still can't remember him. Or can you?"

"No, I have no idea what he looks like, even if I saw him."

"That must be it, then." Graydon moved away just enough so he could look down at his wife. "You going to be okay now?"

"I think so," she sighed. "I'm sorry to be such a pain, Graydon."

She slumped tiredly, like a rag doll in his arms. Her voice sounded smaller. "I don't want to be any trouble to you."

"Shhh. Lie back. You're exhausted." Gently Graydon cradled her down until she collapsed on to her pillow. Already her eyes were half closed and she struggled half-heartedly to stay awake. "Go to sleep. Everything's okay now. Go on to sleep."

"Thank you, Graydon," she murmured. "You're so...." She trailed off.

Graydon looked down at his sleeping wife. In the light from the street lamp outside, she looked very soft, very vulnerable. The sight of her sleeping so trustingly in his arms wrenched at him. This was the woman who tore his heart out by leaving him. Now she was doing it again—by staying.

Gently Graydon leaned down and brushed his lips against her forehead. She slept soundly.

Chapter Seven

That week Elly had more energy and more ambition. Even though she was painfully sore at first, she forced her body to do the things she needed to do. On Monday she did the shopping and cleaned the house. On Tuesday, she did the laundry. While the rain started and stopped outside intermittently, she busied herself inside, dusting, vacuuming, and folding clothes. It felt good to do for Graydon; he had been so good to her.

She fudged though; she bought a flea collar and flea powder for Chester, even some worm caps and dosed him up good. By Wednesday, she figured it was safe to let him in, and with a new collar on, he prowled around behind Elly everywhere she went. She even bought cat food and hid it in the pantry behind the cereal. It was only a matter of days before she realized Chester spent almost all his time with her.

On Wednesday, she had a caller. She was just mixing up a meatloaf when the doorbell rang and she hurriedly put it in the refrigerator away from Chester before she went to answer the door. A salesman? She wondered.

"Hi, Elly. How are you?"

Elly stared dumbly at the young woman on her doorstep. She didn't know her. She'd never seen her before.

"Elly? What's wrong. Are you okay?"

Elly wanted to die. "Who are you?" she asked.

The woman's face fell. "Elly, it's Linda. I just talked to you on the phone last week. Don't you remember?"

"Linda—Dahl?"

"Yes. Elly, what's wrong?"

"Come in," Elly said. "I'm sorry. Come in."

Linda edged around Elly and walked familiarly through the living room. Elly expected her to sit on the couch, but she didn't. She went to the dining room table, pulled out Elly's chair, and sat. Apparently she was used to sitting there.

"Elly, are you all right?" Linda asked. A slender, willowy strawberry blonde, Linda turned questioning green eyes on her friend. She studied Elly curiously while Elly took a seat across from her at Graydon's place.

"Yes, I am. I just have—memory lapses. I'm sorry. I didn't recognize you. It's because of the concussion."

"Gee, how awful. But the doctors say you're all right?"

"As much as I can be. It'll get better. It just takes time."

"How weird." Linda looked around. "It doesn't look like having that cast on is keeping you down. Or does Graydon help you around the house now?"

"No. I do it. I'm getting used to doing things with my left hand." Elly got up. "Would you like something to drink? Tea or coffee?"

"Oh, coffee if you have it. It's nasty outside." Linda took the opportunity to slide out of her ski jacket and draped it over the back of her chair. "I had the day off so I thought I'd take a run up and see how you were doing. After I read that accident report— yuk!"

"I was lucky," Elly said, pouring coffee. She already had hot water for her own tea. "Except for the concussion and broken arm, it wasn't bad. Would you like something to eat? A sandwich or anything?"

"No, thanks. I'm dieting again."

"Dieting? You're so thin now." Elly brought the mugs over to the table and gave Linda hers.

"Thanks," she laughed, "but I don't think so. I've got to lose five pounds. But listen, I want to know what happened. I just found out yesterday who else was in that car with you." She leaned across the table toward Elly. "You didn't tell me you were taking off with Adam."

Elly felt hot. She avoided Linda's eyes and sipped furtively at her tea. "I, uh, I didn't tell anyone."

"I found that out. Even the high mucky-mucks at the district office won't talk. I only saw the report on Adam by accident. But, Jeez, Elly, do you know how that's going to look in your personal record? Involved in an accident where another employee—or former employee—was killed? And you being married, and pregnant besides? I mean, you don't do things half way, do you?"

"I guess not," Elly said. "But I can't do anything about it now."

Linda stared at her. "God, you're cool. I'd be in pieces."

Elly might have laughed. If only Linda knew—Elly's pieces were all broken up inside.

"But, hey," Linda said, jumping to a new point, "what made you do it? I didn't think you liked Adam all that much. I mean, he treated you a hell of a lot better than Graydon did, but the last time I asked you, you said you didn't think you could love him. What happened?"

Elly tried to sound remote. "I'm not sure. It was just impulsive, I guess. To tell you the truth, with my concussion some things are pretty foggy in my mind. It's hard to remember exactly..."

Linda looked skeptical. "Hey, if you don't want to tell me, that's okay, just say so. I don't want to pry, but ever since we met we've been like boarding school buddies, you know?"

"No, really," Elly amended. This time she put her cup down and met Linda's pert green eyes. "I can't remember a lot of things. It's very hazy. That's why I was so blank when I saw you. I'm not putting you off."

"Gee," Linda breathed. "That's freaky. You don't remember what happened before you left?"

"Not entirely." Elly was too cautious to reveal the whole truth to this woman she didn't know and Graydon didn't like. "A lot of it's just not clear."

Linda nodded in understanding. Apparently, Elly thought, she was a more physical-oriented person than an emotional one. "So what about Graydon? Didn't he come unglued over the whole thing?"

"Sort of, at first. He's been real good about it, though. He—he's been trying to understand. We're doing all right."

"What about the baby?"

"The baby?" Elly repeated.

"Yeah. When you told me about it, you said Graydon would just kill you for getting pregnant. Don't you remember that lunch we had after your visit to the doctor? You said he'd have a fit when he found out, that he didn't want any kids. Don't you remember?"

"Oh, that, yes," Elly kept her voice casual. "Well, he's not pleased, of course, but he's getting used to the idea. I guess we'll just wait and see."

"You're not going through with the abortion, huh?"

"No. We talked about that and Graydon didn't want to do that. He said he'd rather I had it and—and we'll just go from there."

"Boy, are you lucky. The way you talked about it before, I just thought for sure he'd beat the hell out of you when we got you home. I almost expected to see bruises on you today."

"No, we're resolving things one at a time. We'll be okay."

Linda shook her head. "I don't know how you do it. You get yourself into jams I never thought of and come out smelling like a rose. I go along just trying to find a little fun and I get stomped on."

"What do you mean?"

"Remember that guy I told you about, Harris? Well..."

For almost an hour Elly listened to Linda. She told dramatic, detailed stories of her one and only escapade with Harris, recounting for Elly how he had used her and left her after a brief evening. Elly gathered from the allusions Linda made that this was not the first time and wouldn't be the last. And although Linda joked and talked openly, Elly felt that this was her way of crying inside. Linda was a very different kind of person.

"Where did you meet this guy?" Elly asked.

"Oh, at a singles bar. And I know what you're going to say, Elly, so don't say it. I can't find guys at 'nice places' like you seem to think I can. All I find at 'nice places' are nerds."

"Sounds like Harris was a nerd, if you ask me," Elly said. Then quickly, "I'm sorry. I shouldn't have said that. If you liked him..."

"Oh, I didn't particularly like him, he was just gorgeous, that's all. Sort of like Graydon, the strong, silent type, except maybe not so grim-looking. But, hell, I knew what I was doing. It's just the way things work out for me. You're different; you had a perfectly handsome hunk right here at home—even if he was an asshole—and out of the blue ... plunk! You find Adam who treats you like a queen. I guess we're just made for different paths."

"Well, where did I meet Adam?" Elly asked. She made the question sound rhetorical.

"Oh, please," Linda said. "That was a one in a million. The chances of the school district employing a free-lance artist to paint a mural, and the chances of just happening to work at that school for a few days and just happening to meet..."

"Mural?" Elly's brain was clanking slowly into gear. She'd seen a mural at a school. When? Where? It was big, bold, with a montage of figures playing games, studying. But where?

"What school was that?"

"Why, Pike, of course. Don't tell me you've forgotten that."

Elly groaned. Graydon had driven her past it on their brief tour the day she came home. It had been the last school he'd driven by, and she'd seen the mural but had been too depressed to comment on it. He had to have known. He had to have been testing her.

"Elly? You okay?"

"Yes. It just all came back to me. What were we talking about? Oh, meeting people."

"Now don't start on me, Elly. Like I said, I just don't circulate in the same crowds you do. The only nice men I find are married, so I'll take my chances at single bars."

"It's not my place to preach to you," Elly ad-libbed, "but it just seems like you don't look for a pumpkin in a watermelon patch."

"I know," Linda sighed. "What can I say? Just chalk it all up to experience, I guess." She pushed herself away from the table. "Well, I gotta go. I didn't mean to stay so long; I didn't want to tire you out..."

"It's okay," Elly said, rising. And it was. She'd learned something. "We'll have to do it again. I just hope next time you'll have good news to tell me about."

Linda laughed, a throaty, full laugh. "You're not the only one." She picked up her purse and headed for the door. "You're going to take your full leave anyway, aren't you? All three months?"

"Uh, yes. I think so. At least until I get oriented a little better."

"And then it'll be time for a maternity leave. Well, call me if you want to get together downtown. I don't have too many days off, you know."

"All right, I will. Thanks for stopping by, Linda. I appreciate it."

"Sure," Linda smiled. "Any time I can help out, let me know."

"I will." That was a promise.

After Linda had gone, Elly went about fixing dinner, but her mind was buzzing at a much faster speed. Linda's casual remarks had answered some questions but also had opened a veritable Pandora's box of other ones. Elly tried to make sense of it all.

It was a blow to her to think that she may not have loved Adam. Why, then, was she running away with him? Perhaps that had changed, though, and she'd hadn't confided to Linda. Maybe Elly had only just realized it before she bolted. Linda said Adam had treated her like a queen. Maybe after Graydon's chauvinism, a little kindness had seemed the only important thing. Why couldn't she remember?

And the mural—Graydon must have known. It couldn't have been just chance that he drove that way. What had he thought when she had made no sign, made no comment about it? Would that have pleased him or made him angry? She had no way of knowing. He was always angry those first few days.

Thinking about Graydon brought a different sort of soul-searching to Elly.

For all his ranting and raving, his fits of temper and jealousy, his angry looks, she realized that she could love him. The way he was sometimes when he held her and comforted her brought an involuntary smile to her. If only she could tame his anger and erase his resentment, she was sure she could love him. But that was a tall order. Elly, the lion-tamer. Little, memoryless Elly going to war against the armies of hate and pain that clamored inside her huge husband. It was a pretty feeble image.

When Graydon came home that night, Elly was subdued. As much as she would have liked to share her internal discussion with him, initiating a conversation about Adam was still not the best idea. Elly served dinner and let the entire matter slide.

"How was school?" she asked. Graydon, she had noticed, was not in a particularly good mood.

"It could have been better," Graydon said curtly. "There's one cadet that I'd just like to take out and beat his brains in."

"The same one?" Graydon had mentioned one boy who was a problem. He nodded.

"Yeah. Warner. He's an Air Force brat, anyway, and he thinks he knows it all. He won't learn from me unless Daddy okays it or some dumb thing."

"What rank is Daddy? General?"

Graydon laughed then. "No, Captain. But I guess Daddies that are Captains outrank Colonels that aren't related at all. That kid has some rough years ahead if he doesn't correct his attitude, though. I just wish I could make him see that."

"You can't make them learn, Graydon. You can offer them the knowledge, but you can't make them take it." Her own advice surprised her a little. "When—before, when I taught—did we compare notes?"

"On what?"

"Teaching. Did we discuss how we taught?"

"Not much. The Academy's a little bit different than third grade."

Elly ignored the cut. "I know, but the basic methods are the same, aren't they? You have to get the kids interested, challenge them, make them want to know. That doesn't change, does it?"

Graydon stopped eating to look across into the wide blue eyes of his wife. On his face was patent disbelief. "Can you remember that? Teaching?"

Elly blushed under his scrutiny. "No, it just makes sense to me. Why are you looking at me that way? Am I saying something stupid?"

Graydon shook his head. "Not stupid but—different. You never talked this much before, and if you did, it wasn't about comparative teaching methods."

"Why didn't I?"

"I don't know. You were always quiet. You're just different now."

Elly met his eyes squarely, her chin tipped ever so slightly up. "Do you mind?" she asked quietly.

Graydon studied her. Sitting that way, her eyes open and honest, she looked almost demure and yet Graydon could see the underlying strength, the steel skeleton that structured her calm. Why had he never seen that before? She was at once passive and yet very capable of resisting. At this moment, she could go either way, and she would—depending on what his answer was. It was disquieting, and yet not unpleasant to see this in his wife. Maybe he had chosen better than he thought. At the same time, though, he could hardly say that to her.

"No," he said in a casual voice. "I don't mind. It keeps things interesting."

For a fraction of a second, Elly held her position, then softened. She returned her attention to her own dinner. "I guess interesting is better than dull, isn't it?"

Graydon didn't answer.

She brought the cat in later. It was the first time since Sunday that she'd let Chester in while Graydon was home, but when he was sitting comfortably on the couch looking over the mail, she came to sit on the hearth, Chester in her lap.

Graydon glanced up. "Put the cat out," he said, then went back to his mail.

"Look," Elly said. "I got him a flea collar and powder, too. Monday I dusted him with it and by now all his fleas should be gone." She hadn't moved an inch.

"He's still dirty," Graydon said. "Put him out."

"No, he's not. And he's such a nice cat. I promise I'll watch him. The minute he starts prowling, I'll put him out."

Graydon put his papers down and glared at Elly. His eyes darkened. "Elly, I said put him out. He's got worms."

"I wormed him Monday."

"He's not our cat. He doesn't belong here."

"But he doesn't belong to anyone else, either," Elly argued. "It's not like I'm trying to take him away from anyone. He spends most of his time here. And he won't hurt anything, not if I watch him."

"Elly..."

"Please, Graydon," she rushed on, "please. He's so much company for me when you're gone. He really is a good cat and he's completely housebroken."

Graydon's eyes widened and Elly knew she'd said too much. She swallowed nervously.

"How do you know he's housebroken?" Graydon wanted to know.

"Uh, well..."

"Elly, you're slipping."

Her face flamed when she realized Graydon was chuckling at her expense. She buried her hands in Chester's fur and waited for Graydon's verdict.

"You've already had him in the house."

"Just to keep me company. Just so I have someone to talk to. He doesn't do anything wrong." She chanced looking up. Graydon's face was impassive. "Please?" she added.

He shook his head uselessly. "Oh, hell. Even if I said no, you'd have him in every chance you got." Elly brightened. "But he's your responsibility. I don't want any little piles left anywhere where I can step in them."

"Promise," she said. "I'll watch him."

"And no scratching up furniture."

Elly nodded.

"And no seven flavors of cat food."

Elly saluted.

"Oh, for crying out loud," Graydon fumed. "Keep the damn cat."

Elly wrapped her arms around Chester and hugged him close. His purring never stopped.

"Thank you, Graydon," she said happily.

He ignored her.

On Thursday of that week, Elly got bored and nothing needed cleaning. She tried to find something to do, but even the bathtub didn't need scrubbing. Finally, after prowling all the safe rooms, she ventured into Graydon's den.

It was a nice room. His desk was old and refinished oak, and Graydon had taken care of it so the wood gleamed. A computer sat on the desk, strangely incongruous with the older piece of furniture. Bookshelves lined one whole wall of the room. His recliner waited patiently against the opposite wall, angled toward the small TV in the corner. It was like a male sanctuary. She wondered if he used to escape here often.

She brushed book bindings with her good hand and tilted her head sideways so she could read the titles. There were a lot of military books, both fiction and non-fiction, war books, documentaries and histories. On another shelf were mysteries— lots and lots of them. Then she found textbooks; psychology, sociology, history and literature. Hers or his? she wondered. And education textbooks—management, discipline, creative learning. Remembering their discussion of the other night, Elly pulled a couple of those out. Anyway, she told herself, if she was ever going to teach again, she'd have to re-learn how to do it. Might as well start brushing up now.

On a lower shelf she caught sight of the photo album Graydon had shown her earlier and wedged in beside it, the envelope of loose photos. On the other side there were three more photo albums. Elly pulled those out, too.

Chester bringing up the rear, Elly carried her booty to the living room and dumped it all on the floor in front of the fireplace. Before she got comfortable, she fixed herself a cup of tea, then stretched out on her stomach and pulled the first photo album up. Chester made a bed in the small of her back and promptly went to sleep.

The pictures had no names. The first ones were old, the people in them from another time. A man and a woman smiling into the sun in front of a wooden two-story house. Graydon's parents?

She found one of the house with snow up to the window sills. Minnesota. Bare trees stood in the yard like skeletal hands. She hoped Colorado didn't have that much snow.

Then there was one of kids, or one baby and two little kids. The oldest girl and the baby were dressed alike, the baby in a cradle between the other two. The boy stood scowling on the right. His dark eyes reflected his displeasure and his black hair shone with the slickness of water. Elly had to laugh. Even then he was ornery.

The kids grew up. Elly found a snap shot of the oldest girl in a school dress, white socks and white buckled shoes. She pulled her dress out on both sides to show it off. Her features were dark like Graydon's, but not so large or commanding. She had a pretty smile.

A dog; a mutt really. It looked like a terrier-and-something cross, with small hairs curling up on the bridge of its nose and over its eyes. Its tongue languished in the picture, as if the dog were waiting for a command from its owner. Elly was sure Graydon had been behind the camera.

The locale changed. In outdoor pictures Elly saw clear skies and hedges. A house with a front porch and nice siding. The youngest girl on a hobby horse at Christmas; Graydon throwing a toy football.

Elly was enchanted. For as long as she had been conscious—almost two weeks—she had seen Graydon as a serious, moody, dominating man. Now she saw him differently; as a boy growing up, learning, experiencing, becoming. There was a birthday picture—eight candles on the cake—and already the handsomeness was there, the strength, yet the smile on his face was young and excited and joyful. Elly wished she could remember Graydon that happy.

From then on, any pictures of Graydon with his sisters showed how he was developing his size. Where before he had been a head shorter than the oldest girl, he was then even with her, and a year or two later even taller. At about twelve, Elly guessed, he began to have the width and depth. Probably he was active in sports all along—a picture in a baseball uniform confirmed that—and his body developed a bulk and maturity beyond his years. In a shot of Graydon in a three-point stance on a football field, Elly calculated he must have been in junior high, yet he looked years older just because of his size. He had probably learned early that he could get his own way by a simple show of strength, and that lesson had survived to show itself even now. Elly had seen evidence of it many times.

The first album ended. Elly pulled the second one over and began again.

High school. A report card showed Graydon's excellence in English, History, Shop and P. E. He got a C in music appreciation, a B in math. His class picture was of a short-haired, unsmiling Graydon—a younger version of the man she was married to.

Elly found a picture of him in an R.O.T.C. uniform. He looked born to it. Then suddenly there were snow pictures again and Graydon in a hockey uniform. His older sister got married; she looked no more than eighteen or nineteen and her husband about twenty. The picture of the wedding party showed a handsome if unemotional Graydon as an usher. His parents, in their celebration finery, looked old.

Back to football. Graydon wore number twelve—first string quarterback?

Elly could imagine his playing any of a half dozen positions. She could also see him as the unreachable captain of the team with his pick of the cheerleaders. Had he been so jealously possessive then? No high school boy in his right mind would challenge him, not when Graydon was so physically superior. Why then, was he so unsure of his hold on Elly? It had to be because of Adam. There was no other explanation.

Next was a picture of a car—a beat-up fifty-something Chevy. One picture showed the car alone, then there was one of Graydon behind the wheel. His first car.

A motorcycle followed, then another, newer car. There was an entire squadron of R. O. T. C. and Elly picked Graydon out as one of the squad leaders. Next a picture of Graydon in a suit beside a girl in a short formal. Elly looked closely at the girl; she was tiny and petite, her freckled face split with a schoolgirl grin. The difference in their heights was at least a foot, more like eighteen inches. Definitely not his type, Elly decided.

There were more pictures of the latest car and a running series of its beautification, even the engine. One picture showed a garage floor completely littered with car parts. The final picture was of a sixty-some Chevy painted a deep metal flake blue. Graydon stood proudly beside his masterpiece.

Then a prom picture. Graydon wore a conservative tux, complete with boutonniere, and the girl, a taller, willowy brunette, languished on his arm in a slinky pastel formal. They looked very good together. Elly flipped the page.

She almost laughed. The next picture was Graydon in an Air force uniform—a very plain uniform—with the shortest haircut Elly had ever seen. His hair couldn't have been more than an eighth of an inch long, and he stood painfully at attention. His face was grim. No doubt he'd just had his first taste of boot camp.

Chester stirred on Elly's back. She glanced at the clock overhead—almost five o'clock and she hadn't even started dinner. The rest of the second album seemed to be just a few pictures of a boot compound, some planes, and one or two of people. Elly thumbed through briskly, then pushed the albums aside. She'd look at the third one later.

When Graydon got home, she was mashing the potatoes.

"Hi," she greeted him. "Dinner's not quite ready. I got the rest of your photo albums out and got so caught up in them, I forgot the time. It'll be another ten minutes or so."

"That's okay." He watched her a moment then retreated to the living room. "Did you look at all the albums?" he called.

"No, just the first two. I think I got up to the point where you had just joined the Air Force."

There was no answer from the living room, but Elly heard the flipping of the heavy pages.

"Did you play quarterback?" she asked.

"Yeah, my senior year. I started as a fullback, though." There was the sound of the albums sliding one on top of another. "I'll put these back for now. You can look at them more later if you want."

"Okay."

When Graydon returned to sit at the table, he leaned back and watched Elly moving around the kitchen. "Did you get those books out, too?"

"Yes, I thought I'd brush up on my education a little. There's no telling how long I'll be off work, but I think I'd like to get back to it eventually. I must have liked it. I wasn't sure if those books were yours or mine, though."

"Most of them are yours. I didn't take much in the way of education theory. The Air Force isn't big on psychology; just pound what you can into the little bastards."

Elly glanced over at him. "Warner?"

"Yeah, Warner. Little creep. I don't even want to think about him."

"Think about t-bones, instead," Elly said. She pulled a broiler pan from the oven and the smell of broiled steak filled the room.

"That sounds great. I'm starving."

"You're always starving," Elly laughed. "Maybe I ought to start getting up with you in the morning and fixing your breakfast. Maybe then you wouldn't be so hungry at dinner time."

"Then I'd be twice as hungry at dinner," Graydon said. "The more I eat, the hungrier I get." He slapped his stomach. "And I've got to watch my weight. I can't let those cadets think the old man's going to pot."

Elly served dinner. "I hardly think they'll get pushy. Looking at those early pictures of you, I'll bet no one ever picked a fight with you in your life."

"Shows how much you know," Graydon said. Elly looked up from her serving, questioning. "You'd be surprised how much pressure big kids get."

"Pressure? What kind of pressure?" Elly put away her pot holders and slid into her chair across from Graydon. Rather than fill her plate, she let Graydon have the potatoes first and waited patiently.

"Pressure to prove myself. It's sort of like the old saw about gunslingers. You know how the star is always the fastest gun and all the young punks come from all over the territory to try his hand? Well, that's how it is if you're big. All the kids are always wanting you to prove yourself, see if you're as tough as you look, see if you can really put someone away. It was a pain in the ass."

"That's strange," Elly said. "I would think all you'd have to do is look cross-eyed at another kid and he'd run away screaming. Did they really press you so much?"

"Constantly," Graydon nodded. "In fact it got to a point where I almost doubted my own ability. I felt that if all these yo-yos figured I wasn't as tough as I looked, maybe I really wasn't. I began to have a real chip on my shoulder."

Elly studied her husband as he talked. Was that why he was so over-bearing, so decidedly dominating? Maybe he had never been able to relax and let his guard down. It would fit in with what she knew of him. It also showed a vulnerability she hadn't seen before.

"What's in the third album?" she asked. "I didn't get to see any of it at all."

"Not much that you would find interesting. Mostly Air Force stuff." He passed her the potatoes. "You must have been pretty bored if you were dragging all that stuff out."

"Sort of," Elly admitted. "That's why I thought I'd brush up on teaching. I was thinking that after the baby's born, I won't have any reason not to go back to work."

"That's true," Graydon agreed. "There wasn't enough around here to keep you busy before. I don't suppose it'll be any different now."

Elly glanced up. Graydon's tone was funny, almost condemning. He kept his eyes down as he ate, though, and wouldn't acknowledge her curiosity. She let it pass.

"Mayfield asked me today if we're still going to be able to make it Saturday night. I told him we would."

"Oh, that's right. I'd almost forgotten."

"You still want to go?"

Elly shrugged. "I guess we should. I'll feel funny, though."

"You'll do fine."

Elly wasn't so sure. "Is tripoly like bridge? I mean, do you play partners?"

"Not really. You each play your own hand, and it doesn't really matter what your partner has. You just play to win."

"Oh." His explanation didn't put Elly any more at ease. She wondered how much she would hold up the game by playing one-handed. "Graydon?" He glanced up. "If you don't have anything pressing to do tonight, would you do me a favor?"

"What favor?"

Elly sighed. "Practice playing cards with me."

His eyes were lit with a quiet amusement. "Sure," he said.

"You'll be a whiz in no time."

Chapter Eight

Saturday Elly was nervous. That morning Graydon had caught her off balance first thing by shoving a wedding ring across the table to her. She looked at it, then up at him questioningly.

"It's yours. You'd better wear it so Don and Clare won't wonder."

She nodded and picked it up. A simple gold band, it matched his. She put it on. How had she felt when Graydon had been the one sliding it on her finger?

"Where was it?" she asked hesitatingly. "Did I...leave it?"

Graydon passed off her question with a shake of his head and a casual sip of his coffee. "No, you were wearing it. The hospital took it off when they admitted you. I got it the day you were released."

She twisted it around her finger, trying to familiarize herself with the feel of it. She might have wished for a more sentimental presentation from Graydon, but she could hardly have expected it.

"More coffee?" she asked.

Graydon had some work he wanted to do in his basement shop—he was building more bookcases for the den—so Elly tried patiently to occupy herself in the house and stay out of his way. After all week in the house, though, she was restless. She stood in front of her closet for over a half hour trying to decide what she would wear that night. She pulled out the sleeves of dresses, the legs of pant suits; nothing seemed right. Twice she started for the door to ask Graydon, but both times she stopped herself. He was busy; he wouldn't appreciate her interference.

Eventually she had to give up on her choice of wardrobe; it was getting her nowhere. With Chester padding after her, she checked the clock. It was going on noon. She wondered if Graydon would like lunch. There was no sign of him from the shop.

She wandered into his den. He had moved the recliner away from the wall in order to take some measurements for his shelves. Very soon, Elly thought, he would run out of room in the small den. He should have taken the other spare bedroom—her room—and left the smaller room for guests. But maybe three years ago when they bought this house, he didn't have so much stuff.

She went familiarly to the place where the photo albums were. She hadn't gotten back to them since Thursday; she'd spent most of Friday leafing through the education books. She had time now to see the last one, even if Graydon said it was boring.

Funny—it wasn't there. The first two were in their place, and the final one, but there was a gap where the third one should have been. It was gone.

Elly scanned the other bookshelves. Nothing else was out of place, no extra books on top of others. What had he done with it? She checked his desk. It was clear. Maybe in one of the drawers.

"Hey! Can a guy get a little something to eat for lunch around here?" Graydon's voice stopped Elly's search and she spun to go meet him. "Elly?"

"I'm here," she said, coming down the hall.

"How about it? I'm—"

"Starving? Yes, I know. What would you like? Soup? Sandwich? Some left over steak?" She stood poised in the kitchen, ready to go in whatever direction Graydon sent her.

"Just a sandwich is fine. Maybe two. What have you been doing?"

"Nothing much," Elly got out the bread and some sliced ham. "Mostly trying to figure out what to wear tonight. What do I usually wear over to their house?"

"Just a pantsuit or something. It's no big deal. I've got to wash up. I've got sawdust all over me."

No big deal, Elly thought. Maybe not to him but he wasn't trying to impersonate himself without knowing how to act. As she made his sandwiches, she resigned herself to guessing and hoped she'd guess right.

"Do you want me to help you pick out something to wear?" Graydon had returned to lean against the kitchen counter. He watched silently as Elly put mustard but no mayonnaise on his ham.

"That's okay," she said. "I've got to try my hand at it sometime. I can't always be running to you to tell me what to wear."

Graydon scooped up one sandwich as she finished it and got himself a napkin as she started to make the other one. "Come on," he said abruptly. "Leave that."

"What?" But he was already gone. Knife in hand, Elly peered around the corner of the kitchen. Graydon was disappearing down the hall. "What are you doing?" she called.

"Come here," Graydon's voice came muffled from the back of the house.

Elly followed. At first she thought he had gone into his own room, but at the end of the hall she found him standing in front of her wardrobe. She moved behind him.

"Graydon, I didn't mean for you to do this," she said. "Really, it's not that important."

"You'll be more at ease if you know you don't stick out like a sore thumb, and if you're more at ease, you'll be more natural. What were you thinking of wearing? Did you have anything picked out?"

"No. I didn't know if I usually wore a dress or pants. I was looking at both."

Graydon pulled out something gray. "This is a nice outfit. It would be okay."

Elly didn't like it. Gray wool pants, gray jacket; it looked very boring.

"With a blue blouse, it would look nice," Graydon was saying. Nice and plain, Elly thought. "What do you think?" he asked. He noted her silence curiously.

"That's what I would normally wear?" she queried. Graydon nodded. "Okay, I'll wear it."

"You don't like it," Graydon said. His voice was a little more brittle than it had been.

"No, Graydon, it's fine. I'll wear it. Come on, I'll finish your other sandwich."

"Why don't you like it?" he demanded.

"Graydon, please, let's not fight over it. I just—gray just doesn't do a lot for me, that's all. I must have liked it, though, if I bought it."

"I bought this for your birthday last year."

Elly groaned. Open mouth, insert foot, she thought. "I'll wear it, Graydon. It's fine. It'll probably look better on than it does on the hanger anyway; lots of things do that. Come on, I'll finish your sandwich."

Before Graydon could agree, Elly had turned and headed down the hall. The last thing she wanted to do was upset the fine balance they'd had lately. If it meant wearing a plain outfit, Elly would do it. Anything to keep from starting a battle.

"Wear whatever you want," Graydon sulked behind her. Sandwich in hand, he followed her back to the kitchen.

"I will," she said. "I'll wear that." He looked ready to argue. Elly rushed on to keep him quiet. "I want to wear it. I do, Graydon. Really."

He didn't look pacified but Elly refused to drag it out any more. Later, when she put on the outfit, maybe he'd accept her decision more graciously. For now she finished fixing his lunch.

"Do you want something to drink? A beer?"

"That's fine."

"Are you almost done with your book shelves?"

"Pretty close."

"Will you need any help?"

"No."

Elly ignored his curtness. "Probably isn't much a one-armed cripple could do anyway, huh? Well, unless you want anything else for lunch, I think I'll go wash my hair."

Not waiting for an answer, she left Graydon to his lunch.

With Chester watching from the safety of the bathroom floor,

Elly soaked in the tub. She wondered if things would ever go smoothly between her and Graydon, or if there would always be friction there. Later, after the baby was born, after she had gotten her memory back—or enough of it to satisfy them both—would their fragile partnership dissolve under the strain? She couldn't see much of a future for them the way things were now. Holding her cast aloft, she ducked beneath the water. Forget it, she thought; what happens will happen.

Later, dried and robed, she attended to her hair. She found that if she blew it dry and then touched it up with a curling iron, she could effect a natural, subtly curly hair style that pleased her. Graydon, of course, had not commented, but she liked it well enough to keep it. The soft, short curls around her face added something to the ordinariness of her features, and by waving it close on the side of her face, Elly found it detracted from the gradually decreasing tilt of her right eye. It looked good.

Next makeup. She took a lot of time with it, not only to keep herself busy but to get it just right. It was not so much because she put a lot on, but because she wanted the most effectiveness from the little bit she wore. By subtle shading, she found she could realize enough natural-looking highlights without ending up looking painted. The less makeup she wore, the more it pleased Graydon, so she made sure she got full benefit from what she had. Finally she was able to view her image in the mirror and pronounce it good.

By then, Chester wanted outside. She followed him to the back door and let him out, noting that Graydon had made progress in the den, but was in the shop just then. She checked the clock—after 5:30. He should be quitting pretty soon. She determined to stay out of his way until time to go.

With Chester safely out, she retreated to her room and took the gray suit out of her wardrobe. Dull, she thought, very dull. But she would wear it. Maybe she could spark it up with some jewelry. Searching the closet, she found the blue blouse Graydon mentioned. It was plain, too. No help there. On a hunch, she snuck into Graydon's room to survey what was left of her clothing there.

Her side of the closet had mostly dresses and suits, teacherish things. She ignored those. Digging deep, she found a few things toward the back that looked less conservative; a loose-necked peasant blouse, a denim jacket, a black halter-necked jumpsuit. Why were these things relegated to the back, she wondered. Maybe these were items she had bought but Graydon had nixed; either that or she had been afraid to show them to him at all. She kept digging.

Ah. Just the thing. She pulled out a gauzy, white, Victorian-style blouse. The material was ribbed with slender threads of thin lace—very innocent but very feminine—and had a high ruffled collar and long sleeves ruffled at the wrists.

An inset bib of ruffled lace gave the blouse a demur look, yet the total appearance was candidly appealing. Elly loved it.

The slam of the basement door alerted her to Graydon's entrance. Quickly she hurried into her room with the blouse, and as soon as she hung it up behind the gray suit, Graydon appeared at her door.

"It's almost six," he said.

"Yes, I was just getting ready to get dressed." Elly pretended complete ignorance of his surliness. "What about you?"

"I've got to shower. Are you done in the bathroom?"

"Yep. It's all yours."

"We'll leave in about a half hour, then."

"Fine. I'll be ready."

Graydon stood in the doorway a second longer than necessary, then went to his own room. Elly shut her door behind him.

Old grouch, she thought. She wasn't in any mood to fight tonight. The only good thing about sparring with him though, she realized, was that it took her mind off the upcoming trial at the Mayfield's. Perhaps if she kept all her concentration on avoiding Graydon's temper flares, she could get through the evening without too much anxiety. Sighing to herself, she took down the blouse. Ready or not, she thought, here I come.

Graydon had changed into black slacks and a nice-fitting blue sweater. When Elly came out of her room, gray jacket buttoned over the blouse, they surveyed each other.

Elly pirouetted. "Okay?" she asked. Graydon's examination, she noticed, took in her entire image, including her face and hair.

She waited but he withheld his approval.

"Graydon? Do I look okay? I'm not overdone, am I?" Don't be obtuse tonight, she pleaded silently. Give a little.

"No. You're not overdone." He gave in grudgingly.

"I look all right?"

"You look fine. We'd better go."

Graydon was already at the door when Elly got her coat and purse. His face was peculiarly stony. Elly, a mischievous glint in her eye, paused in front of him at the door.

"You look nice, too," she said, and skipped outside.

The ride in the car was a little chilly. Elly couldn't quite figure out what exactly she had done to displease Graydon, but she made up her mind that she'd be damned if she'd ask him. She had made her move; let him make the next one. If her overture hadn't set things right, then it was his problem now. She concentrated on noting the way Graydon went so she wouldn't be totally lost. He couldn't find fault with that.

When they turned down a residential street and Graydon began to slow the car, Elly got nervous. What would Clare be like? How well did she know Elly? After the near disaster with Linda, Elly was not sure she could pull off another round of improvisation. She prayed the other three would be caught up enough in dinner and the card game not to notice Elly's uncertainty. Graydon, she was sure, would not be awfully supportive tonight. She'd be on her own.

Graydon pulled in front of a well-lit two-story house and parked the car. The house was more pretentious than Elly had expected.

"Are they rich?" she asked. A Mercedes was parked in the driveway.

"Clare's family has money, but Don makes the same pay I do. They just have different priorities."

Somehow his answer didn't soothe Elly. She was glad she had taken such pains to look good; if nothing else, she wouldn't have to worry about that. As Graydon handed her out of the car, though, all the rest of her confidence evaporated. She felt out-classed and hadn't even seen the competition yet.

"Nervous?" Graydon asked. It was the first sign that he had

noticed and still his voice was unsympathetic.

"A little," she hedged. "I'd feel better if they lived in a bungalow or something."

"Don't worry about it. Clare's big on gold lamé. She overdoes it."

The door opened before they reached it. Clare called out from the brightness within.

"Elly, how are you? Where's your cast?"

Elly felt Graydon's hand guiding her up the step. She tried to make out Clare's features but they were lost in the glare of the porch light. "It's here," she mumbled, "under my sleeve."

"Poor dear. Come in. Don didn't even tell me right away or I would have brought some casseroles or something over so you didn't have to cook. How have you been making out?"

"Fine, really. It's not too much of a problem."

Inside, Elly was better able to see her hostess. Clare was taller than she and bigger boned. Her auburn hair was cut short and puffed in an outdated 'cute' style—too cute, Elly thought, for Clare. At close to forty, if not just past, Clare would have looked better in a more moderate hairdo. Elly felt a small degree of relief that Clare wasn't perfect.

"You look well," Clare said with one raised brow. Quickly she noted Elly's appearance. "Staying home must be agreeing with you." She turned to Graydon. "And how are you, Graydon? You're looking absolutely charming, as usual." She put her arm around Graydon and pressed a coy kiss to his cheek. Elly was a trifle taken back.

"Thanks, Clare. Where's that old goat of a Colonel? Plying the bar?"

"Oh, Graydon," Clare laughed. "As a matter of fact, he's just pouring the wine. Come on in. Let me take your coats."

Graydon shrugged out of his coat and helped Elly with hers.

"What about that jacket, Elly? I've got both fireplaces going. You'll be more comfortable without it." Clare took the coats and stood maternally by as Elly unbuttoned her jacket. Again Graydon helped her slip the right sleeve off her cast.

"That's a beautiful blouse, Elly," Clare said. "Is it new?" The older woman cast a sidelong glance at Graydon. He was staring at Elly.

"It's just something I found back in my closet," Elly shrugged. "After being in the hospital, I needed to wear something a little more exciting than pale green. I'm glad you like it."

"It's lovely. Graydon thinks so, too, don't you, Graydon?"

Graydon was caught off guard by Clare's question. He snapped his mouth shut and dragged his eyes from his wife. "Yes. I haven't seen her wear it in a while."

"I'm afraid you'll have Don waiting on you hand and foot all evening, looking like that. Go on in. I'll put your jackets away. You can find your way to the dining room."

Clare strode away down the entry hall and Elly immediately felt Graydon's hand on her elbow. "This way," he said. "Through the living room."

Elly went as directed. Graydon was right. The living room abounded in jade green furniture and gold lamé.

"You planned that, didn't you?" he said quietly. His grip tightened ever so slightly on her arm.

"Planned what?"

"That unveiling."

Elly turned innocent eyes on her husband. "I wore the outfit you picked for me. I just thought this blouse would look nice. It was in my closet. Don't you like it?"

"Would it matter one way or another? You're bound to draw attention to yourself, no matter what I think, aren't you?"

"Graydon, I only want to look good for you," she argued. "Or don't you think a wife's appearance is a reflection of her husband? Would you be happier if I were ugly?"

"Ah! There you are!" They'd crossed the living room and stood framed by an archway to the dining room. Don was just replacing a wine bottle in a ceramic brique. He came forward to meet them.

"How are you, Elly? Looking lovely, I see." He kissed her cheek fondly and she took the opportunity to escape from Graydon's hold. "I told Clare she'd be jealous at how good you were looking. Come in, come in. I think we can go ahead and sit down. Clare's got it all ready."

Graydon held a chair for Elly at the long side of the table. Don stood at the foot while Graydon walked around opposite Elly. He eyed her moodily across the table.

"Are you—oh, you're already sitting. Good." Clare burst from a side door and breezed through to the kitchen. "I'll get the lasagna."

"Is there anything I can help with?" Since Clare was gone already, Elly asked her question of Don.

"Nah," he waved her off. "Clare's got it all done. Just relax and enjoy."

Not hardly, Elly thought, with Graydon glowering at her.

"Ta da!" Clare entered again, this time holding up a long dish of steaming lasagna. She set it in front of Don's chair and took her own seat at the head of the table. "Garlic bread is in that basket by you, Graydon, and Elly, you've got the green beans. Don, if you'll pass the salad..."

It was a good meal as long as Elly could forget Graydon and concentrate on eating. She ate sparingly, though; the waist of her pants, she had noticed, was snug. Hadn't she heard somewhere that the waistline went first in pregnancy? She hoped Clare wouldn't be offended when Elly passed on a second helping.

"Dieting, Elly?" she asked.

"Just watching it," Elly said genially. "With food this good, I could get carried away very easily. Everything is delicious."

"More wine?" Don asked.

"Thanks, no. I'm fine." Elly had sipped sparingly at her wine, just enough not to draw comment. She was sure the baby wouldn't mind a little, but she didn't want to overdo. Anyway she was already more than comfortably warm.

The table conversation drifted and flowed easily, sometimes with Elly, more often around her. She found it less than difficult to escape any unmasking subjects and no one, except Graydon, seemed to be aware that she was a different Elly. More than once she felt Graydon's dark eyes on her in a commanding stare, but she pretended not to notice.

"That was excellent," he told Clare when everyone had pushed their plates away.

"You only had two helpings," Clare complained jokingly. "How could you even tell?"

"Two and a half," Graydon corrected, "and I think it was that half that really did it."

"Yes," Elly chimed in, "it was delicious. I'd love to have the recipe for it."

Clare looked sharply at Elly. "You do. I gave it to you months ago."

Elly's brain went into high gear. "Oh, I know, but I lost it. If you have time, could you write it out for me again? I didn't have it long enough to memorize it."

Clare nodded, her eyes glittering. "Sure. Remind me later. I'll do it between hands."

Elly kept her eyes averted from Graydon's. She could imagine his criticizing scowl. So much for her attempts to bolster conversation.

"Well," Clare said. "Elly, if you'll help me with the dishes, the guys can go tune up with a game of pool."

Everybody rose. Before Elly could slide sideways from her chair, Graydon was there helping her. There was no chance for words, but he caught her elbow with one hand and pressed his fingers into her flesh. She blushed hotly. What was that—a warning? Was he telling her that she had fumbled stupidly? She stood beneath his hand for a split second then, thankfully, he moved away.

"Eightball, Graydon?" Don asked.

"Is there any other game?" The men disappeared out a side door.

Elly began to stack plates. Before she could pick them up in a clumsy hold, Clare was there taking them from her. "Really, Elly, just relax. I don't expect you to do a full share, not with that cast. You can carry the wine brique, though."

Elly did as she was told and followed Clare through the doorway into the kitchen.

"If you want to get the glasses, you can pour the rest of the wine. I'll do the dishes."

Elly retrieved wine glasses two at a time and metered out the rosé evenly.

Clare directed her to a cupboard where she found a serving tray to carry them on. "You and Graydon haven't been quarreling again, have you?"

Elly almost dropped the tray. "No, why? Do we act like it?" She wondered if Clare were used to butting her nose into their business.

"Graydon does. But he's also very solicitous of you, too. I thought maybe you'd had a fight and had only partially made up."

"No." Elly forced her voice to stay level. "I think he's a little tired. He worked in his shop all day and still didn't get the shelves done like he wanted. You know how moody he is."

"Don't I?" Clare laughed. "You know, for a moment there when he was helping you out of your chair you looked—I don't know—like a blushing bride. And that blouse. You certainly are coming out of hiding since your accident, aren't you?"

"Out of hiding?"

"Oh, you know. I hate to say it, dear, but you did let yourself get a little colorless at times. Of course with Graydon's jealousy the way it is, I suppose it was easier not to draw attention to yourself. But tonight, why you positively shine. Are you sure there isn't anything you'd like to tell me?"

Elly's lips thinned in annoyance. If this was Graydon's idea of a friend for her, thanks but no thanks. She didn't need the interference of an older magpie wet-nurse. Placing the full glasses carefully on the tray, Elly took the time to parry.

"What do you mean?" she asked.

"Oh, Elly. We're friends, remember? And don't forget, I've had two of my own. Now come on, level with me. You are pregnant, aren't you?"

Thank God she had the last glass down. She turned and leaned against the kitchen counter, embarrassed now by her evasion.

"You can tell?"

Clare laughed. "You're talking to an expert, remember? When I was working for Dr. Meyers, you have no idea how many young women like you I saw, all glowing and full of life. You get to where you can recognize it, especially when the husband is around. You'd think Graydon didn't want you to even attempt standing without him there to steady you. But I thought you two had decided not to have children."

Elly fiddled with the stem of a glass. Did this woman know everything about them? She broke through the barriers of tactful etiquette like a bull through a china shop. Elly tried to answer without revealing her annoyance.

"We changed our minds," she said. "It's a long story. I won't bore you with it now. It happened so fast, though, that I think we're both still getting used to the idea."

"Well, I think it's lovely," Clare sighed. "I always thought it would have been a horrible waste of talent for Graydon not to have any sons. He's such a handsome devil."

Bingo, Elly thought.

"Have you been thinking of names?"

"Names? Uh, no, not yet. I'm only two and half months. It's early yet."

Clare cocked an eyebrow at her. "It happens sooner than you think. Just wait. You'll see." She had loaded the last of the dishes in the dishwasher. "That's good enough for now. I'll take the tray. Let's go see how the guys are doing."

Elly managed to jockey behind Clare so the older woman could lead the way. She would have had no idea which way to go, but following behind Clare, she peered through doorways and memorized what could have been bathrooms in case she needed to know later. Clare led her on down the entry hall, around a corner and downstairs.

From below, the clack of pool balls drifted up the stair well.

"Who's winning?" Clare called.

"Who else?" It was Don, grumbling. As the women descended the stairs, they saw Graydon hunched over for a shot, Don standing gloomily behind.

"Losing again, dear?" Clare asked sweetly. A card table was set up at the other end of the basement playroom and Clare breezed by to set the wine down. Elly stood across from Graydon to watch him shoot.

"As usual," Don growled.

"Come on, Don," Graydon cautioned him. "That doesn't count. You scratched on the eight ball." He tapped the cue ball with his cue, sending it into the striped thirteen ball, which plunked neatly into a corner pocket. Graydon stood and grinned at Don. "This time I'll get you on my own."

Elly almost giggled. For a moment Graydon looked eight again, a mischievous little boy knowing full well that he was tormenting his friend—and loving it. Graydon caught Elly's look and raised a questioning eyebrow at her. She sidled to the card table.

"Well, hurry up and finish," Clare said as she set the wine glasses around the table. "We want to play cards. Here, Elly, you sit here. Graydon will have to deal for you. I'll get the poker chips."

Elly watched the game from her seat. Graydon missed his next shot, Don made a short putt into a side pocket and then, without a minute's hesitation, sunk the eight ball.

"Oh, no!" he cried. "How could I do that twice? I don't believe it."

Graydon sighed. "What a coward you are, Don. You just can't stand to let a young whippersnapper beat you, can you?"

He stood his pool cue in the rack on the wall. "Well, come on. We'll see if we can't beat your ass in cards. But no fair throwing away pay cards."

They were just like a couple of kids, Elly thought. Still insulting each other, they joined her at the table, one on either side of her. Don, on her right, patted her hand.

"Elly, you haven't been keeping to our bargain," he said.

"Bargain?"

"Yeah. Remember last time you came over? I promised I'd slip you a five under the table if you'd make sure Graydon was dog tired before you came over again." He leaned close and smiled fondly at Elly. "You're just not working him enough, Elly. How can I beat him at pool if you don't wear him out for me?"

Elly blushed. She tacitly avoided looking at Graydon.

"Unless you quit scratching on the eight ball, it's not even a fair contest," Graydon interrupted. "Maybe you ought to be making your bargain with Clare. Seems like you're the one who's worn out."

"Now boys," Clare said from the stairway. "Let's not get crass. Here's the bank. Who wants money?"

Graydon bought chips and shoved a stack in front of Elly.

Silently she gave a prayer of thanks that he had taught her to play before. She felt a small measure of confidence as she antied up, and watched everyone else from beneath her lashes.

"Cut for deal," Clare said. She cut, turned over a jack. "Elly?" Elly produced an ace. "First ace," Clare pronounced. She shoved the deck toward Graydon. "You have to deal for Elly."

"Fair enough." He winked at Don. "She makes sure I win at pool, I'll deal for her."

Elly was becoming extremely uncomfortable amid all the innuendos. She hoped her embarrassment would pass unnoticed and not look like the avoidance of—for all practical purposes—a virgin. Graydon, thankfully, offered no tip-offs.

"Before you do that," Clare said with a hand on his arm, "let's drink a toast, shall we?" She raised her glass.

"To what?" Don asked. He already had his glass in hand.

Clare beamed at Elly. "To Elly's health—and the baby's."

Elly couldn't keep herself from turning to Graydon. She hadn't done it on purpose, she pleaded silently, she hadn't meant to tell. Graydon's face was surprised, but his anger didn't show. He smoothly covered all trace of annoyance and even managed a husbandly smile for his wife.

"Really?" Don asked. "How wonderful. Graydon, you son of a gun, why didn't you tell me?"

"I, uh, wanted to let Elly be the one," Graydon said. "You know how women are."

"Well, I think that's great," Don went on. "When's it due, Elly?"

"About the middle of May. It's still a long ways off."

"Sooner than you think." He echoed Clare's words. "Just think, a little Graydon to tear around and raise hell with old Dad. I love it."

"It could be a girl, you know," Clare drawled.

Don shook his head. "No, it's got to be a boy. There's just no other way." He turned to Elly. "You were darn lucky you didn't lose it in that accident, young lady,"

"I know," Elly murmured, dying inside. How was Graydon coping with all this talk about 'his' son? She was sure it wouldn't improve his mood any.

"Well, are we going to drink a toast or aren't we?" Clare wanted to know. She raised her glass and the others followed suit. "Here's to Elly and baby Graydon."

"Here, here," Don echoed.

Elly drank. Over the rim of her glass, she could see the darkening glow of her husband's eyes.

The card game went smoothly, thank God. Elly paid strict attention, so much so that she sometimes missed small bits of conversation, but by this point both Clare and Don were ready to chalk off her lapses to her pregnancy. The kidding and speculation continued all evening with Graydon by turns scowling at her and laughing with the Mayfields. By the time they cashed in their chips at midnight, Elly was two dollars richer and practically exhausted.

"Gee, that was fun," Clare said. "We'll have to do that more often." She reached across and patted Elly's hand. "You can start a college fund with your winnings."

Elly managed a tired smile. "Thank you for the dinner and all. I'm afraid I wasn't very good company."

"Don't even think about it. Come on, I'll get your coats. You look beat."

"I am." Graydon held Elly's chair and she edged past him, eyes down. She had a feeling she was not going to enjoy the ride home.

"Now I don't want you to hesitate to call me if you need anything," Clare said at the front door. "What obstetrician do you have?"

"Dr. Weiss. I haven't been to him yet, though."

"Oh, he's a good one. You'll like him. He's very professional. But if you need anything at all, especially with that cast, just let me know."

"Thank you," Elly said.

"And Graydon, you be real careful of her. She's got important cargo, now."

Graydon nodded, his hand at Elly's back. "Yes, mother. Don, do something with her, would you?"

"I've tried," Don said. "Doesn't do a bit of good."

Their goodnights echoed across the lawn. Graydon held the

car door for Elly and she slid gratefully against the seat. She would have loved to be able to close her eyes and sleep, but she was sure Graydon would never allow it. No doubt he had been keeping a running tally of her blunders all night. His weight depressing the seat beside her signaled her to sit up.

He started the car. "Are you tired?"

"A little."

"You should have said something. We could have left sooner."

"I didn't tell her, Graydon, not really. She said she could tell by the way I looked. She asked me point blank and caught me by surprise. But I didn't mean to tell her."

"People will find out eventually," Graydon said flatly. He guided the car around a corner and glanced over at Elly. "How did she say you looked?"

Elly leaned back and groaned. "Like a happy, pregnant lady. She said she could tell. She said she used to work for a doctor."

"She did. She was an R.N. for years and worked for an obstetrician."

"I thought she was rich."

"Her family is. I guess she was a little more idealistic in her younger days, though. She worked until the kids were born, then went back to it when they started school and found out she liked staying home better."

"She said she had two children. Where were they?"

"The boy goes to school back East somewhere, some prep school. He's seventeen, I think. And the girl—she must be fifteen—is on an exchange program. She's in France for a year."

"It sounds like they have a lot more money than we do," Elly observed.

"Are you jealous?"

"Jealous? Not hardly. When I have kids I'm certainly not going to send them all—"

Graydon's head snapped around and stopped Elly in mid-sentence.

"What?" she asked. "What did I say? "

He turned back to the road. "You said when you have kids."

Elly swallowed nervously. "I meant *if* I had kids. Oh, I'm so wound up from pretending all evening, I don't know what I'm saying." She closed her eyes and let the sway of the car sooth her. The tension in the car was still heavy. "I'm sorry if I made you angry tonight, Graydon. I really didn't set out to be annoying."

Graydon was silent. He drove the car carefully around the darkened streets, Elly's slumped posture just visible out of the corner of his eye. He was more angry with himself than he was with her. It was difficult to stand objectively by while his wife bloomed into an attractive—no, pretty—woman and be drawn to her yet still be repulsed by an indiscretion she couldn't even remember. Seeing her blush beneath Clare's compliments, standing innocently in that blouse, looking like a young bride, just as Clare had said—it all caused stirrings in Graydon he would rather not feel, and the only way he could dispel them was with anger. And how much more difficult it was when Elly apologized to him for her lapses when he was the one being unfair? He glanced quickly over at her. Head back, eyes closed, she might be almost asleep. Damn, he thought. Any other night like this, they would go home, laugh about the evening, talk a bit and then make love. Why did he have to think about that? It had been almost a month—stop it, he told himself. Things were not the same, now. This is not the same woman. This was not the woman he married. He gripped the steering wheel a little more tightly and drove home, angry.

At home he let Elly out of the car, walked behind her and let her into the house. She began to shrug out of her jacket and he came up behind to help her. She settled quietly at his touch.

"Thank you," she murmured. "I should learn to do it myself."

"You'll have your cast off soon enough," Graydon said.

She took her jacket from his outstretched hand, laid it over her arm. "Yes, then I'll need help getting out of chairs and low cars." She caught Graydon's immediate frown. "I'm sorry. I shouldn't have said that." She turned down the hall a step or two, then stopped. Uncertainly, she looked back over her shoulder. "Thank you, Graydon. It was nice getting out for the evening." And she went on to her room.

"Damn," Graydon swore quietly. Why did she have to look so damn defenseless when he knew good and well she could be a tower of steel if she wanted to? And she had to know how all the banter at the Mayfield's had affected him—a little Graydon! Damn her! If he thought for a moment it was his child she carried—but she had told him it was Adam's. He still had the note. He shook his head to straighten out his thoughts. They wouldn't keep it. They'd give it up. It wouldn't be his, or hers either, for that matter. It was already decided. Still frowning, Graydon poured himself a shot of whiskey before locking himself in his own room for the night.

Elly's check-up appointment at the doctor was scheduled for Tuesday. She got up early and left the house almost two hours ahead of time. Dr. D'Angelo had drawn her a simple map so she wouldn't have to drive blindly through Denver and with it on the seat beside her, she set off.

She was feeling more and more independent. At least now she had over two weeks' worth of memories and a small stock of familiar names and places. The real memories—Garden of the Gods and, apparently, her driving nightmare—seemed less than real, but she tried to incorporate them into her past. Maybe, she thought, Dr. D'Angelo could tell something about her recovery from them.

The drive to Denver was pleasant—it was a sunny, late October day with the few clouds blown north by the crisp breeze. The Rockies were sharp and pristine on her left, giant stone guardians of her journey. She felt particularly confident.

Dr. D'Angelo's office wasn't nearly as hard to find as she thought it might be. She parked and went inside, giving the receptionist her name. In minutes she was led back to a cubicle and had only to wait briefly there before Dr. D'Angelo came in.

"Hello," he said pleasantly. "How are you, Mrs. Cole?"

"Fine, thank you. How are you?"

"Much better, seeing you smile like that." He sat at the small desk and placed a folder in front of him. "You look well. How are things going? All right?"

"Pretty much," she said honestly. "There are some obstacles, but all in all, I don't think I've done badly."

"Is your husband here with you?"

"No. I came alone."

Dr. D'Angelo took her arm and studied the cast. "No difficulty driving?"

"Not with an automatic. No, about the only things I have trouble doing are tying my shoes and opening jars. Otherwise I manage."

He grinned. "Good, glad to hear it." He released her arm and sat back in his chair. "How about the memory? Any progress?"

She told him briefly about her two flashes of memory, deliberately playing down the horror of the dream. "What's weird is that it didn't feel familiar, I didn't recognize it as a memory, not like the first one. It still doesn't seem the same."

Dr. D'Angelo nodded professionally. "That's normal, though, for a dream sequence. You know how sometimes you dream something that starts out normal and ends up weird or surreal, and it's not until you think about it the next day that you realize the real part was patterned after something you had done the day before? Dreams don't often seem familiar, even if you're dreaming about something you did the same day. So that doesn't surprise me. What does surprise me is that recalling the dream didn't cause any more information to break through."

"It seems like it's going to be a very slow process," Elly mused.

"It could be. But it's not so bad. At least we know you're on your way. Just as an aside, let me explain to you some of the things we do know about memory. Apparently there are several different places in the brain where memory functions are carried out, and some of these are redundant. Also, they've found out there's a difference between the areas for short-term memory and long-term memory. Basically, that's why you remember some things— mostly non-emotional or things not pertaining to your personality. Whatever you damaged in the accident was an area concerned with emotional memory and personality formation. We can safely assume, since you've remembered those two incidents, that it is healing and your memory will be restored. It also looks like any memories you are finally able to retrieve will be emotional ones— possibly traumatic ones. I think, because of that, it's liable to be a pretty unsettling process."

Elly could well believe that. So far, between remembering and not, she'd hit all the highs and lows of an emotional roller coaster. What Dr. D'Angelo was saying was that the ride wasn't over yet.

"I understand," she said.

"But, like I said before, you seem to be a resourceful young woman. I have great hopes for you." She blushed. "Now," he said, picking up her folder for the first time, "How about a few tests?"

Elly drove home feeling quite a bit lighter. Just talking to Dr. D'Angelo was a comfort, and she could almost feel the micro-electrical currents jumping around in her brain, synapse to synapse, trying to bridge the gap caused by her concussion. I will remember, she chanted to herself, I will remember. And this time she believed it.

At the beginning of her second trimester, Elly discovered morning sickness. The first day she chalked it up to a salami sandwich and ice cream just before bed the night before, but the second morning she had nothing to blame. She rinsed her mouth and groaned into the mirror at her pallid face. Why couldn't she have been one of those women who sailed through pregnancy with no more discomfort than an occasional back twinge or, at most, a quick, two-hour labor? But no, she realized, she could look forward to this morning ritual for at least several more weeks. Pregnancy was so fulfilling.

That night she told Graydon.

"Is it bad?" he asked.

"Well, it s not debilitating, if that's what you mean, but it's not fun. I just can't get too far from a bathroom for a few hours after I get up in the morning."

Graydon mulled that over for a minute. "What about going to your folks? Do you still want to do it?"

"I think we should. We already said we would. Which reminds me, I have to write to them and let them know when we'll be there. What do you think?"

"It's almost a six-hour drive. If we left Wednesday afternoon and got there late that night, would that be a good time for you? Or would you rather drive half on Wednesday and stay overnight, say in Santa Fe, and go on in Thursday morning? I'll leave it up to you."

"Thanks," Elly groaned. She leaned down and stroked Chester

where he rubbed against her leg. "I guess with this sickness, we'd better do it all on Wednesday. Then at least I can hole up in the bathroom there if I need to, and I won't be holding you up or anyone else."

"Sounds okay to me. Just one more question."

Elly raised an eyebrow at him across the table. "What?"

"How are you going to write?"

Elly glared down at her own arm. "I don't know. Can I use the computer?"

Graydon chuckled. "Yeah."

"Do I know how to type?" she asked.

"No."

"Good. Then it won't matter if I use one finger. I'll be glad when I get this dumb thing off, but my arm will probably look like a shriveled up prune."

"When's your next appointment?"

"Day after tomorrow."

"And you'll get it off then?"

Elly nodded. "At least that's what Dr. D'Angelo said last time. I sure hope he doesn't change his mind. It'd be wonderful to be able to take a shower and tie my own shoes and do stuff like that."

"And you won't have to worry about throwing up on your cast," Graydon offered.

"Right," Elly agreed grimly. "Then I'll only be a mental cripple instead of a physical one, too. What luxury."

Graydon laughed. "You don't sound very appreciative of your new freedom. Maybe you ought to tell Dr. D'Angelo to leave that thing on for another month and see how good it'll sound to you then."

"Oh, no," Elly said, "I'm appreciative. I just wish he could remove the block from my mind as easily as he can remove the cast."

Graydon stared thoughtfully at her across the table. "Don't worry," he said. "It'll come."

"I hope so," Elly sighed.

The next day Elly tapped out a brief letter on the computer.

She explained, as simply as possible, that she was pregnant and probably wouldn't be worth much of a darn, but that they would arrive in Carrizozo late Wednesday night before Thanksgiving. She mentioned that she was getting her cast off the following day, that she had gained some memory, but for the most part it was a slow process. When she read the letter over she thought it was adequate. It occurred to her that her mother might have wanted a more personal, excited announcement of the impending grandchild—at least a happy phone call—but she was simply not up to that. What else could she say to parents she didn't know— miss you? Wish you were here? She managed to print out an envelope and stood the letter up in the mailbox outside. It was all she could do for now.

On Thursday, she drove back to Denver. When Dr. D'Angelo strode into her cubicle, clipboard under his arm, Elly just held out her right arm to him and smiled. "You're not in a hurry, are you?" he chuckled.

"Not at all. Take all the time in a world, just so long as it doesn't take more than a half hour. Graydon told me I have to be properly appreciative, but he didn't say anything about not being impatient."

"All right. We'll crack this thing open in record time."

Later, they took the time to talk. "How are things at home?" Dr. D'Angelo asked. It was now his standard opening question.

"Fine. We're going to New Mexico for Thanksgiving so I'll be meeting my parents and my brother."

"That should be interesting."

Elly laughed good-naturedly. "Not exactly my choice of words, but yes, it should be."

"Scared, huh?" Dr. D'Angelo smiled.

"Petrified. But I'm hoping it'll jolt something loose—even something traumatic."

"No other breakthroughs since last time?"

"No, none. But then Graydon and I have been getting along better, and I've gotten into a comfortable routine, so not as many things are coming at me by surprise. It seems like my capability for remembering is not so great when I'm at ease—but that will change as soon as we leave for New Mexico."

Dr. D'Angelo nodded. "Well, just take it one day at a time and try to keep a handle on things. Too much excitement for you isn't good for the little one, either."

"As if he's thinking of me," Elly groaned. "I have him to thank for being sick every morning now."

"Fourth month?" He ran his eyes objectively over her stomach.

"Yes, can you tell?"

"Not really. Can you? I mean other than being sick?"

"Unfortunately, yes. I've had to put away all my pants except those with elastic waistbands, and I think before we go on our trip, I'll have to buy some new things—big things. It's a little depressing."

"Don't let it get you down," the doctor advised. "You're doing fine. Judging by your face, I would tend to think that pregnancy agrees with you."

"I'd like to see you say that to me at eight o'clock in the morning," she laughed. "Really, it's not so bad. I'm fine."

"Good. That's the important thing." He rose, signaling the end of the session. "And in five months' time, it'll all seem worth it to you when you have that little guy in your arms."

Elly managed a tight smile. "Yes." She stood, also. "Well, thank you, Dr. D'Angelo. Two weeks next time?"

"Make it a month. You deserve a little time off for good behavior. Take care on your vacation."

"I will."

True to her word, Elly went out and bought some new outfits, all with loose tops or blouses and stretch or paneled pants. It was a pleasure just to be able to try things on like a normal person and not need help getting things over her cast. For variety, she bought a couple of waistless dresses and then some comfortable, crepe-soled shoes. Very practical, she mused. Too bad it was all for nothing.

As she felt her body change, she was more and more aware of the growing life inside. She thought about the little seed as 'him' and that, somehow, made it worse. Five more months of nurturing, carrying, and sacrificing for the little guy and then she'd never see him again. That line of thought led inevitably to depression, so Elly tried not to let it get away from her too often. Lurking not far beyond it, though, was a half-formed idea of keeping the baby. How or why, she didn't know, but occasionally, when she was tired or half asleep, it surfaced. It was what she wanted almost more than anything. And it was ultimately impossible.

To keep from too much of that, Elly tempted emotional imbalance by thinking ahead to the trip to New Mexico. Again and again she dragged out the latest photo album and her own wallet to stare at pictures of her parents and Bryan. Nothing ever came, no flash of memory, no twinge of feeling—nothing. They were just frozen little faces staring absently back at her. Every time she put the pictures away, she felt a sense of frustration and a niggling spark of relief. No traumas. Not yet.

Linda called the Monday of Thanksgiving week.

"Elly? How are you? You haven't called."

"Oh, no, I haven't," Elly stammered. "I, uh, really I've been pretty busy and the time just got away from me. I'm sorry."

"Well, that's okay. I mean I'm not mad, but I just thought you'd be down for lunch or something by now. How're things?"

"Pretty good," Elly said truthfully. "Graydon and I are going to New Mexico for Thanksgiving and then we're going to stop at Telluride on the way back to do some skiing."

"Sounds like fun," Linda said. "How's the baby?"

"Oh, fine. I get morning sickness now, but I hope it'll only last a month or two. I'm coming right along."

"Good. You still got your cast?"

"No. I've had it off almost a week now. It's nice to be right-handed again."

"I'll bet."

"How are you?" Elly asked. "Any new boyfriends?"

"Oh, the usual, you know. One thing, though, Greg was back in town. He's such a fox. I sure wish I could get him to stick around."

"Greg?"

"Yeah, you know, the pilot. He was here three days and that's amazing in itself. I'd like to think he arranged it so he could see me, but I don't think I'll kid myself."

"You never know," Elly said. "How long has in been since you've seen him?"

"Oh, since last time I told you. What's that been, two months? Remember the last time we had lunch and you were agonizing over Adam and I was floating on air? What a pair we were."

"Agonizing over Adam? Was I?"

"Maybe you don't call it that; I do. When you're as torn between two guys as you were then, that's agony. But, hey, I'll let you go. You've probably got packing and stuff to do and I'm just on a quick break. Call me when you get back, though, and we'll get together."

"I will," Elly promised. "We'll have lunch and catch up on everything."

"Sounds like a deal. Well, have a good trip."

"I will. Thanks for calling, Linda."

As Elly hung up the phone, she resolved that she would call Linda later, and go to lunch and catch up on things. She had a feeling Linda knew some things Elly didn't—things Elly should know.

Chapter Nine

Graydon planned to take off early from work Wednesday and be home around one. They had almost everything packed and just had to load the BMW and go. Elly puttered around the house all morning—after being sick—and cleaned and put things away so they would come home to a clean house. After being on the go for a week and a half, the last thing she wanted to do was come home and have to clean.

She stacked Chester's cat food on the kitchen counter for the neighbor lady who would feed him and bring in their mail. Chester padded possessively after her as if he understood all the commotion, and jumped into Elly's lap every time she sat down. She hugged him and let him knead her lap until he dug his claws in.

"It's only for ten or eleven days," she told him. "We'll be back before you know it."

She wished they were back already.

When Graydon came home, Elly had the suitcases lined up by the front door. "All ready?" he asked.

"Yes. I just have to pack my toothbrush, but otherwise I'm ready."

"Okay. Let me change my clothes and we'll get the car packed. We should be on our way by two."

They were. Elly waved goodbye to Chester as they backed out of the driveway, but the big orange cat just glared after them. Before they had started down the street, he turned and disappeared into a hedge.

Elly didn't want to think too much about their ultimate destination, so she took out the road map and kept track of their progress. Some of the names of cities they would pass through were familiar—Pueblo in Colorado, Santa Fe and Albuquerque in New Mexico. Others, like Trinidad and Carrizozo were complete blanks.

"Have we driven down since we moved to Colorado?" she asked.

"Once, two years ago. It wasn't a pleasant trip."

"Why not?"

"Oh," Graydon breathed, "different reasons. I wasn't real keen on going for one thing, and when we got there it sort of sent you into a tailspin. That upset your parents, which made you feel worse and that didn't set well with me. It was just one thing on top of another."

"Why did it upset me? Going, I mean."

"I'm not exactly sure. I think just the fact that you hadn't seen your mother for over a year and you hadn't wanted to leave her anyway. It just all came together. I swore we'd never go back."

Elly studied her husband sitting so normally beside her, his eyes on the road. "But we are," she said.

He looked over. His eyes appraised her. "Yes. Things have changed."

"For better or worse?"

Graydon didn't disguise his own uncertainty. "I'm not sure yet. I guess we'll just have to wait and see."

Going southbound on the freeway, Elly was able to watch the scenery change and undulate. As the sun slipped lower and lower toward the Rockies, she noticed how they seemed to dip too, from the mountains down to the desert. It was all unfamiliar to her. She noted each town they passed and checked it against the map in her lap. They were making good time. Too good.

The sun exploded in a silent blaze just beyond the mountains and the fiery colors flamed against the few clouds huddled over the horizon. As they passed the boundary of Colorado and entered New Mexico, Elly began to fidget. The night fell with a disturbing thoroughness over the desert, leaving the freeway lights to gleam like strung lanterns across the darkness. Elly would have felt much better if she could see the country she was traveling through. This way, without so much to look at, she had too much time to think about the future.

A green highway sign said *Carrizozo - 7 miles*. Elly found herself biting her fingernails. Forcibly she took one hand in the other and kept them primly in her lap. Her palms began to sweat.

From what she could see of the area, it seemed to stretch away in a peculiarly rocky desert. A few miles on down she saw another sign that said *Lava Beds—Viewpoint—Next right*.

"Is that what all these rocks are—lava beds?" she asked.

"Yes," Graydon affirmed. "It's pretty desolate. There are a lot of rocky clefts with sharp edges. It's not exactly good hiking territory."

Elly tried to see more of it. "Did I grow up here?"

"Mostly. I think your parents lived someplace else when you were born, but it wasn't far from here. You have relatives in Gallup that you used to visit. You're pretty much a native New Mexican, through and through."

Elly didn't feel like a New Mexican. She felt like a Martian landing smack in the middle of Peyton Place and being expected to fit in. Lights in the distance conglomerated and became service stations clustered at a cross street; the town lay beyond. She pressed back into the seat.

Graydon guided the car to the right at the small intersection, then left again on another street. Gas stations, motels, bars and liquor stores shed garish light on the streets, showing little activity for not quite nine o'clock. Beyond the limits of the business section, Elly could see the regular pattern of porch lights, window lights, residential street lights. Everyone was home. Elly was going home.

Then why didn't she feel like it? She would much rather have turned around and headed right back to Colorado, not even stopping for curiosity's sake. She felt more like a rabbit crouching in fear as a hawk circled down and down, nearer and nearer. Her stomach flip-flopped as Graydon turned down a residential street; her palms grew slick with sweat as he slowed the car.

Her head began to tingle. She recognized the house. It was stucco with brick on the bottom half, set back off the street on a big lot. Tall, leafless weeds sprouted in clusters like dead sticks on one side of the driveway. The lights were on inside.

Graydon glanced over at her. She looked in shock. He reached over to cover her hand with his. "Scared?"

"No," she croaked, "terrified. Graydon, I'm afraid." Her hand turned under his, gripping it in a desperate hold.

"It'll be okay, Elly. I'll be right with you every step. Just go along. You'll do fine."

"Oh, God," she whispered.

Graydon pulled up in front of the house and parked. There was movement behind a curtain. Elly had a strangle-hold on his hand without knowing it.

"Elly, calm down. Take a few deep breaths. It won't be nearly as bad as you're imagining it. Try to relax."

She nodded dumbly. He managed to pry her fingers loose and slide out of the car so he could open her door. He held out a hand to her and she took it, rising like a sleepwalker.

Her eyes darted from one lighted window to another, then met and locked with Graydon's. Her pupils were huge.

"Hey," Graydon said, leaning close, "it's gonna be okay, Elly. I'm here with you, okay?"

"Don't leave me, Graydon," she whispered.

"I won't. I'll be right beside you. You'll be fine."

The front door opened. Light spilled out, bright and golden, then crowded with silhouettes.

"Eleanor? Graydon? Is that you?" It was her voice, that woman—her mother. Elly knew the voice, knew the face. They came together in her mind.

"Mom?" Elly called hoarsely. She started forward.

"Elly, darling. How are you?"

"Mom!" Before Graydon could react, Elly had torn out of his hold and run across the sparse grass to her mother. They met and hugged and both began talking at the same time.

"Elly! I'm so happy to see you."

"Mom, Mom. How are you?"

Graydon walked slowly across the lawn until he stood behind his wife. Over the heads of the two women he faced Elly's dad. They stared at each other, old adversaries, and nodded a greeting. Graydon turned his attention back to Elly. When she and her mother stood back to look at each other, he put a questioning hand on her shoulder. Elly looked up. Graydon quirked an eyebrow at her and she nodded. In a flash of joy, she turned around and kissed Graydon happily on the cheek. Then everyone began to move.

"Graydon," Elly's mom said. She came forward shyly and hugged him.

Elly went to her dad. She slid her arms around him and pressed against his bulk until his own arms closed the circle.

"Hi, Elly," he said. "How's my girl?"

"Fine, Dad," Elly said. "Gee, you look good."

"How can you tell?" he asked gruffly. "It's so goddamn dark out here."

"Oh, come in," her mom said. "Come in. I want to look at you."

They trooped into the house. Elly walked behind her mother, her eyes roaming over everything they could see. In the entry hall, Elly saw a colonial table topped with a lace doily and a hinged double picture frame. Elly's own face, younger, stared back at her and Bryan looked out of the other side. It was familiar.

The walls were off white, chipped in places or dark where hands touched frequently. Pictures hung along the entry in a hodgepodge—some family, some cheap prints of seascapes or big-eyed waifs. One in particular she recognized, a moonlit surf with gulls wheeling dramatically over the silver breakers. She remembered! Not all of it by any means, but pieces were coming together.

"Now let me look at you," Elly's mother was saying. She touched Elly's arm, turning her into the living room light and stood back.

Peg Hatcher—Margaret Joan Hatcher. She was shorter than Elly thought she should have been, no taller than Elly's nose, and her short waved hair was threaded with grey. Her features were regular, English, her mouth curved in an emotional smile.

"Oh, you're showing!" she said happily.

Elly's hand went to her stomach. "Yes. Is it really that noticeable?"

"Shouldn't you be wearing something more loose?" her dad asked. He and Graydon had come to fill in the circle.

"Oh, this is really comfortable."

"I mean so you don't show," Glen Hatcher said a little harshly.

Elly looked shocked. She flicked her eyes to Graydon and he came a step closer to her.

"I don't look obscene, do I?" she asked. Her father frowned. He was almost as tall as Graydon, his dark hair slicked back and lined with grey. His physique had gone soft and his belly drooped slightly over his belt. His face was florid.

"Glen," his wife said, "women don't cover up nowadays like they used to. They're proud to show off when they're going to have a baby."

Glen didn't look convinced. He eyed Elly's bulge nervously.

"Well, sit down," Peg said. "Relax. Are you hungry? Can I fix you a snack or would you like a beer, Graydon?"

"No, thanks," Graydon answered, and he didn't budge from his place between Elly and her dad. "We had a hamburger not too long ago."

"Mom," Elly said, "can I—would you mind if I looked around the house? Some things are coming back to me. I'd just like to— just look."

"Of course, dear," Peg agreed. "Do you remember where everything is?" Elly turned slowly around the living room.

"Not everything. Just snatches, pieces of things. That's why I'd like to look."

"Go ahead. I'll put on some water for tea. Glen, why don't you and Graydon go get their things?"

Graydon touched Elly's elbow. "Will you be okay?" he asked quietly.

Elly flashed him a grateful smile. "Yes, go ahead. I'll be fine."

The hallway off the living room beckoned to Elly. As soon as Graydon and her dad went back outside, she headed for it. Her head buzzed and her skin prickled.

The hall was dark. She put her hand up on the right wall—light switch, right beneath her fingers. The overhead illuminated the linen cupboards and drawers on the opposite wall, the dreary, worn rug on the floor. Elly turned right.

This was her room. She flicked on the light. One wall was stacked with boxes, piles of magazines. A rose-patterned rug covered the hardwood floor.

"I'm putting you two in here," Peg said behind her. "We bought a new bed last year so we put our old one in here."

Elly swiveled her eyes to the iron bedstead. It was a double, made up with two pillows. Elly felt hot.

"Oh," she breathed.

"It doesn't look like much, but it's really comfortable."

It looked overpowering to Elly. The curved iron head and foot boards rose in a half moon with radiating arms of iron tubing. Her parents' bed—how many times had she peeked at them through the wheeled footboard? She saw herself as a little girl, hands tight around the iron spokes. She saw her father, much younger, scowling at her to go back to bed.

Scuffling behind her snapped her back to the present. Glen came down the hall, suitcases in hand. Graydon was behind with Elly's overnight case.

"I'm sorry about those boxes, Elly," Peg said. "I just didn't have any other place to store those things. Will you have enough room?"

Elly dragged her eyes from the bed and patently avoided Graydon as he came through the doorway.

"It's fine, Mom."

"This room was good enough for her for nineteen years," Glen said. He plopped the suitcases on top of the bed. Graydon put the smaller case on the dresser.

"Yes, it's fine, Mom." Elly edged away from Graydon. She could feel his eyes on her, questioning, but she couldn't meet them. She pretended not to notice. "When will Bryan be here?"

"Tomorrow," she said. Peg started down the hall. "I've kept his room for him, of course, since he comes home more."

Behind her, Elly's dad snorted. She flinched. Escaping down

the hall, she peeked inside Bryan's room.

It looked very familiar. The single bed was against the far wall, the dresser along one side, the closet opposite. The top of the dresser and a shelf all along the top of one wall was filled with trophies.

"Bryan plays baseball," Elly said to herself.

"Of course," Peg agreed.

Elly moved closer to the dresser, touched the trophies with curious fingers. Some had baseballs pinned on them, some had gilt batters, small golden figures of baseball players. The inscriptions were varied: *1st Place District Championship 1990; 2nd Place - Regionals - 1992; All Stars - 1991.*

"He plays first base."

"He's catching now, too," Peg said.

Elly turned. "Catching?"

"Yes, you know. Remember when I wrote and told you how he got cleated so bad at home plate last year?"

"You wrote me?" Elly asked.

"Yes. Don't you remember?" Her mother's expression became concerned.

"No. I don't remember that. Where does he play?"

"Why, Albuquerque of course. He's been there for years." Elly nodded. She didn't remember. "Pro ball?"

"Triple A. He's never been picked up by a pro team, but he's still hopeful."

That was all a blank. Elly could remember Bryan at twelve or fourteen, firing a ball to second base for a double play. She remembered her dad jumping to his feet and bellowing praise for his son, and Bryan's quick, embarrassed smile.

But that was all.

"Come see our new bedroom set," Peg said.

Elly followed her on down the hall to the last bedroom. This room was bigger, brighter than Elly expected.

"What color did it use to be?" she asked.

"Oh, we had it that light green color for years, but we painted it before we got the new furniture. Do you like it?"

A king-sized bed crowded the room. Pale peach walls echoed the peach and green flowered bedspread, the matching curtains. It looked so different.

"It's nice," Elly said. But not at all like she remembered. Pieces, she thought. All I'm getting is pieces.

As in the Garden of the Gods, her depression at not remembering all was equal in degree to her initial excitement at being able to remember anything. She turned and walked quietly back out to the living room.

"Elly?" Graydon sat on the couch opposite her dad. He watched her, concerned by her slumped posture. "Are you okay?"

She nodded. "Just tired, I think."

She came and settled beside him on the couch. He put an arm along the top of the couch behind her. "Anything?" he asked quietly.

"Pieces. Just pieces."

"Elly, some tea?" Peg asked.

"That sounds good, Mom."

Her dad already had a can of beer in one meaty fist. He watched his daughter suspiciously. "When's the baby due?" he asked gruffly.

"In May. Around the fifteenth."

"You going to show it off like that the whole time you're carrying it?"

Elly didn't like his tone. "I'm not showing off, Dad. I'm just not going to cover it up. You act like I should be ashamed of it." As soon as the words were out, Elly regretted them. Her face flushed hot. She felt Graydon's held breath beside her.

"I didn't say that," Glen mumbled. "I just don't think you ought to be parading around like that. Decent women don't draw attention to things like that."

Graydon's hand dropped casually down onto Elly's shoulder. "Times are changing, Glen," he said casually. "People aren't so shocked about natural functions any more."

Outnumbered, Elly's dad backed off. It wasn't a good-natured retreat, though. Elly caught the moody shifting of his eyes. Between that and Graydon's presence so close at her side, she felt trapped. She wished she could remember everything. Had her father always been so old-fashioned? And was it just coincidence that his words seemed to echo Graydon's earlier outbursts? She could feel the tension in the room rising.

"How was your trip?" Peg asked. She brought Elly a steaming cup of tea and sat in a needlepoint chair across from her.

"Long," Graydon said.

"It wouldn't have been so bad in the daytime," Elly added, "but with nothing to look at but darkness, it did seem long."

"How long can you stay?" Her mother's voice was high and hopeful.

Elly glanced at Graydon. "We'll have to leave Friday morning. I shouldn't try to do too much." Elly couldn't face her mother as the lie slipped out. She sipped at her tea.

"Oh, that's too bad. We hoped you could stay until Sunday."

"I really haven't been feeling well," Elly said truthfully. "If it weren't for Thanksgiving and the fact that we haven't been down in so long, I don't think we would have come at all. I've been miserably sick every morning."

Peg nodded understandingly. "I was sick with both you and Bryan, especially him. Luckily, it gets easier. Your next one won't be bad at all."

Elly took another drink of tea. Graydon shifted in his seat and his hand went back up on the couch. Her shoulder turned cool where it had been.

"Um, I'm sure the guys don't want to hear about this stuff," Elly ventured. "What have you folks been doing lately?"

Peg sighed. "Oh, just the same. You know we had that awful windstorm last March and Glen was just busy as a bee for awhile with his roofing business. I think he had to replace half the roofs in town."

Elly looked blank. "I thought—I thought you worked at a lumber yard," she said to her dad.

"I did—five years ago. Then I went out on my own. Don't you remember that?"

"I'm sorry," Elly said shaking her head. "I just don't remember enough. It seems like—I don't know."

Graydon's arm slipped down around Elly's shoulder again. "I think she's mostly tired," he said to her parents. "It's been a long day."

"Oh, of course," Peg said getting up. "How silly of us not to think. It's not quite ten, but we'll be getting up fairly early. Come on, Eleanor, I'll help you unpack your things."

Elly slid out of the curl of Graydon's arm and followed her mother obediently to her room. There they pulled out a few of Elly's things from her suitcase and found her nightgown.

"Things are going okay for you, aren't they, dear?" her mother asked pensively.

Elly closed the bedroom door and unbuttoned her blouse. "Yes. I'm just tired tonight, Mom. I'm still not completely recovered and I—I get confused. But I'm okay."

"Is Graydon happy about the baby?" She held Elly's nightgown for her.

"Well, it wasn't exactly planned, but he's okay with it."

"I thought so," Peg nodded. "But by the time the baby gets here, he'll feel better about it." She sighed. "I wish Bryan and Dana would get married. Dana would love to have a little one, I know."

"Is that Bryan's girlfriend?"

"Yes. They've been going together for years. You don't remember her?"

Elly shook her head and slipped into her nightgown. "I wish I did."

"Well," Peg stood back and studied her daughter, "maybe you'll feel better in the morning."

"I hope so, Mom. I wish I could wake up and remember everything."

Peg stepped forward and kissed her daughter on the cheek. "Me too, dear," she said. "It's so good to have you home, though, no matter how you are."

When her mother had gone and closed the door behind her, Elly fidgeted with the tie of her nightgown. A thin nylon of teal blue, it clung silkily to her body. The bodice was gathered in a variegated stitched smocking with a keyhole tie at the throat. Elly stared at her image in the mirror.

Oh, God, she thought, how can we both sleep in that little bed? Even with her stomach slightly rounding, she looked good—her breasts held the material high, so that it draped seductively down to her knees; her legs were still shapely and slender. She did not look as though sex with her own husband was fearful to her. She looked responsive.

Voices calling goodnights rumbled in the hall. Elly scooted around the bed to the far side and pulled the covers open. She had barely gotten them free of her mother's efficient tucking when the door swung open and Graydon stepped in.

His eyes caught her; she blushed red and looked away, slipping into bed. Her pulse had begun to pound and her blood felt hot. She busied herself with the project of plumping her pillow.

"You're remembering," he stated quietly. After locking the door he moved to the bed and pulled off his shoes.

"Some. Nothing recent. It seems like it's all old stuff, from when I was little."

"It's a start," he said. Elly had difficulty keeping her eyes from him as he unbuttoned his shirt. She'd never seen him without a shirt. His chest was massive.

"Thank you for supporting me," she said raggedly.

Graydon lifted an eyebrow at her. "Don't you mean, thank you for not agreeing with him?"

She shot a glance at him and looked quickly away. "Do you think I'm parading?"

"No." His voice was lighter, softer than she expected. "I think you look fine just the way you are." He moved to the light switch clad only in his pants. "Ready for sleep?"

She nodded.

The room went black. Scuffling noises alerted her to Graydon's blind walk back to the bed, his shedding of his pants. The bed tipped and squeaked and Elly had to clutch the edge of the mattress to keep from rolling toward the bulk of her husband. Even when the bed leveled, she kept her grip. Graydon's shoulder brushed against hers. As her eyes adjusted, she could make out his profile from the corner of her eye. The scent of his cologne mixed with the subtle chemistry of his skin came to her. She closed her eyes and pulled the sheet up to her chin.

"Goodnight, Elly," he said softly.

"Goodnight, Graydon."

Sometime during the night she woke up, alert and tense. She

was on her side and the front of Graydon's body was pressed along the curve of her back. His hand rested on her hipbone.

She held her breath and listened. His own breathing was deep and rhythmic. She moved cautiously, trying to crawl back to her own side of the bed, but as soon as she did, Graydon stirred and his hand slid down to cup the roundness of her stomach. She could feel the heat of his palm through the thin nylon, and he pulled her casually back into the fold of his arm. Eyes wide, she let him settle her comfortably against him; then his breathing resumed its slow rhythm. It was a long time before she could get back to sleep.

Graydon woke first and since it was the rocking of the bed that woke Elly, she had no idea how they had been sleeping. She rolled on her back and chanced a look up at Graydon. He slipped his pants on and turned to face her. His eyes told her nothing.

"Morning," he said brusquely.

"Good morning," she answered as she pulled the sheet up around her shoulders and stretched back into her pillow.

"Sleep well?"

"Mmm, pretty well," she said. "Except this bed squeaks."

"Yes, it does." He pulled on a clean shirt and buttoned it, watching her. "How do you feel? Is it safe for me to use the bathroom?"

"I think so." She rubbed her stomach. "For at least a few minutes. I think my stomach has to wake up first before it figures out that it doesn't feel good. Then watch out."

Graydon nodded. "Okay, I'll hurry. Then I'll see you out in the living room."

He took his shoes and shaving kit and left the room.

Elly watched him go with mixed feelings. How nice it would have been to wake up beside him, have him slip his arms around her and just lie together for a few quiet minutes. Had they ever done that? She let herself remember the way he had pulled her back to him in the night and grew warm. If only she could believe that he had known what he was doing. She sighed. Probably not. He was too objective this morning. Pushing the dreamy thoughts aside, she swung her feet out of bed and stood up.

Better get dressed quickly, she thought, or she'd have to run for the bathroom half naked.

It wasn't until almost an hour later that Elly took a chance on going to the kitchen. She passed through the living room and saw Graydon and her dad out in front looking at the BMW. Her dad, she noticed, asked point blank questions with a quick wave of his hand or a nod of his head; Graydon answered more easily, his stance casual.

Elly's mom peered around the kitchen doorway.

"Oh, there you are. I wondered if you were ever going to come out. Are you all right?"

"Not bad," Elly said, going in. "Will I be in your way if I fix myself a cup of tea?"

"No, go ahead. The water's hot. Do you want something to eat?"

"Oh, no, please," Elly begged. "Just tea. I won't be able to think about food for a couple of hours. Did Dad and Graydon eat?"

"Just a little. I told them I don't want them filling up before dinner."

Elly fixed her tea and skittered past her mother preparing the turkey and went back to the dining room. There she sat in the place she remembered always sitting when she was little.

She sipped her tea and watched her mother. Peg worked efficiently, as she always had. Elly could remember her hanging up wash on the clothes line outside, a wooden clothespin in her mouth, her hands sliding quickly down the line, stopping only fleetingly to put up a corner of a shirt and pin it in place. Elly had been six and too little to help, but she stood at her mother's side and held up more clothespins as Peg needed them.

"Do you need help, Mom?" she asked.

"No, dear. You just relax. Did you sleep well?"

"Fine. What time are you expecting Bryan?"

"Pretty soon. He thought he'd be here around ten or so. You know how he and your dad love to watch football together."

No, Elly didn't know, but she could imagine. The image of Bryan making his double play reran itself in her mind. Then she saw him, tall and gawky, checking her out on a big two-wheeler, his hands on the handle bars in front of her. She was eight, he was ten. He told her what to do, pushed her off and laughed when she crashed into the weeds beside the driveway.

"I asked him to bring Dana, but he said no. He doesn't like the way she and I get in a corner and talk. She's such a dear; I don't know why he won't marry her. She'd be such a good wife for him."

"Do they live together?" Elly asked.

Her mother's head bobbed up in surprise. "Why, what a question! Elly, your father and I didn't raise you that way. Of course they don't live together. What a question."

"Sorry," Elly murmured, but she was thinking, *like hell.* Bryan was twenty-six; twenty-six year olds didn't kiss goodnight at the doorstep. Was her mother blind or just stubborn? Elly sipped her tea and glanced out the window. Her dad and Graydon were coming up the walk. He looked like Mom sounded—old-fashioned, stubborn, entrenched. So she was raised that way. So what? She didn't remember. Was that why she was so bound to break free?

"Well, it's about time you joined the rest of the world," Glen said gruffly. "You spend more time in the bathroom now than you did when you were seventeen."

"I know," Elly shrugged. "It goes with the territory."

Her dad winced at the reminder of Elly's 'family condition;' he turned away as if stung.

"Ready for some football, Graydon?" he asked. Graydon murmured agreement and took a seat at the end of the couch closest to the dining room. He glanced over at Elly but she just smiled bravely. Thank God for his support, Elly thought. She certainly didn't have anyone else's.

Bryan arrived shortly before noon. He pulled in behind the BMW in a low, red sports car and unfolded himself from the front seat. Elly watched out the window.

He had his father's height but his mother's gauntness, with a long face and long frame. His brown hair was cut short and a baseball cap sat back on his head. He had large facial features that seemed to jump out of the narrowness of his face. Elly thought he looked less like a twenty-six year old than a large economy-size sixteen year old. As he shambled up the driveway, Elly crossed the living room and met him at the door.

"Hey, Sis," he said happily. "How are you?"

"Fine, Bryan." She let him pick her up in his long arms while she hugged his neck. "How are you?"

"Great. Where's Graydon?"

"In here." She gestured toward the living room and Bryan set her down, then breezed on by. She stared after him quizzically.

The men exchanged hearty greetings and after a compulsory wave to his mother, Bryan joined them on the couch.

"Elly, get your brother a beer, will you?" her dad said. "Graydon, you want one?"

"Thanks, no," Graydon said. "Maybe later."

Elly did as she was told. When she brought Bryan his beer he took it from her with a careless wink. His eyes barely took in the face and shape of his sister as he argued good-naturedly with their dad over the football game. Elly wandered back to the kitchen.

"Does Bryan know about my accident?" she asked her mom quietly.

"Well, of course he does. Why?" Peg was busy making stuffing.

"He didn't even ask me about it."

"Oh, you know how the men are when they get together. They forget everything but their stomachs and what's on TV. Here, why don't you finish this, and I'll get the turkey pan ready."

Elly took over folding bread crumbs into the mixture Peg had in a bowl. A jar of oysters stood nearby.

"You want these oysters in here, too?" she asked.

"Of course, you know your father. It wouldn't be Thanksgiving without oyster dressing."

Elly easily remembered that she hated oysters. She opened the jar and dumped the slimy things onto the breadboard, then hunted up a knife. Luckily the drawer arrangement was the same as she remembered. Holding onto the grisly things with a cautious thumb and forefinger, she began to slice.

"Does he know I'm pregnant?"

"Yes, we told him."

"He didn't say anything about that, either."

Peg made a scoffing sound. "I hardly think that's surprising.

When I was pregnant with you, your dad and I hardly ever talked about it. Men don't care about things like that."

Why not, Elly wanted to know. He's my brother; why shouldn't he care. And my father—is it normal for him to be more concerned about my 'parading' than my health or sanity? She felt a lump rise in her throat and was afraid she was being over-emotional. A sudden whiff of oysters revealed the cause—holding her mouth, she ran for the bathroom.

She felt disgusted with herself. Retching her guts out, she felt dirty and ugly and unwanted. What was wrong with her? Why did she feel so undesirable in her own parents' home? Had she changed so much that she was being shut out now? Her stomach and sides ached from retching nothing but bile. When the spasms had subsided, she splashed cold water on her face and leaned tiredly on the counter.

"Elly?" It was Graydon's voice, quiet and questioning. The door opened a few inches, and Elly saw one dark eye. He came in.

"Are you okay?" He shut the door behind them.

She nodded. "Remind me not to fix oyster dressing next time I'm pregnant." She was too racked with fatigue to even care about the carelessness of her statement.

"Maybe you ought to lie down for awhile," Graydon said. "I'm sure your mom can manage."

"No, I'm okay." She looked at her pale image. "I don't look okay but I am." Shuddering, she pushed herself erect. "Sorry I interrupted the football game. I'll get back to my woman's work now."

She started past Graydon but he clamped a hand on her arm and brought her up short. "What's that supposed to mean?"

"Nothing," she said.

"It didn't sound like nothing. What's wrong, Elly?"

"I … don't know. Everything is … just weird. I feel … out of place." She looked up at him with genuine confusion. "I'm glad we're leaving tomorrow."

"Me, too," he said. His hand dropped from her arm and he let her by. "Don't knock yourself out, Elly. Just take it easy."

She nodded and opened the bathroom door. Glen and Bryan's

collective roar of excitement assailed her. So much for interrupting the football game, she thought.

From then on, Elly stuck to safe jobs. Peg stuffed the turkey and Elly peeled potatoes. Peg prepared the yams while Elly set the table. Her stomach behaved.

Finally there was nothing to do but wait. The aroma of cooking turkey filled the house and Elly's stomach began to growl. She fixed a cup of tea and retired to the bathroom to see if she could put some color back in her face. She felt drab and hoped seeing a better image of herself would perk her up a little. Anything was better than the way she felt now.

Minutes later, she was back in the living room and wondering what to do with herself. Peg sat in a straight-backed chair in the dining room and crocheted. The men had the couch covered.

"Sit here," Graydon said, and got up so Elly could have his corner seat.

"No, that's okay, Graydon. I'll sit with Mom."

"This is more comfortable. Here, go ahead. I'll pull up a chair."

Elly sat. It did feel good to sink back into the cushions. Graydon pulled a straight backed chair up alongside the end of the couch and lowered himself into it. She smiled her thanks. He flashed her a conspiring grin and returned his attention to the football game.

"Who's winning?" she asked Bryan next to her.

"Dallas, three to nothing."

She tried to watch the game. It was boring. A game of defense, each team went three downs and punted. She looked around the room at all the knickknacks.

On top of the TV were pictures standing in a hodgepodge of mismatched frames. She found her senior picture—she guessed; it didn't look familiar—and one of Bryan in his baseball uniform, a grin on his angular face. There was one of her mom and dad in front of the house, one of her dad's father—she remembered him. He had died when she was ten or so, but she remembered the way he ruled the household whenever he came to visit. A tall, wiry man, he would thunder about the house and send everyone scurrying. Elly had been afraid of him for years. When he died, she was glad.

Her vision blurred. She saw herself sitting in front of the TV when she was twelve, engrossed in an afternoon Western with Bryan beside her. She felt funny, wet and sticky. On an impulse she had gone to the bathroom and discovered her panties soaked through with blood, and little flecks of it had stained the back of her dress. She wanted to die. The blood smelled awful and it seemed that the more she washed herself, the dirtier she felt. She had heard about this—this *thing*—but had hoped it wouldn't happen to her. It only happened to women, she knew and was the sign of woman's suffering. It had something to do with original sin. She felt dirty and ashamed. Scrubbing as much of the stain as she could out of her clothing, she managed to hide the panties in the trash and chanced putting her dress in the laundry. She couldn't sit next to Bryan any more. She smelled.

The roar of her dad and Bryan over a blocked kick revived her. God, she thought, what's wrong with me? She felt like she was losing her mind, wandering through a kaleidoscopic landscape of past and present with no continuity joining the frames. Was it going to be like this much longer? Some day, she prayed, it had to all come together. Please.

It couldn't have been too soon when her mother called her back into the kitchen to start preparing dinner. Together they mashed and sliced and arranged.

"I wish Graydon didn't insist on living so far away," Peg said. "It would be so nice if you could come home more."

"But his work is there, Mom. You know that." Anyway, Colorado was home, not here.

"I know. But he could teach around here, or even go back to Alamogordo. You had a nice apartment there. And it wasn't nearly as cold as in Colorado." She'd never seen snow. She'd never been anywhere.

"Mom, do you and Dad ever go anywhere? I mean on vacation or anything? Do you just get out and go?"

"Of course, dear," Peg said solicitously. "We just spent a week with your Aunt Jane in Gallup this summer, and we drove up to see quite a few of Bryan's games this year. We don't stay at home all the time."

"No, but I mean someplace fun for you and Dad both. Have

you ever gone to Disneyworld in Florida or the Grand Canyon or someplace like that?"

"Oh, no, not like that. We don't enjoy long driving trips. You know your dad's eyes aren't as good as they used to be. No, we're very content to stay right here in New Mexico."

No wonder she'd been terrified at the idea of moving to Colorado. She'd been torn from a nest that had coddled and confined her for so many years that she didn't know any better.

"Mom—"

Her dad appeared in the doorway of the kitchen. He surveyed the two women working, then stepped between them for the refrigerator. He got out two more cans of beer. Elly was aware of a peculiar intensity about him as he casually popped open the cans beside her.

"How's my girl?" he asked.

Elly glanced up from the salad she was making. "Fine, Dad."

He nodded and took a swig of beer. Elly sliced more tomatoes.

"You know your mother and I tried to raise you right," he said. "We tried to instill standards into you—good standards."

"I know," she agreed.

"And if I jumped you about your … condition, I'm sorry. It's just that it's not a real proper thing for mixed company."

"Dad, things are different now. People don't—"

"We also raised you not to paint your face."

Elly put down her knife. She could almost feel Graydon's hand on her arm, twisting, twisting, his voice hard and demanding in her ear.

"Dad," she said evenly, "I'm a grown woman. I'm twenty-four."

"Even grown women don't need to paint up like a whore. Proper women don't need that. It's false, Elly, false."

Elly's mom skittered conveniently out to the dining room and busied herself with arranging the table.

"I look better this way," Elly said.

"You look like a goddamn whore."

"Dad—"

"You know, I've been watching you and you come down here

different. Sure, you were in an accident and I'm sorry, but you come down all fat and proud and showing off and painting your face. It's not the way we taught you, Elly. And we never thought Graydon would allow it neither, even if he was a bad choice for a son-in-law. We thought Graydon was more level-headed than that, at least about some things."

Elly felt that panicky, smothering feeling coming over her. *Don't do this to me, Dad, don't.* She concentrated on wiping her hands, then picked up a fork and spoon to toss the salad.

"What Graydon and I do is our own business," she said slowly. "I'm sorry you don't agree, but—"

"Your own business?" His voice became more gruff. "Like getting married to a sinner? Your own business, too, and you barely twenty? Not even so much as asking us, that's your business? And the way he hauled you off to Colorado so your mother can't ever see you, and she's got no one to help her, what's that if that's not our business?"

"Dad, we have our own lives to live."

"And not so much as a by-your-leave for your parents, is that it? I knew he was a slick talker the first time I set eyes on him but I never thought he'd brainwash you like this. You're turning your back on your family, Elly, that's what you're doing."

"Graydon hasn't brainwashed me," she said with effort. "I'm just being myself. I'm sorry you don't like it."

"Like it? I think he's turned you into a goddamn Air Force whore. He—"

"Dad," Elly said. "He's my husband. Don't talk about him that way."

Her dad's eyebrows slammed angrily down over his eyes. "You defending him? After all those times you called your mother crying because you'd had a fight, and now you're defending him? The way he bulls his way into our home and steals our daughter, makes her cry, and you say don't talk like that?"

"Things are different now." She turned away to get the salt and pepper. Her dad's hand caught her arm and jerked her roughly back around to face him.

"Oh, they are, are they? So different that you can turn away from your dad when he's talking to you?"

"Most of the morning you've hardly spoken two words to me," Elly flared. "All you cared about was if I could bring you a beer. Well, I'm busy now, and I don't see any point in—"

His face hardened and turned dark, like heating clay. Elly was afraid she'd gone too far.

"Elly?"

It was Graydon. He stood in the kitchen doorway, his eyes catching every detail of her father's hand on her arm, the glaring look between the two. "Can I help you with anything?"

He stepped up behind her and put his hands on her shoulders. Glen released her arm and took a deliberate breath, his eyes angry and frustrated.

"You just better think about it, young lady," he said bitterly. Without so much as a token nod at Graydon, he pushed by them both and left the kitchen.

Elly sank back into the comforting strength of Graydon's hands.

"Hey," he said, "are you all right? Did he—"

"No, it's okay," she said quickly. She had heard the dangerous lowering of Graydon's voice. "He's just upset because I'm … different. It's all right." She turned around to face him and looked up into his eyes. She managed a tight smile. "I guess you're not the only one that I'm a disappointment to."

"I think everyone's getting hungry," her mother said suddenly. She hurried into the kitchen and grabbed up the salad. "Come on, you two. Let's get everything on the table and we can start."

The meal was a quiet one. The sound of the final quarter took up most of the slack, but Elly was painfully aware of the murmured requests for food, the clacking of silverware on china. She was grateful for Graydon's silent presence beside her.

She tried to reach back in her mind and find the answers. Why was it all she could see was Bryan? Bryan at the baseball game, Bryan riding a bike, Bryan closing the door of his room in her face. She had wanted so badly to be like Bryan, to be with Bryan. At the baseball game, when he had made the double play and her father had jumped up roaring, she had jumped up, too, and hugged her dad excitedly around the waist.

"Daddy, Daddy!" she had cried. And he had unwound her

arms from around him and continued to yell to Bryan.

"Way to play, son! Way to play!"

Had her dad any idea of how hurt she was or how quickly she had covered the hurt with scar tissue, like the careful embalming of a grain of sand into a pearl? She had carried the pearl within her for years, half the time not even realizing it herself. Bryan was older, Bryan was a boy, Bryan was better.

By the time dinner was over, Elly felt drugged with memories. They flashed through her mind like disconnected dreams, each one with an emotion—envy, hurt, desperation, a crying desire to please. She moved like a sleepwalker from the dining room to the kitchen and took a silent stance beside her mother at the sink.

"You want to dry?"

"Sure," she murmured. "Didn't I always dry?"

Her mother looked at her oddly, then plunged her hands into the dishwater. "You have to understand your dad," Peg said softly. "You're his only daughter. He's concerned about you."

Elly laughed humorlessly. "Why doesn't he ask me how I am? Why doesn't he ask me if I'm happy? Whether I wear makeup or not doesn't prove a damn thing."

"Elly."

"Sorry. I just…don't understand. I feel like I've always tried to please him and he never would let me. Now I'm trying to find out who I am, who I *really* am, and he doesn't like that, either. I don't know what to do."

"He—he doesn't like to feel like he's losing his grip. Things are changing so fast in the world and everything young people do is so different and he doesn't like that. He was always in control, you know. Just like his dad was always in control, always the undisputed head of the house."

"But Dad has to change, too," Elly said, "or he'll lose everything. He can't hold things back. He can't keep things the same. It's not possible."

"Oh, it is a little bit. At least here, at home. We try to keep things the same."

Elly stared at her mother. This unassuming, thin woman, washing dishes like she had for the last thirty years—she was trying to keep the same climate that her husband was used to in the face of radical world changes. How ridiculous, Elly thought—and how touching.

"You really love him, don't you, Mom?" she asked.

Peg looked embarrassed. "Why, of course I do. What a question."

Yes, what a question, Elly thought.

That evening was a blur. The family sat around the living room, eating pumpkin pie in front of the TV set, watching the crop of holiday specials or talking politely. Elly felt as if she were made of photo-sensitive paper and was being bombarded with images. Great flashes of memory would sear across her mind, whole days, and then she would be assailed by the offhand banter of her brother or her mother's quiet concern. She listened to every word, capturing it, analyzing it, filing it away so maybe later she could put all the pieces together and make a picture out of it. Her father rarely spoke. Elly wondered where she had gone wrong.

When the last special signed off, she helped her mother pick up the dessert plates and beer cans. She had a headache. She didn't think she'd ever thought so much in her life.

"Do you really have to leave so early tomorrow?" her mother asked in the kitchen.

"I think it's best, Mom. I'm still not feeling real well, and ... I think it's best. Maybe later, when I'm better, I can come back and spend some time."

"I hope so," Peg sighed. "I don't like to see us drifting apart like this. You may not think so, but I know your father is upset that you quarreled."

Quarreled, Elly thought. Was that what it was? She had thought it sounded more like his trying to make her into something she wasn't. He sounded like Graydon used to. Funny, she thought, Graydon doesn't sound like that any more.

When the kitchen was clean, Elly noticed that Graydon had already gone into the bathroom. Bryan had disappeared into his room. Only her father sat on the couch.

"Dad," she said sitting down beside him. "I'm sorry about what happened earlier. I'm not trying to oppose you."

Glen swiveled his broody eyes to her unsympathetically. She could see the way his eyes took her in—and found her not to his liking.

"I've never been able to please you, have I?" she whispered. "You always liked Bryan best. Bryan was everything to you, and I just couldn't quite come up to standard. That's the way it always was."

Glen scoffed. "That's foolish talk. You're my daughter. Of course you pleased me."

She shook her head. "I don't think I did. I used to wish I was a boy because I thought you would like me better. When I started developing, I was ashamed. I felt like I'd failed you again."

"Stop it," he said roughly. "Don't talk like that."

"Dad, I can't remember it all, I don't understand it all, but I'm trying to be me. It's really hard, though. I'm having to make a lot of decisions, a lot of discoveries that most people make as children. I'm finding out that I can't please you or a lot of other people, but I have to be the way I feel I should be. Am I making any sense to you at all?"

"No. I think those doctors up in Colorado have filled your head with a lot of garbage. You were you all your life. Why do you have to start over—just because you can't remember? That's foolishness."

"No, Dad, it's true. Oh, I wish I could explain to you."

He stood up. "I don't think you can. Sorry." Turning, he called to his wife. "Peg? You coming?"

"Right there, dear."

Glen looked down at his daughter. "I just thought we raised you better than this, that's all."

Graydon was waiting for her in the bedroom. She moved slowly to her suitcase, pulled out her nightgown and started for the bathroom. He let her go.

In the bathroom she stared at her face in the mirror. Why am I so mixed up, she thought. Why am I so plain? Maybe I belong in the background, an obedient daughter to help her mother and bring beer to her father. Maybe I don't deserve to be up front, in the light, happy. Maybe I really am an awful person.

With heartbreaking care she washed all trace of makeup from her face.

Graydon had pulled back the bed covers. She shambled

tiredly to her side of the bed and climbed beneath the sheets. An involuntary sigh escaped her.

"Ready?" he asked.

She nodded. The light went out. The bed creaked beneath Graydon's weight as he settled himself beside her.

"This is why I never wanted to come," he said quietly. "When I see the way your father belittles you, I could just—"

Elly's sobs stopped him in mid-sentence. She forced a hand to her mouth to keep from crying out loud, but whimpers of pain escaped her. Her eyes flooded with tears.

"Elly," Graydon breathed. In seconds he had gathered her into his arms and cradled her head against his shoulder. With his arms holding her tightly against him, he rocked her. "Elly, Elly, God, Elly, why do you let him get to you?"

"He hates me," she sobbed. "Why does he hate me?"

"He doesn't hate you. He just doesn't understand you."

"He doesn't try!"

Graydon corrected her. "He doesn't know how."

She cried harder, her words jumbling. "Well, I don't know, either. I don't understand why I'm so awful for wanting to be myself. I can't be pretty, I can't be smart, I can't go to work, I can't get married. What am I allowed to do, Graydon? What am I living for?" Her sobs choked off her words in a contorted strangle.

"Jesus, Elly," Graydon breathed. He gathered her closer, the wall of his shoulders surrounding her in a high, protective barrier. Her body shuddered uncontrollably against him. Holding her, feeling her shake with the torrential outpouring of her misery, Graydon felt very small.

"I guess I'm as much to blame for this as he is," he said quietly. "It seemed like you were always so unsure of yourself, so eager to please, I guess it was easy to try to mold you. I never thought that you would try to be something you weren't just to satisfy others." He pressed his cheek to her temple. "God, Elly, what have I done to you? I never realized. I'm sorry. I just never knew."

She cried uncontrollably. With each sob, her body shook and seemed to grow smaller in Graydon's grasp. She collapsed by degrees into a tiny, lost little girl with Graydon both her adversary and savior. He held on tightly to her until she could breathe in dry, ragged breaths.

"Oh, God," she moaned. "I'm so tired."

"Just rest, Elly. Try to sleep. I promise you things will be better tomorrow." He would make sure of it.

"No. Things will be just the same. I'll never be what anyone wants."

Graydon cupped her chin with his hand and forced her head up. "You'll be you, Elly. That's all you have to be. That's all anyone can expect you to be."

"Graydon." She slid her hand over his, fumbling with exhaustion.

"Shhh. Sleep, baby. Just go to sleep."

Caught against him in the fortress of his arms, she did.

It was a long time before Graydon could find the same sort of sanctuary.

Chapter Ten

*I*n the morning, they all stood around the BMW, Elly's mother ready to cry. "Mom, Please!" Elly begged. "I'll be back. I'll come back as soon as I can and—and we'll talk."

"What about the baby? You'll need help when it comes."

Crossing her fingers, Elly answered, "As soon as I know I'm coming home with it, I'll call you. We'll fly you up, both of you, if you want. You can make a vacation out of it. Okay, Mom?"

"Okay." Peg blinked to keep the tears back. "Are you sure you don't want to stay a little longer? You don't look well."

That's what no makeup does for you, Elly wanted to say. "No, we'd better go. I feel pretty good right now and the sooner we get home, the better I'll be. But thanks, Mom. For everything."

Bryan stood awkwardly by as they hugged. He was next.

"Good luck with your baseball, Bryan," she said. "And say hello to Dana for me."

"Sure, Sis. You take care."

"I will." She hugged him. "You let me know when you and Dana decide to tie the knot. I want to be there."

"Yeah." His face flamed like a big, dumb kid. Elly was touched.

She turned to her dad. "Dad, I'm sorry if I said anything to upset you. Maybe next time I see you we can talk." He looked properly embarrassed by his daughter's candor. When he seemed unable to find an answer, she took his hands and rose up on tiptoe to kiss his cheek. "You'll always be my father," she whispered. "I love you."

He let her back away without a word.

"Goodbye," Graydon said. He helped Elly into the car and started the engine. The Hatchers stepped back to the curb.

"Goodbye," Peg called.

"Goodbye," Elly waved. It wasn't until they had almost reached the corner that she saw the three small figures turn for the house.

Elly sighed.

"What?" Graydon asked.

"It's awful, but I'm so glad we're leaving. I couldn't have gone through another day. He was just like a stone wall to me."

Graydon patted her hand. "Don't let it bother you. It's his problem, not yours. You're doing fine, just the way you are."

She smiled bravely. "Thanks. I'll try to remember that."

"Think you'll be okay this morning? It's a long drive to Telluride—longer than from Colorado Springs to here."

"I'm keeping my fingers crossed. With any luck, I did all I have to do back at the house. If I feel an accident coming on, though, I'll let you know."

"Fair enough." Graydon headed for the highway.

"I wonder if they thought anything of seeing the skis on top of the car."

"Probably not," Graydon said. "They've seen skis on almost every car I've ever brought here. They probably think I store them up there in the rack."

"Good. I don't feel quite as guilty, then."

"Your father didn't much like the idea of our having a BMW."

"Oh?" she asked. "Why not?"

"He said he wasn't aware the government gave away money so Colonels could buy expensive foreign cars."

"God," Elly groaned. "What did you say?"

"I said the government paid me for my time, but they didn't tell me how to spend my money. He didn't like that much."

"I'll bet." She shook her head. "It's really kind of sad, you know?"

Graydon nodded. "I know. But like I said, that's his problem, not ours. We're going skiing."

"I can't wait." Elly smiled over to her husband and her lake blue eyes sparkled in anticipation. He smiled back.

"You know, you really should have a little color in your face," he said casually.

"What?"

"Well, your eyes are so blue this morning, and I think just a touch of color on your cheeks would really bring them out."

Elly pulled down the visor and checked herself in the mirror. "You think so?" She lifted an eyebrow at her husband.

"Yeah." he said. "I think so. After all, a wife's appearance is a reflection of her husband, isn't it?"

They had to make two emergency stops at gas stations. Luckily Elly felt the rolling queasiness in her stomach in time so that Graydon could pull into a station before she made a complete mess of herself. After the second episode, she felt much better. Looked better, too, with a little blusher on.

She decided the western half of New Mexico was much prettier than the eastern half. Again she sat with the map spread out in her lap and she noted all the landmarks and advised Graydon of the towns coming up. They laughed over some of the more difficult names and Elly queried Graydon about the Indian history.

"Sorry," he said. "History of New Mexico was not one of my better classes. Matter of fact, I think I flunked that altogether."

"But wouldn't it be interesting to know? Look at all the fascinating Indian things. Doesn't it make you curious?"

"No," he laughed, "but obviously it does you. We'll see if we can't find you some answers."

They ate lunch in a tiny cafe and browsed through the little one-room gift shop next door. While Elly was drawn excitedly to the jewelry case by the freeform silver and turquoise, Graydon scanned the book and magazine rack.

"Look," she said when he came to stand at her shoulder. "Isn't it beautiful?" She pointed to a silver pendant in an undulating, exotic form with turquoise embedded in its center. Matching drop-earrings lay alongside.

"Nice," he agreed. "Do you like it?"

"I love it." She dragged her eyes away in expectation of going. "Are you ready to go?"

"Almost." He caught the shopkeeper's eye, a middle-aged Indian with a weather-eroded leather face. "We'll take those," he said, and pointed to the set. The man grinned at Elly as he took the jewelry from the display.

"Oh, Graydon, no, they're too expensive," Elly cried. "I didn't want you to—"

"*I* want to," he said. "They'll look good on you. That dark turquoise almost matches your eyes."

The Indian rang up the sale and presented the sack to Elly as Graydon paid. She thanked him, a child with her first Christmas toy. On the way out of the store she steadied herself on Graydon's arm and leaned up to kiss him on the cheek. He laughed.

"Oh, Graydon, they're beautiful!" She tore the sack open as soon as they got in the car and held up the pendent so it sparkled in the sun.

"Put it on," he said.

Her mouth in an 'o' of excitement, Elly clasped the necklace beneath her hair and threaded the earrings through her pierced lobes. The design of the earrings dropped to just below her hair and swung wildly when she turned to show Graydon.

"How do I look?" she asked.

"Like a blue-eyed Hiawatha," he laughed.

"No," she scoffed. "Hiawatha wasn't a Navaho." She pulled the visor down and examined her new finery. "I just love them. Thank you, Graydon. You didn't have to."

"If I had to, I probably wouldn't have," he said. "Oh, here. I picked this up in there, too." He handed her another sack, one she hadn't even noticed him carrying, and started the car.

"What is it?" she asked.

"Open it."

She did. It was a book on New Mexican Indians. Elly fanned through the elaborately illustrated pages and saw names like Hopi, Navaho, Zuni and Anasazi. The pictures captured her imagination.

"How wonderful! Look at all the funny costumes, oh, and the rugs! Aren't they beautiful? Graydon, this is wonderful!"

"Gee, I'm sorry you don't like it," he chuckled.

"Oh, Graydon!" Again she leaned over and kissed him. "You shouldn't have. You're going to spoil me."

"I doubt it," he said. "I only got you that so you'd quit telling me how many miles it is to the next waterhole."

Elly had the grace to blush and quickly buried herself in the book. "Now I'll bore you with interesting Indian facts," she threatened. "You'll think you've created a monster."

She was so engrossed in her book that she didn't see the thoughtful frown on her husband's face.

They arrived in Telluride right at dusk and Elly got her first glimpse of the little mining town against its backdrop of dimming mountains.

"What a cute little town," she breathed. "How did you ever find it way up here in the mountains?"

"It's been a ski resort for quite a few years now," Graydon said. He slowed the car and entered on Colorado, the only main street in town. "The original idea was to give Aspen some healthy competition, but somehow it's just not quite as chic as Aspen. I like it, though."

Snowy citadels of the San Juan Mountains rose on three sides with the tiny town nestled comfortably in their lap. Snow blanketed everything and piled thickly on the roadside where it had been plowed into muddy barricades. Elly watched fascinated out the window as they drove past huge modern ski lodges and tiny false-fronted shops.

"Here we go," Graydon said. He pulled off the road and forced the car across the snowy parking lot of a ski lodge office. "Why don't you stay here? I'll get the key."

Elly saw several separate buildings behind, each with balconies upstairs and down, all paneled in rough, dark wood. Above them rose the white and tree-streaked mountains. Elly loved it.

"Okay," Graydon said when he returned to the car. "We can just park over here and forget the car for a week."

"Forget the car?"

"Sure. Everything we'll need is within walking distance."

Their room was in one of the distant buildings, one of eight studio apartments. They were upstairs and their balcony faced town, the barely perceptible creek beyond, and the ski slopes.

"It's adorable," Elly exclaimed. They had a full kitchen, separate bath and huge living room complete with fireplace. "I hate to say this, though," she told Graydon, "but there's no bedroom."

"The couch folds out," he said. "Go ahead and look around. I'll bring the stuff up."

Elly did. She opened all the cupboards and found dishes, silverware, towels—even a coffee pot. The refrigerator was empty but all the ice trays were full. Even the oven was clean.

"What do you think?" Graydon asked as he dumped a load of suitcases beside the bureau.

"I love it. Did we come here a lot?"

"A few times. Maybe three or four. Why?"

"I'd like to come every year. I'd like to live here."

"Sorry," Graydon laughed. "Why do you think the town's able to stay so small? Unless you want to work in tourism, there's no industry. And I don't think the Air Force has plans to build any new installations here. But we'll come more often if you want. That wouldn't bother me at all."

They arranged their suitcases and unpacked a few things before venturing out for dinner. Graydon knew of a good restaurant not two blocks away. "What should I wear? My zip boots?"

"Wear your snowmobile boots. Better traction."

Elly rummaged through her suitcase. "Oh, these funny-looking black ones? I wondered why you wanted me to bring them."

"They're great in the snow. And around here, there's very little in the way of formality."

The restaurant was the Silver Jack, named after one of the mines that had sparked life into the little town in the 1800's. The walls were all of rough planked wood with antique mining paraphernalia hung decoratively around. The atmosphere was intimate.

"We're not going to eat here every night, are we?" Elly asked, eyeing the prices on the menu.

"No. Tomorrow we'll go get groceries and set up house in our studio. Unless you don't want to cook?"

"No, that's fine. I haven't cooked for three days, so I won't mind."

The meal was excellent. Graydon ordered a half liter of wine and poured Elly a little bit in a glass. It tasted good and warmed her inside. A little antifreeze for the baby, she thought. Tomorrow, on the slopes, they'd need it.

After dinner Graydon took Elly on a walk around town. It took fifteen minutes.

"This is fascinating," Elly said. She loved the rough-hewn old-time store fronts, the high, gabled houses and the atmosphere of history. "This place is just steeped in early Americana, isn't it?" she asked. "Do any of the mines still work?"

"I think one or two, but I don't know which ones. I haven't read up much on them. I know the main thing that was mined was an ore called Telluride and that's where the town got its name. Maybe tomorrow we'll find you a book on that, too."

Back at the apartment, Graydon fired up the electric fireplace and Elly finished unpacking. The closet in the hall was roomy, big enough for most of their things, and Elly arranged their shoes and boots along the floor. Compact as the apartment was it was very comfortable and it brought Elly a homey contentment just to putter around in her stocking feet.

"Want to watch TV?" Graydon asked.

"Sure. What's on?"

She heard the rustle of paper. "A movie, *Love With the Proper Stranger*. Want to watch that?"

"Have I ever seen it?"

"I don't think so," he said

"I don't, either. Let's watch it."

"Okay."

When she was done with her unpacking, she found Graydon stretched out on the open hide-a-bed, propped up with pillows in front of the TV. He looked as comfortable as she felt.

"Here," he said, and gave her one of his pillows. Elly took it and lay down beside him, the pillow a soft wedge at her back. It felt good to snuggle down in the bed. She found her attention immediately captured by Steve McQueen and Natalie Wood.

Somehow their plight was a dangerously close version of her own.

Graydon let Elly have the bathroom first. Initially she hadn't felt any reluctance since she had been sharing a bed with her husband for two nights running now, but as she put her hand on the doorknob to go out, she became suddenly shy. They were not in her parent's house now. They were alone.

"All done?" he asked.

She nodded and crept into bed on her own side. Graydon left on the lamp on his end table and disappeared into the bathroom. Elly pulled the covers up to her chin and tried to go right to sleep. She didn't succeed.

The sound of the bathroom door opening jolted her eyes open. Her heart began to hammer in her chest and she willed herself to relax. Forcing her eyes closed again, she feigned sleep. She could hear Graydon padding about the room.

The light beyond her lids clicked out. Although this bed didn't squeak, she was still very aware of Graydon's slipping beneath the blankets, the gentle rocking of the mattress and the sudden presence of him beside her. Without realizing it, she clutched the sheet in fisted hands.

"Elly?"

Her eyes flew open. "What?"

Graydon waited a half second to answer, making her turn to face him. "Will you be able to sleep all right?" In the darkness Elly could just make out the edge of his cheek and the rise of his shoulder. He lay facing her.

"Yes." She tried to look away but his eyes, even in the darkness, held her. The electrical charge of a summer storm passed between them.

"Come here." His voice was quiet, gentle, commanding.

Elly's breath caught in her throat. She couldn't move.

He put an arm out almost lazily and gathered her in it. With all the strength and determination of his powerful body, he pulled her inexorably to him. She came like a dead weight and lay motionless against his chest.

"Elly," he called softly. One of his large hands touched her hair, smoothed it away from her face. "Look at me."

She was paralyzed. Her insides felt wound as tight as a coiled spring and her blood pounded thunderously in her head. The only things that existed in the whole world were her and that hand, that big, gently caressing hand that traced soft paths down her cheek and cupped her chin.

He lifted her head. She opened her mouth to protest but found it immediately covered by his. The natural, insistent pressure of his mouth sent rockets shooting through her head and she flushed hot. She became instantly aware of the determined hardness of his embrace, not just in his mouth but along his entire body. He meant to have her.

He released her mouth and pressed kisses on her eyes, closing them. His hand strayed down to her throat, gently caressing. Everywhere he touched sparked nerves to warmth. Elly felt shudders of unbelievable sensation echoing through her. Shyly she slipped her hand around his neck. He kissed her again.

She felt fused to him. He pushed the sheet down off her shoulders but no chill pricked her skin. Instead she felt nothing but heat, all-enveloping, consuming heat. Graydon's hands moved over her like solid, searing flames that melted her against him. She gave herself up to it.

Then her stomach began to knot. Great coils of anxiety writhed and curled like a giant constrictor inside of her. The heat of her body balled up into a breathless, gripping panic and Elly began to fight.

"No, it's a mistake!" she cried. "It's a mistake, it's a mistake, I'm sorry, no, I made a mistake, please, no, it's all wrong, it's a mistake, it's a mistake!" Hardly aware of the words she was forming, she cried out uncontrollably, all the while pushing and fighting out of Graydon's embrace.

"Elly! For Christ's sake, what's wrong with you? Stop it! Elly!"

The image of the headless man fell across her mind, coming toward her heavily in slow motion. His empty shoulders rolled forward, the black gaping hole of his neck yawning like a bottomless, beckoning cavern. In the timeless second of an unbidden thought, Elly saw the black hole closing in on her.

She screamed.

Graydon grabbed her shoulders in a commanding hold and shook her violently. Her head snapped back on her neck and the strangled, incoherent words died in her throat. She went limp in his hands.

"Please," she whispered, "please turn on the light."

Graydon hesitated at first. When he heard her gulping for air, he reached behind him and snapped on the light, never taking his eyes from her.

Her pupils were huge, frightened and clawing in the light. She breathed raggedly, her mouth half open, the catch in her throat still audible. Her eyes shifted about the room like those of a cornered animal, then finally settled on Graydon.

"Elly, my God, what's wrong?" he demanded. "What happened?"

She blinked her eyes slowly and swallowed. "Oh, Graydon," she breathed. "It was awful."

"But what was it? What happened to you?"

"I don't know." Her head rolled listlessly on his arm. "My stomach turned into knots and ... and I saw him again—the man with no head. He—he was coming for me. The black hole was coming for me and I was afraid—afraid I'd fall in. It was awful." She shuddered.

"What did you mean, it was a mistake?"

Elly looked up guilelessly. "What?"

"You said it was a mistake. What did you mean?"

"A mistake?" She frowned. "I don't know. I don't remember saying it. Are you sure—?"

"You said it over and over, practically crying. Yes, I'm sure. You don't know why?"

"No," she said miserably. "I don't understand any of it." Her eyes sought his again. "Graydon, I—do you think I'm ever going to get well? I feel like I'm going crazy. My head and my body do things that I don't understand, I say things that I don't remember. Maybe I—I'm getting worse."

"Stop it," he said. His arms tightened around her and pulled her against his chest. "You're not crazy. It's just taking time and ... and things are surfacing without making connections to any other things. It's just happening this way. You'll remember. It'll all make sense sometime."

She turned into the hollow of his shoulder. "God, I hope so. I hate this. I'm afraid of things I don't understand and I feel like I have no control. I feel like I might just freak out sometime and go completely crazy."

"Don't worry about that," Graydon said. "It's just taking time. You'll get better. In a month or two you'll be fine and you'll look back at this and laugh."

She shook her head. "I don't think so. I don't think I'll ever laugh about it." She looked up at Graydon. "I'm sorry."

"Hey," he said, "don't worry about me." He kissed her nose. "We've got time." He reached back around for the light.

"Graydon?" She put a hand on his arm. "Will you—would you mind leaving the light on?"

"All night?" he asked.

"Yes." Her voice was small. "Please. I don't want it to be dark."

"Can you sleep with the light on?"

"Yes. Do you mind?"

"No." He settled back beside her. "If you can sleep, I can sleep." With her in the crook of his arm, he pulled the sheet up over her shoulders. She laid a hand lovingly against his bare chest.

"Thank you, Graydon."

"For what? Leaving the light on?"

"For everything."

It was late when Elly woke up—or early. Outside the darkness still pressed against the windows. The light from the bedside lamp sprawled across the bed, illuminating Graydon's shoulder and side, pooling shadows where Elly's hand still touched his chest. She moved her head just slightly so she could look up at her husband.

She had never been able to look at him carefully for any length of time. Awake, he could intimidate her with his impaling black eyes or cause a flutter of unease with just a casual raised brow. Now, asleep, he lay breathing deeply, a candid subject for her to study. She took advantage of the rare opportunity.

Even in sleep his strength and mastery were evident. A lock of black hair curled over his high, wide forehead and the chiseled, planed features of his face were illuminated by the soft light. His jaw was square and angular, for once not set in a grim line the way it normally was. His entire face was at once familiar to her and still new. She discovered it contentedly.

Not like the man with no head. Elly shuddered at the unwanted thought. Somewhere, she felt, there was a connection between him and the lovemaking Graydon had initiated. But it had been Graydon tonight, not the other man.

It was Graydon here beside her now—Graydon, her husband. With the light on and her eyes open, she would see no one else. All she would see was Graydon.

She ran her hand softly through the black, curling hair of his chest. Above the powerful muscles there, she found the cord at the side of his neck, the cord that stood out so angrily when he was mad. It was relaxed now. She let her fingertips follow its length up to his chin, to his cheek and his ear. He stirred.

Black eyes opened on her. She read surprise in them, surprise and—pleasure? With more confidence than she felt, she stroked his cheek with the tips of her fingers.

His arm tightened around her shoulders and pulled her against him.

Graydon smoothed her bangs from her forehead, then laid his hand along the side of her face. She didn't wait for him to ask; she turned her lips to him and met his without embarrassment. He moved over her, his hands losing themselves in her hair.

"Elly," he breathed against her mouth, "are you sure?"

She brushed her lips against his. "Yes. Just keep the light on so I can see you, Graydon. I want to be able to see you."

Elly woke facing the window. Sun glared off the snowy mountains across the valley, shining like a brilliant light in her eyes. She rolled over.

Graydon's eyes greeted her.

"Good morning."

She blushed. "Good morning."

"Sleep well?"

"Perfectly."

"Come here."

Elly moved over to him, finding her place in his arms. He kissed her. "Do you know," he asked, "that you have the biggest, bluest eyes in the world?"

"No. I'm glad you like them, though."

"Like them? I married you for them." He bent his head and pressed kisses on her cheeks and nose. Elly slid her arms around his back and felt his body respond. She lifted her face to him, wanting him to want her again.

In the middle of his kiss, as his hands touched and warmed her body, the swelling threat of sickness rose in her throat. She broke away. "Wait," she said. "Let me up."

"What is it?" Graydon asked, concerned. "Are you all right?"

Afraid to talk, Elly nodded and rolled out of bed. She clamped a hand over her mouth and ran for the bathroom.

Graydon fell back on his pillow and groaned.

Fifteen minutes later Elly felt capable of venturing out of the bathroom. Graydon already had pants on and was making the bed.

"I'm sorry," Elly said. She grabbed her robe and slipped into it, preferring not to stand naked while deciding what to wear.

"It's okay," he said. "I'm not usually a morning man anyway. How do you feel?"

"Not very good. If you want to shave or anything, go ahead, but you might leave the door unlocked."

He nodded and grabbed his shirt. Elly waited until he had disappeared into the bathroom, then sank down on the bed. She felt stupid.

She would manage to foul things up. He didn't seem to mind—at least he didn't show it—but Elly felt like a failure again. And right now she wanted more than anything to please Graydon. Not the way she used to, not the wide-eyed puppyish way everyone said she had been before, but on an equal level, as adults, as partners. She was in love with Graydon. She might have laughed, but it would be without humor. In love with her own husband—haltingly, wonderfully, frighteningly in love. She could never tell him.

The sound of the water in the bathroom drew her eyes to the closed door. If not for her illness, they would still be in bed, twined together like coiling honeysuckles, experiencing the sensations she had craved without realizing until last night. But no, her baby—Adam's baby—had come between them, as it so often did. For a split second she wished she had aborted it. Maybe then they would have spent the whole day discovering each other. Maybe then she could have made Graydon fall in love with her.

Disconsolately, she chose her clothing for the day. Bile rose in her throat and she hurried to dress before she had to barge in on Graydon's solitude.

The grocery store was a half block closer than the Silver Jack. They walked down on crunchy frozen snow and blew vapor into the frigid air with their breath. Elly was enchanted with the little town and its huge, guardian mountains. It was like living in a fairy tale.

Graydon pushed the basket. Elly began to protest, ready to insist that she wasn't so pregnant that she couldn't put out such small efforts but decided to leave it unsaid. She would not remind him any more than necessary.

He took an active part in choosing the groceries, too. Elly realized it shouldn't surprise her; Graydon was never one to sit back and watch, no matter what the situation. She let him make the major decisions about meat and concentrated on the smaller, more indispensable articles: sugar, coffee, milk. They had the cart filled in no time.

"Are you supposed to be taking vitamins?" he asked as they came down the last aisle, the pharmaceuticals.

"Dr. Weiss said I should. I keep forgetting."

Graydon grabbed a big bottle of vitamins with iron. "I want you to take two of these as soon as we get back. No sense your running around in the snow with low resistance."

"All right," she murmured. His tone of voice allowed no discussion. As gruff as it was, it warmed her a little. Maybe he did care.

Walking back to the apartment, Graydon had no choice but to let Elly carry two sacks; he couldn't carry four by himself. He hefted each one first and gave Elly the lightest two. They crunched home.

While Elly put the groceries away, she heard Graydon hauling out the ski equipment. He brought two pair of skis into the living room and laid them on the floor. Elly glanced at them over her shoulder; they seemed awfully long. She couldn't imagine being very agile on them. Graydon was preoccupied with his examination of them, checking the edges and bottoms. She couldn't tell if he was pleased or not; he frowned in concentration. She put the rest of the food away and joined him as quickly as she could.

"Which pair are mine?" she asked.

Graydon looked up. "What?"

"Which ones are mine?" She hoped the blue ones were hers; black was more Graydon's color.

"Neither. They're both mine."

Elly felt confused. "Both yours? But don't I use one pair? How can I ski without skis?"

"You don't," Graydon said. "You don't ski."

Elly fought a grain of annoyance working its way beneath her skin. "What do I do—watch?"

"Usually, yes. I offered to teach you to ski once and you said you didn't want to learn. You seemed happy just to watch me."

She tried not to show her disappointment, but it was difficult to keep her face from falling. She didn't want to watch; she wanted to ski. "Can I … reconsider now?"

"You want to learn?" he asked, incredulous. His face grew discouragingly perplexed.

"Yes. I mean, if it's not too much trouble. I don't want to ruin your vacation by asking you to play nursemaid to me, but..."

"No, it's not that. I'd like to teach you. What about the baby?"

Elly glanced down at her rounding stomach. She hadn't wanted that subject to come up again. "I should be okay. After all, I came through that accident, and the first three months are the most uncertain. I think as long as I don't go falling off any mountains, I'll be fine." She met Graydon's eyes in a soft challenge. "I'd like to learn."

His expressionless stare told her nothing. She could only imagine the wheels turning in his brain, weighing what she said against what he thought—or believed. She hoped the blackness of his eyes was only concentration and not the building of a storm.

"All right."

She released the breath she hadn't been aware she was holding. "You don't mind? I won't keep you back, I promise. If you'll just show me the pointers, the main things, I can goof around by myself. I—I won't be ... a hindrance to you."

"Don't worry," he said, rising from the floor. "I won't let you. Come on. Let's go get you some gear."

They walked down to a ski shop. Elly was amazed at the row of varied colored skis stretching the length of the shop, all standing at attention, curved tips up. She walked the row and wondered how anyone was ever able to decide which ones to buy.

"Elly," Graydon called, "over here."

She went to him. He stood in front of a rack of funny-looking plastic boots.

"What are these? They look like Frankenstein shoes."

"Ski boots. Let's see; if I remember correctly, you wear a size seven." He pulled a boot off the rack. "Sit down. Let's try this one."

"But what about the skis?" she asked, sitting. "Shouldn't we pick those first?"

"No. The boots are the most important thing." He unlaced her snowmobile boots and pulled them off, then slid one of the Frankenstein boots on.

Elly wrinkled her nose at them. "Why are they most important?"

"Because if they don't fit, all the rest is nothing. How does that feel? Snug?"

"Yeah," she admitted grudgingly. She wiggled her toes inside. The boots looked like blocks of plastic on her feet.

"Stand up," Graydon ordered. "Walk around."

Elly did as Graydon told her. She walked lopsided, going up on the boot with one step and down on her stocking foot with the next. "I feel like Captain Ahab," she said.

"How does it feel?"

"Okay, I guess. Is it supposed to feel like a regular boot?"

"As long as it's tight. Come here. Let me see if the heel slips." Elly came and stood in front of him. He grabbed the boot with both hands and held it tight against the floor. "Can you slip your heel up at all?"

She pulled up. The heel held tight. "No."

"Good," Graydon said. "Put the other one on."

Elly managed to buckle on the second boot with a few curt instructions from Graydon. It reminded her of the complex strapping of a strait jacket, but she said nothing. When she had the second boot on, she again walked for Graydon and let him hold the boot against her pull.

"How are your toes?" he asked.

"I can move them. Am I supposed to be able to do that?"

"Do they slip down at all? Do they pinch at the end of the boot?"

She shook her head. "No. They're just there."

"Okay." Graydon sat back on his heels on the floor. "We'll take those. Now skis."

Elly clunked over to the far wall and scanned the row of skis again. Graydon stood behind her.

"What kind should I get?" she asked.

Graydon put out an arm that dissected the row. "Anything from here on up is okay. Those ones at the front are children's, and some wood. We'll get fiberglass."

"Are yours fiberglass?"

He nodded. "Mine are Head. It's one of the best brands."

Elly found some that said Head. The colors weren't very pretty, she thought. Black and gold, blue and gold; she didn't want high school colors. "What about those?" she asked. She picked out a pair, red with a grey stripe down the middle and a funny little bird on the tip.

"Those are good. They're Rossingnals."

"Would they be okay?"

"Sure. Is that what you want?"

She nodded. "I like the little bird on the ends."

Graydon's face got funny. Apparently he didn't think much of Elly's unprofessional method of deciding. Then he chuckled.

"Okay," he said, "we'll take the little birds."

A sales clerk hovered behind them, apparently alerted by Graydon's hand on the ski. "Found what you want?" he asked. A small, thirtyish man with curly hair and round glasses, he smiled blandly at Graydon—obviously the decision maker of the two.

"Do you have these in, say, one-fifties?" Graydon asked. He seemed to size Elly up with his eyes as he talked.

"I'm sure I do," the man said. "Let me check in the back."

"One-fifties?" Elly echoed.

"A hundred and fifty centimeters. That's length. You'll start with shorter skis than mine; they're easier to manage. Later you can get longer ones if you want. A lot of people stick with short ones, though. We'll just have to see later on."

The sales clerk returned with Elly's one-fifties. Then Graydon picked out bindings, explaining briefly to Elly how they released her boot if she fell and also how an additional set of straps would keep the skis from running away down hill without her. It all sounded Greek, but she looked and listened and hoped some of it would sink in once she got on the slope.

When Graydon piled all the equipment on the counter, Elly thought they were done.

"Over here," he said. "You have to have poles."

Poles, Elly thought. Was there ever an end to it? Maybe a helmet or flak vest? Wiping the disappointment from her face, she clunked after Graydon. "Isn't that upside down?" she asked. Graydon held the pole handle down and measured it against Elly's side.

"Yes, it's upside down. Here, hold it and tell me if it feels light or heavy or what."

They were surprisingly light. Elly held the leather grips and poked the tips into the indoor-outdoor carpeting.

"They're like feathers. What are they made of?"

"Aluminum. Try these." He handed her another pair.

"These are heavier," she said.

"They shouldn't weigh you down at all. Do this—hold the grips and bring the poles back under your arms." He demonstrated.

Elly chuckled, then immediately wiped the smile from her face. She did as Graydon said.

"Heavy?" he asked.

"No. Are they supposed to be?"

"No, but if they're too light you'll be throwing them around like twigs. Those should be okay."

She handed the poles to Graydon. "Is that all?"

"Almost. All we need now are goggles, gloves and a boot press. That'll do it." Thank God, Elly thought. As it was they were going to walk out loaded up to the armpits.

"Why don't we grab some lunch?" he said as the clerk rang up the sale.

"Lunch? And carry all this stuff around?"

Graydon laughed. "Not hardly. They have to fit your bindings on the skis and fit them to your boots. We can go grab a sandwich while he's doing that, then come back for the stuff. Then we'll be ready to go."

Elly nodded absently. Her attention was taken with the phenomenal prices the clerk was ringing up on the register. The final price staggered her.

"Graydon," she whispered. "Is that right? Is that really how much this is going to cost?"

"Sure," he said pulling out his credit card. "Why?"

"But it's all so expensive!"

"Well, it's not exactly like playing tiddly-winks. This is good equipment." He gave the card to the smiling clerk.

"But, just to learn on? And longer skis later? What if ... what if I can't learn very well? What if I can't do it? This will all be for nothing."

Graydon studied her critically as he put his card away. "Do you want to learn?" he asked.

"Well, yes, but—"

"Then you will. Anyway," he added, "if you want to come on ski trips with me, it's either ski or watch. You said you don't want to watch; this is all that's left. I won't leave you home alone."

Elly couldn't quite tell if that was a threat, a promise or a joke in poor taste. Graydon's expression gave nothing away. She swallowed, nodded and waited patiently while the clerk told Graydon how long it would be. Then he was turning for the door and Elly fell in beside him. They went to lunch.

"We'll take it easy the first couple of days," Graydon said over a sandwich at a little place across the street. "Your legs and back aren't used to this kind of exercise and you'll be plenty sore after just a little bit. It's a good idea to exercise before, but we don't have time for that. Later you'll see what I mean."

Elly was beginning to wonder if she had made the right decision. She had expected Graydon to strap skis on her, point her in the right direction and push. Like riding a bike. He was going on as if this were a major vocation. It couldn't be that hard, could it? Or maybe that was why she hadn't wanted to learn before; maybe she had been afraid of failing.

"How long did it take you to learn?" she asked.

"Not long. I learned young. You have to learn to ski in Minnesota or you don't go anywhere all winter long. But don't worry; you'll do fine."

Elly wasn't so sure.

After lunch they walked back to the ski shop and picked up Elly's gear.

At the sight of her new skis all fitted and ready to go, she felt a tingling of excitement. She put on her new boots and hiked her goggles up on her forehead for the walk back to the apartment for Graydon's skis.

They walked to the bottom of the T-bar. The logged slope of the ski run rose white and gleaming, like a wide, white road up through the throng of snow-dusted trees on either side. The T-bars came down the hill on the right of the elevating struts empty, and rose smoothly on the left side with two people on its bar seats. Down the length of the ski run came all manner of skiers: slow, fast, straight and zigzagging. Elly was awed.

"It looks awfully high," she gulped.

"It isn't as bad as you think. Come on. I'll show you how to put your skis on."

Graydon found a level, fairly trampled place in the snow and stuck his own skis upright in a drift. He took Elly's and tossed them down beside her.

"Watch me," he said.

Elly tried. He buckled and strapped so effortlessly that it was difficult for her to see what the trick was. When he sat back on his heels and looked up at her, she nodded.

He put the loose ski alongside the first and she slid her boot into the bracket. With Graydon still watching from his crouch, she bent down to start buckling. The first ski started to move.

"Oh!" she cried. She did a half split before Graydon caught her ski and checked its slide. By then her heart was hammering in her chest and she was hot with embarrassment.

"First lesson," Graydon said. "Keep your weight over the middle of the skis if you don't want to go anywhere. Bend over like that to adjust your bindings and you'll be downhill before you know it."

"Okay," Elly breathed. Her heart was still thumping but she forced herself to calmness. She tried again, crouching more than bending. She started to buckle, but now she couldn't remember how Graydon had done it. Her gloved hands fumbled with the fittings uselessly.

"I—I don't remember what you did. It looked so easy."

"Here," he said. "Watch closely." And he did it again. Easy. "You can practice at home. Once you've done it a few times, it'll come easier." He rose and handed Elly her poles. "Stick these in the snow so you don't go anywhere while I put mine on."

Elly jammed the tips of her poles into the snow and flexed her fingers on the grips. She felt like a skier—sort of. She wondered if she looked like a skier.

"Okay." Graydon stood beside her, all strapped in, in what seemed like seconds. She realized she should have been watching.

"Now, second lesson. You have to know how to turn. Watch me."

He didn't do what Elly thought. She expected him to push off with his poles and ski around in a nice little turn. Instead he lifted one ski, tip first, and put it at an angle to the second. The back ends of the skis almost touched, like a backward V. When Graydon had planted the first ski back in the snow, he lifted the second and brought it alongside.

"Like that," he said.

Easy, Elly thought. She gripped her poles and pulled one ski up—or half of it. The tip caught in the snow and with the back edge waving around she couldn't seem to get any leverage. She ended up with that ski back almost in its original position except now it overlapped the other by a half inch.

"The tip tends to be heavier," Graydon explained, "so always lift it first. Keep the back down."

Elly tried again. That time was better. Graydon insisted that she practice and he had her turning slow, awkward circles, one ski out, the next brought even, out, even, out, even. By the time the circle was complete, Elly's legs were already beginning to ache.

"That's the step turn," he said. "Now we'll walk. Put your weight on your right ski, then slide your left ski forward a little. Put your right pole out in front to steady you. Good. Now bring your right ski up, and your left pole. Keep your ski on the ground. Just slide it. Good. Get a rhythm."

They walked. Elly felt rather like a mechanical man, sliding one foot and the opposite arm so systematically forward and back, but Graydon did the same thing so she figured it must be right. After a few minutes and about thirty feet, she thought she pretty much had the hang of it, until she came up over a small rise in the snow and very smoothly slid down the other side, off balance, poles waving, body leaning, and keeled over sideways into the snow.

Graydon was at her side instantly. "Are you all right?" He pulled her up out of the snow by her armpits and studied with concern her half white face.

She wiped the snow out of her ear and licked the icy particles off her lips. "I guess so. What happened?"

"You just went skiing," he chuckled. "How did you like it?"

"Not very much. You don't have a lot of control, do you? I mean once you start down a hill."

"You will. Come on. I'll teach you how to wedge. Then you'll be able to slow down and stop."

It was like being back in school again. Graydon explained, demonstrated and drilled relentlessly while Elly watched, listened and practiced—and sometimes fell. Graydon had to abandon his teaching of the wedge to show her how to fall and how to push herself back up out of the snow, but then was able to get back to it. By the time Elly learned the secret of the wedge—putting her weight on the inside edge of her skis and snow plowing to a stop—she was tired and aching. She waited tiredly for Graydon's next lesson.

"How about some coffee?" he asked.

"I'd love it," she breathed.

They ski-walked to a small concession built off the bottom of the T-bar and Graydon ordered hot drinks. When Elly had seated herself securely on the little plastic chairs welded to tables, she relaxed and sipped her hot cocoa

It was wonderful to sit on a solid, non-movable object and loosen the muscles of her legs and back. Unthinkingly, she sighed.

"Tired?" Graydon asked. He peered at her through the steam rising off his coffee.

"A little," she fibbed. "It's not as easy as it looks, is it?"

"Not at first. Later it's more fun than anything. Getting down the basics is always tiring, because you have to concentrate on every little thing you do. Later it's all automatic, you do it without thinking. But you're getting it."

She hoped so. She felt like she was making a complete fool out of herself, but as long as Graydon's jaw didn't tighten, she must have been doing okay. She tried to shrug off her pessimism and just relax. As soon as they had finished their break, she knew they'd get back to her lesson and she'd need all the determination she could muster.

The second session seemed easier. She was geared for it now, frowning in concentration, checking the angle of her knees, the pressure on her ski edges, the placement of her poles. When she pushed herself over the same small rise and flowed evenly down it, stopping in a wide wedge, Graydon applauded. She made a quick step turn, ducked into a formal bow and fell over. So much for pride, she thought.

Graydon explained about the fall line, the imaginary line of gravity that should be taken into consideration in almost everything she did. He created the image of a snowball rolling heedlessly downhill; the path it took was the fall line, the most direct line of gravity. Using that as a base, he showed her the side step, the walking sideways up a hill with her skis perpendicular to the fall line. Elly accomplished that without a tumble.

They practiced endlessly. Skiing back and forth across the clear base of the slope, Elly used all the things Graydon taught her. She watched him covetously from the corner of her eye, not only to see how he received her progress but to watch his method and see if his own style could teach her anything he might have forgotten. By late afternoon, she felt comfortable.

"Ready to go up?" Graydon asked.

"Go up?"

He jabbed a pole toward the mountain. "Up. To the top."

Elly blanched. Step-turning, she came around to face the slope. Less people jammed its whiteness now and some seats on the T-bar went up empty. It still looked high.

"Sure," she croaked.

Graydon bought lift tickets. They climbed to the waiting point, a knoll of packed snow, and watched a few skiers hop onto the bar ahead of them.

"Just grab a hold and jump on," Graydon said. "You've done this before, just without skis. Ready?"

She nodded. They got in line. I've done this before, she chanted, I've done this before.

Even if she didn't remember, her body did and swung easily up onto the narrow bar seat. Clutching both poles in one hand and holding her skis flat, she settled on the seat and watched the knoll fall away behind.

"This is neat!" she called to Graydon. From his own side of the T-bar, he laughed.

"Just wait," he said. "You ain't seen nothing yet."

At the top Graydon cautioned her about jumping off, making sure that her skis were flat and she hit level ground. She would have done fine if she hadn't forgotten about the people coming behind. While she was still straightening her skis, Graydon had to reach over and tow her out of the T-bar's path, barely missing the ski tips of the people jumping off the next seats.

"Don't ever stand there," he said. "Get out of the way of that thing as fast as you can."

"Okay." Her enthusiasm was a little dampened by his gruff order, but she understood it was as much for safety as anything. From now on she'd remember. She wouldn't ever make him tell her again.

They walked along the top of the ridge. Elly took her first look down the slope and became instantly terrified. It was so far!

The people below looked like ants! Even the squiggling, zig zag paths that led from just below their feet seemed to drop away dramatically into tiny, narrow trails.

"What do you think?" Graydon asked beside her. "Pretty exciting?"

Elly had to swallow before she could find the words to speak. "Exciting," she echoed numbly. She tore her eyes from the slope and looked to Graydon. "But it's so far down. Do you really think I can do that already?"

"Sure," he said. "It's easy. Just slide on down, wedge when you want to slow or stop, and straighten out when you want to go faster. We won't do any fancy stuff today. Just basics."

Elly nodded, her throat still too dry to talk. Easy, he said. Basics.

"Come on," Graydon said. "I'll be right with you."

He tipped his skis over the edge of the ridge and teetered down the slope. His skis veeing at a narrow angle, he checked back to watch Elly. His expression called her on.

Elly gulped one last, panicked breath of air, step-turned so she was facing the slope and pushed herself over the edge. Immediately her stomach bottomed out and her eyes widened in terror. The hard white glare of the snow sped up at her, rushing at breakneck speed beneath her skis. She felt paralyzed.

"Wedge!" Graydon yelled. "Wedge! Elly, slow down!"

The words bounded around inside her head but couldn't quite seem to spark a response. Her jaw ached from the unwitting way she was gritting her teeth. Wind whipped her face.

"Elly! Wedge, damn it!" A flurry of dark clothing and flying snow appeared beside her. Graydon. "Wedge! Elly!"

Wedge, she thought; snowplow. Bend your knees. Bring the tips of the skis in. As she repeated Graydon's earlier instructions to herself, she looked down and saw herself doing it. The tips of her skis—the funny little birds—came closer, closer, bumped slightly. She forced the back of her skis out wider. A ridge of snow began to build in front of her ski edges. She slowed.

Graydon cut expertly in front of her and planted himself like a barricade, forcing her to stop or run over him. She brought herself to a halting, unsteady stop, her knees almost cap to cap, her legs bent awkwardly. She jammed her poles into the snow and collapsed against the grips.

"Jesus!" Graydon swore. "What the hell were you trying to do? Kill yourself?"

Elly couldn't talk. She was having enough trouble forcing air down into her lungs. Her throat burned with the effort, and her goggles steamed up until she couldn't even see. With a shaking hand, she pushed them up onto her forehead.

Finally she could hold her head up. Graydon glowered at her, his jaw tight. She shook her head against anything he had in mind to say.

"I...I didn't...I couldn't do anything," she puffed. "It was...so fast...I couldn't...stop."

"Christ," he muttered. "Scare me half to death, why don't you? Are you okay now?"

She nodded, still catching her breath. "I...think...so." She craned her head around to see behind her. "How far...did I...oh."

They were almost a third of the way down the mountain.

"Oh," she said again. "I didn't know I went so far. It was so fast."

"I'll say it was fast. Tucked forward like that, you'll fly. Jesus." He shook his head as if to clear it. "Do you think you can try it a little slower now? Like keep it under fifty miles an hour, maybe?"

"Fifty...?"

"Not really. But I want you to take it slow, do you understand? If you'd fallen the way you were going, you wouldn't have stopped until you landed in the creek in the middle of town. Go slow. Now can you do that?"

Elly pushed herself up straight and nodded. Her head was clearing and her stomach had found its place. She licked her lips.

"Okay," she said. "I'm okay now. I'll go slow."

Graydon looked suspicious, as if he expected her to bolt as soon as he gave the signal. She met his look with wide, blue eyes, waiting and trusting.

"All right," he growled. "Come on."

He flipped his skis around and poled off. Elly followed.

The rest of the way down was slower but infinitely more

instructive for Elly. She matched Graydon's pace, skiing evenly
or wedging to a controlled slow or stop as he did. Once or twice
he stopped her to give her a bit of advice and she would stand
knock-kneed and patient while he talked, then they were off again.
The only problem she had was with turning, her legs still not used
to moving the way that forced her skis on edge, and close to the
bottom she had to stop once to keep from running into a tree. Step-
turning around toward Graydon, she pushed herself on down the
slope and skied modestly to the bottom.

Graydon pulled up beside her as she shoved her goggles up
on her head.

"How was that?" she asked. His expression didn't tell her
anything.

"Better," he grumbled. "At least you stopped when I told you
to. Do you want to make one more run or would you rather start
again tomorrow?" He turned his grudging attention from Elly to
the western sky, already empty of the sun but still azure blue.

"Probably tomorrow," she said, second-guessing him. "Unless
you want to go again?"

He pulled his own goggles off. "No, I think we'll call it a day.
I don't want to have to go chasing you down the mountain side
again today. Can you get your skis off?"

With a little instruction from him, she could. She tried hefting
them up onto her shoulder the way she'd seen him do earlier, but
while she was still struggling with them, he took them and added
them to his own shoulder.

"I can carry them, Graydon," she said. But he had already
started for town.

"Come on. Just do me a favor and don't break your neck on
the way back."

Behind his back, Elly saluted crossly, then shoved her hands
in her pockets and trudged after him.

Back at the apartment, Graydon stowed the skis in the ski
locker outside the door; each apartment had one. Elly went on
inside and collapsed on the couch. Her back ached and her legs
trembled. She felt pulled through a wringer.

At the sound of Graydon stamping his boots outside the door,
Elly pulled herself up and made a project of unbuckling her own

boots. She wasn't sure why exactly Graydon was annoyed with her; she'd thought she'd done fairly well. Just because she got a little stage fright...

"Let me do that," he said when he saw her fumbling with the buckles.

She turned her shoulder to him and kept at it. "No, I can do it."

"Here." Graydon brushed her hands aside and flipped the buckles loose like a pro. "Like this."

He glanced up to make sure she was paying attention and was caught off guard by the shiny-eyed, angry red look on her face.

"What's the matter with you?" he demanded.

"I could do it if you'd let me!" The tears sprang from her eyes and her voice rose in a quivering wail. "You never let me do anything! How can I learn if you don't let me do it?"

"What?" Graydon rocked back on his heels.

"You treat me like a two-year old! You tell me how to do something and if I can't do it right the first time, you don't even let me try. I'm not one of your cadets that you can pound it into my head over and over and over and then expect me to pass a test! You never let me try!" She broke into sobs and buried her face in her hands.

"Christ," Graydon muttered. He wiped at his own tired face with a big hand. "I'm trying to teach you," he said through clenched teeth. "If I let you try to figure everything out for yourself, you'd still be back at the ski shop looking for boots with little birds on them!"

Elly wailed louder.

"Shit." Graydon pushed himself to his feet and began to pace the living room floor. "Elly," he said, "how are you going to learn if you don't do what I say? You've got to know the right way to do things. Skiing isn't something you can fake your way through. It's too dangerous."

"But you don't let me try!" she cried again. "If I don't get it perfect the very first time you treat me like a moron. You don't think I can put my skis on. You don't think I can wedge, you don't think I can carry my skis and you don't think I can take my own boots off! What can I do, Graydon? What is there that's simple enough for a brainless idiot like me to do?" Anger had stemmed her sobs but the tears still ran unchecked down her face. She met Graydon's eyes defiantly.

"That's not it at all," he grumbled. "And you know it."

"I don't know it! You're always mad at me for screwing up something. I was afraid on top of the mountain, but I didn't want to disappoint you, so I went. When I—I froze up, and I couldn't stop, you got mad at me anyway. I'm damned if I do and damned if I don't. I can't please you, Graydon. Everything I do is wrong!" Her chin quivered but she tightened her jaw and refused to look away.

"That's not true," he insisted angrily. "For Christ's sake, Elly, you could have killed yourself up there. Why didn't you tell me you were afraid? I wouldn't have made you go."

"I didn't want you to think I was a failure." Her voice trembled again.

"You're not a failure, damn it! You skied, didn't you?"

"I tried," she wailed. "And you still got mad at me. What did I do wrong? Was I standing wrong on my skis or holding my poles wrong? What did I do?"

"You scared the holy hell out of me, that's what you did!" He raged at her, his face contorted with emotion. "God damn it, Elly, the whole time you were skiing like that, I could just see you lying at the bottom of the mountain with a broken neck."

"So what?" she sniffed. "Would you care?"

Angry strides carried Graydon to her in a flash. He caught her shoulders and shook her roughly.

"Yes, damn it, I'd care. I swore I'd never let you back into my life, that I'd never touch you again except maybe to strangle you with my own hands, but damn it, you're my wife, and goddamnit, yes, I care. Something took you away from me before but now that you're back I don't ever want to lose you again."

Elly stared wide-eyed at her husband, awed by the words she was hearing from him. Even through his anger and frustration she could see the truth in his eyes, the caring and concern. She melted.

"Say that again," she breathed.

Graydon's hands flexed on her shoulders, his fingers digging into her flesh. He pulled her close. "I care. God knows why, but I do." His mouth came down on hers, rough and demanding, and his arms slipped around her in a steel grip. She luxuriated in the force of his revelation and before he released her she was crying again.

"Now what?" he growled, but the sting had gone out of his words.

"I'm just happy," she choked.

He pulled her against his chest and cradled her head on his shoulder. One hand strayed to her face and smoothed the unruly wisps of hair from it. "Women," he muttered. "Are all pregnant women as emotional as you are? I've never seen anyone cry so much over so little in my life."

"I'm sorry," she murmured. "I—"

"No." Graydon stilled her with a finger on her lips. "Don't apologize. I don't ever want you to apologize to me again. You're a capable, responsible human being and you don't need to be sorry about anything. You're not a failure or a disappointment, not to me. Is that clear?"

She nodded, wanting so badly to believe him that her heart ached with it. She burrowed into the warmth of his arms and swore that he would never ever regret this.

Later Elly said something about taking a bath and Graydon agreed that it would probably ease some of her aching muscles to soak in a hot tub. It seemed like the longer she sat, the stiffer she became and by the time she had her bath water running, it was a chore just pulling off her turtleneck. When the tub was mounded high with bubbles she sank gratefully into it and eased back into the hot water. She felt immediately better.

As she soaked, an unknowing smile curved her lips. She repeated Graydon's words over and over to herself so she wouldn't forget, so she wouldn't think it was a dream. He cared—he really cared. The smile broke into a grin. How wonderful it was! A month ago she never would have believed that Graydon could overcome his hatred and learn to care again. She had expected no more than token decency and a quick show to the door once the mysteries were cleared up, but now...now?

Better not to think of it, she cautioned herself. Let it come as it would, but she would do all in her power to ensure that this time her marriage would last.

Cooking odors drifted to her under the bathroom door as she dressed. Graydon—cooking? She pulled on some after-ski stretch pants and a fuzzy sweater, checked her makeup and combed her hair. She wanted to look especially good tonight.

One whiff out the bathroom door told her what Graydon was doing.

"Mmm," she said, "spaghetti?" She rounded the kitchen wall and found him checking the sauce as it simmered.

"You're too early," he scolded. "It won't be ready for fifteen more minutes."

Elly inspected his preparations. The sauce, with meatballs, bubbled merrily, the noodles were cooking and garlic bread lay ready in the oven for quick grilling. Green beans simmered in a fragrant butter sauce.

"Graydon, you didn't tell me you could cook," she said. Everything smelled so delicious that it teased her stomach to growling.

"You didn't ask. I'll have you know that I used to cook dinner at least once a month; maybe more if you were lucky. Anyway, as much as you were groaning over your aches and pains, I figured we'd be eating at midnight if I let you do it. You're moving slow, Elly; that's the first sign of age."

She smiled at his teasing. "If I am, it's only because of you," she said. "You'd probably like to teach me racquetball and tennis and football, too, and then I'd really be groaning."

"Football, no, but racquetball and tennis...?"

Elly stuck her tongue out at him, jumped out of the way of his swiping hand and ran for the dining room.

"Come here," he growled.

"I have to set the table." She pretended innocence and wiped at the table with a flirty hand.

"Forget the damn table. Come here."

She went. He curled one arm around her and pulled her close to his side. Bending his head, he met her upturned face and kissed her. She purred. "Maybe," Graydon murmured, "we won't eat until midnight after all."

Chapter Eleven

Telluride, for Elly, became synonymous with Eden. It was their own private haven and, secluded within its mountain walls, they lived a playful, adventurous week, laughing and loving, teasing and skiing. Elly learned to wedge and to eat mahi mahi at the Silver Jack and that light fingernails tracing a path up Graydon's inner thigh drove him out of his mind. She learned to do kick turns and a herringbone climb and found out after watching movies all night that Graydon was madly in love with Susan Hayward. Everything she did was a discovery and she reveled in it. She felt like she was coming alive.

Graydon, too, seemed more childlike and enthusiastic. He not only watched Elly's antics with a new pleasure but joined in now at the smallest invitation. When Elly tossed a snowball at Graydon's unwary back, he retaliated in kind, dumping big handfuls of snow on Elly's head or wrestling her gently into a snow bank. When they walked through town to the base of the waterfall that came tumbling off the Dallas Divide, Graydon showed Elly how to skip rocks and they broke icicles off the frozen edges of the fall and sucked on them like candy. It was more fun than either of them could remember having. Elly wanted it to never end.

And they talked. Elly asked endless questions and Graydon answered all of them that he could. She decided that if she'd had this sort of environment to come home to directly after her accident, she would have had hardly any problems adjusting at all, but there was no ingratitude in her thoughts. Just relief.

"Happy?" Graydon asked on their sixth night when they cuddled on the couch in front of the TV.

"Mm, yes," she purred. "This week has been perfect. Do you know that this is the first time since my accident that I've been able to forget about who I was or what I was supposed to be like and just be myself? It's a warm, wonderful feeling, like being set free. I'm so happy."

"Good." Graydon squeezed her playfully. "And do you know that I've never seen you so confident and out-going? I wonder if that's a cause or an effect? Or maybe it's like the chicken and the egg."

"I don't know," she mused. "I certainly didn't feel confident at my parents' house, but I didn't feel happy there, either."

"Forget about that. That's past."

"No," she shook her head. "I can't forget about it. Someday I'll go back. I wish my dad could see me now, I wish I could show him how happy I am being myself. But maybe he still wouldn't like me."

"It's not that he doesn't like you," Graydon insisted.

"Oh, I know; he just doesn't understand me. He's not pleased with me, though, and I gather a lot of it's because I married you." She tilted her head up to look at him. "He called you a sinner. Do you know why?"

Graydon shrugged. "I don't think he would have approved of any man you picked unless he was a local yokel who planned to live and die in Carrizozo and didn't mind living right next door so you could run over and bring your dad a beer at night and help your mom with the dishes. He's so set in his ways he just couldn't imagine your having a life of your own."

"What were you like then?"

"I don't know. I don't think I was much different than I am now. Maybe a little more hot-headed, a little more intense."

Elly studied him as he talked, debating whether or not to say what was in her mind. She felt honor-bound, in view of their new candor. "You're very like him, you know."

Graydon frowned and she was afraid she had carried honesty too far. "I know," he said.

"You do?"

"Yes, just since we were there. I don't think I would have seen it before, but that night that he started chewing on you and you fell apart in bed, I realized it. Talk about a shock! I hate your father, and thinking that I'm like him is like a bucket of cold water in the face. I'd never seen it before, and that night I made up my mind that I wouldn't see it again—I made up my mind that I would change."

Elly was quiet. She felt closer to Graydon for hearing his unlikely confession, but a creeping discomfort came on her, too.

"I don't want you to change," she said. "I married you; I must have fallen in love with you like that. You shouldn't have to change."

With her cheek pressed against his shoulder, she could feel him shaking his head. "Everybody can use a little improvement. I just never realized how much I could use until I looked at myself from your viewpoint. I'm not saying it'll happen overnight; I wasn't exactly Prince Charming that first day skiing, but I'll change. I don't want to grow old as a narrow-minded, pig-headed fool."

"I wonder," she breathed, "if I married you because of that—because you're like him. I never could please him. Maybe I thought I could please you and that would make up for it."

Graydon didn't think so. "Like him or not, I hated him and did my best to get you away from him. Sometimes you'd come back from spending a weekend with them and just be miserable from all his nit-picking and I'd get so mad I'd want to run up there and punch him. I used to beg you not to go. Hell, I had to ask you to marry me twice before you said yes."

Elly looked up, smiling. "Really? Twice? Why?"

"I don't know. You were afraid, I guess. You were so quiet and shy and I was big and noisy and your parents hated my guts and ... well, those are pretty good reasons, I'd say."

She touched a hand to his cheek, wondering how she could have said no to him. "Why did you marry me? What did you like about me?"

"Oh, lots of things. You weren't flirty or loose and you didn't carry on with a lot of guys. You were the opposite of what I was used to."

"What were you used to?"

He cleared his throat. "Just different types. It doesn't matter."

"But those were all characteristics I didn't have. What about things I did?"

"Well," he said thoughtfully, "let's see. You were smart. I never did care for airheads. And you were interested in me, in everything I did. You supported me. I liked that. And you were a virgin."

Elly blushed. "How awful."

"Awful? What's awful about marrying a virgin?" he demanded.

"Nothing's awful about marrying one. It's just awful being one." She remembered that horrible panic she'd felt that first night in Carrizozo and then again, worse, here in Telluride. It was bad enough going through the trauma of deflowering once in her life, but twice was more than anyone should have to endure. Just thinking about it made her face flush hot. "I must have been terrified on our wedding night," she thought out loud.

"You were." He chuckled. "We went out with Bud and Sue and ate Chinese food and celebrated all evening and when I took you to the motel I'd rented you were like a block of wood. You locked yourself in the bathroom and wouldn't come out until I pounded on the door."

"You pounded on the door?" she gasped. "Oh my God, you must have scared the hell out of me doing that."

"Probably. But you'd been in there almost an hour and I wasn't in the mood to play hide-and-seek. By that time, I didn't care if you were scared or not."

Elly tried to imagine it; herself younger, frightened, unsure and Graydon, the huge, demanding new husband insisting on his rights.

"How—how was it?" she whispered. "Did I cry?"

Graydon kissed the top of her head. "Yes. I tried not to hurt you but you wouldn't relax. I held you and talked to you and did everything I could to make it right, but it still hurt. When you started crying I felt like the world's biggest bastard."

"How did I feel?"

"I don't know; you wouldn't tell me. You just hugged me around the neck until I thought you'd strangle me and cried and said you were sorry. It wasn't a real pleasant night."

"And later?" she prompted.

"Later?"

"We did make love again sometime, didn't we?"

"Oh. Yeah. The next night, back in my quarters on the base. Matter of fact, I wanted to try again the next morning but you wouldn't in daylight. You didn't want me to see you." Elly blushed again at her own innocence. "That's why you surprised me the first night here by wanting to leave the light on. Before you never would do that."

"But I'm different now," she said contentedly.

"Yes," he agreed, "you are."

"And better?" Her voice was hopeful.

Graydon laughed. "Yes, better. I think talking about it like this, we're both better. And it'll just keep on getting better all the time."

Their last day on the slopes wasn't much fun. Graydon took a fall that, to Elly, looked horrible and she almost skied herself into a tree while trying to turn around and get to him. He was all right—his left wrist was tender, but nothing was broken—and he bent one of his poles to an almost forty-five degree angle. That made him mad.

"Can it be fixed?" she asked when he expressed more annoyance over the pole than his wrist.

"No. It wouldn't be the same. Once this aluminum bends it just doesn't have the strength it should. Damn. I'll have to buy a new one."

It being early still, they skied carefully on down, took off their skis and hiked to the ski shop. The salesman remembered them from the week before and was most anxious to sell Graydon new poles. His ingratiating manner only irritated Graydon more; Elly was glad when they hiked back to the T-bar.

Before going up, Graydon suggested a cup of coffee and Elly voted yes. She stuck the skis in the snow and waited while

Graydon went to the concession. She hoped a hot cup of coffee would warm his disposition.

Standing not far from the lift, Elly was close to the path skiers took to the T-bar and several passed by her. She was caught off guard, though, by two suntanned young men that sauntered by, checked her over appreciatively and issued low wolf whistles in her direction. She blushed violently and looked the other way.

There was Graydon. Cups steaming in both hands, the hot vapor might just as well have been coming from his nostrils. His black brows gathered like storm clouds over his eyes and his jaw was noticeably tight. He approached Elly, pushed the cups at her and continued on after the two men.

"Graydon," Elly cried. "Where are you going? What are you doing?" She ran after him.

"I'm going to tell those punks to watch who the hell they're making passes at," he ground out.

"Graydon, no, wait. It's no big deal." She dropped the cups in the snow and grabbed his arm, slowing him down by making him drag her weight. "They just whistled. It wasn't a real pass. They didn't even stop."

"They're going to learn not to whistle at other men's wives—especially mine. Now let go."

"No! Graydon stop and listen to me. This is ridiculous."

He stopped but he didn't listen. "I don't want other men looking at you like a cheap pick-up," he flared. "You're my wife."

"I know," she soothed. "And I'm right here with you. I'm not going anywhere. I don't care what any other man does, I don't care if they whistle at me or talk to me or what—I'm with you. And I'll stay with you. I love you, Graydon. You don't have to worry about anyone else. Can't you understand that?"

He fumed still, but his eyes settled on her for the first time. "I don't like it."

Knowing she was swaying him, she set her own modesty aside and went for a complete dissolution of his anger. She slipped her arms around his neck and pressed close to him. Even with all their ski clothes on, Graydon wouldn't be able to mistake her intent. She pulled his head down and met his mouth boldly, her hips pressed against his in an unashamed way. She didn't stop until she felt an answering response from him and his own arms had tightened around her.

He quirked an eyebrow at her.

"Would you rather go back to our room and I'll show you how much I care?" she asked huskily.

"I know you care," he said, still a little sullen. But he didn't release her.

"But I want you to know how much. I want you to know that it doesn't matter how many men look at me. I'm yours. Please understand, Graydon. I don't want anyone but you."

His jaw slackened a bit and he put a gloved hand to her cheek. "You don't have to bribe me."

"I'm not bribing you. I'm here if you want me. It's up to you." She met his eyes evenly, the wide round blue reaching out to the black.

One corner of Graydon's mouth quivered, wanting to curve upward against his wishes. "You are a pretty little offering," he murmured. "But I thought you wanted to ski."

"I'll do anything you want," she breathed.

He leaned down and brushed his lips tantalizingly across her mouth. "We'll ski. For now. Later, though, I want to take you to bed and make love to you with every single light in the place blazing. We'll forget all about other people."

"What other people?" she teased happily.

Elly cried the day they left. She had felt it coming on as they packed the car, her eyes straying constantly to the snowy peaks all around. It was like leaving paradise. Her stomach balled and twisted, although she wasn't sick, and in general her condition was miserable. When they pulled out of their parking place and drove out of town, Elly looked back at the scattered trail of snow that had fallen off the car and she cried.

The drive across the state was interesting but Elly found she was no longer starving for sights and sounds and possible memories like before. She sat as close to Graydon as she could and drew more surcease from his presence that she had from her childlike gawking earlier. The map stayed folded in the glove box. Occasionally she thumbed through her Indian book, but even that took a back seat to Graydon. Nothing was better than talking to him, laughing with him, loving him.

"Well, we'll be back to the old grind soon," he said when they could see the back of Pike's Peak in the distance.

"Yes," Elly said. Nothing could ever equal the week in Telluride. "When can we go skiing again?"

"My God, we just had eight days of it and we're still an hour from home. Don't you think you're being a little pushy?" The warmth in his voice took the sting out of his reprimand.

"But it was fun," Elly said quietly.

"I know," Graydon laughed. "Don't worry, we'll go again soon."

It wouldn't be soon enough. Alone with Graydon where no one knew her, she had been isolated from her jigsaw past—interrupted only occasionally by her pregnancy. But here, back in Colorado Springs, it wouldn't be like that. Here there were people to bluff, facades to keep up, dreams to remember. It would be far from idyllic. Still, she sighed, glancing up at Graydon, she had his love and support; that was the important thing. The rest was a string of mountains they would need to climb. Thank God they'd be climbing together.

It was barely sunset when they pulled into the driveway. The house looked shuttered with its drawn drapes and unlit windows. Elly looked for Chester but the orange cat was nowhere around.

"Boy, it'll be nice to get out of the car," Graydon said. "This drive is the only thing I hate. Maybe next time we'll fly."

He unlocked the front door for Elly and then went back for their luggage. Elly busied herself riffling through the mail and noting how many cans of cat food were gone from the pyramid she'd left. Good; at least Chester had eaten well.

"We have any food in the house?" Graydon called on his last trip out to the car. "I'm starving."

Elly checked the refrigerator. There wasn't much. Eggs, a half brick of cheese, a quart of milk. The neighbor lady must have brought it for Chester; it was fresh and more that half full. She also found some salami, still vacuum-sealed and edible.

"How about an omelet?" she asked.

"Sounds great. Make it a big one."

She did.

"Don't expect breakfast tomorrow before I go to the store," she told him as they ate. "Now there's absolutely nothing left to eat. It's a good thing tomorrow's Sunday so I'll have a chance to get the house back to normal."

Graydon nodded, devouring his omelet with his usual appetite. "And I'll have a chance to rest up from vacation before I have to go back to work. Sometimes I think vacations are more work than work is."

"Getting old," Elly clucked.

He grinned. "No. I just have a young wife that needs to be kept happy."

"That sounds like the kind of excuse you'd give Don Mayfield for losing at cards. Which reminds me, should we be inviting them over soon? It's our turn next, I guess."

Graydon shook his head. "No, let it go. What with Christmas coming up and all, we'll wait til things settle down again. Unless you want to."

"No," she said, "not really. God, I hadn't even thought of Christmas. Who do we usually buy for?"

"Your family and us."

"That's all? Not your sisters or any friends?"

He shrugged. "I usually get Mayfield a bottle of something, but that's about it. Just send cards to my sisters. We haven't exchanged gifts for years."

"All right," she said. That, at least, would give her something to do during the coming days. She could buy Christmas cards and decorate the house. Maybe Colorado Springs wasn't the paradise Telluride was, but it would be okay. She rather liked the idea of getting ready for Christmas now that she had Graydon to share it with.

Chester came to the back door later and scratched and Elly greeted him warmly. He mewed at her and sunk his claws into her shoulder when she picked him up, but then his kneading relaxed and he purred gratefully. She carried him around with her until she was ready to shower, then let him tag along behind on his own.

"Graydon?" she called when she went to her room for her things. "Where did you put my suitcase? I need some things out of it."

Instead of calling an answer to her like she expected, he sauntered down the hall and leaned against the door frame.

"It's in your room," he said finally.

"Where?" She turned and swept the room with her eyes. "I don't see it."

"That's because you're looking in the wrong room," he said. "Your room is across the hall—with my room."

Understanding dawned on her. She stepped to the door and peered across the hall. Both suitcases were on the king-sized bed.

"Oh," she said.

His eyes darkened thoughtfully. "We are married," he said, a trifle put out by her forgetfulness. "Married people usually sleep in the same bedroom, you know."

"Yes, I know." She sidled closer and went up on her tip toes to kiss him. "I just...hadn't really thought about it. Don't be mad." She burrowed into his arms.

"Do you want to stay in this room?" he asked.

"No. But you hadn't invited me into yours. You already told me I was being pushy once today. I don't want you to really think I'm pushy." She pressed against him the whole time she was talking and nibbled delicately on his neck. His arm went around her.

"God, but you're a schemer," he said, but his voice was pleased. "I suppose any time I'm mad at you from now on you're going to twine yourself around me like this and weasel out of the argument."

"If you don't want me to..." She tried to pull out of his grasp, but Graydon wouldn't allow it. She didn't struggle long.

"Oh, no," he said. "You're going to have to learn to finish what you start. I let you off the hook yesterday in Telluride but I'm not going to be so lenient anymore. From now on, don't tease me unless you're ready to deliver."

He bent his head to distract her with a kiss, then swung her up into his arms. A muffled cry escaped her but she was no match for Graydon's strength. He carried her effortlessly into the master bedroom.

"Graydon," she said when she could talk again, "I need to

shower. Let me do that first."

"No."

"But Graydon, I'm dirty."

"You're fine just the way you are." He set her down and with one hand still riding on her waist, bent to lift the suitcases off the bed.

She bolted. Knowing she might well be enraging him beyond forgiveness, she sprinted down the hall to the bathroom and locked herself in. In seconds he was there, pounding on the door.

"Elly! Open this door!"

"No, Graydon, really, just let me shower so I'll be clean, then I promise..."

"Open the door! Elly, I'm warning you."

"It'll just take a minute. Listen, I've already got the water on." She raced to the tub and cranked on both hot and cold full blast. "Can you hear it, Graydon? Just a real quick one, I promise. Graydon?"

The pounding had stopped. Graydon didn't answer. Elly listened at the door, half expecting to be blasted away by his outraged voice. There was nothing.

"Graydon?" she called softly. No answer. Surprised that he would give up so quickly, she decided nevertheless to shower and get out of the bathroom, just in case he was really angry and she'd have to appease him. Living with him, she decided, was like walking on eggshells; unpredictable, never boring and really sort of fun.

She pulled her clothes off and left them in a pile on the floor. The water, surprisingly, was almost just right and she adjusted it slightly and climbed in the tub. In seconds she was soaked and lathering.

A noise at the door caught her attention. "Graydon? I'm almost done. I'll be out in just a minute." Another noise. "Graydon? Can you hear me?" Silence.

Better hurry, she told herself. He's getting restless. She turned her attention to her washing, concentrating on how quickly she could soap away the grime of the long drive. It was amazing how grungy she could feel after just sitting in a car all day.

A movement outside the frosted glass doors caught her eye.

She turned toward it just in time to watch the door slide back on its track and Graydon, standing naked and dark, towering over her.

"What are you doing?" she cried as he lifted one leg inside the tub.

"The same thing you are—taking a shower." His voice was threatening, though, and as he advanced Elly shrank back against the far wall of the enclosure. His eyes gleamed at her.

"Graydon, don't be mad. I only wanted to be clean." She wedged herself into a corner and then found her way blocked by his massive body. He put his arms out on either side, penning her in.

"And I said I didn't care," he growled. His face had the characteristic ferociousness she'd seen before when he was crossed. "I told you you wouldn't get off the hook so easily this time and I meant it. And I don't particularly like having to dismantle a door knob to get into my own bathroom, either."

"Dismantle a—? You took the doorknob off the door?" She almost choked. The image of Graydon tearing the door apart was funny, but she really shouldn't laugh—not really.

"What's so funny?" he roared.

"You took the doorknob off the door." She could hardy talk for laughing and Graydon's huge bulk towering over her couldn't effect its normal quieting influence on her. "With what?"

"With a screwdriver, what else?"

Elly realized she shouldn't, but she let herself collapse into giggles.

He stood glowering down at her, completely unmoved. Or almost. Elly tried to catch her breath, wiped the smirk off her face and met Graydon's eyes, then was off into hysterics again. Graydon chuckled. "You're insane, do you know that?" he insisted.

"*I* am?" she said breathlessly. "I'm not the one taking doorknobs off doors." It was impossible for her to keep from laughing.

He brought his arms in behind her and drew her out of her corner. "No, you're the one having hysterics in the bathtub," he said.

She came easily into his arms, quieted by his touch the way she couldn't have been by his frown. He pulled her into the still streaming water and kissed her, bending her head back with his demand. She answered readily.

"I love you, Graydon," she sighed against his neck.

"Crazy woman," he muttered, tightening his arms around her. "I love you, too."

"Say it again."

He held her face in his hands and stared deeply into her lake blue eyes. "I love you, Elly. I never thought the day would come when I would say that to you again, but I do. I do love you."

They sealed their vows in the veil of cascading water.

She slept nestled in the crook of Graydon's arm. She was in Telluride again, riding up the T-bar, looking at the scenery. Graydon sat behind her. She looked back at the next T, saw him and waved. He didn't wave back.

The T-bar extended up and over the hill instead of doubling back down as it should have. Elly could see it continuing on like a giant amusement ride, the empty seats swinging carelessly along. Her own seat approached the top of the mountain. She made ready to jump off.

It was farther than she remembered to the ground. Falling in slow motion, feet first, she looked down and realized she didn't have her skis on. She fell weightlessly down, now turning, now rolling onto her back in the snow as easily as rolling on a feather bed mattress. She was content to wait there for Graydon.

His seat approached. From her place on the ground she could see the bottom of the T-bar and Graydon's heavy booted feet dangling down. His hand flexed on the side bar. He was jumping.

Elly's lazy smile turned to shock, then abject fear. As Graydon's body pitched slowly forward off the T-bar, she could see that it wasn't Graydon now—it was the headless man. His body rolled off the seat and arced toward her, the empty shoulders spinning foremost, the gaping hole always toward her.

Oh God, she thought, not again, please, not again, not again.

"Elly? Elly! Wake up!"

"Please," she begged, "please, not again!"

"Elly! It's a dream! Wake up!"

Graydon shook her to sensibility. Her eyes snapped open and searched fearfully for the shape of his head in the darkness. It was there, just above her, leaning over her in concern.

"The light," she breathed. "Please."

Graydon clicked it on. The room pooled with light, forcing shadows back into the corners. Elly assured herself that she was awake, that Graydon was real and with her, then collapsed weakly back in to her pillow.

"Oh, God," she swallowed. A shudder of residual fear shook her.

"Him again?" Graydon asked. He bent over her on one elbow, his other arm comfortingly around her waist.

She nodded. "On the T-bar at Telluride. I jumped and landed in the snow and he—he was coming down on top of me." Another chill spasmed up her back. "I wish I could stop dreaming about him. It's always so awful."

Graydon pulled her into the hollow of his shoulder. "You probably will. In time it'll probably fade. Just relax. Everything's okay now."

Elly didn't say anything. She didn't think everything was okay. She hated dreaming about the headless man and waking up frightened and she didn't think it would fade. If anything, the dreams were becoming more frequent. She dreaded the thought of trying to sleep again.

"Do you want me to leave the light on?" Graydon asked.

"For a little while, yes. Just until I can breathe normally."

"It can stay on all night if you want."

She started to protest but felt too weak to argue. "I feel so stupid. Twenty-four years old and afraid of the dark. I can't always sleep with the light on."

"You won't," he said. He kissed her forehead. "They'll fade; just wait. Everything will be fine."

Elly let a small movement of her head substitute for agreement. Everything wouldn't be fine. She was going to have to do something to exorcise the image of the headless man, because she couldn't stand these dreams any more. She would ask Dr. D'Angelo. Her last appointment with him was on Wednesday. She would ask him then.

Chapter Twelve

"Who do you think the headless man is?"

Dr. D'Angelo laid his clipboard down on the desk and leaned back in his chair. His sensitive gray eyes watched Elly fiddle with her wedding ring, twisting it forward and back on her finger. She didn't appear aware that she was doing it at all.

"I don't know...I'm not sure." Her voice sounded lame even to her own ears.

He nodded as if she'd said something entirely normal, then shifted in his chair. "Do you think it may be the man who was killed in the accident?"

She fastened her eyes on her ring. "I—I don't know. Maybe. It seems like it, but I just don't know." She looked up. "I don't remember him at all. Graydon thinks that's why I dream of him with no head—because I don't even remember what he looks like. But the dreams are horrible and I don't want to have them. I was hoping you could tell me..."

He frowned in thought. "I'm not a psychiatrist, you know. I'm a surgeon. The kind of eradicating you want to do should probably be handled by a psychiatrist, or even a psychologist. I could refer you to one, if you want."

"No, I don't think I want that." She shook her head slowly. She was afraid to go to a psychiatrist. She didn't want anyone delving into her murky subconscious, dredging up memories and fears best forgotten. She was happy now, with Graydon—for the most part—and she was content to leave the rest of her uncertain past buried. "I just want to stop dreaming about the headless man."

Dr. D'Angelo looked thoughtful. If he was aware of Elly's reason for balking, he didn't presume to pass judgment on it. Instead he leaned his elbows on the desk and spoke softly.

"Do you have any idea what that man—Mr. Wolfford?—looked like? Have you even seen a picture of him?"

"No, nothing." She concentrated on her ring again. "He—he's supposed to have been my lover. I don't remember anything. I had to be told his name."

"Hmm. That may be something you could try then."

Elly didn't understand. "What?"

"His picture. Maybe if you can see him, you'll realize he does have a head and you won't dream like that anymore. Can you get a picture of him somewhere?"

Elly hadn't thought of that. She'd had very little curiosity about Adam; all her thoughts had been so concentrated on Graydon. It was an idea, though—a very good one.

"I don't know. I think I might be able to."

Dr. D'Angelo looked cautious. "Now, I'm not a counselor," he said, "and I'm not trained in psychiatry so I'm not dispensing a professional medical opinion right now. There's no guarantee that seeing a picture of Mr. Wolfford will do you any good at all. It's just an idea of mine. I want to make sure you understand that."

"I do," Elly nodded. "And I know your capacity. Don't worry. I'll think about it for a bit first, then decide for myself. It does sound like a good idea, though."

"I wish you'd agree to counseling," the doctor sighed. "I'd feel much better if you'd talk this over with a professional in those matters. I don't feel good about you trying to work it out for yourself. You could do yourself damage."

"I think it'll be all right," she said. "Except for this, I'm really doing well." He didn't look assured. "I'll tell you what," Elly said. "If I get a picture of Adam and it doesn't help, or if I feel like I'm losing ground, I'll call you and let you refer me to a psychiatrist.

How's that?"

That relieved him somewhat. "You've got a deal. As it is, call me if you have any questions or problems at all, I mean even the slightest thing. Will you do that?"

"Promise," Elly said.

"All right." He stood up. "You've been doing so well, I probably shouldn't worry. I just don't want to see your disorganized healing process foul up the works now."

Elly flashed him a smile. "Don't worry. I'm doing my best."

Elly decided not to say anything to Graydon—not yet. She felt sure that even if he agreed to the unorthodox treatment, he wouldn't like it. Right now he was perfectly happy knowing Elly didn't remember a thing about Adam; no doubt he'd like to keep it that way.

Feeling only slightly traitorous, Elly decided. After all, it was for her wellbeing, her emotional and mental peace of mind. Her happiness with Graydon was marred by the recurring dream and only by being free of it could she be totally happy. After a thoughtful drive home from Denver, she pulled out the phone book and looked up the number for the school district administration office.

"School District Eleven."

"May I speak with Linda Dahl, please?" Elly coached her voice to confidence. She wished she knew more what Linda's job was, just in case she was asked.

"Linda Dahl?" the receptionist said. Elly held her breath. "Just a minute. I'll have to transfer you." Elly listened to the click of the line with relief.

"Linda Dahl." The familiar voice came smoothly over the line.

"Linda? This is Elly."

"Elly! How are you? How was the vacation?"

"Great," Elly said truthfully. "We had a fantastic time."

"Good. I'd love to hear all about it."

"That's sort of why I'm calling," Elly said. "I wondered if you wanted to have lunch one day. I, uh, need to ask you a favor."

"A favor? Well, sure, Elly. What is it?"

"Well, I'd rather explain when I see you. Can you meet me?"

"Let me see. Tomorrow I've got a hair appointment and Friday is bank day. What about Monday?" Elly had hoped they could meet sooner. Now that she'd made her decision, she didn't want to wait.

"Monday's fine," she said evenly. "Where should we meet?"

Linda laughed. "Is there anyplace beside Corky's?"

"Corky's?"

"Come on, Elly, you haven't been gone that long. Anyway, the less time I have to spend hiking down there, the more time we have to talk."

"Oh, of course."

"Hey, look, I gotta go. Old Deacon's on the rag today and I'd better not let him catch me yakking. I'll see you at Corky's, okay?"

"Sure. What time?"

"What time? Elly, you don't think they're going to give me a choice of lunch hours do you? It'll be twelve sharp til the day I die."

"Oh, yeah. I forgot. Okay, I'll see you then."

"Okay. I'm dying to know what the favor is that you want. Oh well. See you Monday."

If not for Graydon, Elly was sure the time until Monday would have dragged by unmercifully. As it was, his attentiveness and blossoming warmth bolstered her and drove all the anxieties away. She found delight in cooking for him, folding his laundry, snuggling beside him in front of the fireplace. She felt heartily domestic and loved it.

"What do you want to do this weekend?" he asked on Friday night. They sat on the floor in the living room, all the lights out but content in the glow from the fire. Outside, early December winds howled around the house.

"I don't care," she said truthfully. "Whatever you want to do." She rubbed her cheek against his shoulder.

Graydon looked down and smiled. "You aren't restless after a boring week at home? I didn't even find any education books strewn all over the floor tonight."

"Huh uh," Elly said. "I'm not bored. As a matter of fact, I wouldn't even care about going back to work except I feel like

I ought to do something constructive. But that's a long way off, anyway. No, I'm fine. Anything you want to do is okay with me."

"Okay," Graydon said. "We probably ought to do some Christmas shopping. December always goes so fast, and we'll need to mail off stuff for your family."

"That's true. I did get Christmas cards yesterday, but I'll need you to help me with them. I don't know who to send them to."

"There's not too many we need to send out. We have a very exclusive circle of friends." He squeezed her shoulders.

Elly looked up at her husband. "You know, before I used to think it was sad that we lived in Colorado away from both our families, but it doesn't bother me now."

"No? Why not?"

She shrugged. "Because we're a family. I'm so happy being with you, I don't need anyone else. I still wish we could be closer to our families—me and my dad, especially—but you and your sisters, too. I guess I feel so good about being here with you that I'd like everyone to feel it. Does that make any sense?"

"I guess," he chuckled. "You sure do go around in circles. Maybe that's why you used to be so quiet; you start out to say one thing and by the time you're done, you're thinking something else."

"Did you like me better quiet?" she asked.

"Don't be silly," he said.

"Then tell me."

"Tell you what? I like you better talking in circles?"

"Yes." She smiled up at him.

"God, you're demanding."

"Tell me."

Graydon pulled her onto his lap and kissed her. "I love you, Elly, just exactly the way you are."

She snuggled against his chest. "I love to hear you say that. I love being with you. I don't want it to ever change."

"Don't worry," he said. "It won't."

The image of the headless man flashed across Elly's mind like an involuntary eyeblink. She shivered.

The stores were crowded. They had to park at an outlying

corner of the parking lot and walk to the shopping center, and once there they jostled among the other shoppers to look at merchandise.

"What a madhouse," Graydon said.

"It looks like everyone else had the same idea we did," Elly agreed.

"Yeah." Graydon glanced around disgustedly. "This is the only part of Christmas I hate."

They managed to get most of their shopping done. Elly found a beautiful crystal wine set for her parents and Graydon agreed that it would be a nice surprise for them. They bought a wool shirt for Bryan and Elly picked out a delicate pearl necklace for Dana.

"Do you like Dana?" she asked Graydon.

"She's nice; probably the best thing that ever happened to your brother. She's a little on the dumb side, though."

Elly insisted on buying something for Graydon's sisters. She found a beautifully etched teak jewelry box and insisted on buying it when Graydon said his older sister, Theresa would like something like that.

"They don't send us anything," he said to Elly's generosity.

"I don't care. It's Christmas, Graydon. Christmas is for giving and not worrying about getting. Now what about your other sister—what's her name?"

"Patricia. She's not as conventional as Theresa. She likes weird stuff."

"Like what? Help me, Graydon. If you don't, I'll buy what I like and she may not like it. Help me."

Graydon finally let Elly cajole him into offering suggestions. When he pointed out a unique, hand worked silver ring with black enamel in the depths of its design, Elly promptly bought it.

"Now that wasn't so hard, was it?" she asked.

"You're crazy," Graydon insisted.

She kissed him. "Flattery will get you nowhere. It's Christmas, Graydon. Don't be a scrooge."

"All right. What do you want?"

"I don't know." And she honestly didn't. "Surprise me. Anything you get me will be okay."

"You always were hard to please," he laughed. "All right, if it's surprises you want, surprises you'll get. Come on, let's get out of this place and go home. I'm tired of rubbing shoulders with all these people."

They spent the rest of the weekend watching football, wrapping gifts for the mail and addressing Christmas cards. Elly liked having Graydon sit beside her as she wrote cheery messages.

"When can we get our Christmas tree?" she asked. "And do we have a lot of decorations?"

"I'll get a permit this week and we can go cut one next Saturday."

"Cut one?" she asked happily. "We don't buy one?"

"Not usually. Do you want to?"

"Oh, no," she said. "I'd love to go cut our own. That'll be fun. What about decorations?"

"We have tons, don't worry. Our first year here we got a huge tree and had to buy boxes of bulbs for it, and we've never had a tree that big since."

"Good. I can't wait. I think I love Christmas."

Graydon chuckled. "You do. You always get excited over it. I don't see why this year should be any different."

That evening while Elly cooked dinner, she wracked her brain trying to think of what to get for Graydon. She loved him so much and she wanted to get him a very special present. No ideas came, though. She decided she'd spend the entire day tomorrow in town and look. She even considered calling off her lunch date with Linda. She'd had no bad dreams lately and she was so happy with Graydon. Maybe everything would be okay from now on.

That night the headless man appeared in the bedroom doorway of Elly's dream. She cowered in her bed, knowing she was dreaming but unable to wake up. He walked toward her, one hand outstretched. The sound of his footfalls on the carpet came like muffled thuds, and each one brought him closer, closer.

Wake up, she told herself, *wake up, please wake up*.

He rounded the corner of the bed. The hole between his shoulders gleamed like a black star. His hand, reaching for her, was drifting closer. He lifted each leg in a frightening, zombie-like movement, and each foot fell like a dead man's. He was beside the bed now, reaching for her, reaching for the sheet. His hand brushed her cheek.

Elly startled awake. The area beside her bed was empty but her eyes darted nervously around the dark room. Her hands clutched the sheet desperately with wet palms and her heartbeat sounded like a jackhammer. Thank God she hadn't screamed; Graydon slept blissfully beside her. She brushed the damp hair off her forehead with a trembling hand and inched closer to the comforting form of her husband. She was a big girl, she told herself sternly; she could go back to sleep without the light on.

But tomorrow she would ask Linda to get her a picture of Adam.

Corky's was a little coffee shop on El Paso, just a block away from the administration office. Elly looked it up in the phone book Monday morning and studied the city map Graydon had bought for her over a month ago. Just to be safe, she left early and told herself she'd do some Christmas shopping down town.

The sky was white with thick, formless clouds and while Elly was looking for a parking place, small snowflakes began to spiral down. She parked and walked briskly past the shop windows, noting how the flakes grew in size and number, and ducked into the door of Corky's. It was only eleven-thirty; she would get a booth by the window and watch the snow fall over a cup of hot tea.

At 12:05 Linda burst through the belled door and shook her umbrella out on the linoleum. She found Elly and lifted her chin in greeting, then pulled her umbrella closed and stood it by the door. Shrugging out of her coat, she stepped over to Elly's red vinyl booth and plopped down.

"Damn snow! Hi, how are you? You been here long?" She fluffed her short hair with her hands and droplets of water fell out.

"No," Elly lied. "Just a couple of minutes. How are you?"

"Oh, terrible. You know how Mondays are. I wish I could be a lady of leisure like you and stay home or just putt around town. God, I'm starving."

The waitress came over and took their orders and Linda collapsed back in her seat. She eyed Elly expectantly.

"Well? What's new? You sounded like you had a lot to tell me on the phone."

Elly found herself amazed by the energy of her friend. Linda moved and talked with so much nervous energy that Elly knew she'd go stir-crazy if she didn't work. Linda was not one to sit calmly or accept life passively. For a moment, Elly envied her spunk.

"Well, come on, give," Linda prodded. "Tell me."

"Everything's great," Elly said with a smile. "We had so much fun skiing. Graydon taught me how and bought me a whole set of skis and boots. It was a ball."

"He taught you to ski? I thought you said he was too much of a perfectionist. You said he'd never be able to teach you without blowing his top."

Elly blushed a little at Linda's correctness.

"Well, we did sort of have it out, but after that he was fine. He really is a good teacher if he just remembers I'm his wife and not one of his students."

"Is that so?" Linda looked skeptical. "The old boy must be mellowing out. I can remember when you got scared just talking about him teaching you to ski. How'd you ever get your nerve up?"

"Oh, it wasn't hard," Elly said truthfully. "I just told him I didn't want to just watch. Now I wonder why I never asked him before. It's so much fun."

"Huh." Linda eyed her friend curiously. "You know, Elly, if I didn't know you so well, I'd swear you're acting different."

"Different? How?"

"I don't know exactly. You're happier than hell, I can see that, and getting fat and sassy. Maybe that's it. Maybe it's just being pregnant. You don't act so scared anymore. I'm glad. I hated to see you cow-tow to Graydon all the time. No offense, but he can be a real son of a bitch sometimes."

Don't I know, Elly thought. "We've both changed. I think maybe everything that happened sort of shook things up and we just started over from scratch. Graydon's really sweet now, and I don't make him as mad as I used to. We're a lot better."

Linda was shaking her head. "You're amazing. You run off

and leave the guy, go back to him when your boyfriend gets killed and now everything's all hunky-dory. How do you do it?"

"I don't know. It's not as easy as it sounds, let me tell you. But what about you? And Greg? Was that his name?"

"Yeah, Greg." Linda sighed and supported her head with one hand. "He's such a doll. He spent a weekend with me, then—whoosh!—he's off to God-knows-where. Sure wish I could get him to settle down. I'd wash his socks any day."

"Why don't you tell him?" Elly asked. "Maybe he doesn't know you care."

"Oh, God," Linda groaned. "I'd never do that. He'd probably never take a flight less than a hundred miles from here. Pilots don't go in for that kind of scene."

"Why not? Pilots are regular men. Some of them have to want to settle down with a woman who loves them."

"Who are you, Pollyanna? Jeez, you get chummy with your husband, start showing off that stomach of yours and you think the whole world's a love story. Give me a break, Elly."

Before Elly could argue, the waitress came and set hamburgers down in front of them. Linda grabbed the catsup and doused hers with it.

"So what's this favor that you want? I've been dying of curiosity."

"Oh." Elly pulled the onions off her hamburger and added a little salt. "It's not a big deal, but—do you think you can get me a picture of Adam?"

Linda dropped her knife with a clatter. "A picture of—? Hey, what's all this romantic shit you're handing me, and now you want a picture of Adam? What gives? I thought you were happy as a clam with old Graydon."

"I am, really," Elly said quickly. "It's not what you think. You see, I have these awful dreams, nightmares really, about Adam, but I don't remember what he looks like—"

"Elly," Linda scolded. "This is your old friend, remember? Don't hand me a line like that. I won't tell if you want to keep a few private fantasies. It's okay."

"No, really," Elly insisted. "It's true. I told you how I don't remember some things since the accident. For some reason I've blocked out Adam's face from my memory and I have these horrible dreams. I dream of him with no head. It's awful."

Linda didn't look convinced. "I think the accident did more than block your memory; I think it scrambled your brains."

"Linda, I swear it's true. I love Graydon, I'm perfectly happy with him. The only thing that bothers me is this dreaming and my doctor suggested—"

"Your doctor? You told your doctor?"

"Sure. Why?"

"My God, you're candid. Weren't you afraid he'd tell Graydon?"

"Graydon knows about the dreams. He has to; I wake up screaming from them. Really, Linda, if I see a picture of him and remember what he looked like, I think I'll stop dreaming about him. That's all I want."

Linda sighed heavily and shook her head. "I don't know why, but I believe you. Sure, I'll get you a picture. The employment ID shot isn't the greatest, but it'll do, I guess. It just won't show those adorable dimples."

"Dimples?" Elly asked.

"Oh, save it," Linda said. "I'll get you a picture, don't worry. Now, tell me about Telluride. See any neat-looking guys there?"

Driving toward home, Elly felt much better. Linda had agreed to put Adam's picture in the mail to her that afternoon, as soon as she could sneak it out of the employee files. Elly'd have it tomorrow, or Wednesday at the latest. Then, no more dreams. It was like a weight being lifted from her. She felt so good she stopped at the shopping center to look for a present for Graydon and didn't even mind the crowds.

Choosing her gift wasn't so easy. She spent an hour in a sporting goods store looking at skis and boots, jackets and snowmobile suits. Nothing was special enough. She stopped at a department store and browsed through the hardware section. He had lots of tools for his shop; that wouldn't be any big deal. She looked at clothes, jewelry and cologne. Nothing seemed right. At three-thirty she gave up for the day and went home. Tomorrow, she told herself. Tomorrow she'd find something.

"How would you like to go out for dinner tomorrow night?" Graydon asked over his pork chops.

"Out?"

"Yeah, you know, to a restaurant."

"Sure," she agreed. "Are we celebrating something?"

His eyes turned a shade darker. "No. We're just going out. Is that any big surprise?"

"No, of course not," she soothed quickly. "It's just that you've never offered before, except on vacation. No, I think that's a great idea, Graydon. Where can we go?"

He looked mildly appeased. "There's a place just down the hill called the Castaways that has excellent food. I thought we'd eat there, do some Christmas shopping and then maybe go to a late show."

Elly looked up in surprise but quickly smoothed the look off her face in response to Graydon's defensive quirk. "That sounds like fun," she said. "But we did all our shopping, didn't we?"

"I don't have anything for you yet," he said.

She blushed. "Oh. And I need to shop for you. How can we do it if we're together?"

"I know where I want to go. I'll just send you off in another direction and we can meet later. How's that for organization?"

"Good idea," she nodded. "Okay, I'll just be ready when you get home?"

"Yeah. We'll make a night of it."

"You've got yourself a deal." She smiled at him across the table and cautioned herself not to show surprise at his unusual invitations in the future. She wasn't sure why, but for some reason he was defensive about it.

The picture didn't come in Tuesday's mail. Since Linda hadn't called to say otherwise, Elly was sure she'd gotten it, but maybe she hadn't had time to sneak it into the mail until late. Elly would be okay for one more night as long as she didn't dream. She prayed that after a night on the town with Graydon, she'd be too tired to dream.

The Castaways was not what Elly expected.

She had thought Graydon would take her to a nice family restaurant or a steak house maybe, but not this. It was a wonderfully dim place, decorated inside like a ship with rugged planking, nets and life rings strung across the walls. Candles flickered in red hurricane lanterns and a piano located somewhere in a smoky corner filtered softly throughout the restaurant. The waiters were men dressed like pirates.

"This is fun," Elly whispered when they were shown to their secluded booth. "Did we used to come here a lot?"

"Not much," Graydon said. "It's always been my favorite place, though. The food is great, but save room for dessert. They have the best cherry cheesecake in town here."

Elly nodded and scanned the menu. Everything sounded good. Why hadn't they come here if Graydon liked it so much?

"Cocktails?" a pirate asked.

Elly passed, a hand laid thoughtlessly on her stomach. Graydon ordered wine.

"What are you going to have?" he asked. "I haven't had lobster for a long time."

The sound of it made Elly's mouth water. "Do I like lobster?"

He laughed. "Yes. Do you want that?"

"I think so. Is that okay?"

"Of course it's okay." He took her menu from her and folded it with his on the table. "You don't have to ask that, Elly. You can have anything you want."

He took her hands and held them across the table, making Elly's blood pump hot. Luckily with the dim candlelight he couldn't see her blushing.

"I want to come here more often," she said boldly.

"You do?"

"Yes. I like it here, and if it's your favorite place, why not? I don't understand why we didn't before."

Graydon seemed to struggle within himself but luckily his moodiness didn't win this time. "You didn't like to go out much before," he said.

"Why not?" She smiled, but her brows knitted in curiosity.

"I don't know; too much trouble, I guess."

Elly wasn't sure why, but she had a feeling Graydon was lying. How could it be too much trouble? She hadn't taken a lot of time for this, just washed and curled her hair and wore a teal blue pantsuit that still stretched around her stomach. That was hardly any trouble at all.

The waiter brought the wine and Graydon ordered for both of them. Elly sipped at her water. She waited until the pirate had gone before she resumed their conversation.

"What movie are we going to see?" she asked.

"I don't know. We'll get a paper at the shopping center and see what's playing. What are you in the mood for?"

Her eyes shone at him. "A love story."

The dinner was excellent, just as Graydon had promised. Elly loved lobster. She was afraid she would pay later for its richness, but that wasn't enough of a deterrent to keep her from eating it all. Her baked potato cooled with hardly a bite of it gone but she was saving room for cheesecake. Thank God her morning sickness had abated somewhat; if not, she'd be miserable tomorrow.

By the time Graydon paid the check and helped her out of her seat, she felt at least fifty pounds heavier. She groaned softly as she slid into the coat Graydon held for her.

"Are you okay?" he asked.

"Fine," she said. "But my stomach thinks it died and went to heaven. I'm so full!"

He grinned at her. "We'll walk it off shopping. You'll be hungry again by the time we get to the show and I'll buy you some popcorn."

"Oooh," Elly moaned.

The shopping center was only half as crowded as before. Snowy Tuesday nights were not normally busy, Graydon explained.

"I want that half of the shopping center," he said, waving a hand. "You can have this half."

Elly noted the stores he left open to her. "Sounds fair. What time should we meet?"

"Eight-thirty. How about right there at the door inside?"

"Okay."

He kissed her. "Don't spend too much."

"Why not? Are we poor?"

"No, but I'm going to spend a bunch on you and I don't get paid for another week."

Elly smiled happily as she walked—or waddled, more like—into her first store. She was so lucky! Graydon was a wonderful man; she couldn't imagine how she had been so lucky as to wind up with him. Don't spend much, he said. As if she'd buy him a tie after he said he was spending a lot on her. She decided she'd get him everything she thought he would like. After all, what else did they have to spend their money on if not each other?

In a clothing store she browsed disinterestedly.

What clothes did he need? She couldn't buy him a new color uniform. She was sure the Air Force would frown on new fall colors. She spied a black turtleneck pinned artfully on a high wall; it reminded her of Graydon, his darkness. She tried to imagine him in it and conjured up an image of a black-garbed pirate, complete with eyepatch and saber. The allusion fit Graydon to a T. She bought the sweater.

She wandered down the mall and glanced into other shops. He didn't need luggage, or shoes. She passed a pet shop and felt compelled to go in. The kittens in the window were so cute. She'd love to have one, but she felt sure she'd have two angry males at home—Graydon and Chester. No sense courting disaster. The thought of Chester and a new cat squalling and running all over the house and Graydon bellowing like a bull after them propelled Elly out of the pet store after only a brief look.

She started by a toy store and stopped carelessly in front of the window. It was too bad she wasn't looking for baby gifts. Her heart wrenched at the realization that next Christmas someone would be buying presents for her baby—but it wouldn't be her. She touched a warm hand to her stomach.

It was a boy; she knew it. A little boy with dimples and a sparkling smile. And he'd like baseball and army men and paper airplanes.

She drifted into the toy store.

Dolls stood in chorus lines near the door, all shapes and sizes. Elly let her eyes trip dreamily over them. A girl? No, it was a boy. She knew it as well as she knew her name. She walked back to the section for boys.

A hobby horse stood motionless in its spring traces. Elly rocked it with a careful hand, imagining the boy on it, crying out in excitement. She shouldn't do this; she shouldn't torment herself. Graydon would never allow her to keep the baby in a million years. He didn't even want one of his own. Better that she forget all about toys.

On the way out, her eye was caught by a model of a fighter plane similar to those she'd seen in Graydon's pictures at home. Only this wasn't a model, at least not a glue-together one. She read the display.

RADIO-CONTROLLED JET FIGHTER

You control it—no wires!

Climb, dive, roll, land! Just like the real thing!

How cute, Elly thought. She wondered if Graydon would think so. He didn't really have any toys, not *real* toys, but this might be kind of fun for him. She checked the price. One thing for sure, this was not a paper airplane.

"Can I help you?" a man asked.

Elly turned to him, her hand on the little plane. "Can you tell me about this? Is it really for kids? It's awfully expensive."

The man smiled sympathetically. "Actually we have more adults buy those than kids. There seems to be no age limit on radio-controlled airplanes. There are even clubs for people who have them and they get together and have meets and races. They're quite a lot of fun."

"Does it do everything it says here?"

"Absolutely. Let me show you the controls." A half hour later Elly walked out with the box under her arm.

God, I hope he likes it, she said to herself. Well, she'd buy him other things, too, but still ... She checked her watch: 8:20. No time to worry about it now. She had to get back down to the other store and meet Graydon.

Her worry over what was in her packages dissolved as she tried to imagine what Graydon had in his. He would have them wrapped, of course, like she did so no one could peek. As she neared the door, she craned her neck to find him. Ah—there he was. But no packages.

"Here," he said as soon as she came up, "let me carry those." His own arms had been conspicuously empty.

"No fair shaking," she said.

"I come from a long line of non-shakers. If you'll open the trunk, I'll put these in there. No point in advertising to any burglars while we're at the show."

Elly did as Graydon asked, still wildly curious about why he had no packages. Finally in the car, she had to ask.

"Didn't you have any luck?"

"Luck? Oh, shopping? No, not really." He acted patently uninterested. "I'll do more later. Why don't you look in the paper there and decide what show you want to see?"

The show was good—a three-hanky tear-jerker that Elly loved. Graydon seemed a little brusque about the way she sniffed on the way home, but when she faced out the side window to keep him from seeing her cry, he took her hand and pulled her over close to him.

"I can't help it," she said with her chin quivering. "Sad movies just affect me like that."

"I know." He held her hand. "I just don't like to see you cry. You've done enough of that for a while."

She melted against him and cried on his shirt sleeve. When they got home she was still sniffling and he undressed her and made love to her slowly until she started to cry again, but not about the movie this time. When she slept, her head pillowed on Graydon's shoulder, she dreamed about absolutely nothing at all.

Chapter Thirteen

The envelope had a printed return address of School District 11. Elly's first reaction was to rip it open and see—know—what Adam looked like, but an overhanging guilt dampened her excitement.

She should have told Graydon. She should have told him what she'd done. But he wouldn't like it, not her seeing Linda or getting Adam's picture or anything. He would expect her to get over her nightmares without that kind of help.

She sank down into the cushions of the couch, Graydon's mail left to slide carelessly to the floor. Chester jumped into Elly's lap and began to purr.

"I can't do it alone," she told the cat. "I tried and I can't." She stroked him with one hand. "We can't go to movies every night and make love until I'm so exhausted I don't even remember falling asleep, much less dream."

All she wanted to do was see. Once she'd seen, she'd throw the picture away. Graydon wouldn't have to know. It was simple, really.

She opened the envelope. It was a small picture, black and white. She held it in the palm of her hand and stared at it.

He was thinner than Graydon, with light brown hair cut more casually long. Only the tips of his ear lobes showed. His eyes were a medium gray—possibly green or hazel, she guessed—and set wide apart. His features were more patrician than Graydon's with a straight nose, wide forehead and rather triangular chin. Not bad looking, Elly mused. And if he'd really had dimples, Linda was right; they didn't show. He looked as if he would have a nice smile, though, a trusting smile.

Her eyes saw the picture but suddenly her brain was seeing a different image—Adam, in full color, bending toward her over a cafe table. His mouth opened, the dimples showing faintly as he talked. His hazel eyes sparked with green lights.

"You're a beautiful person, Elly. You don't have to put up with anyone's bullshit, and I don't care if he is your husband. You have a right to live your life, you have a right to control what you do. You're a human being, not a slave. Don't you see, Elly?"

She dropped the picture and clutched her head with frightened hands. Had she really heard him say that? It sounded so real. It was almost as if—as if he were there with her.

No, she said to herself, no, he's dead, Adam is dead. It was just a memory.

A memory! She remembered Adam! She remembered him leaning across the table toward her, trying to talk some sense into her, trying to instill some confidence into her with his earnest voice and honest eyes. And she had wanted to believe him so badly. She could feel the ache of wanting and the small stirring of hope.

"Think about it," he had said. "What gives your husband the right to dictate to you, what makes him more important than you? You're as good as he is. A marriage should be a partnership, pretty lady, not a master-slave relationship. You should have as much say about your life as he does. It's your right as a human being."

Elly sank back against the couch. It was all so clear, just as if Adam had been sitting right there in the living room. She could even remember the way he stirred his coffee as he talked, absently, the spoon going round and round and round in mindless hypnotic circles. She had finally had to look out the window to keep from being caught in the whirlpool of his coffee cup and dragged down.

"But I love him," she remembered herself saying.

Adam had sighed in frustration. "Sometimes, pretty lady, love isn't enough. Sometimes you need other things, like respect and confidence. Sometimes you need to do things that maybe will hurt the ones you love but that will help you find yourself. Isn't finding yourself worth a little pain? Especially if he loves you. Is it right that he's happy and you're miserable?"

Elly had shaken her head to try to clear it. "But it's a two-way street, isn't it? If I act differently so I'm happy but I hurt Graydon or make him unhappy, what right do I have to do that? And anyway, aren't you doing what he does? Aren't you trying to make me something I'm not?" She'd steadied her huge blue eyes on him, waiting.

"I want you to be you, pretty lady. I don't want you to do anything except a little soul-searching and find out who you are and what you are. I see you as a diamond in the rough and all I want you to do is look inside until you see the sparkle that I see. You have it, pretty lady, it's there. And you can crack off that prison of ordinary rock around you and shine like fire if you want. You can do it."

Elly wiped her eyes to clear away the dreams.

God, he had been persuasive. His eyes had held her like an evangelist holds a cripple and she had wanted to believe so badly. But she loved Graydon; she had loved him then and she loved him now. How could she have left him? How could she have believed that she had to leave him to find herself when he was part of her and his life was her life?

She leaned down to retrieve the picture off the floor. So innocent, she thought, staring at it; a little snapshot was so innocent, yet it was a veritable Pandora's Box for her. Maybe she wouldn't dream of the headless man again, but how many new questions would she have? How many more locked doors would she have to pound on before she knew the answers?

In a lethargic haze, she took the little picture to the bedroom and buried it at the bottom of her underwear drawer. Later, she thought, I'll think about it later. I love Graydon, I don't care why I left, I'm here now and I love Graydon. Nothing else matters.

The closer Christmas came, the more excited Elly got. She led Graydon all over the national forest looking for the perfect tree, then cried when he cut it down. She counted its rings; it was only fourteen years old.

"Do you want the damn tree or not?" Graydon demanded crossly. She had been so crazily happy when they were tree-hunting and now her tears over his felling of the tree made him feel like a villain. It was hard for him to keep up with her emotional curve.

"Yes," she sniffed. "We can't just leave it here lying like a carcass. Poor little tree."

Graydon muttered obscenities under his breath as he dragged the tree to the car and tied it to the ski rack on top.

At home, he lugged boxes up from the basement all marked *Xmas* and let Elly plow through them while he set the tree in its stand. She had managed to stop sniffling since the tree was no longer lying like a dead body on the ground and now with decorations in hand she became excited over that part of it.

"There's so many ornaments!" she exclaimed.

"I know. I told you there were." His voice came muffled from behind the tree as he jammed rocks into a bucket to hold it up.

"We must have had a huge tree."

"It was. This living room has a twelve foot ceiling and that first tree came right to the top. I even had to cut off a few inches for the angel."

Graydon worked carefully positioning the tree but kept an expectant ear out for Elly's next burst of enthusiasm. When it didn't come, he turned to peer through the branches at her.

She sat on her heels on the floor, a small glass ornament in her hands. One side of the globe was concave and a silver star glittered from the recess. The ball itself was red except flakes of color had come off leaving shiny patches underneath. Elly stared at it as if mesmerized.

She looked so strange. Graydon had never known Elly to sleepwalk, but if she had, he felt certain her face would have looked like it did now. Her eyes were wide but unseeing, her mouth partially open and her chest rose and fell in rhythmic breathing. She was not here in this room. She had gone somewhere.

"Elly?" His voice was soft, questioning. He drew her back slowly. "Elly? What are you doing?"

She blinked and looked up away from the ornament, then

turned to Graydon.

"I—I...This ornament—it's mine, isn't it? It's from when I was little."

Graydon nodded. "Yes, it's yours. You asked your mother for it our last Christmas in New Mexico."

She held it up so Graydon could see the star. "I used to wish on this star. When I was big enough to help decorate the tree, I always hung this on a bottom branch so I could lie on the floor beneath the tree and look up and wish on the star. It was the first star I saw every night, so I wished on it every night. I always wished the same thing."

"What was that?" he asked.

"I wished that I could be happy."

Elly's plaintive voice echoed in the silence. The sad softness of her words tore at Graydon.

"What would you wish now?" he asked.

She fastened her eyes on the star and for a brief moment they got that far-away look again. Her lips moved. "I would wish... I would wish..." She glanced at him, abruptly normal. "I don't think I have anything to wish for," she said. "I have you. That's all I want."

Graydon studied her. Her face looked normal, yet somehow he sensed an avoidance in her eyes, a confrontation that blocked off something else like a...like a mother bird dragging a wing to lead a predator away from her eggs. It made Graydon uneasy.

"Are you sure?" he asked quietly. "There's nothing that you want?"

She looked down, away from his stare. "No. I have all the things that are the most important to me. I have you." She looked up again. "No matter what else I had, without you I wouldn't be happy."

He knew Elly. He knew she was telling him the truth but there was a piece missing somewhere, as if it weren't the whole truth she was telling him. He didn't like feeling this secretiveness coming from her and he started to say something.

"We need icicles," she said, dismissing the subject busily. "Maybe when you're done there we can run down to the store and buy some. Which ornaments do you think we ought to use? These gold ones are pretty, and I really like the blue ones. Or how about all red and green?"

Graydon let the uncertainty slip away. "It doesn't matter to me. You can have it any way you want."

Elly looked sharply at him. "It's your tree, too Graydon. I want us both to like it."

He forced the last rock into place and felt the tree's sturdiness with a sure hand. Good enough. Rising from behind the tree and walking to Elly, he laid one hand along the side of her face. She stared up at him, the warmth of her cheek pressing against his hand.

"I've always liked the way you do our trees," he said quietly.

Elly lowered her lashes slightly, absorbing the tenderness in Graydon's voice.

"All right," she murmured. Her blue eyes met his black ones and for a heartbeat it seemed as if they looked into each other's souls.

Graydon's fingers brushed the tips of her lashes. "Blue has always been my favorite color."

Elly did the tree in blue and red and green. Graydon strung the lights on, then drove to the store for icicles while Elly decorated and they finished it by the time Elly needed to start dinner. Graydon's chair at the table faced the living room anyway, but Elly had to turn in her seat to see the tree while she ate.

"It's pretty, isn't it?" she asked.

"Yes, it's nice."

Elly sighed. "Poor little tree. But I guess if you have to go, you might as well go as a Christmas tree."

A scratching on the door drew her eyes from the tree. She got up and let Chester in.

"Watch him," Graydon ordered. "I don't want him trying to climb the tree."

Elly let Chester wander after her into the dining room and his attention was immediately caught by the unfamiliar object in the living room. Holding his tail straight out behind him, the tabby strode casually to the tree. Elly stood by her chair, ready, and watched.

Chester sniffed an icicle and eyed it curiously when it flickered away at the touch of his whisker. An ornament hung on a low branch called for inspection and he sniffed it, too. It didn't move, though. He examined the bucket, now wrapped in a white sheet, and circled around behind the tree.

"You'd better get him," Graydon said.

Elly didn't move. "I will."

Chester attended to the back of the bucket and touched his nose to another icicle. He glanced at Elly from behind the tree, his eyes half closed in approval. The rumpled sheet made a nice, comfortable place. He began to knead, circled once and coiled himself into an orange ball at the base of the tree.

"Isn't that cute?" she asked, sliding into her chair.

Graydon scowled. "Just keep an eye on him. I don't trust him."

"I will," she said. She finished her dinner in contentment.

The packages began to accumulate under the tree. Elly had put her two presents for Graydon there first, and then a package came in the mail from Carrizozo. The following week Elly bought some presents for Chester—a catnip mouse, catchovies, a little plastic caged ball with a bell inside—and wrapped those, too. One day she realized that Graydon had snuck a big, luxuriously wrapped box beneath the tree and she shook it furtively. It didn't rattle.

Elly was surprised and unhappy to discover they had no stockings to hang over the hearth, and bought three on her next trip to the shopping center.

"Three?" Graydon asked archly.

"One for Chester. It's Christmas for him, too."

She pounded thumbtacks into the back of the door and strung thin wire across in level strands to hold Christmas cards. She bought bayberry scented candles and burned them constantly so the house always smelled good when Graydon came home. She even tied a swatch of sleigh bells to the front door knob.

"What next?" Graydon asked. "Reindeer in the backyard?"

"No," she answered slowly, "but I would sort of like to have Christmas lights on the outside of the house. Maybe in the big tree in front? Would that be hard to do?"

Graydon sighed helplessly. "No, it wouldn't be hard. How many lights do you want?"

The week before Christmas Elly was like a child. She drove Graydon crazy with her constant rearranging of the Christmas presents, and she was perfectly happy in the evening to sit in front of the tree and glory in its electric beauty. Graydon found it a strange, disquieting contrast to see her so wide-eyed and childlike while her belly rounded more every day. Even the smocks she wore couldn't hide the basketball shape of her stomach.

"Why don't we invite the Mayfields over?" she asked Graydon one night.

"The Mayfields? I told you, you don't have to worry about that. We can catch up on our turn after the holidays."

Elly couched her next words tactfully. "But it would be kind of fun to share our Christmas with friends. And since you guys don't have to work, I mean since there are no classes this week, they could come over any night."

Graydon studied her with surprise. "I got the impression you weren't overly fond of Clare."

"Well," Elly hedged, "I don't think I'd say she's my best friend in all the world but that doesn't really matter. Don't you think it'd be fun to have them over for a little get-together?"

"Sure, if you want. I'm going in tomorrow to work on finals, and if he's there I'll ask him. If not, I'll give him a call at home."

"Good." Elly felt proud of herself. She would get Graydon into the Christmas spirit yet.

She bought him more presents: a pair of soft, pigskin slippers, a calendar filled with fantastically photographed ski pictures, an Irish coffee mug for after the slopes. More presents appeared under the tree for her, too—a very small one and another big one. She couldn't wait until she could open them.

The Mayfields came over the Saturday night before Christmas. They had declined dinner so Elly just fixed a plate of cheese and sausage sliced thin and bowls of popcorn and peanuts.

"Hello, hello," Clare said cheerfully when Graydon answered the door. She pecked him on the cheek and gave him her coat. "What a lovely tree. Did you cut it?"

"After looking at every tree in the forest first, yes," Graydon said. "Come on in, Don."

While the men said their hellos, Clare made a beeline to the kitchen where Elly was finishing up the cheese plate.

"Elly! Let me look at you!" She took Elly's arm and turned her so she could see Elly's bulging stomach to full advantage. "My, you are getting rollie-pollie, aren't you?"

"I'm afraid so," Elly sighed.

"Well don't say it like that," Clare scolded. "You look lovely. I'll bet Graydon can hardly wait until the little tyke comes. He'll probably want to put him on skis right away."

Elly hoped Graydon was being adequately distracted by Don not to have heard that. She led Clare out of the kitchen, cheese plate in hand.

"Where are your children? I thought they'd be home from school for vacation."

"Oh, they are, but you know how teen-agers are. And you'll know more about how they are later." Clare laughed at her own joke. "Debby just had to stay home by the phone in case any of a hundred friends called and John went out with his friends earlier. They'd do nothing but fidget here."

"Sit down," Elly offered. "Can I get you something to drink?"

"That's my department," Don broke in. He came to give Elly an affectionate pat on her stomach. "Let the little mother sit down and take a load off. I've got the makings for a nice hot buttered rum for everyone."

Elly couldn't keep her eyes from sliding to Graydon. Maybe having the Mayfields over wasn't such a good idea after all, she thought. If Graydon resented the allusions to Elly's pregnancy, though, he kept it from his eyes. Elly lowered herself into a chair and let Don have the run of the kitchen since he obviously knew his way around.

"No rum for me," she called.

"What?" Don came back. "No rum?"

"No." She glanced down at her stomach.

"Oh, he won't mind," Don said with a wave toward the bulge. "We just won't let you overdo."

"No, really, I—" But Don had already disappeared into the kitchen, bottle in hand. Elly let him go and made up her mind to hold the drink good-naturedly and just not drink any.

"So when do you go back to work?" Clare wanted to know. Her eyes sparkled at the chance to hear something interesting.

"I haven't really thought too much about it," Elly confessed. "I've been so busy here at home I haven't felt the need to—"

"Plus with the baby coming, why bother?" Clare interjected.

Elly realized Graydon was standing behind her chair because Clare's clever eyes lifted from Elly up to her husband in conspiracy.

"It's not even that so much," Elly said firmly. "I'm just happy at home. I don't feel like I have to go do something else to be satisfied with my life." She was surprised and wonderfully warmed to feel Graydon's hand sliding onto her shoulder in a casual caress. Instinctively she put her own hand up to cover his and he squeezed her shoulder.

"Oh, you two love birds," Clare sighed. "I think it's positively nauseating the way you two act after four years of marriage. It's downright indecent." She chuckled.

"All right," Graydon said, "I can take a hint. I'll see if Don needs help mixing up those drinks." He moved toward the kitchen, letting his hand trail across Elly's shoulder and brushing against her hair.

She watched him go.

"You know," Clare said, "men are always like that. No matter how much they rant and rave about kids, as soon as it's *their* wife having *their* child, they turn to mush. I've never seen Graydon so mellow, but it doesn't surprise me a bit." Her eyes glittered. "Have you picked out names yet?"

Elly shook her head. "No. There's still plenty of time yet."

"Don't wait too long." Clare wagged a finger at Elly. "It's like Christmas; it gets here before you know it."

"All right," Don called, "break up the girl talk." He came from the kitchen bringing two mugs steaming with fragrant spices, and Graydon followed with two more. Don handed one of his mugs ceremoniously to Elly while Graydon gave one to Clare.

"Dr. Mayfield's special elixir of hot rum," Don explained. "It's good for what ails you." He lifted his mug in a friendly toast. "Here's to Christmas spirits."

"I think you have that wrong, dear," Clare said. "It's supposed to be singular, as in Christmas spirit."

"Singular, plural, it's all the same, right, Elly?"

She was cooling her drink with small breaths of air. "Oh, right."

Don winked at her. "Don't worry. I gave you a virgin drink."

She smiled at him and sipped her drink. Graydon settled himself beside her and draped a hand over her knee. She liked the warmth that she felt coming from him.

"Sit down, Dr. Mayfield," Graydon said. "You've sold us, now relax."

"Oh, wait," Clare said. She stopped Don from sitting by holding a hand out to him in a traffic stop. "Go out to the car and get our present, first. Then you can relax."

"Present?" Elly repeated. "But, Clare, you shouldn't—"

"Tut, tut. I know we shouldn't, but that's okay. We wanted to." She took Don's rum while he let himself out the door. "Just consider it an early birthday present."

Elly glanced sideways at Graydon. She didn't think she was going to like this. She was beginning to realize that, as time went on, it was going to be more and more difficult to pretend like eager parents. They had no names picked out, no plans for a nursery, not even so much as a safety pin in the house. How long would it be before people like the Mayfields noticed the Coles' negligent behavior? It was something to think about.

Don returned with a flourish and a cold blast of air from outside. At Clare's eager gesture, he carried the present to her while he took his rum and warmed his backside at the fireplace.

"Here," Clare said. "I want you both to open it." She passed the present to Elly.

Elly set down her mug hesitantly. She took the gaily wrapped box and set it on her lap. Stealing another guilty glance at her husband, she pulled at the ribbon.

"Both of you, I said. Come on, Graydon, get in there. It takes two, you know."

Graydon pulled on another end of ribbon and drew it off the package. Elly loosened the scotch tape and smoothed the paper aside. The box was wide and flat. Elly pulled off the top.

Her throat closed in an anxious gasp. As she expected—a

baby blanket. She felt Graydon's stillness beside her, contrasted by Clare's delighted smile across from her and Don's indulgent grin.

"Well? Take it out," Clare prompted. "Don't you like it?"

Elly moved hesitant hands to the tiny blanket. "Of course, I love it," she said breathlessly. "It's beautiful. Did you make it?" She held it up. It was knit of bright white yarn with a border trim of navy blue—or Air Force blue, she guessed. Matching booties lay underneath.

"Heavens, no," Clare laughed. "But I know a woman who does beautiful work and I just told her what I wanted. After all, I think the little guy ought to get used to wearing dark blue right away, don't you?"

"Yes," Elly agreed helplessly. She refolded the blanket and laid it back in its nest of tissue. "It's beautiful, Clare. Thank you."

"It's never too early," Clare clucked.

Elly put the top back on the box and wondered what she ought to do now. "No," she murmured, "it's never too early."

Graydon surprised her by taking the box out of her lap. She looked at him sharply. "Here," he said, "let's put it under the tree."

"Oh, yes," Clare agreed. "But leave it open, why don't you? It's too pretty to cover up."

They did. And all evening long, Elly felt the awful, smothering pang of despair. She wasn't sure which emotion was dragging her down most, her fear of Graydon's reprisal or her own sadness because her baby would never see that blanket. She avoided looking at it, but still her eyes seemed always aware of the glowing whiteness that was just beyond her vision.

When the front door clicked solidly behind the Mayfields, Elly fell immediately to gathering up mugs and glasses and straightening the kitchen. She worked diligently, knowing Graydon was behind her but not wanting to acknowledge him. His presence at the kitchen doorway was like a looming black cloud.

"I'm sorry," she apologized without looking at him. "If I'd had any idea, I wouldn't have insisted on inviting them over. I just didn't think—"

Graydon moved up behind her and slid his bear-like arms

around her. She melted against him, tears swimming in her eyes. "I'm sorry, Graydon." She felt his cheek against her hair.

"Shhh. Didn't I say I never wanted to hear you say that? I love you, Elly."

Her chin trembled threateningly and she forced it down against her throat to steady it. "I love you, too, Graydon."

"Then don't worry about anything else. We'll get through it. No matter what, we'll get through."

Christmas was on a Thursday. The night before, Elly had difficulty keeping her eyes from straying to the mound of presents—she'd removed the baby blanket and hidden it away— and she hoped Graydon wouldn't want to stay up too late. If she could just go to sleep, Christmas would come faster.

"Aren't you tired?" she asked calmly when it came close to eleven.

"Tired?" Graydon echoed. His dark eyes sparkled at her. "No, are you? I thought we'd watch the Late Show."

Elly groaned.

"Come here," he said. Elly left her place beside Chester and went to sit in the hollow Graydon made for her inside the circle of his arm. "Are you anxious to go to bed?" He lifted her chin so she couldn't elude his knowing smile.

"Well, it is late," she said lamely. She pulled the hem of her nightgown down over her knees and tucked her feet beneath her. "We usually go to bed around eleven."

"That's true," he said, "unless you want to go to bed early for some reason." He slid his hand down to her waist, pulling her closer and drawing her thin nylon gown up with the same movement. The material stretched like a blue veil across her breasts and stomach. "Did you have anything in mind?"

"Oh, Graydon," she sighed, "I can't think of anything but opening presents. You know you're torturing me."

He laughed. "All right. I'll make a deal with you. Let me watch the monologue and then we'll go to bed."

"Okay," she agreed. She leaned into him and laid her head on his chest. He seemed undisturbed and went back to watching his program on TV. His hand slid from her waist to her hip and rested there for the evening.

At 11:45 they went to bed. Elly slid over next to Graydon and worked her way inside his arm. "Graydon?" she said softly.

"What?"

"I didn't mean we couldn't make love. We can if you want."

His body moved with a silent chuckle. "Go to sleep. It's almost Christmas."

"No, really," she said, "I—"

"Shh. Don't tempt me. In fifteen minutes it'll be Christmas. We'll have time for all our presents tomorrow." He kissed the top of her head. "All of them."

"I love you," she sighed.

"Go to sleep."

She woke up at six-thirty. Her eyes flew open like window blinds and she was instantly awake. She rolled her head over to see what Graydon was doing.

He was sleeping.

She let out a breath of frustration. He seldom slept past seven on a day off; maybe she could go back to sleep. She forced her eyes shut.

The click of the digital clock at her side relayed the passing of every minute. She heard the wind brushing against the house. The heater came on and pinged. She let her eyes flip open again and checked the clock. Six-thirty-five.

She couldn't do it. She couldn't lie there and let the minutes crawl by for a half hour or longer. She had to get up and do something. Taking care not to wake Graydon, she slid from bed and padded down the hall.

When Graydon finally came out after her, she was seated at the base of the Christmas tree, a cup of tea in her hand and Chester in her lap.

"Merry Christmas," he said sleepily. "You're not in a hurry, are you?"

Elly made a face. "You know I can't stand it, Graydon. Don't tease me."

"All right," he laughed. "Let me at least get a cup of coffee and we'll start."

When they both had taken up positions near the tree, Elly

forced Chester out of her lap. "Hand me Chester's stocking," she said. "There's something in there that will keep him busy."

Graydon unhooked all three stockings from over the hearth and handed her Chester's. She took out the catchovies and gave the big tom one. He crunched it down daintily and looked for more.

"Not yet," Elly cautioned with a stern finger. "You'd probably eat them all and make yourself sick. Here." She took out his new catnip mouse and let him get a good whiff. His nose wrinkled in concentration and when she would have teased him by pulling the mouse away, he slapped a quick, clawed paw on the toy and held it firm. "Okay," she said, "take it." Chester did. In seconds he was rolling on the floor, pillowing his head on the mouse, his claws still sunk possessively into the gray felt.

"So much for Chester," Graydon said. "Now open yours."

Elly did. She spilled out a half dozen of her favorite candies—chocolate kisses—and several small boxes.

"Oh, Santa was busy," she noticed. She reached for a box and started to open it. "Aren't you going to open yours?"

"Sure." Graydon dumped his, too. They pored over the contents like two kids over a game of marbles.

"Oh, how cute!" Elly cried. She unwrapped a tiny ceramic cat, glazed with orange tabby stripes and with a devilishly innocent expression on its face. "Oh, Graydon, where did you get this? It's adorable!"

"I found it downtown. There's a gift store that has all sorts of cat things. I'll take you down there some time." Meanwhile he was unwrapping his first gift—new ski goggles complete with interchangeable lenses in different colors for varying conditions. "Hey, great! These are just what I've been thinking of buying."

"Oh, good," Elly said. "The man at the store said they were the best."

"They are." He leaned over to kiss her. "Thank you."

"Mmm, thank *you*," Elly said. "But don't stop now. We've got lots to go."

One by one, they demolished the presents. Elly unwrapped her parents' package and pulled out a full set of kitchen towels and hot pads. "How domestic," she said, then, "that's not nice. They are pretty, and I can always use towels."

"Sure," Graydon said. "Anyway, last year they sent a canning rack and that big blue pot that sits in the back of the cupboard. Anything's an improvement over that."

They laughed and Elly put the towels aside. "I'll have to write them a nice letter. It would be nice to think we could see eye to eye sometime."

"Here," Graydon said, closing the subject. "Open this."

Elly did and drew out the most beautiful ski sweater she'd ever seen. It was frosty white with delicate teal blue snowflakes embroidered across the bust line. "Oh, Graydon. It's gorgeous!"

"It matches your eyes," he said.

"Oh, I love it! It's beautiful." She held it up to her and smoothed a hand over it.

"You'll have to try it on," Graydon said. "You can give me a fashion show."

In retaliation Elly gave Graydon the box with his black turtleneck, and that seemed to please him as much as her sweater did her.

"For my night commando raids?" he asked devilishly.

"Or anytime you feel the urge to smuggle something."

"If we wear these things together, we'll look like walking salt and pepper shakers. Or an advertisement for Black & White."

"Or a devil and angel," Elly laughed. "Did you buy me a halo, too?"

"You don't need one," Graydon said. "You're perfect just the way you are."

Elly opened a box and found warm, fluffy after-ski boots and a new pair of gloves with rabbit fur lining. She gave Graydon his Irish coffee mug, then, hesitantly, his radio-controlled airplane.

"Elly," he said, "is this really what the box says? Is this really an airplane?"

She couldn't tell if it was excitement or disbelief in his voice. "Yes. Do you like it?"

He laughed as if at a very large joke. "Do you have any idea how long I've wanted one of these but I just couldn't bring myself to go out and buy one? This is great." He pulled the Styrofoam pack out of the box and began the unblocking of his plane.

Elly breathed in relief. "Why wouldn't you buy one? It's less expensive than skis."

"Just because," Graydon said, already immersed in his project. "It's a toy. Grown men don't buy toys."

"If they like them they do," Elly insisted. "Who cares if it's a toy?"

Graydon looked up and nodded. "You're absolutely right. This is great, Elly. You couldn't have gotten me anything better." He leaned across the tangle of empty boxes and crumpled paper to kiss her and Elly gloried in the love they shared.

"It's a good Christmas, isn't it?" she asked.

"The best," Graydon agreed. "But it's not over yet."

"It's not?" Elly looked around at the mounds of torn paper, punctuated by strands of loose, coiling ribbon. Somewhere beneath the mess was Chester but she was sure there were no unopened boxes.

"Here." Graydon plucked a tiny box from its hiding place on a low branch of the tree. "Open this."

Elly took the box. She hadn't seen it before and now her curiosity was aroused. Graydon had even stopped tinkering with his airplane while she ripped the silver ribbon off the red-wrapped box.

"They say good things come in small packages," she murmured. She lifted the lid and a sheet of protective cotton. A jewelry box of burgundy velvet met her eyes.

Her heart was already pounding in her ears as she lifted the smaller box free of the big one.

The lid of the velvet box had some sort of crest on it; she lifted the hinged lid and gasped.

A ring glittered at her. But not an ordinary ring. It was a delicate circlet of snowflakes, each a perfect creation of tiny diamonds and sapphires nestled in platinum settings. It shone like something out of a fairy tale.

"Oh, Graydon," she breathed, and there was a definite catch in her throat. "It's beautiful. Oh, my God, where did you ever find this? It's the most beautiful thing I've ever seen."

Graydon sat grinning like a Cheshire cat. "Do you like it?"

"Like it?" Clutching the ring box, she hurled herself at him and practically strangled him with her unbelievable happiness. "Oh, Graydon, it's fantastic! You shouldn't have. It's so beautiful."

"Like you," he said, untangling her arms. "Aren't you going to try it on?"

Elly pushed the box at him. "Will you put it on me?"

Smiling indulgently at her romanticism, Graydon lifted the ring from its velvet slot. He took her right hand and held it gently, fingers outstretched. The ring glittered like blue fire.

Elly's heart surged as she watched Graydon slip the ring on her finger. She felt a wash of wonder and happiness and—yes, fear—break over her, and a trembling set in. She tried to focus on the bright fire on her finger but her eyes were misting. The ring was a promise, a brand, the start of the future and the end of the past. It was at once her freedom and her prison; it was both joyful and frightening.

"Elly?"

Graydon's voice was curious, prompting.

She raised her eyes to his, all the brightness in the room blurred by the veil of tears. His eyes were dark and bottomless, like a secret well from which she could draw life—or drown.

"Elly?"

She shook her head once to clear it. The tears fell free of her eyes. "I do," she whispered, "but I'm afraid." *Graydon, I'm afraid, I'm afraid.*

"Elly, hey, what's wrong? What are you talking about?" His hands clutched her shoulders and shook her gently. "Elly, wake up. You're dreaming. Elly?"

The lights in the room went in and out of focus, then sharpened to alarming clarity. Elly looked around and found Graydon's face, worried and intent in front of her.

"Graydon?" she whispered. "What was I doing? What did I say?"

He cleared the floor between them with a sweep of his hand and pulled Elly into his arms. "I'm not sure," he said, "but I think you were dreaming—or remembering. You're okay now, though. You're safe." He kissed her hair. "There's nothing to be afraid of."

Afraid. She had been afraid. She stared down at the new ring and saw it as a blazing seal on her finger.

"The ring," she said. "It's the ring."

Graydon frowned. "What about the ring? Elly, you're acting crazy. You look cornered. For a minute you almost reminded me of the day we got married."

Married, married, married. The word echoed off the walls of her brain and ricocheted around maniacally. "I'll try, Graydon, I'll try, I'll try." She caught at the words, already out, and put a hand over her mouth. Married.

"Elly? For God's sake, what's wrong?"

She turned her face into his chest. "I see...candles. Bud is standing behind you; Sue is behind me. The chaplain is smiling. They're all smiling, even Graydon is smiling. But I'm afraid. What if I can't do it? What if I can't? I'm afraid, I'm afraid I won't do good. I'll try, Graydon, I'll try, I promise I'll try."

"Elly!" Graydon clawed her shoulders with angry fingers and shook her body so that her head snapped. "Stop it!" he roared. "Wake up! That was a long time ago. This is now, Christmas. Wake up!"

Her eyes widened in alarm, then caught at Graydon's face. They flicked to the bright lights of the Christmas tree. She seemed to gather in the images, seeing for the first time, and her body slackened its tautness. Her nostrils flared in restored breathing.

"Oh, God," she said weakly. "I'm doing it again, aren't I? I'm dreaming when I'm awake." She turned frightened eyes back to Graydon. "I'm sorry. I don't know what happened to me."

Graydon gathered her protectively against the wall of his chest. "No, it's all right. You just scared me. Jesus, I hate to see that frightened-rabbit look in your eyes. You looked like that when we got married. You made me feel like your protector and your persecutor all at once. Elly, I love you. You don't have to be afraid. I love you."

"Hold me, Graydon," she pleaded. "Just hold me."

The rest of the day was subdued, although both Elly and Graydon steered valiantly clear of references to Elly's visions. Graydon insisted on taking a picture of Elly in front of the Christmas tree with her new sweater on and Chester in her lap, and she demanded a similar one of him. Because of the fitful rain and snow outside, they couldn't try out Graydon's new toy, but he tinkered with it contentedly while Elly cooked a small turkey and fixed all Graydon's favorite dressings. Their dinner was warm and quiet, made more so by the interruption of a phone call from Los Angeles. Graydon's younger sister Patty called to thank them enthusiastically for their gift. While Graydon didn't subject Elly to role-playing with the sister-in-law she didn't know, he still made it clear to Patty that it was Elly's desire and thoughtfulness that prompted the gift. Elly picked absently at her turkey, glowing under the praise Graydon spoke of to his sister. When they'd both eaten their fill and the dishes were done, they lay on the floor between the fireplace and the Christmas tree and talked in murmurs until Graydon undressed Elly of all but her rings and made gentle love to her in the light of the fire. Twined together like growing vines, they rested cheek to cheek and watched the firelight play on the icicles of the tree.

"It was a good Christmas, wasn't it?" she breathed against the moist skin of his shoulder.

"Still is," he said. "For about another hour or so."

"And each one will get better." Her words were softly spoken, but beneath them was a promise. Graydon tilted his head so he could look down at his wife.

"Elly, tell me what you remember about our wedding day," he asked. "Don't go away from me, but tell me. I want to know what you were feeling."

Her eyes went instinctively to the circlet of blue and white on the hand at Graydon's neck, but she dragged them away before she could sink beneath the spell of the stones' blaze. She concentrated on the square strength of Graydon's chin instead.

"I felt...all sorts of things. I was very happy because you wanted me, although it was hard for me to believe. I was afraid maybe you saw more in me than I actually was, and that later you'd find out and not want me anymore. I was glad because... because I was not going to be single anymore, I wasn't going to be only my parents' daughter. I was going to be your wife. That made me feel very good. But at the same time..." She trailed off, thinking.

"What?" Graydon prompted. "Talk to me, Elly. Don't go

away. Talk to me."

She redoubled her concentration on his jaw.

"I wondered if I wasn't...trading one set of fences for another. I had been so restricted by my dad, by his image of me and what I should or shouldn't do, and I wondered if I wasn't just escaping his constraints to be bound up in yours. Not that I didn't want to be, but I felt as if...I had never known freedom. And at the same time I didn't even know if I wanted to, or if I could handle it." She lifted her eyes to his. "I was happy and afraid and free but not free and I was determined to make you a good wife and make you happy. Most of all, I was afraid I'd fail you. I didn't want to do that. More than anything in the world I didn't want to do that."

Graydon took her hand from his neck and kissed her palm. "You won't fail me. Don't ever worry about that. And don't be afraid of me, Elly. I think I used to...well, *enjoy* knowing you were afraid of me, that I could reduce you to fear with a look or a word. I don't anymore. I want you beside me as an equal, not as a possession or a slave. You're much more important than that. I guess I just never realized before."

"We're both changing a lot, aren't we, Graydon?"

"Yes," he said, "we are. A lot."

Chapter Fourteen

The month after Christmas things quieted and the days merged smoothly into weeks. The tree came down on New Years and Graydon packed away all the decorations. The Academy resumed school. Elly was left to steer her growing belly quietly through the house and pursue her simple distractions. The roundness of her stomach grew hard and lumpy by turns; Dr. Weiss found a heartbeat.

Cold weather set in. Where before the winds and scattered showers were forgiven for the clear, cold days in between, now a blanket of heavy gray clouds stretched from the Rockies out onto the plains and it snowed. When six inches covered the undisturbed ground, the temperatures plummeted to below freezing and the softness of the snow turned to brittle ice.

Although the main streets were plowed, Elly kept to the house most days and took any chores she had to the living room to do in front of the fire. She answered the brief, unfamiliar notes that came from Graydon's sisters after Christmas as well as she could, and composed cautious, understanding letters to her parents. Even Dana wrote for herself and Bryan; when Elly read her tiny, scroll-like script, she drew a memory of Dana out of her mind—small, petite, long-suffering Dana, who loved Elly's brother so much she was enslaved by it. Elly felt genuine pity for her; she knew the insecurity such love produced. Thank God she didn't have to battle with it anymore.

She took to wearing Graydon's athletic tube socks. Luckily he wore black socks during his work week and only thundered for his tube socks on Saturday morning if Elly had neglected to wash on Friday. She kept meaning to buy some for herself, but somehow it was easier to steal Graydon's. She once attempted to wear a pair to bed, but Graydon wouldn't allow it. He insisted their combined body heat was sufficient to keep her warm and most of the time he was able to win her over easily. Her sleep on those nights was deep and tranquil, punctuated only rarely by dreams she never remembered the next morning.

It seemed almost a daily occurrence now to remember something, and she didn't feel the throat-tightening apprehension that had come with the early memories. Often she surprised herself by pulling memories as if out of a hat, casually and without conscious thought.

"Damn," Graydon exploded one evening out of his basement shop. "Would you believe I locked my damn tool box key *inside* the tool box? Now I've got to see if I can find the spare and I don't have any idea where I put it. Someplace safe so I wouldn't lose it, probably."

Elly calmly untangled Chester from where he lay along her leg on the couch and waddled to the kitchen. "Isn't it here, in the cup?" She opened a cupboard and went up on tiptoes to reach a cracked mug on the top shelf. Her probing fingers rattled several keys.

"I didn't think of that," Graydon said. "Let me." He nudged Elly gently aside and pulled down the cup. "Ah ha! Good thinking, Elly. I never would have remembered. I probably put that there two years ago."

Elly smiled smugly. "Mind like a steel trap," she said, tapping her forehead.

They both laughed.

She remembered more and more of Adam. One day in the mail she got a two-page newsletter of School District 11 and highlighted on the back page was the mural at Pike School and a brief reference to the artist's untimely death in a car accident shortly after its completion. Adam's name leaped out at her from the obscurity of the article, and her brain clicked into a memory response.

She stood before the chalked and one-quarter painted mural, a swarm of second-graders around her, all staring at the thin, casual-looking man who painted and stepped back, painted and stepped back.

"What's he doing?" a shrill-voiced boy asked.

Elly calmed the ready-to-burst children with a quieting motion. "I don't know, probably checking to make sure he's doing exactly what he wants. It looks different close up than it does far away."

She wasn't sure if it was the boy's gusty question or her own moderated voice that caught the artist's attention, but he glanced over his sweatshirted shoulder and smiled genially to the group.

"How's it look?" he asked.

"Good!"

"Funny!"

"Pretty!" The children took advantage of the opportunity to shout good-naturedly.

"Maybe," Elly said in a stage whisper, "if you ask nicely, the man will explain why he paints that way."

She flashed him a smile and stepped back behind the children in her best substitute's manner.

After that she lost track of Adam's explanations to the children. His green-flecked hazel eyes sparkled enthusiastically as he spoke to the second graders, but they seemed to take on extra shine when he swept them over Elly. His smile was friendly and encouraging, but it seemed to deepen into responsive dimples when he met her stare. Instead of listening as she should have, Elly found herself experiencing strange pins and needle sensations all along her body.

When Adam's impromptu speech was over, the children all turned expectant faces to Elly and she shook herself out of her cocoon of feeling and stepped forward, gray skirt swinging.

"All right, children. Thank the man and we'll go back to class and have our art period. Remember, no running."

A chorus of mismatched voices called thanks to the artist, then the children closest to the building began to file toward the door.

Elly turned to the man professionally. "Thank you so much for talking to the children. They're very excited about the mural."

The artist smiled. "Anytime you want to bring a group of kids out is okay by me. I could talk to kids all day as long as I have a pretty lady to look at."

Elly blushed furiously, her lips tight in an embarrassed parody of a smile. The simple compliment was enough to elicit churning anxiety, and Graydon wasn't even there! She ducked her head nervously and began to twist her ring.

"Yes, well, I, uh, have to get back to class now. Thank you again—for the children."

Skittering away like a spooked colt, Elly could feel the man's eyes on her back all the way to the door.

Even the memory evoked strains of nervous fear and anxiety in her. Through her father's repetitive brow-beating and Graydon's explosive, possessive temper, no wonder she ran from so obvious a compliment. It was a wonder she didn't go out and smear mud all over herself just so she could avoid such situations and their attendant emotions. Shaking off the thought, she tossed the newsletter in the fireplace. It had served its purpose. She remembered—and she learned.

Linda called on a Friday afternoon late in January.

"Elly? How are you? What have you been doing with yourself?"

"Hi, Linda. Not much, just keeping busy here at home."

"I don't blame you. I wouldn't go out in this damn snow if I didn't have to, either. How fat are you?"

Elly groaned theatrically. "Pretty fat, and getting bigger all the time. I'm into my sixth month now. Dr. Weiss says I'm right on schedule as far as gaining weight goes. He can hear a real strong heartbeat."

"Neat," Linda enthused. "I'll bet Graydon's getting excited. No man can resist the idea of having a kid. I don't know if it's the size of the little thing or the fact that it's their own flesh and blood, but even the biggest diehards fall to it."

"Yes," Elly murmured. Didn't Linda know this wasn't Graydon's child? Hadn't Elly told her? She'd told her everything else, even the fact that she was going to leave.

"Hey, how are the nightmares doing? Did you get the picture?"

"Oh, yeah, I did. Thanks for sending it. I meant to call you. It did the trick completely. I haven't had a single nightmare since I got it."

"Good," Linda said. "Did you happen to catch the article in the District paper last week?"

"About Adam?"

"Yeah." Linda giggled devilishly. "When I heard they were going to run it, I just kept my mouth shut. Liz came and got that file and went through it at least a dozen times looking for Adam's picture to run with the article, but of course it wasn't there. I finally couldn't stand to watch her anymore and suggested maybe we gave it to the cops after the accident."

"And she believed that?"

"She had to. What else was there?"

Elly remembered Liz, an older, fastidious woman who liked everything in its place and had taken to supervising the other clerks. Linda loved to goad her.

"That's mean, Linda," Elly said.

"I know, but she asks for it. If she didn't get her back up so easily I wouldn't be tempted to tease her. But I don't want to talk about her. Guess what?"

Elly had no trouble guessing. Linda had a new love interest—"His name's Ron and he's absolutely gorgeous!"—and she expounded to Elly all his virtues and her speculations about his love-making abilities.

"Linda," Elly sighed, "don't you think you ought to slow down? You just met the guy. Has he asked you out?"

"No, but he called me last night. I'm sure he'll call tonight, and if he does I think I'll ask him over. God, he's a hunk. Tall and blonde and tan. He almost looks Scandinavian. I can't wait."

Elly laughed hopelessly. "And what about Greg?"

"Oh, Greg. I haven't heard from him in months. I can't sit around on my butt every weekend and wait for my quarterly or biannual visit, you know."

"But you love him."

"Sure I do, but he doesn't have to know that. Anyway, Ron is so beautiful. God, I'd love to see him naked. I'll be he looks like a Norse god."

"Oh, Linda," Elly sighed.

"Okay, okay. I don't want to bruise your middle-American sensibilities. Not that you've never done anything impulsive or romantic," she drawled sarcastically.

"Touché," Elly admitted. "Thanks. I needed that."

"Sorry. It just slipped out. Speaking of slipping out, I've got to get back to work. Hey, call me, okay? Or if this snow ever melts, come on down. Maybe by then I'll have something juicy to tell you."

"All right," Elly promised. "Just do me a favor and slow down. I can't keep up with you, you know."

"That's my problem," Linda sighed. "No one can."

Elly shook her head as she hung up the phone. Poor Linda. Would she ever learn?

Saturday morning Graydon insisted on driving Elly to the market since the streets were icy and she hadn't gone yet this week. She argued with him in bed, facing him across the pillows, but he wouldn't hear of it. Right in the middle of her best defense, the baby let out a kick that punched her right in the bladder and she balled involuntarily to keep from urinating.

"What is it?" Graydon asked. "What's wrong?"

"It's okay. Just—he kicked me." She straightened slowly and rubbed her stomach to soothe the little guy. "Any more like that and I'll have to start wearing rubber pants."

Graydon's eyes darkened slightly. "See? If you were driving just then, you wouldn't have any control for a few seconds. It's settled. I'm taking you to the store."

Rather than let the argument simmer around her growing burden, Elly gave in. She realized her guilt grew along with the baby, and so rather than face it, she backed away from a confrontation whenever possible. Anything to keep the peace.

She dressed and took her still sore body to the bathroom, leaving Graydon to the bedroom. When she left him, he was digging in his top drawer for socks.

Staring into the mirror, she smoothed her smock top over her belly. It was getting so big! And now her belly button was starting to protrude, so far just a little, but later it would stick out like a sore thumb. Thank God the rest of her didn't look so inflated. She turned her face to the mirror. Nope; still looked pretty good.

"Elly!"

Graydon's voice sounded funny; harsh but not loud. It twisted her name, almost as if he were in pain. She waddled into the hall.

"Graydon? What is it? Are you all right?" While she called to him she made her way back down to the bedroom. "Graydon, what—"

He stood enraged, his face black and angry; in one hand he held a pair of tube socks and in the other—Adam's picture.

Elly felt her heart fold in like a dying animal.

"What the hell is this doing in your drawer?" he snarled.

Elly's face went chalky at the accusing tone of his voice and her legs threatened to buckle. She held herself up with a hand on the door frame.

"Graydon, it's nothing really. I got it for the nightmares. Dr. D'Angelo thought a picture—"

"What the goddamn hell does Dr. D'Angelo know about anything?" Graydon's attack was uncompromising, matching the flinty hardness of his eyes. "If you were really recovering the way you seemed to be, you wouldn't need anything like this."

Elly hurried to reassure him. "Graydon, it was just the nightmares. I couldn't stand them, I was afraid to go to sleep. As soon as I saw the picture, though, they stopped. I swear to you, that's all it was. I swear." Her voice was weak and breathless, not at all the way she wanted it to be.

Graydon's eyes remained unmoved. "Then why," he asked, "didn't you throw the goddamn thing away? Why was it hidden here in your drawer?"

"It wasn't hidden, I—"

"Goddamn it, Elly, I want answers!" He blew and the air vibrated with the force of his bellow. His whole body shook and Elly recognized the awesome rage that was clamoring for release—and vengeance. She began to be afraid.

"I'm trying to answer you," she practically sobbed. "It was only for the nightmares, I swear it. I was going to throw it away as soon as I was sure I was over them. I just—forgot. I didn't even think about it, that's how much it matters to me. I forgot all about it."

"And you expect me to believe that?" he snarled. "Jesus, Elly, he was your lover, you're carrying his bastard; do you really expect me to believe you've kept his picture just because you *forgot* to throw it away? You must really think I'm some kind of fool if you think I'm going to go through this again. It was bad enough the first time, and don't think it was easy for me to let myself fall in love with you again, but goddamn it, I trusted you! I shouldn't have but I did. And now....now I see. You'll never be happy with just one man, will you? Not anymore; not after you were 'liberated.'"

Elly stepped toward him, unmindful of the way his lip curled savagely.

"Graydon, no, you're wrong. I love you, only you, I swear. I am happy with you. Please." She felt the tears start, bitter, salty tears. She put a pleading hand on his arm. "I'm not lying, Graydon. I've never lied to you, ever. I love you."

He shoved the picture into her face.

"And this is how you show it, right?"

With a breathless sob Elly batted the picture away; still tight in Graydon's fist, it tore.

"It's *nothing!*" she cried. "I swear, it's nothing!"

Graydon didn't soften. If anything he tightened his jaw and with a rough shake of his arm, freed himself of Elly's hand.

"That's right," he said in a cold voice. "It's nothing. But that's what you wanted; that's what you've got."

"Graydon, no! I'm sorry. I should have told you about it from the beginning, I know that, but I didn't want to upset you. I didn't want you to think about me having his picture, even if it was to help me." She reached for him but he stepped back, removing any support she might have found. She crumpled to her knees on the floor in front of him and sobbed.

"I'm sorry! I was wrong, I should have told you. Graydon, I swear I would never do anything to hurt you. I haven't lied to you. I love you, Graydon, only you. Please, please believe me! I'm telling you the truth!" She cried into her anguished hands, the dark form of her husband blurry and indistinct before her. "Please," she keened, "please."

She heard the harsh intake of breath above her but couldn't find the courage or strength to look up.

"I'm going out," he said bitterly, "but when I get back, I want you gone—"

"No!"

"You call your swinging friend Linda and tell her to come get you out of my house. You can do your fucking and fantasizing somewhere else, because you're not going to do it here anymore. I want you *out*."

Elly grabbed despairingly for Graydon's leg but he moved deftly away, his bare feet carrying him to the closet for his shoes. Elly folded in on herself in a flood of tears.

He stood behind her.

"Take anything you want," he said. "I don't want anything here that will remind me of you. And here. You'll probably want this."

Elly wrenched herself into a sitting position only quick enough to see him disappear down the hall. His footfalls echoed on the floor; the front door opened, then closed hard. In seconds the blue Ford was starting.

Adam's picture lay staring at her from the carpet.

She didn't know how long she stayed huddled on the floor, crying. Long after the sound of the blue Ford faded away, long after Chester gave up scratching at the back door, long after the mail slot rattled under the mailman's hand. When her legs cramped from kneeling she rolled heavily onto her side and finally sprawled hopelessly beside the bed. Graydon's tennis shoes lay near her head; without understanding why, she pulled one across the floor and cradled her cheek on its laces. Still crying, she slept.

It was bright when she woke up. The afternoon sun threatened to break through the snow clouds and the ethereal, diffused light flooded the bedroom. Elly opened her eyes and stared across the floor at the open closet and Adam's picture in front of it. She groaned.

Her body ached. Not that it mattered—nothing did—but she was still aware of the soreness. She moved listlessly, hauling herself upright. Her jaw ached and she felt welts on her cheek from the shoe laces she'd been lying on. Her head pounded and the baby felt like a lead weight dragging her down. She wiped damp tendrils of hair from her face.

What was she going to do? The question brought a flow of thoughts—*please, Graydon, please believe me, I love you*—but no answers.

I want you out. Take anything you want. I don't want anything that will remind me of you. A weak sob caught in her throat. No! I don't want to go. This is my home!

Her chin trembled but she had no more tears that she could shed. She was dry—unrelieved, unconsoled and dry. The only thing she got for her half-hearted attempt was an aching throat and burning eyes. There was no way she could wash away the bitter despair that mushroomed inside.

Tea, she thought. I've got to get something down my throat. She couldn't even swallow. Sighing heavily, she pulled herself off the floor by the bedpost. Graydon's bed. She turned away.

As soon as she began to move about the kitchen, Chester scratched at the door. Automatically she let him in. He rubbed against her leg and purred, unaware that the world had stopped. She didn't know how to tell him.

When her tea was brewed she took it into the living room and huddled on the hearth. The fireplace was cold and black. It didn't matter. Nothing would warm her now. Chester came and insisted on coiling in her lap. He preened himself while she sipped her tea and stared down the hall with sightless eyes.

She had failed again. With one simple, stupid, unimportant lapse of memory, she had destroyed her entire life. At least before she had gone out with a bang, she had left the old for something new, she had been going to something at the same time she was going away. This time she had destroyed it all with careless ease, and she had no place to go.

It wasn't fair! How could she have lost so much over something so small? It *was* small, Graydon, it was nothing compared to what they had. She'd endure nightmares every night from now on to have it back, and better yet, not even sleep. She'd be deliriously happy to lie beside him in bed and do nothing all night but watch him. What good was dreamless sleep to her now when her waking world was dead? It wasn't fair! She'd come so far, fought for so much, too much to let it slip away from her so easily.

And with that thought, a resolution began to form. She had overcome countless obstacles in the past three months, had clung to and fought for and recreated the life that, for some reason, her former self had destroyed. She wasn't going to give it all up now. She couldn't take the thread and fabric and design of her life and throw it away because of a minor detail; no one could force her to do that unless she chose it, not Graydon or anyone else. She would fight for what was hers, and by God she would keep it together. If Graydon wouldn't hear the words that she said, he'd have to acknowledge the way that she acted and she would show him how important he was to her. She would not give up.

I will not fail, she chanted to herself. I will not fail; this time I will not fail.

It was after midnight before Graydon came home. Elly had planned and resolved and bolstered her ideas with impulsive, nervous bouts of pacing, had eaten sparingly, and finally had collapsed into bed shortly after eleven that night. The idea occurred to her that it might be safer to remove herself back to the spare bedroom, but she discarded it. She was Graydon's wife; her rightful place was beside him, and until she did something to unseat that right, she would sleep next to him. And, she promised herself, nothing would ever happen that would change that.

He flicked the light on and stood glowering at her from the doorway.

As hyper as she had been, she had been able to fall asleep almost instantly and the bright light shocked her out of obscurity. She blinked, forcing her eyes to adjust. One hand instinctively shielded her face from the glare.

"Graydon?"

"What are you doing here? I thought I told you to get out."

Elly sat up in bed, fully aware of the savagery of his voice. She met his stare.

"I'm staying," she said.

He seemed to rouse, his hackles coming up like a challenged wolf, his entire body inflating with the huge breaths he took. His hands balled into fists.

"I told you to get out of this house," he said threateningly, "and I meant it. Now get out. Call Linda and do whatever you have to do, but get out."

She shook her head, not defiantly, but sadly. "I can't do that, Graydon. You're wrong about me, and I'm not guilty of whatever you think I've done. I'm not going to run. This is my home, this is where I belong. I'm staying. With you."

His expression was patently shocked. Her quiet refusal was the last defense he had expected.

"No!" he roared. "You're a lying, scheming spoiled bitch and you're not going to use me as a base for your sexual adventures." He fairly snorted in rage and moved restlessly in the doorway.

"I never have," she said. "I still don't remember or understand everything about my life before the accident, but I know everything since then, and you're the only man I love, the only man I have ever loved. I made a mistake by not telling you about the picture, but I've done nothing else wrong. I haven't, Graydon. And I won't go."

"And you expect me to believe that?" he demanded. "You expect me to take you at your word—"

"Not my word, no," she interrupted. "Take me at my actions. Take me at my living, the things I do, the way I behave. I love you too much to let you drive me out. Take me at what I am doing— staying and fighting for my home and my husband. Because if I didn't love you and I didn't cherish what we have, I wouldn't stay."

"What we *had*, you mean." He fixed her with a hateful stare.

"I'll fight for it again, Graydon. I won't let it go that easily. I promise you that."

Her calm had begun to wear down his inflamed anger and he raked a hand through his black hair. His eyes still glowed with an abnormal fury but he didn't lash out at her so quickly. Instead he turned in a quarter circle and faced the hall.

"God damn it, Elly," he swore.

"Let it rest, Graydon. I can't prove a thing to you tonight. Let me stay and let this rest and I promise I *will* prove it to you, maybe not tomorrow or the next day, but I will. If I have to argue with you every single day to make you understand, I'll do it. I love you."

He refused to acknowledge her, but kept his face averted and shook his head slowly. His hands, so restless at his sides, came up to fist impotently at his waist. He straightened and looked over his shoulder at her.

"You're going to *have* to prove it to me," he said harshly, "because right now I don't believe a word of what you've said."

She nodded. "I understand that."

He let out an angry, frustrated breath. His eyes flicked from her to the empty side of the bed.

"It's your room, too," she said quietly.

He shook his head. "Keep it. Keep the whole goddamn room. I'll sleep on the couch."

His hand passed over the light switch and blackened the room. When Elly's eyes had again adjusted to the darkness, he was gone.

She awoke dreading the day. Why, she wasn't quite sure at first, but when she rolled her head instinctively to Graydon's side of the bed and found it empty, she knew.

He was sleeping fitfully on the couch when she had dressed and walked silently through the living room. The blanket he'd thrown over himself was untucked and half of it trailed on the floor. She thought of pulling it back over him but decided to let it be.

She fixed coffee as quietly as she could. Chester demanded in. The snow clouds of yesterday had torn apart and bright windows of blue dotted the sky. The snow sparkled.

A sighing breath behind her alerted her to Graydon's presence. She turned to face him across the kitchen. His eyes looked tired and his thick black hair was unruly from a restless night. He hadn't bothered to change out of the clothes he left the house in yesterday.

"Morning," Elly said quietly. "Coffee's almost ready."

Graydon's eyes flicked to the coffee maker, then back to Elly. They weren't kind. He turned around and walked away.

Elly listened to the rummaging sounds that came from the

bedroom, the closing of the bathroom door. The pipes knocked shallowly at the rush of water being called to the shower, and Elly could hear the steady drum of water on tile. She fixed herself a cup of tea and settled into her chair at the dining room table to wait.

It was a half hour before Graydon returned to pour himself a cup of coffee. He held himself stiffly and instead of coming to the table or leaning against the counter, he stood aloofly in the middle of the kitchen. Even as much as his distrust hurt Elly, she recognized his own pain and confusion and she couldn't blame him.

"The Super Bowl's on today," she offered. "If you don't think you'd like a heavy lunch, I thought I would pop a big batch of popcorn."

Graydon stared unflinchingly at her over the rim of his cup. "You don't like football," he said.

She half shrugged. "Not a lot; after all season, though, I'm getting to where I understand it. Once it starts making sense to me, I like it more. I wouldn't mind watching it." She paused, gauging his reaction. "Or if you want, I can find something else to do and you can watch it alone."

"I told you to get out." His brows thickened in a frown, but his voice lacked the irreversible conviction it had last night.

"No," Elly said, shaking her head. "I told you I won't do that. I'll do anything for you but that, Graydon."

"Anything?" He twisted the word into a diabolical threat.

"Yes, anything." She lifted her chin slightly. "Anything you want. Anything that will make you realize how much I love you and how important you are to me. But I won't leave."

Graydon sipped his coffee, thinking. "Go wash your face. Get that crap off."

Without a word, Elly set her tea cup down and went to the bathroom. She ran warm water and scrubbed the scant makeup from her face. Glancing at herself in the mirror as she toweled dry, she saw that her face looked plainer, but nothing could dim the determination in her eyes.

She returned to the dining room and sat down to her tea again. When she turned her face to Graydon, awaiting his next test, her expression was clear, confident and forgiving.

"Put that damn cat out," he directed.

Elly rose from her chair and scooped Chester up off the floor. He protested, clawing her shoulder, but she carried him to the door and tossed him out. Moving by Graydon soundlessly, she regained her seat.

"Where's that picture?" Graydon demanded.

"Gone."

"Gone where?"

"Torn up and thrown out. I can dig it out of the trash if you want. It'll probably have coffee grounds on it, but I can find it for you."

He scowled into his coffee. "No. Forget it. Listen, all this means nothing, you know. It doesn't prove anything. Doing what I say doesn't mean everything's okay."

She nodded. "I know that."

"Well, then, goddamn it, why are you doing it?" He exploded, setting his cup down and pacing the kitchen. "Why are you acting like this, why do those things if they're not important?"

"Because," she explained simply. "That's the reason—they're not important. Nothing's as important as my love for you, not makeup, not Chester, not my wearing different clothes or working or Adam or this baby. It's all nothing compared to you and what we have. I'd give it all up in a second if it meant keeping you."

He didn't look at her, but paced the small area in front of the stove. "This doesn't make sense. Nothing makes sense. Why do I feel like I'm the one who should be apologizing? You're the one who's been harboring a picture of your dead lover and every time I look at those goddamn blue eyes of yours I feel like *I'm* the one who needs to be forgiven. This whole thing is insane."

Elly couldn't see that there was anything to say to that so she remained silent.

"Why didn't you tell me? Why didn't you just tell me about the goddamn picture? Why hide it?" He stopped pacing and pinned her with his eyes.

She had to look down at that. "I was stupid. I was afraid you'd think I was weak because I couldn't get over the nightmares." Humbled, she lifted her eyes. "I made the mistake of not being honest and I should have known better. I'm sorry for that, Graydon.

I'll never make that mistake again. Whatever I do, whatever I want or need, I'll trust you to understand, and I'll never hide anything from you again."

Where she might have expected her confession to spark anger or reprisal, she was surprised to realize that her humility had actually taken the wind out of Graydon's sails. His eyes lost their cold certainty. He reached for his coffee restlessly, then pushed it away again.

"Goddamn it, Elly. I wish just once that I could feel sure about you. You act one way, you do everything I could ever ask, and then something like this happens. You make me so mad I could strangle you but instead of cowering from me the way you should, you sit there calm as a cat and make me feel like I'm the one who's wrong. Once, just once, I wish you'd be a normal, average, predictable wife." He turned on her. "Why can't you do that?"

"I will if you want," she said quietly. "Just say the word. Do you want me to wear gray all the time? Do you want to take the BMW away from me so I can't go anywhere without you? Say the word and I'll be as dull and boring and predictable as you want."

He shook his head uselessly. "You know that's not what I want. I didn't marry you for that."

"Why did you marry me?" she asked.

Her question brought his eyes flashing over her. "Because I loved you. Because you are—were—sweet and scared and fun and pretty and everything I wanted."

"And have I changed so much because I made a stupid mistake?" she asked.

He frowned angrily. "I don't know. I can't tell. I'm not sure of anything any more."

She stared down at her cup. It was as much as she could expect.

"Jesus," Graydon swore impatiently. He pointed a commanding finger at her. "Look, just because I'm not tossing you out on your ass doesn't mean everything's okay. You can stay, but it's not like it was. I don't know if it can ever be that way again."

"All right," she breathed.

"And don't pressure me. I don't want you killing me with kindness, I don't want you acting like nothing happened. You stay on your side of things and leave me to mine. I'll decide in my own time whether or not I believe you, whether I can trust you."

"Okay."

Her agreement only seemed to provoke him more.

"And if I have any questions, if I ask you anything at all about anything, I want a truthful and honest answer. I don't care if you think I'll flatten you over it, I want the truth."

"You'll have it."

"Shit." He paced the kitchen once more, pushed his coffee cup further back on the counter and breezed by her into the living room. He grabbed the remote, punched on the TV and concentrated on changing channels. "Go put some makeup on. You look like a ghost."

Chapter Fifteen

The day was stiff at best. Elly left Graydon the couch and ensconced herself in the chair. They watched the Super Bowl without conversation, and in fact the only words spoken were short, necessary questions and monosyllabic answers. Elly made sandwiches for lunch and lasagna for dinner, announcing to Graydon in a low, undemanding voice. After dinner he disappeared into his basement shop and stayed there for hours. Elly understood. She watched TV for a while, then took a shower and went to bed alone.

She fell asleep before she ever heard Graydon come to bed.

Monday morning he was gone before she could manage to drag herself out of her exhausted sleep. His side of the bed was unmade, though, and his pillow was indented where his head had lain. She told herself that was progress.

For a brief moment, the clarity of morning was devastating. Wasn't she fooling herself? She'd won him back once, and then only grudgingly; was it really possible to do it again or was she just too stubborn and stupid to admit defeat? She lay in bed and stared out the window. No, she could do it. She had to.

One foot in front of the other, she told herself as she got dressed. No miracles, no breakthroughs, just one foot in front of the other. Step by step.

Her single-minded concentration was broken at noon when the phone rang. She left off warming up a bit of leftover lasagna and answered it. Graydon?

"Elly, Linda. You busy?"

"No," Elly breathed. "I was just fixing myself some lunch."

"Oh, okay." Linda's voice lowered conspiratorially. "I wanted to tell you about my weekend. You'll never believe it."

"Sure I will," Elly said. "I know you, remember?"

"No, but that's just the point. This wasn't like my normal weekend. God, I don't even know where to start."

"The beginning, maybe?" Elly suggested.

"Yeah, the beginning. Ron called me Friday night and we were just talking, you know? Well, I invited him over but he said no. That was kind of difficult for me, I mean what red-blooded American male turns down an invite to a not bad-looking if I say so myself red-blooded American girl's apartment, right? So anyway, I let it slide for a while but we kept on talking. I kept expecting him to say he had to go, like maybe he was busy or going out someplace else, but no, he just kept on like he had all the time in the world. Finally I asked him was he doing something else that night and he said no. So I said again why didn't he come over and he said no. I mean turned down twice in one night with not even a flimsy excuse! I was starting to get paranoid."

"Hmm," Elly murmured. She could tell Linda about feeling paranoid.

"So anyway, I couldn't stand it and I said how come? How come he wouldn't come over if he had nothing else to do? Well, talk about knock my socks off, know what he said?"

"No."

"He said, and I quote, 'You're too beautiful a person for me to come over and make love to you because I have nothing else planned for tonight.' I mean, God, can you believe that?"

"Nice," Elly said sincerely.

"Nice? My God, if he'd been there I would have attacked him. After that I couldn't even talk anymore, I mean my brain was so hypnotized that I couldn't even make sense. We didn't talk long after that." She paused.

"Okay."

"Okay, so he calls me Saturday night. By this time I don't even care that he's found out I stayed home alone both nights, I mean normally I'd give 'em an excuse like I was on my way out the door or something, but when I heard his voice I didn't even care. So we talked for awhile and something was said about not doing much and I almost—almost—asked him over. But I caught myself. So that passed and finally he said he had something he'd like to do Sunday evening and would I care to join him?"

"And did you?"

"Did I? Holy shit, yes. He picked me up last night at seven and we went to dinner, had a marvelous lobster, and then we drove."

"Drove where?"

"Just drove! All over! And he didn't even look twice at any dark alleys. I mean, I was on pins and needles all night, I'll tell you. It was incredible. Then, about eleven, he took me home."

Here it comes, Elly thought tiredly.

"I unlocked my door and started in, expecting him to follow, you know, but I turn around and he's just standing there on the porch. When I asked him what was wrong he said it was late and we both had work tomorrow and he was going home. I couldn't believe it. So I went back outside and stood there and said it was okay, I didn't mind, he could stay. So then he said, 'I'm not staying because you don't mind. Not minding is not a good enough reason.' Well, that just blew me away, I felt like he'd slapped me or something, so I said, okay, go. He stood there for a minute, just staring at me and he's got those gorgeous blue eyes like a fjord, you know, and he made me feel like an idiot and when I was about ready to go slam the door in his face, he puts one finger under my chin and very, very gently kisses me. Wow! What a kiss! I mean, he just brushes my lips with his, but Jesus! The old adrenalin starts pumping and the sparks flew. It was so erotic I just wanted to melt into his arms. I mean, he could have laid me out on the concrete and I wouldn't have known the difference."

"Mmm," Elly agreed.

"So then he left."

"Left? Just like that?"

"Just like that. Kisses me, says good night and leaves. I couldn't believe it. I think I almost broke my toe stumbling inside.

I've never, ever had a guy put me off before and still make me feel so good. It was amazing."

"Sounds it," Elly said.

"But that's not all," Linda went on. "He just called and asked me if I want to go to the zoo on Saturday!"

"The zoo?"

"The zoo! Can you believe it? And what's really freaky is—I want to. God, Elly, I think I'm finally flipping out. Can you believe it?"

"Barely," she said. She was glad for Linda, but her enthusiasm was limited.

"Hey," Linda said, "are you okay? You haven't been making your usual goody-two-shoes comments."

"It's nothing," Elly said, but she knew her voice was giving her away.

"Hey, come on, pal. You help me, I'll help you. Come on, what is it? You guys have a fight?"

Elly sighed. "Yes. Graydon found the picture of Adam. I forgot to throw it away and he thought I was hiding it."

"Oh, shit," Linda said. "Did he hit the ceiling?"

"To put it mildly." Thinking how close she had come to losing everything gave Elly the shivers. "In a way I can't blame him but he started dragging up everything from before, including the baby. God, it was awful."

"The baby?" Linda's voice was perplexed.

"Yes. Oh, you know, I've always meant to ask you about that. Did I ever tell you this was Adam's child?"

"Elly, are you crazy? What's the matter with you?"

"No, listen," Elly rushed on. "You've said things about it being Graydon's but to tell you the honest-to-God truth, I don't know whose it is. Remember when I said things were fuzzy and I didn't have clear memory?"

"Yes."

"Well, that wasn't the whole truth. I woke up in the hospital with amnesia—total, blanked out amnesia. I didn't even know my own name."

"Elly!"

"No, just listen, Linda. I tried to pretend, and most of the time

I could, but like the first time you called me and when you came over that day? I had no more idea who you were than the man in the moon. Most of the time I just let you talk and I made the right responses. Do you remember?"

"Well, now that you mention it, yeah, you acted funny. But *total* amnesia?"

"Total. Imagine waking up in a hospital not knowing who you are. Then add a huge, angry husband who accuses you of leaving him for another man but that man is now dead, but you're pregnant with that man's child."

"But it's not. Why would Graydon think that?"

Elly sighed. "Because apparently before I left, I wrote him a note and I told him the baby was Adam's."

"You didn't," Linda breathed hopefully.

"I did. I must have, but I don't remember. It's only now that things are starting to come back, like my wedding day, things Graydon and I did, the day I met Adam. But I don't know whose baby this is. Do you? I mean, for certain?"

"Hell, yes," Linda said. "It's Graydon's."

Elly crossed her fingers and tried not to let the spark of hope in her flare too high. "How do you know?"

"Because the day you found out you were pregnant you stopped by at lunch and we went out and cried together. You knew Graydon would just be furious at you for letting it happen."

"But ... did I...know Adam?"

"Sure. You'd met him, I don't know, maybe a week before."

"Then how do you know it wasn't his?"

"Because, ninny, you'd never let Adam so much as pay for your lunch or hold your hand, much less take you to bed. You tell me everything. That kid is no more Adam's than I am. It's Graydon's."

The words were a prison reprieve to Elly's ears. Graydon's child! She felt as light as a feather, drifting ecstatically up and out of the chains of doubt that had encased her. She could keep the baby! He'd have to let her now. He couldn't make her give up his own child. But something else sparked a new idea and Elly pierced the veil of joy she felt wrapped in and forced her mind to tend to it.

"Linda, answer me one more question. Since I told you everything, did I ever—I mean, as far as you know—did I...sleep with Adam?"

Linda snorted impatiently. "Are you kidding? Miss Virgin of the year 2000? The first time he kissed you I thought you were going to have a nervous breakdown. But to answer your question, as far as I know, which is up to the time you took off, no, you hadn't ever slept with him."

"Oh, thank you," she whispered.

"Which brings us to the original question I had for you in October. Why did you run off with him? I don't understand."

"That makes two of us," Elly said. "I wish I could remember!"

"Me, too," Linda said. "Well, at least we got a few things resolved. God, I wish you'd leveled with me before. It sounds like I could have saved you a whole lot of trouble."

"I know. And to think if we gave the baby up and then—"

"Gave it up?"

"Yes. You see Graydon and I agreed I'd have it—I almost didn't—but that I would give it up for adoption. We were going to tell everyone it was stillborn. He'd never allow me to keep it if it was Adam's."

"Jesus! Elly, you've got to tell me these things from now on. My God, you almost blew it."

"Yes," Elly agreed quietly. "I almost did. But I haven't and I won't, not now or ever. From now on, it's all going to be different. I can't wait to tell Graydon. He'll be so relieved."

"I'll bet," Linda said. Elly could imagine her shaking her head. "Whew! What a pair we are. Me screwing up because I'm too forward, you screwing up because you're too bashful. I think we both could learn a little from the other, you know?"

"Yes," Elly agreed, laughing. "It probably wouldn't hurt. Oh, Linda, I'm so excited!"

"God," Linda said, "I've created a monster. I can tell I'm not going to get any more intelligent conversation out of you today. Well, I ought to go get something for lunch, even if it's just a salad. Hell, I've only got ten minutes left of my lunch hour."

"I'm sorry," Elly said, but her voice was light. "I didn't mean to take all your lunch hour."

"Forget it. My pleasure. Just you make sure Graydon knows the score from now on. That's my godchild you're carrying."

"I will," Elly laughed. "And thanks, Linda. I can't tell you how much."

"So buy me lunch."

"You've got a deal."

Elly walked around in a dream state all afternoon. She hummed and pet Chester and kept a warm hand on her ripening stomach and smiled. Twice she reached for the phone and almost called Graydon at the Academy, but she stopped herself. She wanted to see his face. He'd be so pleased!

She started thinking of names. She prowled the spare bedroom, imagining soft curtains with calico stitching or maybe baby blue with playful animals.

They'd need a crib and a bassinette and—she ran and got out the blanket Clare gave her at Christmas. There was so much to think about!

She knew it was a boy, and she knew he'd look like Graydon. He had to. Dark hair, dark eyes. Feeling marvelously impulsive, she went to the den and pulled out Graydon's first photo album. There he was, at four. Graydon—and now their baby. Entranced, she followed the progress of Graydon's growth all over again, but this time imagined it was their son.

When she had finished looking at the second photo album, she started to reach for the last one and remembered, curiously, that the third one had disappeared. She'd never gotten around to asking Graydon about it, but it was still gone from the bookshelf. Maybe it was something he had found especially interesting and had kept out. She wanted to see, too. She began to search for it.

It wasn't in his desk. She riffled carefully through all the drawers, but no photo album. She scanned the other bookshelves again, but it wasn't there. The small closet held their bulky ski clothes and some outdated things they'd never thrown away; she searched through the boots and things on the floor. It just wasn't there.

Then her eye caught the gleam of light on vinyl and she reached up to the shelf across the top of the closet. Feeling proud of her ingenuity, she pulled down the photo album and settled into Graydon's chair to look through it.

More Air Force pictures. Some had a definite southern flavor, and occasionally she would see one of everglades or ocean breakers. She tried to think of an Air Force base in the south, but her knowledge was too limited.

She turned a page and was suddenly frozen by the picture before her. Her breath escaped in an abrupt arrest of her lungs and her eyes blurred. Her heart thumped like a warning rabbit. With suddenly trembling hands, she smoothed the plastic over the picture and forced herself to see clearly.

It was a picture of Graydon's wedding day—to someone else.

Elly's brain was too numb to make sense out of it. This was impossible. He was married to her. She'd seen pictures, she remembered the wedding. How could he have married someone else?

It was earlier, of course. She saw the youthful intensity in Graydon's face. He couldn't have been more than twenty-two or twenty-three at the most. And the girl was young, too.

Elly looked closer at her.

She was pretty. She had shoulder-length blonde hair, caught half back and softly laced with pale green ribbons. Her dress was a creation of lace and satin, white of course, and set off by the bouquet of tiny pink roses and green ribbon trim that she held at her side. Her eyes were a matching sea-green, set pertly in her joyous, smiling face. Graydon grimaced stiffly for the camera, but still it was obvious that he was embarrassingly pleased. They looked very nice together.

Elly had to blink and look away. This was insane. Why hadn't Graydon told her about this? She'd had no idea. And what happened to the girl? Had she died? Had they divorced?

A light went on in Elly's memory. Her father's voice swam back: "It was bad enough you marrying a sinner..." Divorced. That was it. Her family was Catholic, although casual about most of the ritual, but marrying a divorced man was adultery. No wonder her parents hated Graydon.

An ineffectual anger grabbed her. Why hadn't he told her?

After they'd left New Mexico, she'd asked him about her father's reference and he'd passed it off. He'd purposely kept it from her, right down to hiding the photo album. She balled her fists and tried to reason it out, but the aggravating unfairness of it wouldn't dissipate. How chastising he had been over the discovery of Adam's picture! It was so unfair!

She flipped through the rest of the pictures. There was Graydon in uniform again, and the girl in front of a military bungalow—their first home? Christmas pictures, Graydon and his wife and an older couple and a teen-aged boy. Elly could see the resemblance between the girl and the older woman. They all smiled a lot, and it looked like they were having a wonderful time. She turned the page.

The next pictures had a European look to them. There were a couple of peasant-flavored countrysides and narrow, cobbled streets. Small European cars and funny-looking taxis appeared indifferently. Elly searched for something to tell her where this was, but only some shop names were even partially readable. Was it German? She couldn't be sure.

Back to the everglades. There were pictures of professional water-skiers doing pyramids and easy-looking ballet arrangements. A crocodile hissed dramatically for a portrait. A couple of pictures of swampy-looking jungle had an angular border across one corner, as if taken from a boat. There was one of the girl holding up a hot dog and laughing. She looked very pretty.

Then nothing. The rest of the album was empty.

Elly closed it and laid it on the floor, her head pounding. It was like a bad dream, only it wouldn't fade away. She closed her eyes but that only made an ominous backdrop for the image of Graydon marrying someone else. Her eyes flew open. It wasn't fair. She'd tried to be honest—even if she had made a cowardly mistake—but Graydon hadn't. He'd deliberately lied to her and hidden away the evidence. She felt righteous anger coursing through her and below that, pain. But she wouldn't cry. No, she wouldn't allow that.

When he came home that night, the aroma of fried chicken greeted him at the door. Elly made sure she was too busy in the kitchen to lean around the corner to say hello. She heard him hang up his coat in the hall closet and then, unhurriedly, he came to stand in the kitchen doorway.

She glanced up from her industrious mashing of potatoes, but failed to greet him.

Graydon stood resolutely silent for a moment, watching her work. He seemed half resolved not to speak first, but Elly's lack of friendliness was like an unexpected assault. He shifted restlessly against the counter.

"How long til dinner?" he asked.

Elly hesitated, too busy to answer right away. "About five minutes," she said finally.

He nodded, not liking the coolness in the kitchen. "Any mail?"

"On the end table," she said. "Mostly junk."

He took the excuse to move away from the kitchen. Elly finished her preparations and set dinner on the table.

When they sat down across from each other, there was no doubt that a challenge was in the air. Elly coolly smoothed her napkin over the bulge of her stomach, but every time she lifted her eyes to Graydon, they snapped blue fire. He recognized the aggravation and frowned.

"Why do I get the impression that you have something to unload on me?" he asked.

"Do you?" she retaliated quietly.

He picked up a piece of chicken and tore it apart with his fork. "All right," he said, "let's hear it. But if it's about Saturday, I'm not in the mood to rehash all that again. There's nothing else to say."

"It's not about Saturday."

He glanced up, suspicious. "Then what? I don't like the way you're looking at me as if you'd like to bite my head off."

Elly clasped her hands beneath the table just so she would have something to hold on to. She didn't trust herself to hold a fork or knife.

"Tell me about your first wife," she said.

Graydon's jaw ticked and his eyes darkened. "What's to tell? You knew about her. I told you about her before we got married."

"Maybe you did," Elly said, leaning toward him. "But you didn't tell me about her since the accident."

"So?" he challenged. "It wasn't important."

"It was important enough for you to lie to me about it. It was important enough for you to hide the photo album with her picture in it." She unclenched her hands and brought them up to the table to push herself back in her chair. "I want to know why, Graydon."

"That's over, Elly. It was over a long time ago. Forget it."

"No, I won't forget it. You lambaste me for having a picture of Adam and all the while you're sitting high and mighty on pictures of her! How dare you be so smug and righteous when you've out and out lied to me! You knew when my father called you a sinner, you knew what he was talking about. Why didn't you tell me?"

Graydon refused to acknowledge her charges and returned his attention to his plate. "It wouldn't have helped matters any, not right then. Anyway, what I did before we were married is quite a bit different from what you've done while you were my wife. I'm not guilty of anything."

"Neither am I," her voice rang. "I've leveled with you, Graydon, I've told you everything I can, everything I know. Now it's your turn. I want to know about her."

He quirked an eyebrow at her. "Are you jealous?"

That was an unexpected hit. She drew in a shaky breath. "I don't know. Should I be?"

"No. Just forget it. It's better this way." He dismissed her.

"Damn it, no, Graydon! I want to know. You're my husband, I have a right to know about you. I have a right to know why you've deliberately hidden it from me."

He set down his fork carefully and met her eyes. "It's over, Elly. What happened before has no bearing on us now. I'd prefer not to talk about it." His jaw was tight, his words final.

"Why not?" she pressed.

Now he was angry. "Because I don't! Did I ask you for full details of all your boyfriends before me? Hell, no. Karen and I were divorced years before I met you. It's history, Elly; forget it."

"Karen," she mused. "Karen what? Where was she from?"

"Elly," he warned. "I'm not going to talk about this. Let it be."

"Why did you get divorced? What happened?"

"I've told you as much as you need to know," he said.

"Which is nothing. Graydon, you can't badger me about being honest with you if you aren't honest with me."

"Like hell," he said angrily. "What you want to know about happened before I met you. What I want to know about happened now. Anyway a previous marriage can't compare to bearing another man's child."

Elly nodded. She'd known that it would inevitably get back around to that; it always did. But this time she didn't have to shrink away from it.

"I'm not," she said.

He frowned impatiently. "Not what?"

"Not bearing another man's child."

He glared at her, the black of his eyes reaching out like dark things in the night. "What the hell does that mean?"

"Just exactly what I said." She drew a steadying breath. "It's not Adam's child. It's yours."

There was no change in his expression, no flicker of emotion. Except for the rhythmic rise and fall of his chest, he might have been carved of stone.

The silence hung almost tangibly in the air between them.

"You're crazy if you think I'm going to believe that," he muttered finally.

"It's true."

"That's not what you told me before. You said it was Adam's." His voice was still flat and unconvinced.

Elly shrugged. "I lied before."

"Why?"

"I don't know. I can't remember."

Graydon pushed himself out of his chair and began to pace. His jaw was so tight Elly was afraid he was grinding the surfaces from his teeth. His hands, although not fisted, flexed restlessly.

"Damn it, Elly, this is insane. You can't expect me to believe that. You're just saying that to throw me off. You're just trying to smooth things over."

She shook her head. "No, I'm not, Graydon. It's true. I found out today."

"Found out? From who?"

"Linda."

Graydon made an uncharitable face. "And you believed her? That slut?"

"She's not a slut. She's a very unhappy, lonely woman, and she's a good friend. Anyway, when I mentioned the baby she couldn't believe I ever thought it was Adam's."

"Why not?"

"Because," Elly said, and rushed on before she had time to think about it, "she said I had never slept with Adam when I found out I was pregnant."

Graydon had stopped pacing but his expression didn't improve. He scoured Elly's face, searching for a crack in her facade. He seemed disturbed that he could find none.

"How do I know that?" he growled.

She sighed. "You don't. But I imagine when the baby's born you'll see."

He looked away. "We're giving the baby up, remember? We'll never see it."

Elly felt as if he'd slapped her. Even the sag of his shoulders and the obvious guilt in his voice couldn't ease the sense of betrayal she felt, or the outrage.

"No," she choked. "You can't mean that. It's our baby. I'm not giving it up."

He impaled her with his eyes. "What if it comes out with hazel eyes? What then? I'm not raising another man's brat."

"It's *yours!*" Elly almost screamed. "Can't you understand that? It's not Adam's, it's yours!"

He turned his back on her. "You're shouting, Elly. You're getting overemotional. I think you ought to calm down."

She was fighting tears of frustration, but Graydon's denial coupled with his heartless lack of concern was almost too much. She shook with gasping breaths.

"I'm not giving up our child," she said slowly. "You can't make me."

He stared out the window now, his eyes sightlessly piercing the dark. "You going to raise it alone?" he asked.

Her outrage crumbled. The tears welled up and over her lids, coursing down her cheeks. She wiped at them weakly.

"Graydon, no," she sobbed. "It's ours. I want us to raise it together. Please, Graydon, don't do this to me. We were happy once. We can be happy again."

He leaned heavily against the window sill, his hesitation like a knife in Elly's heart.

"I don't know," he murmured. "I can't even think. God, what a mess."

"But—"

"No," he stopped her. "Leave it, Elly." He shook his head as if to clear it. "Just let it be for now. I don't want to talk about it anymore." He turned away from the window and swept her with his eyes. "I'm going to the den for a while. I want to be alone. Just let me think about it for a while, okay?" His voice, although firm, was not unkind. Elly had to swallow a protest, but she managed.

"Okay."

He held her gaze for another second, then walked slowly to his den. The door clicked shut behind him.

For the first half hour, Elly could keep herself busy by clearing the table, wrapping up the uneaten dinner and putting it in the refrigerator, doing the dishes. After that, she had nothing to do but wait.

The closed door of the den was like a magnet, drawing her eyes constantly or looming at the edge of her vision. She sat on the hearth where she could see the first movement of the door knob and let Chester sleep in her lap. The clock above her ticked ominously.

It was almost like the way she was drawn to the mural. After that first encounter with the hazel-eyed lively artist, Elly had found her eyes wandering to the mural whenever she was close to a window. That teaching assignment had lasted two weeks straight; long enough to leave her susceptible to Adam's optimism. He hadn't wasted any time, either.

Two days after she had trooped her second graders past the half-painted wall, she walked a circuitous route to her car after school and had seen Adam again. He was engrossed in his work and she thought she might tiptoe past while still remembering the touch of his eyes, but he'd seen her and called for her to stop. She did.

"How do you like it?" he asked in a friendly voice. His eyes sparkled with green lights as he studied her face.

"It's going to be very nice," she said. "I like the colors and the line movement. It's perfect for the school." Embarrassed by his attention, she kept her comments impersonal.

The artist seemed to look right through her unsteady professionalism.

"What's your name? I'm Adam Wolfford."

"Elly Cole." She kept her hands rigidly on her purse, not offering any contact. Adam appeared not to notice.

"You in a hurry?" he asked. "I'd like to buy you a cup of coffee."

"Oh, no," Elly blushed. "I can't." She started to back away.

"How about tomorrow? Lunch. I'll tell you all about my mural and you can tell your kids. They'd like that, wouldn't they?"

"Oh, probably, but I can't really. Thanks, though." She kept moving backward, almost panic-stricken now by his offer. Even with Graydon far away she could feel the sick fear his jealousy caused in her.

"Hey," Adam called. "I don't bite. What's the matter? Just a cup of coffee won't hurt." His optimism was dampened by surprise at Elly's fearful rejection.

"No." She shook her head. "I can't. I—I'm married." With that, she spun away and headed rapidly for her car.

Still the mural had drawn her like a flame draws a moth. The next morning she had cautiously avoided walking anywhere near the wall, but in class she watched out the window as Adam added bold strokes to his creation. Occasionally he would turn and scan the classroom windows, and Elly would duck instinctively away. Not that he was looking for her, she chastised herself; no one would look twice at her. She was plain. But married women shouldn't talk to strange men anyway. She wouldn't talk to him again.

At lunch she had no choice. Seated alone at a small table in the faculty cafeteria, she was startled to have someone plop a tray full of food across from hers. Her bite of sandwich went unswallowed as she watched Adam fold his tall, thin frame into the opposite chair.

"Hello, pretty lady. Mind if I join you?" She almost choked in panic. Her eyes darted around the cafeteria nervously.

"Don't worry," Adam said. "You're not the only teacher I've picked on. I imposed myself on someone else yesterday."

"No," Elly said in a hoarse voice. "It's not that, it's not you. I—I..."

"Yeah, I know," he smiled brightly. "You're married. That's okay, I only want to have lunch with you. That's not considered adultery, is it? Having lunch with a married woman?"

Elly felt her panic recede under his good-natured teasing. He flashed an adorable dimpled smile at her and she returned it hesitantly. "No," she said finally. "It's not. I'm sorry I acted so foolishly."

Adam unwrapped a triangular-cut sandwich and added salt to the beef inside. "That's okay. You're pretty flighty, though, you know. What's the matter? You get accosted by a weirdo some time?"

Elly looked down at her own food in embarrassment. "No, I...my husband is extremely jealous. There have been too many times when I've seen him breathing fire over another man's casual remark. I suppose I'm just conditioned to it."

Adam chewed thoughtfully. "I see. That's his problem, though, you know. Not yours. And he's not here." He smiled again.

Elly felt the pangs of guilt return. No, Graydon wasn't here; she was. And she was having lunch with another man.

"I can see where he'd be pretty busy keeping you isolated, though," Adam continued amiably. "Anyone ever tell you that you have gorgeous eyes?"

Elly blushed furiously at the compliment and became so disoriented she dropped her napkin and almost spilled her milk trying to retrieve it. When she had straightened herself out, she ate as if Adam had never said a word. She kept her eyes resolutely down.

"You're pretty strange, pretty lady," he said more quietly.

"Please," Elly said, "don't call me that." She stabbed at her gelatin nervously.

"Why not?"

"Because I'm not pretty and I know it. And I don't like being complimented."

She felt Adam's eyes on her, the weight of them bowing her head. She wanted to get up and leave but was afraid he'd call after her. She couldn't bear to have everyone in the room staring at her—at them.

"Boy," Adam said finally. "Someone sure did a number on you." He munched his sandwich thoughtfully, no longer demanding any kind of answers from Elly.

"You know," he said, "I used to be sort of like you. Everyone had always told me the days of the freelance troubadour artist were gone and that if I wanted to support myself I had to settle down, get a job and trade hack work for hack pay. And I believed them. The only thing I didn't know was that none of those people had ever tried it or, for that matter, even understood what I was or what I wanted. I don't know exactly how it happened, but I thought a lot about it and it made me mad. I finally realized I had let others put restrictions on me, restrictions that held them in but shouldn't—didn't—apply to me. I looked at the work I was doing—billboards, yet—and hated it. So one day I broke loose, took my acrylics and my brushes and headed out. I left behind me all the don'ts and can'ts and impossibles of other people. And I became what I thought I could be."

He swung his eyes back to Elly, catching her staring at him. She looked quickly away.

"That's nice for you," she said in a small voice.

"It's nice for you, too," he said. He waited until she looked up. "I'm a person and you're a person. Both of us can do or be whatever we want. You have the capacity for beauty in you, just like I had the capacity for art. No one's stopping you but you. Dump those restrictions other people have put on you." He leaned forward. "You *are* a pretty lady."

The flustering embarrassment returned to sear Elly's face. She fumbled with her napkin, holding on to it this time, but crumpling it on her tray.

"I have to go," she said, and rose to leave.

"Great," Adam said. He pushed his tray away smoothly and fell in beside her. "It's much nicer outside, anyway."

Elly was almost blind with embarrassment. She hurried from

the cafeteria, her heels clicking nervously on the floor. Adam caught the door and held it for her, but she almost ran through it without a glance.

"You see," Adam said, "you've let other people tell you you're not pretty; your husband for example." She flashed him a strangled look. "Bull's eye, right? Well, what does he know? What gives him the right to impose his opinions or cockeyed beliefs on you? You're a grown up adult, you can think for yourself. What do you think?"

"I think you're crazy and will you please leave me alone?" she cried.

"You shouldn't listen to him. He's obviously got some kind of insecurity complex and he's scared to death some guy's going to look at you and you're going to look back and there goes husband by the wayside. So he concocts this story that you're—not ugly— let's say plain, and that keeps you in line. How am I doing?"

"Please," Elly wailed, still charging across the school grounds, "please leave me alone."

"That way, you see, he doesn't have to be there to guard you all the time; you guard yourself. Like now. Most guys would take your word for it that you're not pretty and, therefore, not worth getting to know. But I'm a little different. When I look at you, I see a pretty lady, and nothing you or anyone else says will make me see you differently."

Elly stopped and faced him, her anxiety growing into panic. "Please leave me alone. You don't know me. You don't know what you're saying." She shifted her eyes nervously to his and away, then darted off again.

"Think about it," Adam called. "You'll realize I'm right."

And she had thought about it. As she looked back on it now, she could view dispassionately the way she had anguished over the forbidden glimpse of freedom, the potential that Adam had seen and offered her in his cheerful, lunatic way. She had wanted very badly to believe, to let Adam's simple, resounding truths become true for her.

Then she found out she was pregnant and she knew she had failed Graydon again.

The click of the den door brought her back to the present.

Graydon stepped into the hall, a tired, haggard look on his face.

"Are you still up?" he asked, not unkindly.

"What time is it?"

"Almost midnight. What are you doing?"

She rose from the hearth. "Waiting for you. And remembering."

He quirked an eyebrow at her.

"I can remember, Graydon. I remember when I first met Adam, and I can remember when I found out I was pregnant. It wasn't him. It's always been you."

The slow shaking of Graydon's head stopped her. "Do you know how many times I've gone back over this in my mind? One time I think it doesn't matter and the next time I know it does. It's not my way to trust blindly, to let my guard down. I did it with you—twice—and got burned for it. I can't let myself do it again. I can't believe you."

"But—"

"No," he stopped her. "You'll have the baby, there's no question there. If I see it and have any doubts—any at all—we'll give it up. I won't take the chance that I might be made a fool again."

"You'd rather take the chance of giving away your own child?" she asked.

"I can't help it." He shrugged tiredly. "I guess that's just the sort of man I am. This isn't easy for me, Elly, but neither is it easy thinking of you in bed with another man—with or without conceiving a child. But this is the way it's going to have to be."

Elly had to swallow before she could talk; her mouth had gone dry. "And by doing this," she asked, "you expect us to have a close, loving relationship? Living on the edge of doubt?"

Graydon looked at her sadly. "All the time you were regaining your memory you kept telling me you had to be you, whether I liked it or not. Well, I have to be me now. If we can work it out, fine; if not..."

His voice trailed off, timelessly sad with the finality of his unfinished statement. Elly felt the weight of it descend on both of them, locking them into the double yoke of a long, hard pull. She squared her shoulders and clenched her jaw.

"All right, Graydon," she said. "I'll be me and you be you. Let's just hope we can work something out before it all falls apart."

Chapter Sixteen

The days were disjointed after that, permeated with a tenseness that grated on Elly's nerves. She did her best to ignore the strain, bringing home color chips to mull over for the nursery, leaving a baby name book on the end table, telling herself Graydon would come around before too long. But his despondent lack of spunk nagged at her. He was calm, usually agreeable, and practically unflappable. It was demoralizing to Elly. She began to be afraid that she had actually pushed him too far and that his feelings for her—love, hate, whatever it was—had lapsed into apathy.

As she started her seventh month, she became more and more aware of the baby. He did summersaults and kicked carelessly, even upsetting a book she had propped on her stomach one night in bed.

"What was that?" Graydon asked. He glanced over from his perusal of a skiing magazine to see Elly rubbing her sore abdomen and relocating her page in the book.

"Just the tiger," she said casually. "He's gotta be a field-goal kicker. No quarterback has any business having power like that in one leg."

Graydon let his gaze slide from Elly's face to the mound of her stomach, now calm, and regarded it intently for a second. Then he turned back to his magazine. Elly released the breath she was holding, put aside the hope she'd been harboring and returned to her book. Give it time, she thought; just give it time.

One day early in February she was dusting Graydon's den and noticed the third photo album was back in place. At first she ignored it, telling herself she was strong enough to resist its pull, that it didn't matter who Graydon had married or why. As she dusted, though, she moved about the room in a lazy, haphazard way, yet every slow step took her closer to that shelf. When finally her feather duster swept away the invisible traces of dust from the top of its tightly closed pages, she knew she would look again. She wanted to see the girl that Graydon loved before her and now refused to even discuss. Maybe something in the girl's face would tell Elly what Graydon wouldn't.

The pictures were gone.

The pages were marked with faint lines framing the shapes of the pictures, but everywhere there had been anything reminiscent of Karen, even down to the Southern jungle, was emptiness. Elly flipped through the album twice to be sure. Gone. Every picture was gone.

She wasn't sure if she felt relief or annoyance. Did he think hiding them would make her forget about them? Would it erase the fact from his life or eradicate the unpleasantness that was stoppered inside him? She snapped the album shut and returned it to its shelf. She would ask him. Tonight.

"I threw them away."

His voice was calm, normal, yet not encouraging. Elly heard the suggestion that the subject be dropped. She ignored it.

"When?" She was doling up t-bones on plates and used the diversion to keep from meeting Graydon's eyes.

"That night. I should have done it along time ago."

She set his plate down in front of him and added a steaming baked potato. "You weren't married long, were you?" she asked.

Graydon raised an uncompromising face to her. "Drop it, Elly."

"There's no harm in that, is there? How long you were married? What, a year? Two?" She turned away for her own plate and let him spend his frown on her receding back.

"Not quite two," he muttered.

She settled across the table from him and knifed butter on her potato. "You must not have been back from Europe very long."

"Elly," he warned.

"Well, it's just that there were so few pictures after that. Only one or two of her, I think." His glaring eyes seemed to have no effect on her casual table manners. "You never told me you were in Europe," she continued, undaunted. "At least not lately. How long were you there?"

"Nine months. Pass the salt."

"In Germany? Was that where you were?"

"Yes. But some of those pictures are of Austria." Even though he answered her, his voice was still surly.

"I remember seeing *The Sound of Music*. I loved the pictures of the meadows just below the Alps. Did you go any place like that?"

He cut his steak with somber attention. "Once."

"Was it as pretty as the movie showed it?"

Graydon forked a tender piece of steak into his mouth and chewed absently, his black eyes boring into Elly. "No. It was prettier. And that's all I'm going to say."

She shrugged, dramatically unruffled. "I was just wondering..."

"That's *all*, Elly. Drop it." This time she did.

Valentine's Day was looming. Elly did a lot of thinking and finally decided she'd make an occasion out of it whether Graydon did or not. It was getting difficult for her to jockey her stomach behind the steering wheel of the BMW but she spent a day in town and ended up buying Graydon a box of dark Danish chocolates and a heart-shaped, ruffled pillow that had its own scented cachet of wild flowers inside. She hoped to spark some emotion into him with her gifts.

He had made love to her twice since the blow up over Adam's picture, both times late at night and both times leaving her less than satisfied. Not that he made love badly; regardless of the rift between them, he knew how to excite her and the touch of his hands brought her immense pleasure, but emotionally he held her at arm's length, and the closeness they'd had was missing. Even when Elly's body was subdued by sexual satiation, her heart and mind were left still wanting when Graydon rolled away. She hoped she could change that.

On Valentine's Day she baked a cake and decorated it with red and pink hearts. She managed to concoct one of Graydon's favorite meals—fried shrimp and egg foo yaung—and even put Chester out before Graydon was due to arrive. She lit candles in the living and dining rooms and left most of the lights off. When she heard the Ford pull into the driveway she smoothed her pleated-front blouse over her bulge and patted her hair into place.

"Hello," she called. "Did you have a good day?"

"Not bad," he muttered, not yet alert to the fact that Elly had plans in store. "Now that Warner has gone on to flight training, it's not near as difficult as it was. These kids I've got now are a lot less bull-headed."

"Good," Elly said. She slipped him a quick kiss on the cheek as she crossed into the dining room with her covered Oriental dishes. Graydon left the mail where he had been glancing through it at the kitchen counter and followed her to the table.

"What's this?" he asked. He went to lift the cover off of one of the pedestal dishes but Elly slapped his hand away lightly.

"You'll see," she teased. "You haven't washed your hands."

Graydon glared at her passively and strode to the sink. "What are you, my mother?" he growled.

Elly ignored the dig and seated herself cheerfully at the table. When Graydon took his place across from her, she lifted both covers and presented the meal.

"Ta da!"

"Hm," Graydon said, eyeing the feast. "Looks good."

Proud and relieved, Elly watched as Graydon heaped his plate with food. "You aren't very hungry are you?" she asked.

"Starving. This is enough for me but what are you going to eat?"

Elly made a playful face at him and began to serve herself.

After dinner, Elly cleared the table and said nothing when Graydon took the mail to the couch and settled in to go over it. Quietly she set the cake out on the table and then, making sure he wasn't watching, laid out her presents for him at his place. She stuck a lone pink candle in the center of the cake and lit it.

"Would you like some dessert?" she called casually.

"Dessert?" He questioned her but didn't raise his eyes. They didn't normally have dessert; Graydon liked to keep fit and Elly didn't need any help gaining weight.

"Yes, dessert," she said. She got a couple of small plates and a knife, and this time when she walked to the table, Graydon was staring over the back of the couch.

"What's this for?" he asked. He got up slowly, interested but not willing to show it.

"It's Valentine's Day," she said.

He came and stood at his chair, his eyes taking in the hearts on the cake and the presents. "Hmm," he said unemotionally, "so it is. I'd almost forgotten."

Elly brushed away her hurt at his lack of sentimentality and cut two pieces of cake. She set one piece in front of him and tried not to think how badly she had hoped he would remember. It wasn't that he hadn't bought her a present; that was not important. What was important was that he hadn't even thought of her. She focused her eyes on her cake and blinked back unsteady tears as she ate.

"Am I supposed to open these?" he asked.

Elly kept her eyes down. "If you want."

The rattle of crushed paper made her lift her eyes. He casually slipped the wrapping off the smaller package and crumpled the paper into a ball. Not looking at Elly, he opened the box. The chocolates lay assembled neatly for him.

He seemed at a loss for words and Elly felt herself sinking deeper into depression. His hesitation told how uncomfortable he was with her presents.

"Danish?" he asked finally.

Elly nodded, miserable.

He picked one up, looked at it, then returned it to its paper nest and replaced the top of the box. He reached for the second present.

Elly didn't want to see anymore. She slid from her chair.

"I can't eat anymore," she said as she cleared her half-eaten cake from the table. Moving nervously from the dining room, she took her plate and scraped the rest of her cake into the trash. While Graydon was still crumpling paper, she made a production of rinsing her plate and putting it in the dishwasher.

When she turned half-heartedly back to the dining room, Graydon was gone.

She swore at herself. Why had she done this? Had she really thought her sentimental silliness could bring out the love he didn't trust her with? The baby kicked restlessly, perhaps as a result of her anxiety. She smoothed a hand over her stomach and sighed; so much for Valentine's Day.

Then the front door opened. She was surprised to see Graydon striding in—she hadn't heard him leave—and wondered at the curiously arranged expression on his face. He walked up to her and, with a slight hesitation, produced a red-wrapped box from behind his back.

Elly gaped. "What's this?" she asked in disbelief.

"Didn't you just tell me it was Valentine's Day?"

"Y-yes."

"Well, this is a Valentine's Day present." He gestured toward the table. "You know, like those things over there, the pillow, the chocolates. Remember?"

Elly had to study his face to be able to read his voice. His words were mocking, teasing her, but his mouth curved ever so slightly and his dark eyes were velvet soft. Elly smiled.

"Thank you, Graydon," she breathed. She took the present with reverent hands.

"Don't thank me yet—you haven't seen what it is." He guided her back to her chair at the table and while she tore the paper off the package, he finished his cake. His eyes danced at her excitement.

Elly produced a box, pulled it open and drew out a beautiful heart-shaped music box. Made of heavy silver filigree, it stood on miniature claw feet and when Elly opened the red enameled lid, it played soft tinkling notes of a familiar song. She lifted her eyes to Graydon.

"Lara's theme," he said.

Elly felt the tears coming again, a different kind of tears. She forced them back. "It's beautiful, Graydon. Thank you."

He smiled. "Not as beautiful as my pillow," he said, "but I'm not very good at those sorts of things." Elly couldn't hold back anymore. Clutching the music box, she circled the end of the table and fell emotionally to her knees at Graydon's chair. Her eyes shone up at him in gratitude.

"Hey," he said softly. "What's this?"

"I can't help it," she said in a breaking voice. "I love you, Graydon. I love you so much."

He lifted her gently off the floor, standing them both so he could frame her face with his hands only inches from his.

"I don't want you on your knees, Elly," he whispered. "That's not where you belong."

"Where do I belong?" she asked.

He smoothed a finger over her cheek adoringly. "Beside me. Always beside me."

March was a horrible month. The early spring storms rolled up from the south and buffeted the east slope with rain, hail and tornadoes. Graydon didn't like Elly going anywhere by herself, so most days she and Chester huddled together on the couch. A fire was out of the question—too much danger of downdrafts—so Elly turned the heat up and kept Chester close, even on top of the baby if she could manage it. Around them the house creaked and moaned against the constant pressure of the wind.

One day she propped herself up on the couch with pillows and, while Chester purred contentedly beside her, tried to think of good names for the baby. She stared out the front window at the curtains of rain that came in ever-advancing ranks, like armies of shimmering silver. It was a quiet, thoughtful day.

She was sure Graydon would not want to have the baby named Junior. He was a self-made man, and he would want his son to be the same way; no Junior. Maybe Graydon for a middle name. That would be okay. But she had to think of something that sounded good with Cole.

She liked the sound of Nathan. The only problem with it was that it was too similar to Graydon; Nathan Graydon Cole. No, that wasn't good. She scratched Nathan. What about Randall? Randy Cole. She liked that.

The rain sheeted in a northerly slant outside, driving from left to right across the window. Then, with an abrupt change in the wind, it drove directly at the glass pane, riddling the window like bullets. Elly jerked back against her pillows instinctively, the sight of the flattening pellets drawing fear from somewhere inside of her.

It was so hard to see, she thought restlessly, so hard to see the road. She was looking for a bus depot, scouring the obscurity out the car window for a neon bus sign. But it was dark and blurred and so hard to see.

And then there were lights—red lights, flashing brighter, glaring at her through the rain, saying *stop, stop, oh please, stop.*

She jerked herself into a sitting position and inadvertently rolled Chester off the couch. He landed, cat-like, on his feet, but stood and glanced around irritably at finding himself awake on the floor instead of asleep on Elly's warm stomach.

She felt similarly disoriented. The dream—vision?—was less pictures than it was feelings, and the aftertaste of fear lingered. She knew it had to be the accident; it was too similar to the dream of the headless man to be anything else. The rain had triggered it, just like it had the night of her first dream, just like it had flattened her against the car seat on the way home from the hospital. The driving, blinding rain took her back and made her afraid.

She breathed deeply to calm her racing heart. She'd be glad when she could remember fully and less emotionally, so the impact of what happened wasn't so real. Now, she still couldn't piece it all together. Had she really been looking for a bus sign? Or just any sign, a neon landmark in the gray sea of night? She couldn't remember with any certainty. A shiver crawled up her back. She pushed away the memory and went to get herself another warm cup of tea.

That night she told Graydon, briefly, about the waking dream. She had taken to sleeping on her side with a pillow beneath her stomach and she lay that way now, facing Graydon. He bracketed her and watched her in the darkness as she talked.

"No headless man?" he asked.

She shivered. "No, thank God. But I'd sure like to know exactly what I was looking for."

"You will," he said. "In time."

"I suppose so. It's awful remembering only half, though. If I could understand them, the memories wouldn't be so hard to cope with. I'd like to be able to analyze them, take them apart bit by bit and then I know they wouldn't bother me so much."

"Do you think so?" His voice was unconvinced.

Elly tried to read his expression, but it was impossible in the dark.

"Yes," she said, "I do. If I can understand why I acted a certain way, why something affected me a certain way, I can analyze it and see if it's really valid or if I had any other options. I know it."

"Hmm," Graydon said. "Maybe. Maybe it would work for you. Are you ready to go to sleep?"

She recognized the suggestion in his voice. He didn't want to talk anymore. "Yes," she lied. After he kissed her goodnight and dropped into deeper breathing, she lay awake and thought for a long, long time.

Graydon's birthday was March sixteenth. It was also the first day of Elly's eighth month, and she felt almost intolerably heavy. It was a chore to steer her bulging medicine ball of a stomach around the house.

Still, she had plans for Graydon's birthday. She made reservations for them at the Castaways and carefully wrapped the watch she'd bought him. It was gold with a black face, set with one shining diamond at the twelve position. It reminded her of Graydon—dark, unreadable, but lit by a flashing fire.

Unfortunately she realized that it reminded her of Adam, too. Maybe not specifically Adam, but what he had called her—a diamond in the rough. As conditioned as she was to shrink from his compliments, that one had touched her emotions and fired a nerve of pleasure and warmth she hadn't known she had.

After the ghastly lunch in the cafeteria, Elly had eaten her sandwich furtively in her car for two days. On the third day Adam had found her. Letting himself into the passenger side of the BMW, he had grinned pleasantly at Elly.

"Hi. Found a new place to eat lunch, huh? How's the food?"

Elly's face flamed in agony. "Oh, please," she said, glancing around, "what if someone sees?"

"Sees what? All I want to do is talk to you. You're a very intriguing lady."

"But it looks so...so..."

"Intimate?" he supplied. Elly closed her eyes in painful embarrassment. "I'll tell you what," Adam continued amiably, "there's a little lunch place not far from here. We could drive over there in about two minutes and no one would see us. Would that be better?"

"No," Elly said shaking her head. "Please leave me alone." She stared down at her half eaten sandwich and realized she was no longer hungry.

"Hey," Adam said softly. "I'm not trying to annoy you. I like you. I think you're a nice lady."

"Then why won't you leave me alone?" she wailed.

"Because I also think you're an unhappy lady, and I'd like you to know that you don't have to be."

Elly met his eyes, her own terrified blue ones against his serious, sparkling hazel ones. "Please go away. Can't you see that I'm not happy knowing anyone could see us?"

Adam's eyes darkened slightly in conspiracy. "Then let's go to that place I mentioned. Come on, just lunch, I promise. I won't even make you late."

Elly recognized an unyielding firmness behind Adam's light suggestion. It was akin to the strength she saw in Graydon, and her father—and everyone, it seemed, except her. She started the car.

"Which way?" she sighed.

Adam tried to buy her lunch but she had insisted on separate tickets when the waitress took their order. While Adam made casual, offhand conversation, she toyed with her water glass, making rings on the plastic table top. She was still in agony over the thought that someone might recognize her.

"You see, the thing is," he said, "everyone's equal. You know, the old 'all men are created equal' bit? And that doesn't mean civil rights necessarily, or opportunity. It means no one is better than anyone else, no one has any more right to direct your life than you do. When I look into your big baby blues, I see someone who believes *everyone* has a better idea than you do of what to do with your life. And I think that's a real shame."

The waitress brought napkins and silverware, giving Elly a chance to glance shyly at Adam while he sat back in his seat. He really did look kind, not like a loony. But she couldn't understand what he wanted with her, or why.

"Are you a..." she tried to ask when the waitress left but realized she didn't know the word she was looking for.

"A what?" he grinned.

She shook her head. "I don't know. A cultist? A hippy? Why do you care if I'm happy or not?"

His eyes bored into hers. Suddenly the lighthearted comic was gone. "Because I don't like to see people unhappy if they don't have to be. Some people like it, they create their own hell, but you—you're a victim. You're a blue-eyed doe with hunters running you ragged by their potshots at you." He leaned forward. "You don't have to let anyone run you around if you don't want to. If you started standing up to people, they'd take a second look and they'd have to say, 'hey, this is no deer. This is a capable adult human being. And not a bad looking one, either. Maybe I won't shoot at her anymore.'"

Elly blushed and concentrated on her rings of water. "You're insane," she said, but her voice smiled.

"And loving it," he added. "Tell me about you. What do you like to do?"

"Oh," she brushed it off, "not much. I'm not very interesting."

Adam smiled. "Yes, you are. You like kids. You like to teach. What else do you like to do?"

Surprisingly, Elly had started to tell him.

It wasn't until the waitress brought their food that she realized she'd been talking about her teaching, how challenging it was, how fulfilling it was to instill knowledge into the children. At the arrival of lunch, she had stopped abruptly, embarrassed.

"And?" Adam coaxed.

"That's all," she insisted.

"No," he said slowly, "I don't think so. What about your personal life? Have any kids of your own?"

The offhand question brought a sickness to Elly, like a hard fist in her stomach. Involuntarily she doubled up.

"Hey," Adam said, "are you okay?"

"It's okay," she managed. "It's nothing." She had tried not to think about why her body was acting funny, why she had skipped a period when she *never* skipped. Knowing she had an appointment the following Monday to find out for sure didn't ease any of the tension. She had to have a period soon, she just had to. Graydon would never forgive her.

"Now," Adam said when Elly had regained her color. "What'd I say?"

"Nothing," she insisted. She tried to eat her cottage cheese, but only succeeded in playing at it.

Adam was unconvinced. "I'm sorry if you lost a child," he said quietly. "I shouldn't have asked."

Elly was immediately contrite. "Oh, not, it's not that. Nothing like that." He waited silently for her to go on. She swallowed first. "I'm—I'm afraid I'm pregnant."

"That's great," he said happily.

"No." She shook her head. "It's awful. My husband doesn't want kids. Ever. At all."

Adam's expression sobered. "Does he know?"

"No. I'm not even sure yet."

"You going to the doctor?"

"Monday."

Adam nodded, taking it all in. "I see. No wonder you feel sick. Why doesn't he want kids?"

"I don't know," she shrugged. "He just said he doesn't believe in bringing them into this screwed-up world. He won't say exactly why."

"Sounds like a hell of an optimist," Adam said sarcastically.

"No, really," Elly said quickly, "he's not that bad. I mean, he's a good man, a good person. He's just very...opinionated."

"Hmm," Adam tried to sound noncommittal. "What are you going to do? If you are?"

Misery closed in on Elly like a damp fog. She shivered. "I don't know. I haven't thought about it too much. I've tried not to, until I know for sure." She looked up at Adam, her eyes limpid with sadness. "He's going to be very disappointed in me."

Adam's face softened in sympathy. "What about you?" he

asked. "How do you feel about it?"

"I don't know." Elly's mouth twisted harshly in an effort to keep away the quivering. "Why did I have to be so stupid? It was my fault. I didn't—"

She stopped herself in time. She had been about to tell Adam about that night she'd been too tired to put in her diaphragm and how, when Graydon pulled her to his side of the bed, she hadn't gotten up to do it because it annoyed him to have to wait for her. But she stopped herself and blushed red.

"It's okay," Adam dismissed her embarrassment. "I don't need to know the details." He sipped his coffee. "You know, I wouldn't find it hard to believe that if you told him—your husband—"

"Graydon," Elly supplied.

"Graydon—that he'd be thrilled. It's one thing not to want kids and not have them; it's another to not want them and find out you are having one. It changes your viewpoint pretty quickly."

"Not Graydon's," Elly sighed. "He never changes his mind. He's like a block of granite."

"Is that why you married him?" Adam's voice was quiet.

Elly looked up, instantly annoyed, but then somehow clearseeing. Adam didn't need an answer; the look in her eyes told him. Her shoulders slumped.

"I try so hard," she said. "I want to please him, to make him happy, but I never seem to be able to do it."

"Why not?"

She fidgeted with the ratty corner of her napkin. "I don't know, I can't figure it out. The thing is, he was married before. It didn't last, but the girl was very pretty, very sociable. Sometimes I feel like I'm competing with her, but I never measure up."

"Does he talk about her?"

"Oh, no," she shook her head. "That's just it. He never, ever mentions her. But I know he thinks about her. And I can't be like her. I'm just not the same, but I feel like I should try, like if I could be just a little more like her, I wouldn't be such a disappointment to him." She sighed hopelessly. "But I guess I can't change. And he's going to be so angry. I can't even imagine how upset he's going to be."

Adam put a comforting, paint-dappled hand over hers. "If

I were him," he said in a low, serious voice, "I'd count myself very, very lucky. You may not shine on the outside like some women, but you've got diamond-fire inside. You don't have to measure yourself short against anyone. You're an all-right lady, Elly Cole."

Elly remembered how Adam's kind words had sent surges of warmth through her, and how she had smiled her thanks to him through the haze of her misery. She had passed it off as sympathy, but later, when they returned to school and she went back to class, she had remembered his words over and over again. They made her think.

She finished curling the ribbon on Graydon's birthday present. It was amazing what memories were still locked inside of her, and what odd things brought them out. She hadn't realized, until today, that she had harbored those feelings of competition against Karen. No wonder she felt inadequate.

No, she told herself, I'm not inadequate. I'm a capable, not-bad-looking, loving woman, and she didn't care how many times Graydon had been married. She'd show him. She'd make him see.

When Graydon got home there were no warm, enticing smells coming from the kitchen. The kitchen was, in fact, clean and empty. Damn, he was hungry!

"Elly?" he called irritably.

"In here," she answered from the bedroom.

Graydon strode back. A curt demand for dinner died in his throat as he found Elly fastening a last earring, turning toward him dressed in a black dress that gathered artfully beneath her breasts and fell in soft folds over her round stomach. The neckline curved down in a wide, feminine line that showed the white skin above her breasts and her delicate collarbones. The Indian necklace Graydon had bought for her in New Mexico nestled in the soft cleft above her breasts, and the earrings glittered occasionally from her hair. She'd caught it back halfway, then left the rest to fall in casual curls about her shoulders. When she had gotten the earring fastened, she stood waiting for his approval.

"What's this for?" he asked. He was suspicious—she didn't dress that way for nothing—and still vaguely hungry.

"Your birthday," she said happily. "It is today."

He scowled. Of course it was today. Did she think Mayfield didn't remind him at least ten times? Mayfield, at forty-five, thought it was a great joke for Graydon to be turning thirty-three.

"I know it's my birthday," he said.

"Well," she turned away to gather up her gray coat with the rabbit collar, "we have reservations at the Castaways. I knew you'd be hungry, so I made them for 6:30." She held her coat out for him. "We'd better go."

Graydon's annoyance was transformed into surprise. He held Elly's coat for her, smelling the special warmth of her perfume as she slid into it, noticing over her shoulder how the necklace rested on the soft rise of her breast. His hunger for food turned into another kind. When she had pulled her coat on, she stood beneath his hands and looked back at him.

"Ready?" she asked.

No. He wanted to drag the coat off of her and take her to bed. She looked so...so...delectable. He let his hands slide off her shoulders.

"Yes."

She turned and kissed him lightly on the cheek. "Happy birthday." Before he could reach for her she had skipped out the door.

At the restaurant Elly pretended not to notice the way Graydon looked at her. She pored over the menu excitedly, wanting to try everything she hadn't tried before but finally settling on scampi. When she folded her menu and shook out her napkin, Graydon was still staring.

"Is something wrong?" she asked.

Graydon looked down at his own menu for the first time. "No. You just look...different." He glanced up again. "Is that dress new?"

"Yes. Do you like it? I had this dinner planned and I didn't want you to be seen here with a frumpy-looking fat lady, so I bought this. It's guaranteed to make me look svelte. Do I?"

Graydon eyed her suspiciously, waiting for the punch line.

"Well? Do I?"

"Do you what?" he asked.

She looked disappointed. "Look svelte."

He shrugged in an effort to be casual. "I suppose."

"Humph," she said disgustedly. "I guess I'll have to take it back and get my money refunded. The lady at the store guaranteed no man would be able to keep his eyes off me." She smiled sweetly at Graydon.

He seemed disturbed. "Are you trying to make a spectacle of yourself again?" he asked.

She leaned forward, her eyes round with surprise. "Spectacle? No, I'm just trying to look good for you. What's wrong with that?"

She had seen Graydon's quick glance to the booth across from them but thought little of it until he spoke again, his voice low and commanding.

"Sit up. If you lean over any further, that guy across from us will start drooling and I'll personally ram my fist down his throat."

Elly sat up. She flicked her eyes nervously to the man across the room and saw that he was, as Graydon said, practically drooling. Elly's face flamed.

"That's what you wanted, wasn't it?" Graydon asked.

Elly felt her embarrassment flood into defensive anger.

"It's better than feeling like a gray wall," she shot. "Anyway, you should be pleased that another man finds me attractive enough to stare at. Your first wife was very pretty; I should think you'd like me to look my best, too."

Graydon's eyes darkened with the clouds of a sudden storm. His jaw hardened into a dangerous set. "Let's not talk about it."

"I'll tell you what I remembered today," she continued smoothly. "I remembered how inadequate I used to feel because Karen was so pretty. I always felt as if I had to compete with her, and I never quite measured up. Like everything else I tried to do for you, I failed miserably. I couldn't be like her no matter how I tried."

Instead of the angry retort she expected from Graydon, she got nothing for her confession but a disbelieving, icy stare. It chilled her, although she wasn't sure why. She choked back the smug remarks she had waiting.

"Are you ready to order?" A costumed pirate waited, tablet in hand. He seemed oblivious to the play of emotions across the table.

"Yes," Graydon ground out. "Elly? What are you having?"

She forced out her order with a tied tongue, having to fumble open her menu to remember what she had decided on. Graydon ordered for himself, then added a bottle of wine, and the pirate disappeared. Elly smoothed her napkin around the base of her bulging stomach and tried to regain her calm.

Graydon left her alone, content to sit and gaze about distractedly while she sipped her water and fiddled with the stem of her glass. It was an uneasy truce, but one that, this time, Elly accepted graciously.

The waiter brought salads and poured wine for Graydon. Elly declined any at all. She made a project of spearing lettuce with her fork. Wondering how she had managed to botch up the evening so early, she ate listlessly.

"You got a card from Patty," she said after a few silent moments. "At least it looks like a card, long and thin."

"Hmm," Graydon acknowledged coolly. "They don't usually bother. Your Christmas presents must have sparked some guilt into them."

Elly heard the casual dismissal of the subject and, getting ready to broach her own, took a deep breath.

"Speaking of presents," she said, and drew the small box out of her purse. She laid it at Graydon's plate.

He glanced at her curiously but she seemed fascinated by her salad. After a second of tense silence, Graydon picked up the package and unwrapped it. He lifted the lid off the box and stared down inside.

Elly squirmed at his lack of comment. She tried to appear unconcerned, but failed. Finally she had to ask.

"Do you like it?"

Graydon lifted the watch out of its velvet nest and held it to the faint light of the hurricane lantern. "Yes. It's very nice." His voice was quiet, a shade more kind than Elly had expected. She hoped to see forgiveness in his eyes but he had already turned his attention to unstrapping his old watch and putting on the new.

Elly watched. The new timepiece looked rich and elegant next to the sleeve of Graydon's uniform.

It looked as if it were made for him. She felt a small degree of pleasure knowing she was able to choose so well.

"Yes," Graydon said, turning the watch in the dim light. "I like it." He looked over at Elly. "You seem to have a knack for picking out what I like. You never used to be able to do that."

Elly accepted the hidden compliment quietly, reaching for Graydon's old watch. "I gave this to you, didn't I?" she asked.

He nodded. "You remember?"

"Yes. It was my wedding present to you. You didn't like it. You tried to tell me that you did, but I could tell you were lying. I felt awful."

Surprisingly, Graydon reached across the table and cupped Elly's hands, and his old watch, in his. He forced her to meet his eyes.

"Elly, listen to me. I know I'm not easy to live with, I'm not easy to please. It's never been my intention to browbeat you." He took a long breath, gathering his strength in order to be gentle. "I do love you. God knows I don't want to, but I do. It just seems like things are so uncertain."

Elly's eyes looked dark turquoise in the lamplight, shining like the stone around her neck. She recognized Graydon's effort and smiled weakly.

"You know what I wish? I wish we could be totally honest with each other. Maybe then we wouldn't have these uncertain thoughts holding us back."

"Honest?" he asked. "We are honest with each other."

She shook her head. "No, we're not. We hide things from each other. And it's not good for us." Graydon's eyes shuttered instinctively and Elly saw him drawing away. She knew what his next words would be.

"I don't know what you mean," he said. Just then the waiter brought their meals, and Graydon pulled his hands back to allow the man room to set down their plates. Elly smiled sadly across the table.

"I know," she said quietly.

They ate in comparative silence, each making the appropriate remarks about the food but offering little in the way of conversation. Why, Elly thought, did they always seem to hit this same stone wall? She felt as if it weren't just the two of them eating dinner, but four—Adam peering over Graydon's shoulder and Karen over Elly's. Somehow, she realized, they had to eradicate these ghosts of the past; only then would they be free to belong only to each other.

The drive home was cool. The cold March air had chilled the car so that Elly sat with her hand clenching the fur collar of her coat tight around her neck, shivering until the heater warmed up. Graydon laid one large, warm hand on her knee.

"Thank you," he said. "If I have to be thirty-three, I may as well be a full thirty-three. It was a good dinner."

Elly slid over closer to Graydon and kissed his cheek. "You're welcome. Next time, though, I think I'll wear ski pants and a turtleneck."

He smiled absently as he watched the road. "You look nice, though."

"Do you really think so?"

"Yes. If you hadn't had reservations made, I probably would have made us at least an hour late. You looked too good to pass up."

Elly warmed under the compliment, but the wheels were turning. "You don't mind that that man was staring at me?"

"I'll always mind that," he said more seriously. "I can't help it."

Elly nodded at his expected answer. She slid a sidelong glance at him. "Did you mind when men stared at Karen? There must have been plenty of times; she's much prettier than I am."

Graydon's jaw tightened immediately and although his facial expression didn't change, Elly felt his annoyance. "Forget about Karen."

Elly sighed, shaking her head. "I can't. Even after you threw those pictures away, I can still see her face. She was perfect, wasn't she? Petite, pretty, lively; all the things I'm not. Do you know how awful it is to try to be like someone else and know that you'll never in the world be even close?"

"Elly," he warned. "I don't want to talk about it." He lifted his hand from her knee, ostensibly to wheel around a corner, but he didn't replace his hand. Elly's knee turned cold.

"I know you don't," she conceded, "but I have to. I don't think you know how difficult it's been for me. Everything I've tried to do falls short. She's tiny; I'm just average. She's pretty; I'm plain. She had no trouble with birth control; I got pregnant. You have no idea how hard it is to try to be like a perfect model."

"You don't know what you're talking about," Graydon said through clenched teeth.

"I know," Elly laughed humorlessly. "You won't tell me. Maybe if you told me more about her, I'd know more what you want in a wife."

"You know what I want," he said. "You don't have to compete with her."

"But you loved her very much, didn't you?" Elly asked. "It shows in those pictures. It shows in the way you won't talk about her."

"Damn it, Elly, would you leave it alone? I don't see any point in this. Quit worrying it. You're like a terrier lately, latching onto something and never letting go."

"That's probably true. Since I lost my memory I feel like every grain of truth is precious, and I want to know. You probably can't understand that, but truth is foundation to me, Graydon. I need it for my sanity. I want to know about Karen. I want to know where I stand, how I stack up to her. You can tell me that, Graydon."

"You wouldn't want to know," he snarled.

Elly was taken back for a half second. "I'm failing that badly, huh?" She sighed hopelessly. "Why did you marry me if I was so different from her?"

"Because," Graydon said, "I wanted someone different. As a matter of fact you're getting more and more like her every day, and *that* is what I can't stand." For a split second he pinned her with his eyes and his voice was bitter with remembered anger. Elly swallowed.

"I—I don't understand," she stammered.

"Obviously."

"But what do you mean? How am I getting like her? Tell me, Graydon, I don't understand! Tell me."

For a tense moment, Graydon devoted his attention to pulling the car into the driveway, and he switched off the engine. As the car lights dimmed, he turned to Elly sharply.

"She left me," he said tersely, "because she needed the attention of more than one man. *That's* how you're alike."

Elly sat stunned. Even when Graydon jerked open his door and slid out of the car, Elly sat paralyzed by his revelation. It couldn't be true; the woman she had felt in awe of for so long had left him—just like she had. All along Elly had felt so inadequate and eventually, finally, she had become like Karen—without even knowing it.

Her door was pulled impatiently open. "Are you coming?"

She turned toward Graydon's dark face. "Yes. Yes, I'm coming."

Inside the house, Graydon shrugged out of his jacket and offhandedly helped Elly with hers. She was thoughtful, knowing how carefully she had to proceed.

"Will you—can you—tell me about it?" she asked quietly.

"There's not much to tell," he said bitterly. "She was pretty, she was a model. Not a super-model, not a household name, but she did all right. She was used to having men stare at her, to having their eyes on her. She couldn't stay married to one man, not when there were so many men that wanted her."

Elly watched him remember, standing with his feet planted and his fists clenched. She ached for him.

"Did she...love you?"

He flicked his eyes to her. "She said she did. But it didn't matter. She couldn't stay married. She had never stayed married, not even at first."

"What? I don't understand."

"Then let me spell it out for you," Graydon said, tossing their coats on the couch. He stalked to the kitchen and pulled out the coffee as he talked. "She was nineteen when I met her; I was twenty-one. She told me she was a virgin, even made me wait to find out until we'd set the wedding date, but then she explained how she'd lost her hymen due to horseback riding at an early age. I believed it; she rode a lot. Her dad owned a big spread in Florida, even raced a few horses. The story didn't seem strange.

"She insisted on working after we were married, although I didn't want her to. I didn't like the creeps she worked with. All the photographers and ad people seemed too familiar with her. I went to a couple of sessions and almost broke up the set, so after that she scheduled all her jobs while I was gone. She had excuses for it all."

Elly watched as he dumped spoonfuls of coffee into the filter, ran water into the carafe and poured it into the coffee maker. With a quick jerk of his wrist he snapped on the unit.

"Then I got orders to go to Wiesbaden, Germany. She didn't want to go. She said all her friends were here, her family, her job. She cried until I gave in. She made a good show of acting upset when I left, but I never could shake the idea that she was more relieved. Whenever I came home, things seemed fine."

"How long were you there?" Elly asked.

"Nine months. I did well, impressed a few people with my ability and retention and requested an early transfer. They gave it to me. I thought everything would be great from there on out. I even planned to surprise her; I came home unannounced."

Elly waited. "And?"

"And," he continued bitterly, "I caught her 'entertaining' a photographer friend of hers. In my bed."

Elly put a hand to her mouth in shock. "No," she whispered.

Graydon paced like an angry bull. "Yes. The classic scene, and it was happening to me. It hit me like a ton of bricks right between the eyes. I could have broken that guy up into little pieces, but Karen grabbed me and held onto me until he jumped out the window, clothes in hand. If it weren't so shitty it'd be funny."

Elly didn't see the humor. "What did you do?"

"Not much," he said. "She cried, said it wasn't anything, she was just lonely. She swore she loved me and it only happened that once and it would never happen again." He smiled in memory, a humorless, derisive smile. "She even turned it around so that she was the one angry with me."

"With you? Why?"

"Because she said if I hadn't left her alone she wouldn't have had to turn to someone else. She blamed me for it all."

"Oh, my God," Elly said. She lowered herself into a dining

room chair. "And you..."

He shook his head. "I believed it. I guess I wanted to. It was either that or kill her." He cast Elly a sideways glance. "I had a worse temper then than I do now. The only thing was, I was more gullible, too. But I did love her, and I wanted her. She swore it wouldn't happen again."

"But it did," Elly supplied.

"Yes," Graydon's voice hissed. "It took me a long time to figure it out. She was busy—with her job, she said—and I didn't put the pieces together right away. Anytime a man dropped her off at the house, it was a photographer or a go-for or something like that; never any big deal. I think I wanted to believe so bad I just closed my eyes. Then one day she dropped the bomb on me."

Elly stared at him, watching him assemble his courage to face what he had put away for so many years. The air was thick, but the only sound was his breathing.

"One evening when I got home she was waiting for me. She'd always had a lot of energy, but that night she was like a bundle of nerves attacking me. She said she couldn't live with me anymore. She said it was all my fault; I wasn't home enough, I didn't pay enough attention to her. She had to have more. She was barely twenty-one and she was wasting away. Fifteen minutes later, some guy came and picked her up."

Elly felt sick. As Graydon talked, she ached for his younger self, for the twenty-three year old that loved and chose the wrong woman and let her destroy his trust in all women. She ached to hold him and comfort him and rebuild his trust, but she knew she couldn't. He wouldn't let her.

"There's not much to tell after that." He shrugged off the memories and got a cup for his coffee. "I moved out of the married officers' quarters, of course. There were a few fist holes punched in the walls, but no one seemed to notice. I mean, a lot of people get divorced, right?"

"Oh, Graydon," Elly whispered. "I'm sorry. I'm so sorry."

He poured his coffee and frowned. "Don't be. It was a long time ago." He returned the coffee pot to its warming plate and turned to face Elly, leaning restlessly against the kitchen counter. "Now do you see why I'm the way I am?"

She nodded, too weighted down by his burden to speak. She thought of all the pain she'd caused him because she hadn't understood before.

"If only I'd known," she breathed.

"Would it have made a difference?" Graydon eyed her suspiciously.

Elly raised sorrowful eyes to him. "Yes, it would have made a difference. You don't know how anxious I was to please you at first. I wanted so badly to be the perfect wife to you, and I tried so hard. But it's difficult to please a stone wall. You were like a fortress of granite, hard and unyielding. For years I thought you never ached, you never felt pain. And so when I never seemed able to please you—and especially when I got pregnant—I couldn't face you. I felt like I couldn't hurt you, but I could make you very, very angry at me, and I couldn't stand it. God, if I had known about Karen, I might have felt closer to you, I might have been able to explain. It's easier to talk to someone if you know they have feelings, too."

Graydon looked unconvinced. "I wasn't that closed," he said.

Elly laughed, just slightly hysterical. "You don't think so? I was terrified to tell you I was pregnant, especially after that fight we had up at Pike's Peak. I couldn't bear to see that look on your face. I even talked to the doctor about abortion, but he was against it."

Graydon's eyes seemed to clear slightly in understanding. "That last month before you left...you were so depressed. You cried over anything."

"I can't remember it all," Elly said, "but, yes, I was depressed. I had to decide whether or not I could stand up to another one of your ego-crushing tirades."

"What about Adam?" he demanded.

Elly shook it off. "I don't think I loved Adam. At least from what I remember so far, I didn't. But he was sympathetic; he was a shoulder to cry on. I could talk to him without him treating me like a child."

Graydon looked angry. "I didn't treat you like a child."

She smiled sadly. "Maybe you didn't think so. You aren't easy to talk to, Graydon. Even now."

"I suppose it's all my fault," he said sarcastically. "Again."

"No, it's not all your fault. It takes two, and I was too introverted by my fears to try to break through yours." Her eyes glittered with unshed tears. "But don't you see how it all could have been avoided? God, we've wasted such precious time sitting in our own little corners of doubt. I feel very sad for what we've done, Graydon—and for what we've done without."

Graydon stared at Elly thoughtfully over the rim of his cup.

Understanding did not, as Elly might have hoped, clear the air immediately. Graydon proceeded cautiously, seldom letting his guard down but still showing flashes of new awareness, new empathy. Elly was careful to tread lightly and always allowed Graydon his pride. He needed that after his catharsis that night.

She had been communicating regularly with her mother since Thanksgiving, and shortly after Graydon's birthday got a letter asking when Elly wanted her to come up and help with the baby. Elly broached the subject gently over dinner.

"Anytime you want," he said unemotionally.

"Are you sure it'll be all right? I don't want to invite her if you'll be uncomfortable with her here. It's your home; I won't drive you out of it."

Her response sparked a cautious glance of surprise. "No, it's okay. Invite her. You two can get a lot done together, and I don't think we'll have any problems. Go ahead."

Elly smiled warmly in relief. "Thank you. How long? A week? Two?"

"As long as you want. However long you think you need."

"Well," Elly said, "we can start with a week and see how it goes. I can always ask her to stay longer if it goes well and if not—well, she can leave." She eyed the letter lying on the kitchen counter. "I think she's really getting excited. She said she was beginning to think she wouldn't be a grandmother before she was sixty-five."

"Now watch her put the pressure on Bryan," Graydon joked.

"Yes," Elly laughed. "I'd like to think something would influence him to marry Dana. Maybe this will."

Meanwhile, Elly's visits to Dr. Weiss increased, as did her

girth. The heartbeat was clear and strong and Dr. Weiss always gave her a clean bill of health for herself and the baby. The only thing was, he warned her, the baby was big and she was built relatively small in the pelvic area. With luck it wouldn't be a problem, but it was worth knowing.

After her visit early in April, Elly stopped by Corky's and met Linda for lunch. They'd talked on the phone often, but hadn't seen each other for over a month. Linda made a dramatic play at fainting when she saw Elly waddle in.

"My God, you're huge!" she exclaimed.

"Thanks," Elly laughed. "I love flattery."

"No, really, are you sure you're not due in April? You can't go another month!"

"Five weeks," Elly corrected. "Yes, I'm sure. Just remember who the daddy is."

"This kid's going to be a real bruiser," Linda said. "It's downright scary."

"Scary? Why? Are you pregnant?"

Instead of flashing back an appropriate flip answer, Linda settled into uneasiness. "No," she said.

"But?" Elly heard the hesitation in Linda's voice and prompted.

"Oh, shit," Linda said. "Things are starting to get serious with Ron. I mean *real* serious. Even more than with Greg."

"Oh?" Elly pressed. "Has he asked you to marry him?"

"No. Unfortunately, it's not serious like that."

"I don't follow you," Elly said. "How is it serious?"

Linda sighed. "Well, he hasn't asked because, well, because he likes to make me wait. You know how it was when we first met and he insisted on taking it so slow, going to the zoo and all that? Well, he loves to make me stew, and he knows he can do it to me. So he hasn't asked. What's pitiful is that I've been thinking about it all by myself. I mean, Christ, I've even had thoughts that I'd like to have his baby. Can you believe that? Isn't that awful?"

"No," Elly laughed. "I think it's wonderful."

"You would," Linda said sarcastically. "Little Miss Mother of the Year."

"Truth now," Elly said, "doesn't it make you feel good inside to think about getting married and having a baby?"

"It did until I saw you. I would die if I got that big. I mean, Linda, the all-time champion dieter—pregnant? God, I can't even stand the thought of it."

Elly chuckled at her friend. "It's not so bad. You'll see. If everything else is right, it makes a lot of sense."

"It makes sense to you, doesn't it?" Linda asked. Suddenly serious, she watched Elly.

"Yes, it does."

"You guys are okay now?"

"Well, maybe not perfect, but doing better. It's going to take time to chase away all the ghosts—" she'd told Linda about Karen— "but I think we'll manage."

"I don't know how you did it," Linda sighed.

"It wasn't easy," Elly said, "but it wasn't real difficult to figure out. I love him. I won't let him go."

"Yeah, but all the hassles..."

Elly shrugged. "We both made mistakes, and we've both gone through a lot of changes. The important thing is that I love him. He's the man I want to spend the rest of my life with."

"Jeez," Linda said, "you sound like a soap opera. Let's order lunch, okay? I'm starving."

Elly began to realize she didn't have much time. The middle of May was closing in on her and she had done hardly anything in the way of a nursery. Up to now, she had respected Graydon's small, clinging doubts, but as the baby began to drop and press more uncomfortably on her bladder, she knew she had work to do.

The spare bedroom was off white and that color was fine with her; she could do more with trim and decoration this way. She bought curtains for the one window, pastel stripes in circus colors, caught back by matching fabric ties. Immediately the room looked cheerful. She was heartened.

One Saturday she got her nerve up and asked Graydon if he would move furniture for her. Although he eyed her noncommitally, his gaze sliding to the heavy burden she carried, he agreed. While Elly directed, he shoved the spare bed against the far wall and slid the dresser into the large closet. The night stand was okay; Elly left that.

"Now all we need is a crib," she said.

Graydon still looked a trifle skeptical, but Elly figured it was more out of habit—or image—than anything. She was right.

"You want to go get one?" he asked.

"Yes, I think that's a good idea," Elly agreed. "Will you go with me? I'll need help."

He growled a bit, but agreed. Elly tried not to look too smug as they drove to town.

"Graydon," she asked timidly, "tell me the truth; aren't you getting the least little bit excited?"

He drove silently, mulling over her question. When he glanced her way and saw the lights of excitement dancing in her eyes, he couldn't keep his mouth from curling up in an unwilling smile.

"Not like you," he said finally.

"That's not what I asked." She slid over closer to him and took his free hand. "I know you never wanted kids, but now that it's really happening, aren't you looking forward to it?" He had to be, she thought. He'd be inhuman not to feel something.

"Oh, I guess I am," he admitted. "It's strange, though, thinking of having a baby. It'll be someone who's totally dependent on us." He looked down at Elly. "It'll mean you can never leave. Even if we fight and you hate my guts, I won't let you leave. My baby's not going to grow up without both parents."

Elly's heart soared. It was the first time Graydon had talked about the baby being his. She smiled happily.

"That sounds like a deal to me," she said. Then, "I guess it's just as well that you didn't have any kids with Karen, since that didn't last. But this time it's different."

Graydon sobered. "Yes, it's different, all right. When Karen and I got married, I couldn't wait to have kids. Now I thank God that she was too selfish to accommodate me."

Elly's mouth dropped open. "What? You wanted kids? But you said—"

"I said I didn't want to bring any kids into this screwed-up world, and I meant it. If life is so uncertain that what looks like a perfect marriage can fall apart so quickly, it's too shaky a place to have kids. I used to think about what would have happened if

Karen had gotten pregnant. First, I'm not sure she would have kept it, and that makes me crazy just thinking about it. Then, when we split, I don't know who would have gotten custody. Karen didn't care about kids but mothers are funny; she might have gotten real protective if a baby'd been involved. If she had, I shudder to think what that kid would have been subjected to—baby-sitters, boyfriends, maybe even left alone or abused. Karen would not have been a good mother."

Elly sat quietly and listened, recognizing the painful tone of Graydon's confession.

"So rather than go through all that emotional turmoil, I just decided it'd be easier not to have any, period. No strings, no worries. Lots of people do it. No big deal."

Elly laid Graydon's hand on her stomach. "And now?" she asked.

The baby moved under Graydon's hand. He rubbed the restless spot gently.

"Now—it's a big deal." He smiled down at her. "What kind of crib do you want?"

At first Elly found a white one with cartoon ducks laminated on its head- and footboards, but Graydon said no.

"No ducks."

They looked at a maple one, tooled and stained to look colonial, but it was a style neither of them liked. Then Elly found a blue one, powder blue, with different colored beads that turned on segments of rod between the wooden ribs. She liked it.

"What if it's a girl?" Graydon asked.

"It's not." She shook her head. "It's a boy."

"Are you that sure?"

"I'm positive."

They bought the blue one. And a bassinette, and a diaper hamper and a changing table and a diaper bag. And Elly insisted on buying a small stuffed blue elephant.

They spent the afternoon setting up the nursery. Again, Elly supervised and Graydon did the work, and by dinnertime the room was to Elly's satisfaction. She stood proudly in the doorway, her stomach looming out in front, and surveyed their work.

"I like it," she pronounced.

Graydon stood close behind her and wrapped a gentle arm around her neck. "Do you?" he asked.

"Yes."

"The only thing I don't care for," he said, "is that spare bed. I don't want you getting any ideas about sleeping in here. You're my wife and you belong with me. I won't even share you with him."

Elly turned in Graydon's arm and snuggled sideways to him—the only way she could get close. "Jealous of another male?" she asked coyly.

"You're damn right," he growled. "I think I'll take that bed out, just so you don't get any ideas." Elly settled contentedly under his arm. "All right," she said. "I won't mind."

Graydon liked the name Nathan.

"But I wanted his middle name to be Graydon," Elly said. "Nathan Graydon doesn't sound good."

"So think of another middle name. He doesn't have to be named after me. What about your side of the family? There's got to be other names."

They were lying in bed, nose to nose, Elly with her stomach nested on her extra pillow. Graydon had to curl his body around hers in order to get close.

"How about Nathan Bryan?" she asked. "That doesn't sound too bad."

"It sounds fine," Graydon said.

"Or how about Nathan Allen? That's my dad's middle name."

"Sounds like a colonist," Graydon joked.

"Oh, Graydon. Really, what do you think? Don't you think Dad would be pleased? Maybe he wouldn't feel like I was being so obnoxiously independent."

In the darkness Elly could see Graydon's eyes narrow in seriousness. "You don't have to try to please him, you know. Don't name the baby just to placate him. I won't stand for it. Any name you pick, I want it to be because you want it and not as an apology or a peace offering to your dad."

"I know," Elly murmured. "I already thought of that, but that's not why I suggested it. I just think it would be nice."

"It's up to you, Elly. I already voted on Nathan."

"All right, I want it. Nathan Allen."

"Nathan Allen," Graydon echoed. "You promise it won't be a girl?"

"I promise."

He kissed the tip of her nose. "You'd better be right. I don't want to have to go through this all over again."

As Elly's time neared, they seemed to become closer. Occasionally Elly could sense a moody withdrawal in Graydon, as if he had to re-examine the lessons of the past and convince himself he wasn't inviting another emotional upheaval, but generally he was cheerful and thoughtful and more open. Elly might steer a casual conversation around to Karen or Graydon's life before, and where he might have balked, he usually didn't. They found things less traumatic in the daylight, and even the black spots in Elly's memory lost most of their aggravating tendencies. When she did remember something, they talked about it.

"Do you know, Graydon," Elly said one evening in front of the fireplace, "when I found out I was pregnant I just pictured you expanding and puffing up like a huge black storm cloud with your eyes flashing fire. It seems so silly now."

Graydon had the grace to look uncomfortable. "Maybe I was a little dogmatic," he said.

Elly shivered. "I can still see the picture I had. It was awful. I could no more have told you I was pregnant than I could have approached a fire-breathing, snarling bull."

For a thoughtful moment Graydon let the subject lie then, uncomfortably, picked it up again. "Did you always see me like that? Didn't you ever think of me any other way?"

Elly might have gone to sit at his feet then, but she had too much difficulty raising her heavy body. Instead she gazed serenely over at him.

"Yes, I saw you other ways. I love you, Graydon. I know you can be kind and thoughtful and sensitive. I think, then, that I loved you so much that I was just terrified of your disapproval." She smiled. "I think now the raging bull has quieted. Now he's content to be a father and a husband, and I'm content to be a mother and a wife."

Knowing her disability, Graydon made the move to sit beside her on the couch. Chester, on her other side, looked up irritably at the sudden dipping of the cushions under Graydon's added weight.

"You'd better be content," he growled more playfully. "Because you're stuck, now. No more hiding from me, no more running to cry to someone else. Only me."

Elly purred under Graydon's mock reprimand. "I don't need anyone but you," she said.

Graydon nibbled at her earlobe. "Well, if that's true," he said slowly between bites, "how about coming to bed with me?" He glanced down at the mound of her smock, where his hand lay on the baby. "Or are we supposed to quit doing that sometime?"

"Dr. Weiss said there's no hard and fast rule," Elly giggled. "He just said whatever's comfortable and not painful or too difficult." Her eyes were bright. "We haven't had any trouble up to now."

"Then let's not start," Graydon said, taking her hand.

Chapter Seventeen

Clare planned a baby shower for Elly and invited all the other Air Force wives. It was a surprise to Elly, perpetrated by Graydon's story about Don needing Graydon's expertise on a cabinet he was building. When they got to the Mayfield's, Graydon left Elly at the front door while he went the back way into the basement to find Don. Clare led Elly into the jumble of suddenly familiar faces.

When the shock and embarrassment waned, Elly was excited to realize she recognized all the women, even knew their names. They oohed and ahed over her stomach and played silly, laughing games. When it came time to open the gifts, Elly was dumbfounded by the nice things she received. She cried.

"Oh, Graydon," she said on the way home, "wait'll you see all the nice things. We got blankets and sleeper sets and a car seat and crawlers and a mobile and—"

"Okay, okay," Graydon laughed. "I'll see when we get home. You're so wound up you're about to burst. Is it okay for you to get so excited?"

"The baby doesn't care," she said. "He's sleeping. He was so good tonight; he didn't kick once."

"Maybe the kid's finally learning some manners," Graydon said. "That's good. There's nothing worse than an Air Force brat that won't mind."

They spent the next weekend placing and rearranging everything in the nursery—after Graydon removed the spare bed—and Elly waddled around happily examining it all. The mobile spun and danced in front of the window, its soft pieces of clouds and rainbows shining in the sun. When she turned and gazed around the room, she felt at peace.

Elly's due date loomed ahead like Christmas morning. Every day she sipped her tea over the calendar and counted down. May fourteenth shone on the page, lit with a glow only Elly could see. She waited patiently for the day her burden would become a child.

Her mother called on the tenth. "How are you? Any sign?"

"No, Mom," Elly laughed. "Not yet. Dr. Weiss said it's not unusual for the first one to come later."

"But is it dropping?"

"Oh, it's dropping," Elly affirmed. "If I sit for more than twenty minutes in the same position, he cuts off my circulation and my legs to go sleep. But no pains yet."

"Do you think I should wait or come now?" her mother asked.

"Why don't you wait?" Elly said. "It could be days, or it could be a week or more. I'll call you as soon as we know anything at all and we can plan then."

"All right." She tried to hide her disappointment. "I guess that's best."

"Sure. How's Dad?"

"He's fine. He's out in the garage now or I'd call him to the phone."

"That's okay." Elly understood. Her mother was the buffer between father and daughter, shielding each from the other's irritating traits. Elly sighed. "Did he read my last letter? About the baby's name?"

"Oh, yes, he did. I'm sure he was pleased."

Elly saw him, reading the letter, his face blank and unemotional, then tossing the paper down without a word. Her mother was so good at reassuring her; she'd done it for years.

"Well, anyway, I'll call you, Mom. I'd like to talk but I don't want to run up your phone bill. I promise as soon as anything happens, I'll call."

"All right, dear. Make it soon."

Meanwhile, spring had come full blown to Colorado Springs. The flowers Elly now remembered planting came up thick— daffodils, hyacinth, crocus and tulips. The borders of the front and back yards were riotous with color. Every day Elly and Chester would stroll contentedly around the back yard, gently brushing the dew off the flowers or cutting selected ones for vases in the house. Elly felt in tune with the nature around her; May was the time of birth.

On the fourteenth, Graydon almost insisted on staying home.

"I'll call you the minute I feel anything," Elly reassured him. "Go ahead. I'll be fine."

"Well, how accurate are these due dates, anyway? When the doctor says the fourteenth, does he mean the fourteenth?"

"Sort of. It could be anytime, even a week or two different. Don't worry, Graydon. I'll be fine."

He kissed her where she lay in bed, his eyes unsure.

"If you're absolutely positive..." he said.

"Positive. Go ahead. If anything happens, I'll call you immediately."

She could tell he wasn't reassured, but he went. She wasn't exactly reassured herself. Patting her stomach, she thought, come on, Nathan. Don't be late.

The day passed slowly. The dropping weight of the baby put a strain on Elly's back and she couldn't seem to do anything for very long and be comfortable. Walking through the yard—planning a play area with a sandbox—or sitting in the nursery just staring at all the things, she had aches and pains and cramping knees. Finally she stretched out on the couch and let Chester curl up in the crook of her arm.

Now that the birth was so imminent, she couldn't imagine how she had ever entertained thoughts of abortion. The smallest restless turning of the baby made her smile. She could remember the awful feelings of failure she had back in September and October, but she couldn't quite recapture the unthinking panic of the time. It was like a half remembered nightmare.

That Monday she found out she was pregnant was the blackest day of her memory. After crying her story to Linda, she had gone home and moped around the house all day, ashamed and afraid. As transparent as she was, she knew she could never hope to convince Graydon that nothing was wrong. She was a terrible liar, but at least it wouldn't be a lie to say she felt awful. That much was true.

She'd laid dinner before him silently, aware of his examining stare but unable to fend it off. By the time she sat down to join him, he was already perturbed.

"What's the matter? You're not talking."

Elly shrugged listlessly. "I don't feel very well."

"Why not? You catching something?"

"I'm not sure. Maybe. You should eat while it's hot." She tried to turn his attention away from herself, but only partially succeeded. Even as he served himself, his eyes flicked to her.

"You should take vitamins," he said. "Especially in fall when the weather changes."

Elly nodded in noncommittal agreement. Even Graydon's brusque concern was too good for her. She died a little inside when she thought how he'd react if he knew the truth.

Luckily he appeared content to let the subject pass without any more comment. Elly cleared the table and did the dishes while he read the mail and took a closer look at the newspaper. Chester sat patiently outside the kitchen window, but that night Elly was too morose to even wave to him.

"You know this guy?" She was startled out of her self-pity by Graydon's sudden appearance at her side, half the newspaper folded and held close to her face. A grainy, pointilistic picture of Adam stared back at her.

"What?" Elly croaked. Her throat had closed in panic, and a hot embarrassment flooded through her. How did he know?

"This guy. He's an artist, doing a mural at Pike School. That's where you've been teaching the last two weeks, isn't it?"

Elly still couldn't tell if Graydon was angry or not. His clipped attitude could be a holdover from dinner, or …

"Yes," she whispered hoarsely.

"Have you seen the mural? It says it's as big as one whole

wall." He pulled the paper back and resumed his reading of the article. As soon as his eyes slid off Elly she could breathe again.

"Yes," she managed, "I've seen it. It's not done yet."

"That's what this says. Should be done by the middle of October." Graydon scanned the article, his eyes resting only momentarily on the picture of the artist. "Hippy-looking guy, with that long hair. You wouldn't think they'd hire someone who looks like that."

Elly tried to sound casual. "His hair's not really all that long. Some of the kids have longer hair."

"It's practically to his shoulders," Graydon snorted. "No wonder the kids do it when they see grownups like that." He shook his head and folded away the paper. "Well, I guess everyone doesn't see things the Air Force way." He left Elly to her dishes then. She sagged against the counter in relief.

That night Graydon had found Elly's hand beneath the bed covers and pulled her to him. She shrank back. "What's the matter?" he growled.

"Um, nothing, I just...I'm not..."

"You having your period?"

"No."

"Then what?" Even while arguing he insisted on folding her into his arms. She had little strength to resist.

"I'm sorry," she said shakily, "I'm just not much good tonight."

"Oh. You still feel under the weather?" His voice calmed somewhat and Elly felt guilt wash through her. His touch became gentle and persuasive. "I'll make you forget about that," he said. "Just relax."

As it always did, his lovemaking aroused and excited her, surprising in its ability to draw her out of her morass of pity. She found herself unable to keep from him and they came together in the combustive manner so typical of Graydon. Before the last tremor had vibrated through Elly, though, she felt the first chink fall out of her defenses, and in minutes tears were streaming down her face.

"Hey," Graydon said softly in alarm, "what's this? Did I hurt you?"

"No." She shook her head and tears seeped down the sides of her face.

"Then what?" he asked. "Tell me."

"It's...it's nothing. It's just a mood. It'll pass."

"Elly, I want to know. If things aren't right, if I hurt you—"

"No, it's all right, Graydon. Really. I told you, I just don't feel very chipper. I'll feel better tomorrow. I promise."

He pulled her against him so the dampness of her cheek cooled his shoulder.

"I don't like your feeling this way, Elly. If you feel bad you should go to a doctor. Do you feel sick?"

"No, just...I don't know. Maybe I'm just tired. I'll feel better in the morning. I'm sure I will."

The lies contorted her mouth, even in the dark.

"I hope so," Graydon grumbled. "I don't like it when you cry."

"I know," she breathed. "I won't do it any more."

But she did. She cried more and more often, until Graydon stopped asking and turned moodily away at night. But that was as much as she deserved.

Elly shivered at the memory of how she withdrew from Graydon. If only she'd known then what she knew now! If only they'd talked to each other. But instead, his silent anger armored him while her fear kept her from reaching out. She just hadn't been strong enough to see it through.

A sudden, grabbing cramp caught Elly by surprise. She put her hands to her abdomen and soothed it. It wasn't bad, like a small charlie horse. Probably just gas. She rubbed it away.

She wished she could remember those last few days. After she found out she was pregnant, her job at Pike ended and for a few days she was idle. She was aghast and terrified when Adam called her at home.

"What are you doing?" she asked. "You shouldn't call me here."

"Why not?" Adam returned lightly. "Is your husband home?"

"No, but—"

"How'd he take the news? I was kind of worried about you, especially when you didn't come back to the school. I checked with the office and they said your substitution was over. I wanted to check and make sure you're okay."

"I'm fine," she lied.

"And proud papa?"

"I—he doesn't know. I couldn't tell him."

Adam whistled low. "You're really terrified of him, aren't you? That's not the greatest basis for a marriage, you know. What are you going to do? Wait until you show?"

"I—I don't know," Elly stammered. Half formed thoughts flitted across her mind, too drastic to mention. "I have to think. I have to decide what to do."

"Tell you what," Adam said, "come on down here to the coffee shop. We'll talk."

"No. I can't do that." Her eyes fell on the closed door of Graydon's den and she shivered.

"Why not? Sounds like you could use a sounding board."

"No, I—I can't. You shouldn't even have called."

"Hey," he laughed lightly, "I'm not propositioning you. I just want to offer you my ear. This is old Adam, the hippie artist, not a wolf on the make. Come on, pretty lady. Let me buy you lunch. It'll do you good."

"No," she said, but her voice was hesitant.

"Come on, Elly. Meet me there in twenty minutes. You could use a friend."

"I—I shouldn't."

"That's debatable. Will you meet me?"

"Not for lunch. Just...maybe a cup of coffee. Just for a minute."

"Whatever you want," he agreed. "Twenty minutes?"

"All right. Twenty minutes."

And it had gone on from there. Adam had been so kind, so supportive while just the thought of Graydon's reaction to her pregnancy sent her cowering. Adam had listened patiently while Elly related her fears, her thoughts, her broken plans. He called her every day and invited her to lunch more often than not, watching her go through the throes of agonizing decision-making with sympathetic hazel eyes. The day she broached the subject of abortion, he reacted slowly with cautious words of advice.

"I know how upset you are, Elly, but you've got to think about how things are going to be in a month or a year or five years down the road. Don't do anything you'll regret later. Do you want the baby?"

"Oh, yes," she said sorrowfully. "More than anything. But Graydon..."

"You might try telling him," Adam offered. "He just might not react the way you think."

"No." Elly shook her head. "I know him. I know how he feels. He'd be furious. You've never seen him, but if you did, you'd understand."

Adam looked perturbed. "I can't believe that, Elly. I can't believe that any man in his right mind would be upset over you having his baby, or that he'd take the chance of losing you over it." His laughing eyes turned serious. "You are a wonderful lady, Elly. Any man would be proud to have you for a wife."

That was the first time Elly saw it in his eyes—he was in love with her. She shrank back, at once ashamed, afraid, surprised and embarrassed. And pleased?

"I—I have to go." She gathered up her purse and slid out of the cafe booth.

"Elly." Adam's hand on her arm stopped her. "Don't. I'm not asking you for anything. I only want you to be happy. Don't run from me."

"I don't like the way you—you look at me. It's not right."

"It's a fact," he said simply. "I can't help it, and I don't want to. But I'm still not asking anything from you except that you be yourself and be happy. No matter how else I feel, I'm still your friend. If that's all it'll ever be, that's okay, too. I understand."

"But—I can't—I don't..."

"Don't worry about me. I can take care of myself. I'm just worried about you." He took her hand. "Trust me?"

Elly had no choice. She had no other person that she could talk to as freely as Adam, no other friend who would support her as selflessly as he did. She nodded.

"All right," he said. "Now, you can go if you want. I don't want to make you uncomfortable."

He wanted her to stay; she knew that. But she had to go, she had to think. "Call me tomorrow," she said. "I just need to be alone for a little bit."

"Sure." He released her hand. "Promise me you won't do anything ... permanent. Not yet."

Elly nodded. "I won't."

"Good." Adam stepped close and brushed Elly's lips quickly with his own. "I'll call you."

Chester looked up sharply as Elly doubled over another pain. Her memories shattered like a mirror before a thrown ashtray. Elly grabbed her stomach and gasped out loud at the pain.

"Oh, God," she moaned. Chester stood up, irritated by Elly's restlessness, and glared at her. "I'm sorry, Chester," she whispered as the pain ebbed. "It's not on purpose. You'd probably be more comfortable on the chair, though."

The cat seemed unimpressed and began to lick his forepaw for cleaning.

When the pain had passed, Elly lay back and tried to decide if she was really going into labor. How long ago had the first pain hit—twenty minutes? More like a half hour. She'd wait and see. Two pains weren't enough to go by.

She got up and fixed herself a cup of tea, thought about going outside but decided against it. Instead she retrieved the mail from the front porch, scanned through the letters briefly and dropped the last one as a third pain hit her. Luckily she hadn't been holding her tea. She lowered herself into a dining room chair and checked the clock. Twenty minutes.

Well, Nathan, she thought, at least you're punctual.

She called the doctor. His nurse told her to time her pains, both their actual time and the time in between, and to come in when they were five minutes apart. No, her water hadn't broken yet. The nurse thought that was good. She seemed optimistic and unruffled, and her casual instructions eased Elly's mind. Elly hung up the phone with one eye on the clock. This was one thing she'd do right.

She was thinking of calling Graydon when the next pain hit. This one wasn't so bad, just a twinge. She wouldn't call him yet. It was already after two. He'd be home in three hours; she had plenty of time. To keep her mind off things, she waddled carefully to the bedroom and made a final check of her suitcase.

Graydon was home at a quarter to five.

"Elly?" His booming call resounded through the house when she wasn't immediately present.

"I'm here," she called from the bedroom.

Graydon strode urgently down the hall. "How are you? Are you—"

His jaw dropped at the sight of Elly doubled over on the edge of the bed, a nightgown slipping carelessly through her fingers to the floor.

"Elly! My God, are you all right?" He hurried to her, then immediately lost control, unsure if he should hold her or touch her at all. She had one arm circled about her stomach in a soothing cradle, and she managed to nod slowly.

"Yes, I'm okay," she breathed as the pain subsided. "It's ten minutes now." As drawn as she looked, the smile she turned on Graydon was happy and proud.

"Now?" he barked. "How long have you been having pains?"

"Just a couple of hours. I called the doctor. When they're five minutes apart we have to go in."

"Jesus, Elly," Graydon swore, "why didn't you call me? You promised you'd call."

"I know," she nodded. "But there was nothing you could do. I didn't want you to come home just to watch me. I'm okay, really, Graydon. I still can't go in. We have time."

"Jesus." He stood upright, his hands pulling nervously at his tie to loosen it. "Damn it, Elly, I wish you wouldn't scare me like that. What should I do? Anything? Can I get you anything?"

She laughed at him. "No. I was just trying to decide which nightgown I want to take. I'm afraid I haven't even started dinner."

"The hell with dinner," Graydon said. "You shouldn't be on your feet anyway, should you? Shouldn't you be lying down? Just let me change my clothes and then I'll help you do whatever you have to do."

Elly thought they sounded like a vaudeville comedy act. While she rested on the bed, Graydon tore around like a crazy man, pulling off his uniform, yanking clothes out of his closet and running hesitantly to the bathroom. When he was in comfortable clothes he helped her stuff both night gowns into her suitcase and then put it near the front door.

"Graydon, you don't have to rush around. We have lots of time. Slow down."

He arched an eyebrow at her as if she'd just asked him to stop breathing. "Are you hungry? What can I fix for you that's fast? Soup? That would be good for you, wouldn't it?"

"Really, I'm not hungry," she said. "You go ahead and fix yourself something. I—"

Her voice broke at a new pain, a bad one. It squeezed an involuntary gasp from her and had Graydon leaning protectively, anxiously over her.

"Elly? God, Elly, I can't stand this! I'm taking you in now!"

"No," she whispered weakly. "It's not...time. Only...seven minutes."

"I don't care if it's seven hours!" he roared in frustration. "I'm taking you in! Where's your coat? We're going."

Elly was no match for him. Even if she had been at full strength she couldn't have withstood his loud, half-angry blusterings and his unstoppable determination. He refused to listen to any of her weak protests and got her coat, wrapped it cautiously around her and carried her to the car. While in his arms, she flinched at a new pain and all the blood drained from Graydon's face. He laid her gently on the car seat and ran back for her suitcase. In seconds they were on their way.

"What the hell's the matter with those doctors, anyway?" Graydon wanted to know. "Don't they have any more sense than to let a woman sit around in pain for hours and hours?"

"Graydon, it doesn't matter," Elly explained. "It's either sit in the hospital or sit at home. They can't do anything until I'm ready; or I should say, until *he's* ready."

"Well, we'll see about that." His jaw was tight with stubbornness. "For Christ's sake, today's your due date. You're supposed to have the baby today. Don't they understand that?"

Elly sighed and kept still. There was nothing she could say to Graydon's protective rantings. Instead she tried to keep herself sitting upright as Graydon took turns on less than four wheels. She glanced furtively behind for the sight of a police car. There was none.

He had her to the hospital in minutes, but not before another contraction wracked her. It was all he could do to keep from coming to a screaming halt at the front emergency doors, and only his one-sided caution for Elly kept him from bouncing her on the seat at the sudden stop. She was still hissing air between clenched teeth as he jerked the passenger door open.

"Elly! Are you all right?"

She nodded. "Just wait a minute. I'll be fine."

"Do you want me to carry you? Or I could get a wheelchair."

"No. It's going now. I can walk."

The scene at the admitting desk was a nightmare. Aware of Graydon's short fuse, Elly tried to answer all the receptionist's questions but when the girl handed her a clipboard and fact sheet, Graydon ripped it out of her hands.

"Call the doctor," he commanded her. "My wife's in labor. Can't you see that?"

The girl paled under Graydon's intimidating stare and reached for the phone.

"Graydon, please calm down," Elly said. "Let me do this. Will you get me a cup of water?" She pulled the clipboard out of his hands at the same time as she propelled him toward a water cooler. At first he stood rooted, unwilling to leave her, but at her weak insistence, he went.

"I'm sorry," Elly told the girl. "He's upset."

The receptionist was still dialing. "No, it's okay." Her eyes followed Graydon's hulking form. "Better to have Dr. Weiss yell at me than him."

Elly had begun to fill out the form when another wracking pain interrupted her. Graydon returned to find her leaning against the counter, one hand clawed white around the clipboard. He blew.

"God damn it, get a *doctor* here!" he bellowed at the receptionist. "Can't you see she's in pain?" Unmindful of the stares of people in the waiting room and hall, Graydon shored Elly up with an iron arm and scowled dangerously at the girl behind the counter. "I don't care what you have to do, but get someone here and do it quick! I won't have my wife go through another pain out here in the goddamn hall!"

The girl scurried around at her console, wide-eyed. With the phone still at her ear, she called into an intercom for an orderly, then quickly switched back to the phone when a voice squawked out of it. While Graydon gave all his attention over to Elly, the receptionist gathered her reinforcements. She'd handled irate fathers before, but she'd never seen one as dark and devilish as this one.

"Graydon, please," Elly sighed. "Please calm down. I'm okay. Don't yell at people."

"Damn it, Elly, I won't calm down until they get you to a room. There's no excuse for this. I don't want you delivering here on the floor, for God's sake!"

Things began to happen. From down the hall, a gurney squeaked toward them, pushed by a pale young man in greens. His face sober and drawn, he headed for Elly. The receptionist finished speaking into the phone and hung up.

"Doctor's on his way," she said to Elly. "The orderly will take you up to the third floor." She glanced skittishly at Graydon. "If you could just fill out the rest of the form ..."

Graydon grabbed the clipboard out of Elly's fingers. "Later," he snapped. The orderly had drawn up beside them, gurney waiting, and with Graydon's thin-lipped help, eased Elly up onto it. She lay back and soothed her sore abdomen.

"Graydon, please," she said. "She's only doing her job. I'll be all right."

"The form can wait," he said. To the orderly, "Which way?"

"This way, sir. To the back elevators."

Poor kid, thought Elly. He was no more than eighteen, thin and pale, and he fairly cringed beneath Graydon's black stare. Elly sighed and closed her eyes.

The elevator ride was, at least, uninterrupted by pain. Elly let the rising of the car distract her, feeling still Graydon's explosive simmering and the orderly's quiet deference. Graydon had one hand in hers, the other clutching the clipboard.

On the third floor, Elly was wheeled down the hall and to room 312. There, a tough-looking nurse met them, took in the trio with a knowing glance and signaled the orderly on by. She stepped in front of Graydon to hold him back.

"Just a minute, sir," she said in a calm, commanding voice. "You can go in there in a minute, but first … "

Elly heard the swish of the door closing behind her and prayed Graydon would behave. The orderly, she was sure, was greatly relieved to have left Graydon in the hall.

"Can you get into bed?" the boy asked. "Or do you need help?" He pulled the gurney up beside a hospital bed and put a helpful hand on Elly's arm.

"No, I'm okay. I can do it." Wielding her bulk awkwardly, Elly shifted from the gurney to the bed. The boy eased the gurney away. "Thank you," Elly smiled.

The door whispered open and a young nurse Elly's age strode in. "Mrs. Cole? How are you? What pains are you having?"

Elly grimaced. "I'm afraid it's not near the emergency my husband thinks it is. They were seven minutes apart when I—"

A contraction brought her up short. The nurse took control at Elly's side and turned to the orderly. "Do you know how long?" she asked.

He figured silently. "About that, maybe less. Just before I picked her up at admitting."

The nurse nodded. "All right. Thanks." Dismissed, the orderly seemed to hesitate. The nurse had turned her attention to Elly, but glanced back questioningly.

"That big guy outside—her husband. Is he still—"

"Ironsides has him," the nurse smiled. "Go ahead." He appeared slightly relieved and put his shoulder into pushing the gurney toward the door.

Elly felt the pain ebbing and was able to regain her breath.

"Who? What?" she whispered.

"Ironsides. That gray-haired nurse who nabbed your husband. She's the best husband-tamer we've got. I'm just glad she was on duty. You've got yourself a real bruiser out there."

Elly smiled. "I know. And I think I've got another one just like him on the way."

The nurse grinned back. "Well, let's see how you and the little guy are doing. Here, let me help you out of your coat."

It was quite a contrast to her last stay in the hospital. Before, Dr. D'Angelo was the only one who seemed even remotely concerned about her and here she felt practically suffocated with attention. She wasn't sure if it was the normal treatment for laboring women or if Graydon's antics were responsible. Either way, she sank into a blissful state of relaxation and let the nurses do what they had to do.

The young, dark-haired nurse seemed in command. She administered the preliminary blood-pressure test, a quick stethoscope check and began documenting Elly's pains. Another younger girl came to help get Elly out of her clothes and into a hospital gown. After a half hour or so, Dr. Weiss stepped in.

"Mrs. Cole. How are you?"

"Fine, I think," she said. "I'm sorry we rousted you. I hope you weren't eating dinner."

"Actually, no," Dr. Weiss said. His gray hair waved back from his high forehead and crows feet wrinkled the corners of his light blue eyes. "I hadn't quite sat down to it when I got your call." He kept his expression blank. "Your husband's quite a handful, isn't he?"

"Yes," Elly sighed guiltily. "I'm sorry. Is he still upset?"

"You might say that. It's not very often I see Ironsides threatening to chop a man's kneecap."

"Oh," Elly groaned.

"No matter. I'll just check you out, see how you are and then he can come in." Dr. Weiss peered down at her through his glasses. "He'll be all right with you, won't he?"

"Yes. He's just .. . not used to this. He's very protective."

"So I gather."

When the doctor finished his examination, he began to make notes on her chart. Offhandly he recited a canned speech on epidurals. "Now if the pain gets too bad, we can give you an epidural at any time, so if it starts to get unbearable, just say something. The only drawback is that epidurals do tend to slow down the delivery process. Yours is already going slowly, so you'll have to decide what's most important, avoiding the pain or letting your body do its work unimpaired. Just remember that there is no right or wrong to this, it's all just personal preference."

By the time Graydon was allowed into the room, Elly was propped up and resigned. Graydon, although calm, was clearly not happy and anything but resigned. He came to Elly's side and took her hand anxiously.

"How are you?"

"Fine," she said firmly. "The doctor said I've got a long way to go. I've hardly dilated at all." She decided not to tell Graydon that what Dr. Weiss had actually said was that normally he'd send a woman in her condition home for a few more hours. Somehow they both knew that course of action wouldn't go over well with Graydon. "He did say I could have an epidural anytime I want, but it could slow down the process, so I told him I'll hold off on that."

He pulled up a chair and sat head-level with her. "What about the pains?"

"They've eased off a little," she said, "or else I'm just getting used to them." She smiled bravely. "I think little Nathan is going to be like daddy and do things his own way, in his own time. Really, Graydon, there's just not a lot we can do now."

"Jesus," he breathed, shaking his head. "Is it always like this? Did you know it would be like this?"

"I had an idea," she nodded. "It's not exactly like clockwork." She studied the drawn look on her husband's face. "You look tired."

He fumed at the reminder. "That battleaxe of a nurse out there kept me at bay for almost an hour. My God, she even threatened to inject me with some kind of damn dart gun. That woman's crazy. I don't know why they let someone like that run loose in a hospital. She's like some crazy little dog snapping at your heels."

Elly giggled at the picture, but stifled it at Graydon's arched brow. "Sorry. But you have to admit, you were blustering."

"Blustering? I was not! I was trying to see that my wife was getting the attention she needed. No one else seemed to give a damn if you were in pain or not."

"It's not that, Graydon. I'm just not special, that's all. All women do this; it's no big deal."

He made a face. "No big deal. The hell it is—"

A flash of agony tore across Elly's face and Graydon was

instantly on his feet.

"Elly? Should I call the doctor?"

"No," she puffed. "It's okay. It's not bad. Just...ignore it." She breathed deeply, letting the air soothe her body.

"Ignore it? I can't ignore it! How long is it going to be like this?"

Elly waited until the pain had subsided. One of them had to stay calm.

"Graydon, sit down," she commanded gently. "You can't go berserk at every pain. It's going to take a long time..."

"How long?" he demanded.

"Hours. It could take many hours." She pressed Graydon's hand at the stricken look on his face. "Don't look like that. There's absolutely nothing wrong with it. It just takes time."

"Jesus, Elly. I don't know if I can stand this. I'll go crazy watching you..."

"I know," she said. "I want you to go home."

He pulled himself up as if slapped. "Go home?"

"Yes. Go home. Chester hasn't been fed, and come to think of it, neither have you. Go home and warm up one of those casseroles I put in the freezer for you. Read your mail, correct test papers, watch TV. You can't stay here, Graydon. You'll just tear yourself apart."

"Elly, I can't leave you."

"You can't stay."

Her words landed like a blow on him. He slumped.

"Graydon, listen to me," she whispered. "I love you, you know that, but you can't help me here. I have to do this. Once I start, I can't stop, I can't change my mind and say, sorry, my mistake, I don't really want this baby after all. And it's not going to be fun. But that doesn't mean there's anything wrong, and it's all going to happen the way it has to. I just don't want you beating your head against a brick wall over me. The best thing you can do for me is go home."

"But—"

"No buts. Your staying here won't do anyone any good. Go home, Graydon. I'll call you as soon as anything definite happens."

"I can't," he argued. "I can't resign myself to that."

"But you can't stay and jump up and down every time I have a contraction or pull the doctor off his other patients for me when I don't need him. You can't tie up the whole nursing staff with your bellowing. Graydon, be sensible. By staying you'll only make it worse for yourself."

"I don't care about me..."

"But I do. And I don't want to see you hurting over my pains or, God forbid, injected by Nurse Ironsides. You can't help me, Graydon. You can't take my pain away. I want you to go."

He stood up and strode restlessly to the window. Outside, city lights were blinking on.

"Jesus, Elly. Do you have to say it like that?"

"I'm sorry," she sighed. "But you've got to understand. Please, Graydon."

For a long moment he said nothing, just stood staring sightlessly out the window. Except for the rise and fall of his burly chest, he might have been made of dark stone. Elly hurt for him.

"All right," he said helplessly. "I'll go. But I can't promise I'll stay away." He turned back toward her. "I'll go home and feed Chester and maybe grab a bite. Then I'll be back."

Elly accepted the compromise. "Okay. And also, will you call my mom? Just tell her I'm here but nothing's happening yet. Tell her we'll call her later when there's news."

Graydon nodded. "All right."

A new pain seared Elly and she clamped her teeth shut on the words she'd been about to say. Graydon was at her side instantly.

"It's...okay," she gasped. "It's okay. It's a little one."

Graydon's eyes reflected the horror he felt at Elly's ordeal. His eyes looked haunted.

"God, Elly, if I'd known..."

"No, don't. It's okay. I'm fine." She relaxed back into her pillows to illustrate. "Really I am. Go on. Go home and eat. I'll call you the second anything happens."

He looked unconvinced. "Are you sure?"

"Positive. Go on. Call Mom. And don't forget Chester. He'll probably wonder where I am."

Graydon leaned down and kissed Elly lightly on the forehead.

"I don't want to go."

"I know." She smiled bravely. "It'll make the time go faster, though."

He shook his head. "I don't think so."

Elly kept still. She'd never seen Graydon's eyes so full of emotion.

"I love you, Elly," he whispered fiercely. "God, I love you."

She wasn't sure if the pains really got worse or if not having Graydon there to worry about left her more susceptible to them; in any case, they hurt. She began to think fleetingly of biting on bullets and tying pulling ropes to the footboard of the bed.

She hadn't really been prepared for this, either. She'd always suspected that labor pains were subject to gross exaggeration and not really as bad as everyone made them out to be; now she knew she'd been wrong. After being in labor for over two hours, she was ready to believe anything.

The nurses checked her periodically, taking her blood pressure and testing her for dilation. There wasn't a lot of change.

"Three centimeters," the dark haired nurse said. "You've still got time."

Elly groaned. The nurse laughed and patted her hand. "Hang in there. You'll make it."

"I'm not worried as much about myself as I am my husband," Elly said. "He'll be back soon and I'd like to get as much over with while he's gone as I can."

The nurse nodded understanding. "I know what you mean. When I had my first one, my husband insisted on coming into the delivery room with me. As soon as things started happening, he fainted dead away. I might have been upset if I hadn't been so busy." She laughed. "On the second one, he waited outside."

Elly liked her. She had to have been Elly's age or less, and she had an easy, earthy calm about her—almost like Linda, but not quite so abrasive. Elly felt better hearing her anecdotes.

"I'm sure Graydon won't faint," Elly said. "I'm just afraid he might get too protective and make a nuisance of himself."

The nurse plumped Elly's pillow and adjusted the blinds. "Yeah, he could sure do that if he wanted to," she agreed. "You been married long?"

"Almost five years."

"Hmm. He acts more like a newlywed. Well, I've got other ladies to see to. Take it easy. I'll be back."

Elly tried to take it easy but the contractions wouldn't let her. They came in groups; hard, hard, hard; easy, easy, easy. With every one she willed herself to dilate so the baby would come soon.

Come on, Nathan, she begged silently. Three more hours and you'll miss your due date.

Graydon called from the house. "How are you? Anything?"

"No," Elly sighed. "Still the same. What are you doing?"

"I just finished eating. I called your mother. She's going to fly up tomorrow. I told her to wait but she wouldn't hear of it."

"Okay. I don't mind. I'll probably be conked out when she gets here, but she'll be able to see the baby right away. How's Chester?"

"Spoiled rotten. I fed him and he ate a little, but then he insisted on sleeping in my lap while I ate. Every time I tried to push him off, he clawed my legs to shreds. What do you do with him during the day—carry him around on your shoulder?"

"No." She had to laugh. "He just likes to be near a warm body whenever he can."

"Well, he'd better get used to being cold. He's not going to come in after the baby's born."

"But Graydon—"

"No. I've heard about cats and babies. He'll stay out and that's that."

Elly decided not to argue. She recognized the flat finality of Graydon's voice; anyway she'd have time later to convince him of Chester's innocence. Lots of time.

"What about the Mayfields?" Elly asked. "Have you told them?"

"No. I'd better call, though. I'm going to take tomorrow off, anyway; Mayfield can cover my last class."

"Graydon, you don't have to—"

"I am. I'll have to pick your mother up at the airport anyway."

"All right. Well, there's not a lot of point in your coming back right now. Nothing's happening."

Graydon was quiet for a minute, thinking. Elly knew he was trying to stay cool-headed.

"I'll call Don. Then, I don't know; maybe I'll find something to do. But I'll come back pretty soon. Can I bring you anything?"

"I can't think of anything. Oh, maybe some magazines or something. I—"

A pain grabbed her.

"Elly?"

"Wait...just a minute. Oh, that's not so bad." She caught her breath. "Yes, if you could bring me something to read. It's hard not to think about it and just watch the clock. Would you mind?"

"No. I'll pick up something on the way. Anything else?"

"Um, oh..."

"What?"

She hesitated. "Would you, um, mind calling Linda? Just to tell her I'm here?" Graydon made an uncharitable noise. "Please, Graydon. She's my friend."

"Some friend," he grumbled. "Yeah, I'll call her. Is her number in the book?"

"Yes. Tell her I'll call her tomorrow after things have calmed down."

"All right. Now, anything else?"

"No, that's all."

"You're sure?"

"Positive."

"Okay. Well, I guess I'll clean up the mess I made in the kitchen, then I'll be down. If anything happens and you call and I'm not here, you'll know I'm on my way."

"Okay."

"Okay. Well..." He trailed off.

"Graydon?"

"What?"

"I love you."

"I love you, too."

"And I'm going to make you proud of me."

Chapter Eighteen

He arrived back at the hospital about ten. Elly was just getting her half-hourly blood pressure check. The young nurse had gone off duty but a motherly-plump woman had taken her place and she smiled cheerfully at Graydon as he edged inside the room.

"No news yet," she told Graydon and Elly both. "Looks like that baby of yours can't make up its mind whether it wants to come out now or not."

Graydon stepped around the nurse and took Elly's hand.

"How do you feel?"

"Okay. I wish something would happen, though. This is getting old real quick."

"There," the nurse said as she slipped off the arm bag. "Relax. I'll be back." She winked at Elly and strolled out.

Graydon pulled up a chair and laid a pile of magazines on Elly's nightstand. "I got all different kinds; I wasn't sure what you'd be in the mood to read."

"Thanks. They look fine." She sighed. "I wish Nathan would do something. They said he hasn't even started to turn yet."

"You're sure nothing's wrong?" Graydon asked quickly. "There's no problems?"

She shook her head. "No. I guess this kind of thing isn't

unusual for first babies. It's just long and tiring."

"Has the doctor been back lately?"

"No. He should be here pretty soon, I think. He said he'd check back later, and that was two hours ago."

A sudden wrench of Graydon's hand signaled a new pain. Elly tensed but was able to keep from looking too agonized. Graydon's instant reaction was to stand, but he caught himself and settled on the edge of his chair instead. He waited silently for the pain to pass.

"Oh," Elly breathed.

"Bad?"

"Not too. I probably shouldn't fight them, but it's hard not to. Maybe we should have taken one of those birthing classes after all."

Graydon dismissed the subject. "You still don't want the epidural?" he asked.

"No, not yet." She smiled at him. "I want to encourage Nathan to do his own thing as much as we can."

The time passed slowly. As long as Graydon was determined to stay, Elly urged him to do the talking. What had Mom said, and Linda? His narrative was interrupted every few minutes by a contraction and he would wait, either wide-eyed with alarm or just quietly depending on whether the pain was a bad one or not. After each, Elly reassured him.

The nurses came around and checked Elly every half hour, shooing Graydon into a corner when they measured her dilation. It was a slow process. She didn't seem to be dilating any more at all.

Shortly after ten-thirty, Dr. Weiss came back and examined her himself. "Barely three and a half," he told Elly and Graydon. "It's going to be a long night."

"Isn't there anything you can do?" Graydon asked.

"Not at this point. Not until Mrs. Cole's body and that baby decide what they're going to do." He turned to Elly. "How do the contractions feel?"

"Not as bad as they were. Some are no worse than gas pains."

Dr. Weiss seemed to expect that. "The baby's not dropping yet, so maybe your uterus has decided to relax a bit. That's good. You might be able to get some sleep." To Graydon, "Mr. Cole, I would suggest you do the same. There's no telling when everything will start to happen, and you both ought to get as much rest as you can. When the time comes, you'll want to be wide awake."

Graydon frowned down at his wife. "I want to stay."

"Your wife needs her rest, Mr. Cole. You'll be doing her a disservice by keeping her up. We want her strong and healthy when that baby finally comes."

Elly met Graydon's eyes, soft and pleading. He relented.

"All right. But I'm not going home. I'll stay down in the waiting room."

"You'd be more comfortable at home," Dr. Weiss reasoned. "It could be hours."

"No. I'm staying here. I want to be here if anything happens."

"Suit yourself." The doctor shrugged and turned to go. "Try to get some sleep, Mrs. Cole. The nurses will be around regularly and if things start moving again, they'll call me."

"Fine, thank you," Elly said. She watched the small, casual man leave, knowing Graydon was angry.

"He sure doesn't seem very damned concerned," Graydon muttered when the door had whispered shut.

"He is," Elly replied, "he just knows it's going to be a while. And you would be more comfortable at home."

Graydon refused to consider it. "No. I'd just as soon pull up a chair right here, but I'd probably keep you from sleeping." He studied her. "Are you sure you'll be able to sleep?"

"I won't know until I try. I'd like to, though. Just these last eight hours have tired me, and that wasn't even hard labor."

Graydon shook his head. "I don't see how it can get worse."

"We'll see," she said pressing his hand. "Go on, see if you can sleep. With any luck Nathan will start acting up again if he thinks he's being ignored and we'll be in business."

"All right," he said heavily. "I'll be in the waiting room."

Elly was able to sleep fitfully. She dozed between pains or, if they were light, tossed restlessly and slept on. She dreamed quick, fleeting images and the pain she felt physically was sometimes incorporated into her dreams, into twinges of emotional pain.

She saw Adam, his eyes shining with hurt for her and her confusion.

"I think you should tell him. If he loves you, and he'd be crazy not to, he'll take it okay. You're tearing yourself apart."

"I can't. Every time I even think about it, I can see him just raging over it and I can't face that."

Adam's eyes held more than concern. "I wish it was my child you carried. I'd show you how a man in love acts."

Elly was jerked awake by a wrenching pain.

After it subsided, she checked her watch—11:50. Come on, Nathan. You're missing your own birthday. She rubbed her aching abdomen. It felt stretched taut as a drumhead. How could her body possibly eject this medicine ball of a baby? When it was all over, she'd need plastic surgery just to get her stomach back where it belonged.

The nurses came around for her periodic blood pressure test. At 12:30 the short, plump one stopped to talk.

"Looks like you've stopped," she noticed.

"Stopped?"

"You're not dilating any more."

"But I still have pains." She'd just had a slight one not three or four minutes ago.

"Yes, but not like hard labor. I've seen women do this, particularly with a big, first baby."

"What usually happens?" Elly asked.

"Nothing for a while. Depends on the baby, and the doctor. Dr. Weiss might want to put you on an I.V. in the morning if you haven't made any progress, or maybe break your water. That usually gets things going. The only thing is, your baby hasn't even turned." The nurse shook her round head. "Can't do a thing until it does."

Elly felt depressed after the nurse left. Come on, Nathan, she pleaded silently. Don't do this to me. Turn around and drop, please. We're all waiting for you.

She slept. The contractions diminished to aching throbs, sometimes hardly perceptible.

In the waiting room below, Graydon sprawled uncomfortably

in a chair and dozed in spite of himself.

"Augh!"

A grabbing contraction doubled Elly up out of her sleep, jerking her body into a ball of pain. It seemed to slice across her belly like a knife and for an agonizing moment she actually thought she was ripping in half. Sweat popped out on her forehead and she ground her teeth against the pain. In a slow, timeless moment, it passed.

She sank back into her pillows, damp and exhausted. A strange, rumbling feeling churned her abdomen. She put pensive hands on her bulging stomach and felt hard knobs and pulsing soft spots.

"Nathan?" she breathed.

Afraid to move too quickly, she reached for her watch. Just after 3:30. Had this whole thing really started over twelve hours ago? And how much longer before it was over? If that last pain was a preview of what was in store, she didn't want to know.

Her eyes roamed the dark room. Only a slit of light glowed beneath the door. At this hour there wasn't even a whisper of crepe-soled shoes outside in the hall.

Elly knew another pain would be coming soon, and she felt alone.

She glanced at her bedside phone. It would be a simple matter to raise the front desk and have someone send Graydon up. She could almost picture him draped over a styleless couch or chair, his expression eased by sleep. No, she couldn't wake him. That would be unfair. The last twelve hours had been harder on him than they had been on her; she'd let him sleep.

A second pain pierced her, unbelievably sharp, seemingly enough to draw blood. Elly wrapped her arms around her stomach and balled up into a gasping, straining heap. She couldn't believe this was actually happening, that the pains were actually this bad. She'd never felt anything so awful in her life. Surely they couldn't continue like this?

When she felt it ebbing, she lowered herself carefully down on her back, still gasping for breath. She could still feel the throbbing ache of the pain, a phantom echo, and she could feel the baby move.

God, Nathan, what are you doing to me, she thought. What if she couldn't handle the pain? What if she decided she'd rather lie down and die?

She imagined Dr. Weiss confronting Graydon.

"Sorry, Mr. Cole. Your wife couldn't take it. The pain killed her, and your son, too."

Elly gritted her teeth at the gruesome picture. No. She'd proven she could do a few things, like hold her marriage together. She'd prove she could have a baby, too. No amount of pain was going to make her give up.

Another one hit. Like a plummeting puncture wound, it drove the breath from her. She grabbed for her stomach with one hand and the nurse's button with the other. She was bound to do this, but right now she needed help.

"Four centimeters," a new nurse said. "And the baby's turning."

"Then...it'll be soon?" Elly panted.

The nurse clucked her tongue. "Not necessarily, but let's hope so." She watched Elly go through another hard contraction. "Looks like we'd better get you down to the delivery room."

"My...husband," Elly gasped. "He's down...in the...waiting room."

"Okay. You just relax as much as you can. We'll get you to delivery, then get your husband up here."

The delivery room was less comforting than her regular room, but Elly didn't spare much energy studying it. There were several large machines, graphs and meters and things, and more room for nurses and doctors to do whatever might need to be done. It was midway between a regular room and an operating room.

Once she was wheeled in, her blood pressure was taken again and her dilation checked.

"Yes, four," a second nurse confirmed. "Who's your doctor?"

"Dr. Weiss," Elly managed.

"He's gone home. We'll see how it goes. Once you get to six, we'll call him."

Fifteen minutes later, Graydon was ushered in. His black hair was rumpled, his clothes wrinkled, but his eyes were wide open and alert. He strode quickly to Elly.

"How are you? What's happening?"

Elly didn't try to hide her apprehension. "It started again, worse. But the baby's turning."

Graydon frowned. "Is it bad?"

"It's awful. But we'll make it." She tried to squeeze his hand but she was too weak. "Somehow or another, we'll make it."

At her next contraction, Graydon seriously doubted it. He'd never seen a woman's face so contorted with agony, so red and running with sweat. Elly's hair was soaked, clinging to her forehead and neck, and the cords of her neck tautened with the awful clenching of her jaw. Graydon let her squeeze his hand until it turned white. When the pain eased and Elly sank back, exhausted, his first concern was her.

"Jesus, Elly, are you sure this is normal?" he breathed.

She nodded slowly. "Sure. Look at the nurses. They don't think it's anything unusual." She turned her blue eyes on Graydon, huge with the awareness of her commitment. "It's not going to be easy, Graydon. I know that now. I'll need you."

"I'm here," he said immediately. "I won't leave you."

She was shaking her head. "No, I don't mean that. I mean I'll need you to help me, to give me support. You can't go off bellowing at doctors and nurses and ranting and raving. Just help me get through this."

His eyes darkened and Elly was afraid she'd angered him. He seemed to mull over what she'd said. "Okay," he agreed finally. "Whatever you say. Just..."

"What?"

"God I wish I could help you! I wish I could take some of the pain."

She smiled weakly. "You can't. Just be with me and love me."

"I do, Elly," he said. "Believe me, I do."

The next few hours were hell. Elly's contractions came regularly and hard, pulling her into a contorted ball and pushing Graydon to the limit of his patience. One nurse or another was always present, but they offered little in the way of reassurance. Elly could tell by Graydon's tightening jaw if he were growing antagonistic, and unless she was in the throes of a contraction, she squeezed his hand sharply to remind him of his promise. It wasn't easy.

By 5:00 a.m. Elly had dilated no more and the pains began to lessen again. Instead of feeling relieved as she had before, this time she groaned in disappointment. A nurse confirmed her fears.

"You're really having a time of it, aren't you?" she said. "Dr. Waldron is here; I'll ask him to look at you."

"He can damn well do more than look at you," Graydon muttered when the nurse had gone.

"Graydon, please," Elly sighed.

"I know, I know." He smoothed the wet strands of hair off her forehead. "I'll just be so glad when this is over. I know you will, too, but I don't ever want you to have to go through this again."

At first Elly lay quietly and relaxed under his hand; then the gist of what he'd said hit her. Her eyes flew open.

"But, Graydon, this is only one. What about another one? What about a girl?"

Graydon shook his head, frowning. "I don't care about another one, no matter what it is. I don't want you having to do this again. It's too much."

"It gets easier," Elly said. "They say each one gets easier."

"No." His voice was final. "One is enough."

"But—"

"Elly, no. I won't see you torn apart like this again. My God, we just got your mind back together and now this." He leaned down and kissed her lightly. "You've been through enough."

Elly settled under his hand. She felt foolishly pampered, like a Victorian lady who was simply too delicate to bear children, but she had to admit to herself that she wasn't sorry. This ordeal was more than she had bargained for. And anyway, as long as Graydon had his son, that was all he needed.

Dr. Waldron came to see Elly. He was as tall as Graydon but only half as wide and probably ten years older. He seemed not the least intimidated by Graydon's glowering bulk.

"The baby's getting into position," he told Elly after a quick, knowing examination. "We just need to jog it a bit. I'm going to ask you to walk."

"Walk?" Graydon exploded. "She's in pain just sitting! How can you expect her to walk?"

Dr. Waldron faced Graydon squarely. "You can help her. I

realize it sounds unprofessional to you, but it's the best we can offer right now. If we can get that baby to drop normally, that's what we want to do. Mrs. Cole," he turned to Elly, "I want you to put all your weight on your husband, but walk as much as you can."

"Where?"

"Out in the hall, just up and down. Do you have a robe?"

"In my room."

Dr. Waldron dispatched a nurse to retrieve it.

"You don't have to walk fast, no jogging or anything, just one foot in front of the other. Do you think you can do that?"

"I—I guess." Elly kept her eyes on Dr. Waldron, knowing Graydon was fuming. She prayed he could keep control until they got out into the hall.

The nurse returned with Elly's robe and between her and the doctor and Graydon, they managed to slip it on her. Dr. Waldron and Graydon helped Elly swing her legs over and stand. Elly gritted her teeth against the ache of straightening.

"Lean on your husband, Mrs. Cole. Let him carry your weight."

Graydon circled Elly's waist with one hand and offered her his other arm. She grabbed onto it as if it were a lifeline. Fat, bent and exhausted, she let Graydon lead her through the doorway and out into the hall.

"He's a real helpful son-of-a-bitch, isn't he?" Graydon muttered angrily.

"Please, Graydon. Dr. Weiss would have probably done the same thing." Talking took too much energy, so she concentrated instead on carrying her stomach one more step, one more step.

"Does it hurt?"

She shook her head. Actually, it wasn't as bad as she'd expected. Her lower back ached, but there were no tearing pains. She was just thankful it was so early; the halls were practically deserted. As awful as she looked, she didn't want to be seen.

They walked. Graydon leading as if in a slow, awkward dance, they walked the hall to a corner, turned and walked back past delivery to the opposite corridor. They covered probably a hundred feet in twenty minutes or so. At one point Elly had to stop, signaling Graydon with a viselike grip on his arm, and she curled shaking against him as a medium pain spasmed through her. When it was over, she motioned Graydon to walk again. The soles of her feet left damp prints on the floor.

"Elly, that's enough," he said.

"No. Keep walking."

"But you're contracting again!"

She gasped for breath. "Not enough. Keep going."

They made slow, impatient progress, Elly hobbling like a half dead beggar on Graydon's arm. Occasionally a nurse would step out of delivery to check on them, then slip back inside. Another woman had been wheeled in and she was closer to delivering than Elly. Probably her third, Elly thought, or fourth, or ...

They walked to the corner, turned, walked back to the corridor, turned. Elly suffered more pains, none of them crippling or promising more than momentary discomfort. She grew exhausted and had to have Graydon ease her down into one of the chairs in the hall.

"Should I get the doctor?" he asked.

She shook her head no. "Just...rest," she panted. Unwittingly she rubbed her abdomen with a sweaty hand.

Dr. Waldron stepped out once to check Elly's progress. They were walking again and he met them halfway back to delivery.

"Any progress?" he asked.

Elly didn't have the strength so Graydon answered for her. "No." His voice was flat.

Dr. Waldron looked unperturbed. "I think I'll call Dr. Weiss. If she were mine, I'd start her on an I.V., but I better check with him first."

A nurse poked her head out of delivery. A pained wail escaped out the door.

"Doctor!"

Waldron turned and signaled the nurse. "Okay." To Elly, "I've got one coming right now. I'll get Dr. Weiss down here as soon as I can." He strode quickly back up the hall and disappeared inside the delivery room.

Elly wanted to cry. Why couldn't that be her in there? Why couldn't she be built like a stout heavy peasant and have the baby with hardly a whimper? She bit her lip to keep back the urge to cry and gripped Graydon's arm with a desperate resolve.

They walked.

Sometime later they heard the woman's groan heighten into a high-pitched wail. Elly let Graydon lead her to the farthest end of their circuit and then sank gratefully into a chair. Graydon paced.

"They've got to know how demoralizing that is," Graydon said. "Can't they soundproof those rooms?"

"It doesn't matter," Elly lied. She shuddered under a light contraction.

A nurse exploded from the delivery room, urgency hurrying her steps. Before Elly had a chance to protest, Graydon was after her. He caught her halfway to the main hall, but by that time Elly was too miserable to care what he was saying to her. All she wanted to do was curl up in a ball and sleep.

Graydon's shoes stepped into her field of vision. She looked up.

"Dr. Weiss is on his way."

It was almost seven when Dr. Weiss appeared, and he helped Graydon ease Elly back into the delivery room.

The other woman had delivered while Elly sat huddled outside, and the delivery room was being cleaned and disinfected in her aftermath. Elly hadn't watched the half-conscious woman being wheeled down to recovery. She didn't care anymore.

"You're at five centimeters," Dr. Weiss said. "Halfway there."

Halfway! Elly wanted to die. How could she go through as much again as she'd been through? She pushed back in her pillow and began to cry.

"There's got to be something you can do," Graydon insisted irritably. "She can't take any more of this."

Dr. Weiss nodded. "We'll give her an epidural for the pain and go with an I.V. If nothing else can induce her, that should." Dr. Weiss became more serious. "There are things to be done here, Mr. Cole. Why don't you go down to the coffee shop and have a cup of coffee? Come on back in, say, a half hour or so."

This time Graydon didn't need Elly to plead with him. Whatever they had to do couldn't be done fast enough to suit

Graydon. He nodded once to the doctor and pressed Elly's hand.

"I'll be back."

Elly didn't care what they did. She offered her arm when told to, lay calmly beneath more examinations and turned obediently away at the insertion of the I. V. in her arm. She tried to imagine the fluid dripping into her vein, carrying the magic formula that would end her ordeal. She couldn't seem to drum up any enthusiasm or hope.

"It won't be long now," Dr. Weiss said.

Elly waited.

But not for long. She wasn't sure how many minutes had passed—ten? twenty?—when a pain broke across her back, slicing as neatly as a butcher knife and hurting twice as much. She raised up, arching, crying, almost strangling on the scream that caught in her throat. Dr. Weiss came to stand over her, his face compassionate as Elly slowly died of a broken back. The pain seemed to go on and on, reverberating across the small of her back, shock waves of pain.

"God," Elly gasped. "It...hurts!"

Dr. Weiss put a hand beneath her back to support her. It didn't seem to help. Only with time did the awful wave pass, echoing slowly away.

"My...back!" Elly panted. "Why does it hurt my back?"

"The baby's dropping. Don't worry, it's normal. Relax as much as you can between pains. Breathe deeply. Relax."

There was no way, not when she knew another one was coming. The most she could do was consciously unclench her jaw, straighten her clawed fingers and try to breathe deeply.

When Graydon returned, he was horrified to find Elly arched grotesquely against a contraction. His concern turned to explosive anger.

"What the hell are you *doing* to her?" he roared at the doctor. "My God, it's killing her!"

Dr. Weiss seemed unexcited by Graydon's outburst. "Mr. Cole, we are trying to deliver a baby. It's not pleasant. If you can't help your wife calmly, you'll have to leave."

"Jesus, does it have to be like this?" Graydon demanded. Awful hissing noises escaped from Elly's tightly clenched teeth.

"Unfortunately, some women are resistant to the epidural, and it seems your wife is one of those," Dr. Weiss sighed. "No matter what else modern medicine has done, it hasn't found a better way of delivering babies. But the choice is yours, Mr. Cole. Stand quietly or leave. I don't have time to attend two patients."

Graydon behaved. Taking up a station on Elly's far side, he let her strangle his hand in a death grip and watched as her huge blue eyes dissolved into incredible pits of anguish.

"That's better," Dr. Weiss said later. "We're getting somewhere now. Six centimeters. You're doing fine, Mrs. Cole."

The words were meaningless to Elly. Her brain had ceased to function except to regulate the purely animal processes of her body. There was nothing but the pain and, briefly, the aching absence of pain. All else was a gray blur.

"Doctor!" a nurse called sharply. "Her water's breaking!"

The staff scurried into action. Graydon was relegated to a safe place at Elly's shoulder, out of the way of the doctor and three nurses that seemed to perform innumerable small acts, none of which seemed to help Elly. Mesmerized by the procedures, Graydon held Elly's hand and gripped her shoulder.

"Come on," Dr. Weiss said beneath his breath. To a nurse, "She's too slow. She's not dilating fast enough."

Graydon heard the words in panic. What did that mean? Elly drove the blood from his hand with a viselike squeeze and arched spasmodically. The cry that escaped her didn't sound human.

"It's no good," Dr. Weiss said. "We'll have to take it. Nurse, call Dr. Waldron up here. Get the operating station ready."

Graydon was paralyzed. "No good?"

"We'll have to take it, Mr. Cole. She can't do it without tearing in half." Dr. Weiss was too busy to notice Graydon's stricken look. "Wait outside, Mr. Cole. We'll let you know as soon as we're done."

"But..." A nurse was already prying Elly's fingers free of Graydon's hand, propelling him toward the door. He went, too thunderstruck to protest. Elly caught a last, blurred glimpse of him before she was wheeled beneath the lights.

Everything was white, bright and blurry and soft like sunlight through sheer curtains. Elly was floating in it, drifting on a sea of whiteness.

"Elly?"

The word reverberated through her mind, soft and questioning. The voice was familiar. She tried to open her eyes, but they were heavy, so heavy. The dim image of a man's face was over her.

"Elly?"

Who was it? She wanted to know, but didn't have the strength to find out. It couldn't be Graydon; Graydon never spoke so softly to her. Was it...

"Adam?" Her voice was inaudible, just the movement of her lips forming the name. Yes, it was Adam. The motel room was white, white walls and light curtains, not dark the way it should be. She had expected blood red curtains and dark, dingy walls, a faded rug and the bed—the bed.

"Oh." Of course a bed. She'd left Graydon, fled before him in her failure, and Adam had taken her away. She'd left Graydon a horrible note. Afraid yet to admit her failure to him, she'd attacked him, harangued him with her misery at his hands, left him hateful and angry because she'd found happiness and fulfillment with another man. Adam, the first man.

It was all a lie, but she'd had to. She couldn't tell Graydon, not even in a note. She wasn't strong enough. She never had been. Adam didn't care. Adam didn't demand strength from her. Adam loved her.

But the bed. How could she? She'd never, not with anyone but Graydon. Adam was so kind, so gentle. He came to her, slid in beside her, kissed her. He was so kind. He'd taken her away. He expected nothing, he'd told her that, but she knew, she knew. He kissed her. She lay still beneath him, knowing she owed him, she was grateful for what he'd done. And he loved her. Not like Graydon.

His hand was feather light on the column of her neck. No one but Graydon, no one had... She turned toward him, buried her face against his shoulder. His bare shoulder. He was naked. God, so was she! He kissed her, called her name over and over, and his hand...on her breast. No one but Graydon, no one but Graydon. On her waist. She balled her hands into shaking fists, her whole body shaking. She was afraid, God she was afraid! Adam was so kind, she owed him, he had been so kind, but only Graydon, only Graydon, no one but Graydon.

"No!" she cried. "No, I can't, I can't, I'm sorry, it's a mistake, it's all a mistake! I can't, Adam, I can't! Please, don't touch me, don't touch me. I'm sorry, I never should have, it's a mistake, I can't. It was wrong, it's all wrong, I never should have left, I'm sorry, I'm sorry, I'm sorry..."

Sunlight warmed her eyelids. Her head rolled instinctively toward it, eyelids fluttering. The window was so bright, but it felt good. The warmth felt good.

She opened her eyes on the hospital room. Like last time. Who was she? A surge of panic shot through her like an electric shock, but she willed it away.

I'm Elly Cole, she told herself. And I'm happily married and I love my husband and I just had his baby.

Instantly alert, Elly flipped her head around to the other side of the bed. Graydon.

He sat sprawled back in a chair at her side, his arms loose, his head back and settled uncomfortably against the wall. His face was haggard, even in sleep, dark and frowning. Elly put a hand out to touch his knee.

"What?" He jerked awake, already half out of his chair before his eyes fell on Elly's face. "Elly? Are you okay? Was I sleeping?"

She smiled dreamily. "Yes, but I think you needed it."

"How are you?" He crouched over her, her small hand caught in both of his. His eyes searched her face.

"Fine, I think. What time is it?"

"Almost three."

"In the afternoon?"

He nodded. "God, I'm glad you're all right." Elly put a hand to her stomach. It was tender, tight and funny-feeling, but somewhat smaller.

"The baby?"

"Fine."

"You've seen him?" Elly asked.

"Yes. But Elly—"

Immediately her eyes widened in panic. "What? Is he okay?"

Graydon smiled and shook his head at her reaction. "She's fine."

"She..." Stiff with surprise, Elly fell back on her pillows. "She? It's a girl? But I knew, I could tell. Are you sure?"

"Positive."

"Oh, Graydon," she wailed. "I wanted to have a son for you!"

"Hey," he said softly scolding. "I don't care if it's a three-headed Martian. The main thing is that you're okay and she's okay. That's all I care about."

"But, but—" She sighed helplessly. "We'll have another one, a boy, this time."

"No. One's enough."

"But a boy," Elly said again.

"No." He was firm. "No more. One daughter and you is all I want." He kissed her. "You're all I care about."

Elly quieted. "What does she look like?"

He shrugged happily. "I don't know. I haven't seen her up close."

"Why not?" she asked, surprised.

"I've been with you. She's fine, they told me that. I wanted to be here with you."

"But," she paused. "Don't you want to see what she looks like?"

The unspoken past crouched behind Elly's question. She studied Graydon's eyes for a crack, a doubt. There was none.

"It doesn't matter what she looks like. She's ours."

"Are you sure?" Elly breathed.

Instead of answering, Graydon patted Elly's hand playfully. "Do you know that you talk under anesthesia?"

"Talk?" She wrinkled her brow at the question.

"Yes. And you talked about Adam."

Adam. It all came rushing back, half dream, half memory—the motel, the bed, Adam, her crying.

"Oh, God," she breathed. "Did I talk about—that night?"

Graydon nodded. "Now I know why you went crazy that first

time I tried to make love to you up at Telluride. It didn't make any sense then, but it does now."

Elly felt embarrassment stain her cheeks. "I couldn't even manage to have an affair, could I?" she blushed. "I couldn't—I didn't love him. He offered to take me anywhere I wanted, so the next day I told him I wanted to go to New Mexico. He would have driven me, but I insisted that he take me to the bus depot. That was when the accident happened. It's hard to believe I can actually remember it all now." She sighed. "I felt so guilty for what I'd done to him."

"What about me?" Graydon asked. "Didn't you feel guilty about that?"

She faced him guilelessly. "I wanted you to hate me. That's why I wrote that note, so you'd hate me so much you'd think you were better off without me. That was better than disappointing you again."

He shook his head slowly. "You sure suceeded—for a while." He pulled his wallet out of his pocket and opened the billfold, took out a piece of worn, folded paper.

"Is that...?"

"Yes."

"May I see it?"

He handed her the note. She didn't remember everything she said in it, but she remembered crying so hard that she could barely see, and she had to be careful about not letting the tears fall on the paper.

Graydon, she read silently, *I have to leave. I can't please you, I can't be what you want, what you need. You're too strong, too demanding, and I'm too weak. Adam is taking me away. Adam— the first man to love me just the way I am, the first man to plant a seed in me and encourage it to grow, the first man to really believe in me. I am sorry, Graydon. In time, you'll see that it's better this way.*

"Shameless lies," she said, shaking her head. "Every word of it." She handed him back the note.

Graydon took it, wadded it up into a ball and tossed it blithely in the trash can.

He smiled. "That's all over now. And I still haven't seen my daughter up close."

Elly lay back contentedly as Graydon rang for a nurse. In minutes one pushed through the door.

"My wife's awake now," he said. "Could we see the baby?"

"I'll get her." The nurse flashed Elly a grin and disappeared.

She was beautiful. From the thick black hair that Elly saw first as the nurse brought her in, to the tiny, round face that came into view when laid at Elly's side, she was beautiful. Her face, round and red, shone alertly from the bundle of blankets. Her nose was tiny and buttonish, her eyes, awake now, were huge and milky blue. They startled restlessly at the faces and hands above her.

"Oh, Graydon," Elly breathed. "Isn't she beautiful?"

"Just like her momma," Graydon agreed. "Even big blue eyes."

Elly didn't tell him that all babies had blue eyes. Maybe they wouldn't change.

"Look at all that hair!" Elly exclaimed. "And fingernails! Little tiny, long fingernails! Isn't she amazing?"

"She's perfect," Graydon said. He put his arm around Elly and the baby both. "Now, what are we going to name her? You promised me we wouldn't have to go through this again, so you pick."

"Oh, I don't know," Elly groaned. "She's so pretty. Tina?"

"Tina's are ballerinas."

"Kathy?"

"Too close to Karen."

"Patricia? Theresa?"

"No. My sisters have their own kids to carry on their names. Give her a name that's all her own."

Elly thought. She watched the baby wiggle and jerk, so aware, so alive. "Tracy," she said finally.

"Tracy? That's not bad."

"Tracy Cole."

Graydon rolled it around on his tongue. "Tracy Cole. Tracy Eleanor Cole." Elly made a face. "That's it, then. Tracy Eleanor Cole." Graydon pronounced it proudly. "My daughter, Tracy."

"Our daughter," Elly said.

"Yes," Graydon agreed. "Our daughter."

Peg Hatcher fidgeted in the elevator. Forgotten at the airport, she'd waited for twenty minutes before calling the house. No answer. She called the hospital. A Mrs. Cole? Yes, she was listed in delivery. No, that was the last word. Nothing yet.

She'd hauled her suitcase outside to the street and hailed a taxi. She'd never ridden in a taxi before. Afraid of the strange man driving at first, she told him her destination, then proceeded to talk a blue streak about her daughter and son-in-law until the man gladly deposited her at the front door of the hospital.

Now she waited impatiently for the elevator to reach the third floor. In recovery, the receptionist said, 302. Yes, she'd delivered, but by Caesarian. Mother and baby were fine.

She dragged her suitcase out of the elevator and tapped down the hall. 310, 308, 306, 304. There it was. She lunged through the door.

The family turned at her arrival.

"Oh, my God," Graydon breathed. "I forgot!"

"Mom, look!" Elly said. "Look at her. Isn't she beautiful?"

"Elly? Are you all right? Let me see. I want to see my grandbaby."

They all talked and laughed at once. Elly found tears leaking out of her eyes as her mother cooed over Tracy.

"Oh," Peg breathed. "She's beautiful."

"Isn't she?" Elly wasn't too proud. "Her name is Tracy."

"Tracy." Peg picked the bundle up gingerly. "Hello, Tracy," she cooed. "This is Grandma."

Elly laughed and squeezed Graydon's hand.

"You pretty, pretty thing," Peg said. "You're just precious, aren't you?" She smiled at Elly. "You know what? I'll bet your dad would be real proud to see her."

Elly caught her look, surprised. "Do you think so, Mom? Do you think he'd come to see her?"

Peg settled the baby back in Elly's arms and winked at Graydon. "I don't know, but I can sure try."

"Try, then," Elly said. "Try."

Printed in the United States
87261LV00003B/170/A